# *Anne de Bourgh's Best Friend*

*A Pride & Prejudice Variation*

*By Shana Granderson, A Lady*

I

# CONTENTS

# DEDICATION

This book, like all that I write, is dedicated to the love of my life, the holder of my heart. You are my one and only and you complete me. You make it all worthwhile and my world revolves around you. Until we reconnected, I had stopped believing in miracles, but now I most certainly do, you are my miracle.

## *Acknowledgement*

First and foremost, thank you E.C.S. for standing by me while I dedicate many hours to my craft. You are my shining light and my one and only.

I want to thank my Alpha, Will Jamison and my Beta Caroline Piediscalzi Lippert. To both Gayle Surrette and Tish Holmes for taking on the roles of proof-readers and detailed editing, a huge thank you to both of you. All of you who have assisted me please know that your assistance is most appreciated.

My undying love and appreciation to Jane Austen for her incredible literary masterpieces is more than can be expressed adequately here. I also thank all of the JAFF readers who make writing these stories a pleasure.

Thank you to Rob Bockholdt: wyndagger@gmail.com, who was commissioned to create the artwork used for the cover.

**Please Note**: No AI Tools were used in the writing of, or creation of this work of fiction.

# INTRODUCTION

This is a story of friendship which defies all the odds, and survives and flourishes regardless of the impediments which arise.

The friendship is born out of an almost tragedy and extreme bravery by one Elizabeth Bennet. In saving the lives of those in peril, she thwarts the designs of one of the villains of this tale and makes an enemy of the person.

As in canon, our Anne is sickly. In this variation it is because has suffered a bad case of childhood scarlet fever. For the purposes of this story the disease has seriously weakened her cardio-vascular system. It is not a secret her life will not be a long one. We see how our Lizzy, aided by her sisters and others, improve Anne's quality of life and give her friendship and happiness she never thought she would find.

All of the principal characters from canon are present, as well as some of my own invention, including two rather large (and I dare say popular) footmen-guards.

Through Sir Lewis and Anne de Bourgh the Bennets (very different from those in canon) meet the Fitzwilliams and most of the Darcys. Do the connections they make change the initial meeting typically depicted between Elizabeth Bennet and Fitzwilliam Darcy? How do Lady Catherine, George Wickham, Mrs. Younge, and the Bingleys factor into this story?

The above questions and many more will be answered as you read my tale.

# PROLOGUE

Sir Lewis de Bourgh was the living embodiment of *decide in haste, repent at leisure.*

During the season of 1785, he met Lady Catherine Fitzwilliam, who was in her ninth season without anyone offering for her. As he thought back now, he should have recognised that fact as a warning sign.

At the time, he had been attracted to her forthright manner—which he now knew was pretentious and overbearing—and the fact she was the daughter of an earl, while he was only a baronet. The news of her father increasing her dowry from fifteen thousand pounds to five and twenty thousand pounds had also played a major factor in his decision to offer for the lady.

Lewis de Bourgh was no fortune hunter; however, his late father had been somewhat of a gambler, and a bad one at that. The family estate of Rosings Park, near Westerham in Kent, was in trouble thanks to a mortgage his late father had taken out on it to pay for his debts of honour. As the mortgage was close to fifteen thousand pounds, Sir Lewis needed an influx of funds to relieve his estate of its encumbrance. The balance would be used to replenish funds his father had lost before borrowing against the estate.

Sir Lewis decided to pursue Lady Catherine. She was not exactly homely, but she was not a very comely woman. Another warning sign should have been the now late earl's willingness to make marriage to her more attractive by adding a further five thousand pounds to her dowry. At the time, he had ignored the fact Lady Catherine only accepted his suit once she and her father came to see Rosings Park. With hindsight, Sir Lewis now knew how important wealth and status were to his wife. Again, he had ignored the warning signs as he so wanted to have the estate free of debt.

They had married in July 1785. As Sir Lewis was the last of his line, he had no family in attendance when he had married Lady Catherine at Snowhaven—the main estate of the Earls of Matlock—in Derbyshire.

Friends of his attended. On Catherine's side were her parents, the now late earl and countess, her brother, Viscount Hilldale, Lord Reginald Fitzwilliam and his wife Lady Elaine. The latter couple had two boys, Andrew born in September 1781, and Richard who was just beyond one. In addition, her sister Lady Anne attended with her husband, Robert Darcy. They had a son who had been born a little more than six months after Richard. Fitzwilliam, or William as they called him, was in the nursery at Pemberley less than ten miles from the Fitzwilliams' estate, also in Derbyshire.

They had spent ten days at Lakeside House, the Fitzwilliams' house overlooking some of the lakes in the Lake District. By the end of the wedding trip, Lewis knew what an enormous error he had made.

By then, it was far too late to do anything to correct his misjudgement. Yes, he had gained thirty thousand pounds, the mortgage was satisfied, and the estate coffers were once again flush, but he was leg shackled to a virago of the first order.

Too late he discovered she was an uneducated woman with no accomplishments. That fact, however, did not stop her from pontificating on every subject as if she was a genius. She was anything but. Only now he understood why his father-in-law had been willing to pay so much money to have her taken off his hands.

Sitting and thinking back on the interactions between Lady Catherine and her siblings at the wedding breakfast,

Sir Lewis could clearly see how her brother and sister would listen to her pronouncements and advice without comment. Once she was done issuing her useless and uninvited advice, Hilldale and Anne—as they had invited him to call them—would go back to what they were doing before as if Catherine had not said a word.

On the way to the lakes, she had spewed vitriol against their brother-in-law Robert Darcy for being untitled. It was the first, but certainly not the last time Lewis had heard his wife pontificate about the distinction of rank and how it had to be preserved at all costs.

It was almost a year later when the family had got together at Snowhaven for Easter of 1786, where Sir Lewis had heard the truth of why his wife loved to aim her vitriol at Darcy.

Even though she decried the fact Darcy had no title, evidently as soon as Anne had begun to be courted by him, Lady Catherine had tried to divert Darcy to herself. She had gone as far as an attempted—and failed—compromise.

From what he had been told, two things had motivated Lady Catherine's attempt to turn Robert Darcy to herself. One, she could not sit by and allow her younger sister to marry before her, and two, he was one of, if not the, wealthiest non-titled man in the realm. In fact, what the Darcys had rivalled, and in some cases exceeded, the wealth of many peers of the realm.

With her failed entrapment and Darcy's repudiation of her, Lady Catherine had turned her venom on the man. On a visit by Lady Catherine to Pemberley not long after Darcy married Anne—where the younger sister had attempted to find peace between herself and Lady Catherine—Darcy's favourite pointer, one who was more pet than working dog, disappeared.

He was found drowned a day or two later. The suspicion

was it had been Catherine's handiwork, but nothing had been proved. It was the last time his wife had been welcomed at Pemberley.

~~~~~~~/~~~~~~~

Life at Rosings Park had become intolerable for Sir Lewis. Each time he denied his wife's unreasonable demands to redecorate the home in a gaudy, ostentatious fashion, she would caterwaul and screech like a fishmonger's wife. Thankfully, her machinations had no effect on him, and he always stuck to his resolve.

He also had refused her entreaties to have the formal gardens reorganised. She felt there were far too many roses and they were very untidily planted. Sir Lewis had point blank denied her requests pointing out it was forbidden for anyone to remove the roses which had given the estate its name.

Even her demand to have the rest of the flower beds organised by colour and type of flowers had been roundly denied.

During the season, they would spend a few months at de Bourgh House on Cavendish Square in Mayfair. It soon became evident to Sir Lewis that regardless of her protestations to the contrary, his wife had no friends. She was no more palatable to members of the *Ton* than she was to her brother, sister, and their families.

Sir Lewis would see Darcy and Hilldale at White's, Boodle's, or at Angelo's School of Arms, in Carlisle House. By the time he married Lady Catherine, the fencing establishment had been in existence for twelve years.

All three men loved to fence and were very proficient at the sport. Although none of them had beaten him, they would challenge Domenico Angelo to a match from time to time. Darcy had so far come the closest to beating the master swordsman.

As long as his wife was not with him, Sir Lewis was

welcome to visit both Matlock and Darcy Houses on Grosvenor Square.

Invitations to soirées, unless they were for men only, did not arrive at de Bourgh House. Of course, his wife blamed everyone for slighting her. She neither could nor would ever, accept it was her character which drove everyone away from her.

Notwithstanding the dearth of callers and invitations, Catherine insisted they come to London each year.

The first year in London after his mistaken marriage, Sir Lewis had called on his solicitor, Mr. Horrace Rumpole. After the not-so-subtle hints, in actuality demands, his wife had made that on his passing, he leave ownership of the estate, the houses in London and Bath, and any funds in his accounts to her, he had a new will written. The new will was, as much as it was possible to be, incontestable, and left all to his son, or daughter if no son was born, when that child reached their majority. If he died without a child, the estate would become his brothers-in-laws' property. Between them, they would be allowed to give his estate to whomever they chose or to sell the estate and houses, if that was their decision.

Added were clauses codifying his denial of permission to redecorate the house or reorganise the gardens.

Not trusting his wife, he filed a certified copy with the Court of Chancery. In addition, copies were given to his solicitor, Hilldale, and Darcy. It was stipulated in the new will the latter two would act as his executors in the event of his death.

~~~~~~~/~~~~~~~

Lady Catherine did not become with child for the first four years of their marriage. He was sure allowing him to visit her no more than twice a month had something to do with the fact they had no children.

Rosings Park was unentailed so either a son or daughter

could inherit, but there needed to be a child for that to happen. If no child was born before he was called home to God, then the de Bourgh line would end with him, but the estate would not become his termagant of a wife's property—ever!

In the years since he had written his new will, his parents-in-law had passed away. The late countess had passed first, about a year previously, and then the Earl had followed her two months later. That left his brother-in-law as the new Earl of Matlock and, much to his wife's chagrin, Lady Elaine was the new Countess.

Lady Catherine could not accept that one who had been the daughter of a lowly country squire was now above her as a countess. Like everything else she railed against, her vitriol affected nothing.

In late April 1789, Catherine had informed him that she had missed her courses and locked her door to her husband as she stated she was with child. In June of that year, she had reported feeling the quickening. She had condescended to allow the local physician to examine her, all the while telling him how to do his job. The man had confirmed her state and at the same time had requested Sir Lewis find a new doctor to care for his wife.

If she had been irascible when not with child, while she was in the family way Lady Catherine de Bourgh was always on a rampage. Staff and servants knew to keep out of her way as she had not a few times, without any provocation, struck the nearest servant to her.

Sir Lewis had to spend money to placate those not treated well by his wife. Thankfully in the more than four years since his wedding, Sir Lewis had reversed the fortunes of his estate and there was no trace of his father's neglect remaining. Not only was the estate earning at, and above, the eight thousand pounds per annum level again, but he was investing most of the profits and building up the reserves which he had begun to replenish with the balance of his wife's dowry.

On the twelfth day of January 1790, Lady Catherine de Bourgh bore a daughter. She was a small babe, born bald except for a tuft of brown hair on the crown of her head. Like all babes, she had blue eyes at birth. His wife wanted to name her Catherine after herself, but de Bourgh refused. He named her Anne after his mother, and the fact her one aunt was an Anne did not hurt at all.

Within a week of his daughter's birth, Sir Lewis hied to London and Mr. Rumpole's offices to change his will to reflect his daughter Anne as his heir.

He did not hesitate making the changes given his firm belief his wife would never unlock her door to him again. Having congress with Lady Catherine was not something he would miss, so he would not demand his rights.

The new will was filed with the court like the preceding one and copies were left with the same men who had received them before.

When he returned to Kent, his wife had already begun to write letters to her brother and sister to demand they engage one of their sons, preferably Andrew as he was a viscount, to Anne.

Lewis had forbidden her to mention it again and had written to his brothers to apologise and tell them to ignore his wife's ravings.

To say Lady Catherine was displeased would be a vast understatement.

~~~~~~~/~~~~~~~

Thomas and Frances Bennet—called Fanny by all—were the master and mistress of an estate called Longbourn in Hertfordshire, about one mile to the east of the market town of Meryton.

Bennet was the only child born to James and Elizabeth Bennet. His mother had never fallen in the family way again after Thomas's birth.

Thomas and Fanny had married in October 1786, after a three-month courtship followed by a two-month engagement. Although his wife was the daughter of a solicitor and not born into the gentry, Bennet had fallen in love with the beautiful and vivacious Fanny Gardiner.

His eyes were fully open to her faults, she was not the most intelligent of ladies and had a penchant to gossip. She was however willing to learn and with his late mother, Elizabeth Rose's—called Beth by all—assistance, Fanny had learnt to be a creditable mistress of the estate. Beth Bennet had assisted her daughter-in-law until her passing in early 1797.

Thankfully, Fanny loved her husband as much as he loved her which had made her willing to learn anything and everything that she needed to know to become a capable mistress of an estate.

She would never be a great reader like her husband, who was an academic as much as he was the master of an estate. Fanny did, however, enjoy novels and fashion magazines. When her husband would read to her on occasion, she very much enjoyed it. Whether it was the subject matter or his sonorous voice was not known.

The one thing Fanny feared was the entail to heirs male on the estate, and that without a Bennet son, Longbourn would pass to one in the Collins line. Bennet had soothed his wife's fears by explaining to her that although at his passing if they were not blessed with a son, anything he had saved and invested as well as any chattel and jewellery not belonging to the estate would remain with his wife and whatever children they had.

He informed her that he had invested her dowry of five thousand pounds with her brother Edward who had opened Gardiner Imports and Exports in London. Added to that was a legacy of seven thousand five hundred pounds which had been gifted to him by his beloved mother after their second daughter had been born. In addition, he sent Gardiner one thousand pounds from Longbourn's income of three thousand pounds each year. Fanny understood and accepted that even if her Thomas was called home before her, she and any daughters, if there was never a son, would be very comfortable. She was finally able to relax and the fear of the entail was pushed to the back of her mind.

Gardiner, who was three years Fanny's senior, was very successful and was building a strong business. To date, the returns on money invested with him produced an average of about ten percent per annum. In June 1792, he married a woman he dearly loved, Madeline Lambert.

Fanny's older sister, Hattie Philips lived in Meryton with her husband Frank. He had been the late Elias Gardiner's clerk, and when it had become clear Edward had no interest in the law, Frank had been trained to take over the practice.

When the Gardiner patriarch followed his beloved Jane to heaven in April 1788, Philips assumed the management of the practice. Hattie and Frank had no children.

~~~~~~~/~~~~~~~

In mid-February 1788, a daughter was born to Thomas and Fanny Bennet. She was named Jane for Fanny's late mother. She had been born with golden blonde hair and the bluest of eyes.

Fanny was with child once again, and hoped for a son, but would be happy as long as the babe was healthy. Elizabeth Rose Bennet had been born in March 1790, just a little more than two years after Jane. She had the same dark colouring as her Grandmama Beth. By the time Lizzy—as she was called by all—was five months old, her eyes had turned from blue to the vivid emerald-green like her namesake.

Mary arrived in August 1791; she was followed by

Catherine—called Kitty—in May 1793. With each successive girl, Fanny offered profuse contrition to her husband for not birthing an heir. Each time, Bennet gently told his wife all he cared about was that she and the babe were healthy and reminded her of his provisions to make sure she and any daughters were always well cared for.

To emphasise his insistence all was well, between the births of Mary and Kitty, he had the neglected dower house restored as the entail stated the previous mistress and any of her unmarried daughters had lifetime rights to the house.

His action allowed Fanny to completely forget about the entail, as she would always have a home on Longbourn's land, no matter what.

Both Bennet and Fanny loved their four daughters and with the aid of Beth Bennet, they made sure they were educated. As soon as Jane reached the age of six, a governess was employed. Even though Lizzy was only four at that point, she had insisted she wanted to begin lessons with her *Janey*.

Having identified a broad intelligence in their second daughter, her parents allowed her to join Jane in her lessons. By the time their fifth daughter, Lydia, was born in December 1795, Lizzy was reading as well as, if not better than, Jane. Like Lizzy before her, Mary had requested to join the classes before her fifth birthday and seemed to be almost as intelligent as Lizzy.

Sadly, less than a month before Lizzy turned seven in 1797, Beth Bennet was called home to her final reward to rejoin her beloved James in God's Kingdom.

She was mourned as much by her daughter-in-law as she was by her son and granddaughters. Fanny thanked goodness each day for the fact she had learnt so much from her now late mother-in-law.

# CHAPTER 1

Against her mother's vociferous complaints, Sir Lewis took charge of his daughter's care and education. He was horrified that Lady Catherine did not have a single maternal bone in her body.

His wife's idea of education was to try indoctrinating Anne with the same nonsense about the distinction of rank Catherine held inviolate, while not having her educated at all. As she had never bothered to learn herself—mainly because she was tone deaf—she had insisted Anne was too delicate to learn to play an instrument.

Like he did with most of her ridiculous notions, Sir Lewis simply overruled his preposterous wife. He ignored her while she ranted and raved about how wrong it was for a father to take an interest in his daughter, because daughters were of no use to their fathers.

Before Anne turned five, Sir Lewis employed a nursemaid who would, when Anne reached the age to start learning, become her governess. The lady was Mrs. Mildred Jenkinson, a young widow who had been left destitute when her profligate husband had lost all of their money at the card tables. He had been shot for cheating in an attempt to recoup some of his losses.

Mrs. Jenkinson's addition to the household was another thing that unleashed a stream of vitriol from Lady Catherine de Bourgh. Not only had she not been consulted, but the lady was young and pretty, so she was convinced her husband had brought a paramour into her household.

Regardless of how much Sir Lewis disdained his wife, his honour would never allow him to contravene the vows he had taken when he married the termagant. He was not a member of polite society who held the vows only applied to the wife. In addition, he felt nothing but scorn for men who imposed themselves on those they employed in their households.

Living with his wife year round had become unbearable. Her brother and sister and their families refused to visit Rosings Park any longer thanks to his wife's continued campaign to engage either Andrew or William to their daughter. Further, they no longer desired to be around her while she tried to—as she put it—be useful.

What she considered useful was to try inserting herself into her siblings' lives and making ridiculous pronouncements while she issued orders—which she called *suggestions*—without being asked to—about anything and everything.

Given Lady Catherine would never admit to her complete ignorance (even had she recognised it), in her mind, she should be obeyed as she was always right.

The only way Anne could visit with her cousins was if Sir Lewis took her to London or one of their estates—without Lady Catherine. As much as he disliked prevarication, when he and Anne travelled without her, Sir Lewis only told his wife it was for business.

On his last visit to Town in late 1794, Lady Anne and Robert Darcy had shared the former was with child again. They were ecstatic about this fact as over the more than ten years since William had been born, other than four miscarriages, there had been no more Darcy children. Sir Lewis had been sworn to secrecy as the last thing his sister-in-law wanted was nonsensical and unwanted advice from Lady Catherine in the form of a stream of imperious letters.

Knowing he needed a haven where he and Anne could

be away from Lady Catherine, on some of their travels, Sir Lewis had been looking at estates for sale. He only considered ones in counties that were not adjacent to Kent. He had primarily been seeking possibilities in Buckinghamshire, Hertfordshire, and Bedfordshire.

In February 1795, he found what he was looking for. So unbeknownst to his shrewish, overbearing wife, who claimed she knew all, a month after Anne turned five, Sir Lewis purchased a medium-sized estate, Oak Hollow in Bedfordshire.

By summer of 1796, Sir Lewis and Anne—with Mrs. Jenkinson—resided at Oak Hollow more than they did at Rosings Park.

Even though she had interrogated her husband relentlessly, Lady Catherine's complaints had all but ceased due to the fact, in her mind, when her useless husband was away, she was the one managing Rosings Park.

What she was not aware of was the senior staff had been told to listen to her respectfully and then follow Sir Lewis's orders regardless. That being the case, it was still necessary for Sir Lewis to spend some of his time at his estate in Kent to fix the issues caused by his wife and make sure his best tenants did not seek another situation.

Towards the end of 1796, Anne was struck with a serious case of scarlet fever which swept through Kent. It was pure bad luck Sir Lewis and his daughter were at Rosings Park at that time.

They were supposed to be at Oak Hollow but Rosings Park's steward had written an urgent letter to the master informing him that Lady Catherine was causing much trouble with the largest of the tenants. She was demanding higher rents, to be paid directly to her to circumvent the *paltry* allowance she was given. In her mind, three hundred pounds per quarter was not nearly enough for one of her rank.

Anne had teetered between life and death while Sir

Lewis had experienced worry like he had never before. He prayed, multiple times a day, beseeching God to not take his daughter home. No expense was spared when it came to physicians.

As much as he would have liked to hear something else, each doctor told him it was just a matter of time. Sir Lewis spent most of his waking hours at Anne's bedside.

The only thing Lady Catherine cared about was whether she would be *importuned* if Anne passed away. With her daughter so very ill, her demands that Sir Lewis name her the benefactor of his will increased significantly.

~~~~~~~/~~~~~~~

Much to his relief, Anne did recover—slowly. By the summer of 1797, she was as well as she would ever be.

The doctors had opined that the infection had damaged her heart and lungs so for the rest of her life, Anne would have to take care and not overexert herself. The result was that she could not walk far without feeling exhausted or speak too much without having to gasp for breaths.

So that his daughter would not be stuck close to the house due to her physical restrictions, Sir Lewis purchased her two pony-pulled phaetons. One was at Rosings Park and the other at Oak Hollow. Of course, his wife was only aware of the one in Kent.

She had railed against her husband indulging *her* daughter in such a way. Her complaints were two pronged. Firstly she thought it undignified for a daughter of hers to be driving a small carriage, and secondly, in her opinion (she was never wrong) given Anne's delicate health, she should not leave the house, and most of the time, not even leave her bedchamber.

As he always did when his wife spouted drivel, Sir Lewis overruled the nonsense emphatically, and then ignored her.

~~~~~~~/~~~~~~~

It had taken her some years to admit her husband would not bend to her will. His ignoring her after their daughter was taken ill was the last straw for her. Hence Lady Catherine had begun to save as much of her pitiful allowance as she was able. She would have to take things into her own hands and make sure everything would be as she desired.

Her traitorous husband and family would all see she would have things as she decided they must be. All she had to do was bide her time until she was ready to take action. One of the first things she would discover is where the 'nest of sin' was where her husband was having his trysts with Mrs. Jenkinson —as she was sure he was.

As soon as she discovered the truth, she would know how to act!

~~~~~~~/~~~~~~~

# Hertfordshire, June 1800

Elizabeth Bennet loved the outdoors, especially if she was rambling all over Longbourn or riding her beloved pony, Hector. With her vivid imagination and love of books—she had read the Iliad a month before she had been gifted her pony for her ninth birthday—Elizabeth imagined her pony to be a great warrior, just not of the Trojan army.

On this particular day, Elizabeth was on Hector's back (riding astride as was her wont) with a small cart being pulled behind him.

Papa had asked her to collect some materials that had been borrowed by Mr. Humbolt—one of Longbourn's tenants— and return them to the barn next to the manor house.

Miss Lizzy was known among the tenants as one who would always assist them when she could. Her father had purchased her the small cart which could be hitched to, and pulled behind Hector, so she could satisfy her desire to be of service to others. On this day, among other items, there was a sturdy length of rope in the cart to be returned to her father.

The Humbolt farm was in the southeastern corner of the estate, close to the roadway which was often used by those on the way to or from Meryton and beyond. Not far from where Elizabeth found herself at that moment, was a rather sharp turn in the road, with a steep drop into a gully on the one side.

She was riding next to the fence that marked the end of Bennet land when she saw a carriage, a rather fine chaise and four, pass her on its way towards the corner.

Elizabeth stopped to admire the team of four bays and was watching as the coachman drove his team around the corner when there was a very loud cracking noise. To her horror, she watched as the conveyance first teetered and then began to tip over.

As brave as she was, Elizabeth closed her eyes as she was convinced the poor souls would shortly be at the bottom of the gully on the jagged rocks that waited for them there.

She heard no sound of the coach crashing onto the rocks, but she did hear a girl's wailing.

Slowly, she moved her small hand from in front of her eyes and gradually opened them. What she saw horrified her. The carriage was resting against something, the two wheels closest to her in the air. The team of horses were being pulled towards the gully and were getting more and more frightened. Where the coachman who had been driving the carriage, or the footman she had seen on the rear bench were, Elizabeth knew not.

She did know she had to attempt to help them. How? She was not sure. "Hector, go boy," Elizabeth commanded her pony.

She wheeled him around and made for the gap in the fence close to the corner.

As much danger as she was about to place herself in,

Elizabeth knew the first thing she had to do was release the team of horses from the traces. The more perturbed they became, the greater the chance the coach would careen down into the gully, pulling the magnificent animals with it.

"Please, help me," Anne managed. "My Papa hit...his head and I think he is...alive but is not conscious."

Anne had thought they were about to die. By some miracle, the conveyance had not fallen down the incline. A second miracle was she was basically unharmed. Just when she thought no one knew of their plight, a girl, mayhap around her own age, had come into her field of vision, riding a pony.

"I will try," Elizabeth responded.

She thought about unhitching her cart and riding for help, but she discounted that, especially after she dismounted and looked around the back of the coach. The footman was lying prostrate, his one arm at an unnatural angle. His head seemed to have hit a rock when he was thrown from his place. Of the coachman, there was no trace.

The equipage was precariously leaning against what was left of a tree, which reached about two-thirds of the way up the side of the carriage. It was obvious the tree's trunk would not hold for too long.

"I am Lizzy, who are you?" she asked to try and calm the poor girl.

"My name is...Anne," was the timid reply between tears.

"Anne, I must free the horses first. If I do not, they will move the coach and cause it to crash down into the gully. Please be brave and wait for me, I will be as fast as I am able," Elizabeth told the girl.

She did not wait for an answer. As she approached the horses, she made clicking noises with her tongue just like she had heard the Bennet coachman do many times. Thankfully she had paid attention the times she had seen her father's team hitched and unhitched to the traces.

The noise calmed the horses somewhat as Elizabeth approached them gingerly from the front. She knew they needed to see her and accept she meant them no harm before going behind them to free them.

As soon as she felt she had *introduced* herself to the horses, still making clicking noises, and adding in some clucking ones as well, Elizabeth made her way to where the team was fastened to the traces.

She would not be able to disconnect them as even though the team had somewhat calmed, there was still forward pressure. With difficulty, she had the horses take a step back to take the tension from the buckles.

It took some minutes, but Elizabeth managed to free the team. She took the reins the coachman had held, and led them some yards away to the other side of the road and fastened the reins to the trunk of a tree. The horses sensed they were safe and seemed to nicker their thanks to their saviour.

"Please help...me, Lizzy," Anne called out as the coach slid some inches towards the gully as the remains of the tree began to give way.

Elizabeth knew there was only one way to save Anne, and hopefully her father if he was still alive. She ran back to her cart and retrieved the rope. "Anne, if I pass you some rope through one of the windows, are you able to pull it and then pass it back to me from the window on the other side of the door?" Elizabeth enquired.

"I-I think so," Anne averred.

With the tilted angle and the fact she was rather petite, Elizabeth knew she would not be able to reach the window as things stood right then. She reached a decision, there was only one way.

She tied the end of the rope into a loop and inserted her left arm into it. She had seen one rear wheel and its axle were broken, so she went to the front wheel and used it to climb up

—slowly so as not to cause the coach to move.

Elizabeth made her way onto the step. "Anne, I am here, can you take the rope from me?" Elizabeth called out.

A petrified looking girl showed her face at the window, she had straight brown hair and deep blue eyes. "I-I a-am...h-here, Lizzy," Anne managed.

Very slowly while holding onto the door handle with her right hand, she allowed the loop to slip down her left arm until she caught it in that hand. Elizabeth handed the loop to Anne.

Now she had a line of sight into the cabin, she could see Anne's father lying on the floor with blood on his head.

"Now Anne, I will jump down, you pull the rope until you are able to push the loop through that window." Elizabeth inclined her head to the smashed window she intended.

With that, she jumped down and saw how the rope began to be pulled into the interior. Her problem now was Hector was not large or strong enough to pull against the weight of the carriage. There was only one option, the team of carriage horses.

Anne screamed in fear as she felt the coach move again, just as she slipped the loop out of the window Lizzy had instructed her to.

Knowing she had no time to calm Anne now, Elizabeth pulled the rope and then made a loop at the end without one. As quickly as she could, she untied the team from the tree and led them to stand with their tail-ends towards the side of the coach.

She buckled the loops to the tack at the point where it had been connected to the traces. Climbing atop the lead horse, she urged the team forward and tested her loops as they pulled against them. They were holding. At that moment the remainder of the tree gave way. Thanks to Elizabeth having had the team take up the slack, the carriage hardly moved.

Seeing the tree give way, Anne thought her and Papa's last moments in the mortal world were nigh. The coach barely moved! As scared as she was, Anne looked out of the window on the roadside to see the team of horses pulling against the ropes.

Slowly, but surely, Elizabeth had the horses pull until the wheels on her side of the carriage were back on solid ground. She did not stop the horses until the other wheels were situated on the road, even the rear one which was shattered.

Before she released the horses, Elizabeth dismounted and went to the other side of the conveyance to make sure nothing remained hanging over the edge. With that confirmed, she backed up the team a little and then released the rope. As fast as she could, she tied the horses to the tree again and then pulled the rope out of the cabin.

Without the coach impeding her field of vision, Elizabeth had seen the coachman's broken body on the rocks below. She decided to say nothing to the fearful girl within the conveyance.

When she opened the door she could hear Anne's father moaning. He was alive!

"Anne, you are safe now. I need to get help," Elizabeth stated. "I will ride Hector to Mr. Humbolt's farm, it is but a half mile from here, and he will send some of his sons to call my papa and go into Meryton to call Mr. Jones and other men to help."

It was hard to accept she and Papa were alive and not at the bottom of the gully, but Anne nodded. "Thank you, Lizzy," Anne said quietly as she cried tears of relief.

It was the work of moments for her to unhitch Hector from the cart. Soon Elizabeth was galloping on her way to get help.

# CHAPTER 2

When one of Humbolt's sons arrived at the manor house to inform him Miss Lizzy needed him, men, and the large cart at the corner in the road near the Humbolt farm, Bennet was momentarily panicked something had happened to Lizzy.

"Wait, you said Miss Lizzy came and requested help, and you saw her? She was well?" Bennet verified worriedly.

"Aye Sir, I seed 'er an' she be well," the lad confirmed.

As soon as may be, Bennet was on his stallion, Plato, leading the menservants, which included the footmen, grooms, and his coachman, to where he had been asked to come. Hill, Longbourn's butler was driving the cart being pulled by two of the farm horses.

Bennet and the group of men from Longbourn arrived at almost the same time as Mr. Jones—the apothecary and doctor in one person—and several other men from Meryton which included his brother, Frank Philips.

Much to Bennet's relief, he saw Lizzy next to Humbolt, looking unscathed. She was hugging a girl he did not recognize.

While Bennet approached his daughter to discover what had occurred, there was no missing the broken rear axle and one of the smashed rear wheels of the chaise, Jones was attending to the two men Bennet now saw who were lying on the ground.

"Lizzy, what happened here?" Bennet demanded.

"Your daughter...saved our...lives," Sir Lewis managed.

He waved Mr. Jones away to attend to his footman first.

"She did, Sir," Anne stated timidly. "If it were not for… Lizzy, Papa and I would…be with the coachman…in the gully now."

"Please tell me what you did, Lizzy. Were you in danger?" Bennet queried concernedly.

Elizabeth was the most fearless of all of his children. She could be impulsive and rush into danger without fully considering all the risks. At least from what he could see, there was no harm to his second daughter.

She obediently related all from the instant she saw the coach for the first time until she had gone to Mr. Humbolt's farm for help.

"Lizzy, you ride Hector, who is a pony, you do not have experience with carriage horses. What if one of the team had kicked when you were behind them?" Bennet enquired.

"I promise Papa, I calmed the team before I unhitched them. I have seen our coachman and grooms do that many times," Elizabeth mollified her father.

Before Bennet could react, John, his coachman approached him. "Master, I needs to show ya summins," the man stated after removing his cap.

Bennet nodded and followed his man to the rear of the damaged carriage. His coachman pointed to the rear axle. The bottom part of the break was as one would expect to see something that broke on its own, with jagged and splintered wood. The top third was a clean break. The axle had been partially sawn through!

He approached Jones who was attending to the man who was obviously the owner of the coach. "Jones, will this man and his daughter be well?" Bennet questioned.

"The gentleman…" Jones began to aver.

"Lewis de Bourgh," Sir Lewis managed.

"Mr. de Bourgh lost consciousness. He will need to be watched for a few days, so he should not be travelling on yet," Jones responded.

"Longbourn is closest, and it seems," Bennet cocked his head to where Lizzy and the girl she identified as Anne stood, "Mr. de Bourgh's daughter and Lizzy seem to have become friends. We can transport your patients to my home in the cart. They are welcome to remain with us until they are well enough to travel." Bennet paused, looking at the coach. "Until that is repaired, I do not see the gentleman and his daughter going too far. How is the footman?"

"He has a broken arm and also lost consciousness. With some rest and recuperation, he will make a full recovery, as will Mr. de Bourgh," Jones averred.

"Surely there is an inn in the town where we will not be a bother..." Sir Lewis stopped when he saw Anne's disappointment.

Other than her cousin Georgiana Darcy, who was only five, Anne was almost never with girls close to her age. The bravery and obvious good character Anne told him about which this young girl had displayed would be a positive influence on his daughter.

"If that is a sincere offer, then Anne and I would be pleased to accept your generous invitation to host us," Sir Lewis decided.

"Lizzy, please take Anne to the cart," Bennet requested. Once the two girls were out of earshot, Bennet looked at Mr. de Bourgh seriously. "This was no accident..."

"I doubt whether I will ever be able to prove it, but I have a feeling I know who would have orchestrated such a thing," Sir Lewis stated. He did not elucidate, and Bennet felt it was not his place to push for more information.

"As this was not an accident, we will have to notify the mayor, Mr. Lucas who is acting as magistrate currently,"

Philips opined after hearing what Bennet said to the injured man. "I will ride to go see him in my gig." Philips inclined his head to his brother and the prostrate man and made for his small carriage.

"There is a wheelwright in Hatfield, however, we will need to send to Hertford for a man who will be able to fabricate a new axle for you," Bennet informed his guest. "I will dispatch a groom to both men's businesses on the morrow."

As soon as Mr. Jones permitted it, the two men were carried to and placed in the bed of the cart.

Bennet stood close to Mr. de Bourgh and extended his hand. "Thomas Bennet of Longbourn, the estate past the fence line. You already met Lizzy, the second of five daughters."

"Sir Lewis de Bourgh of Rosings Park and Oak Hollow, and you met my dear daughter, Anne," Sir Lewis responded.

"So not Mr. de Bourgh. A knight or baronet?" Bennet asked.

"The latter," Sir Lewis averred. "As I will be your guest, Mr. Bennet, please address me as de Bourgh."

"As long as I am Bennet to you," Bennet agreed. "I will inform our daughters."

"Anne you will meet my Mama and sisters," Elizabeth enthused after Papa told her and Anne the news.

"How many sisters...do you have?" Anne had to take some deep breaths given her diminished lung capacity.

"Are you well, Anne?" Elizabeth enquired concernedly.

"Almost four years past, I...was afflicted with a very bad...case of scarlet fever..." Anne explained her illness to Elizabeth and the fact she had a weakened heart and lungs. "I am reconciled to...the fact I will not live a long...life, but as long as...I am with Papa, it...will be a good life."

"You have not mentioned your mother," Elizabeth noted. "I have the best Mama."

"My mother is different..." Anne gave Elizabeth a brief summary of her mother and the lack of motherly warmth Anne felt from her. "At least I have...Mrs. Jenkinson."

"Mrs. Jenkinson?" Elizabeth looked around and saw no one else.

"She is my governess. She...was visiting a friend so she...will meet us at Oak Hollow." Suddenly, Anne remembered it would be some days before they arrived at the estate in Bedfordshire. "I need to remind Papa...to send a note to the estate...so my governess will join...us at your estate and...not sit at Oak...Hollow without knowing...where we are."

"I am sure she will enjoy meeting our governess, Mrs. Annesley. Her husband used to be an officer who was lost in India. She is ever so nice. Do you play any instruments?"

Before Anne could answer, Bennet approached the two young girls. They were about to retrieve the broken body of the coachman and neither he nor de Bourgh wanted their daughters to see it.

"Lizzy dear, it is time to ride Hector home. I am sure your mother and sisters would like to know you are well," Bennet stated. "If Anne agrees, she can ride in your cart back to Longbourn."

"Anne, would you like to ride with me? I will be careful and go slowly, I promise," Elizabeth enthused.

"Did my Papa give...his permission, Mr. Bennet?" Anne verified.

"He did," Bennet averred.

"In that case, yes...please I would like...to go with Lizzy," Anne smiled.

Bennet first hitched Hector and then helped Anne into the cart, which had plenty of room as the rope was no longer in it. Next, he lifted Lizzy onto her saddle. With one of the

Longbourn grooms as escort, Elizabeth turned Hector towards her house.

~~~~~~~/~~~~~~~

Seeing Elizabeth arrive on Hector in front of the house and her not having gone to the stables as she normally would, Fanny led Jane and Mary outside to meet Lizzy in the circular drive.

"Lizzy, you came home with a girl?" Fanny queried.

"She saved my...Papa's and my life," Anne blurted out before shyness overtook her, and she dropped her eyes to the bed of the small cart.

Fanny held up her hand to stem the questions about to flow from her eldest and middle daughters. There was much she wanted to know, but not while the shy girl was sitting in the cart.

"Come my dear, surely you would be more comfortable in the house and not sitting in Lizzy's cart," Fanny stated gently as she extended her hand for the slight girl to take.

Anne took the hand warmly offered to her and climbed down with Lizzy's mother's steadying assistance. Elizabeth came to stand next to her.

"Mama, Janey, and Mary, this is Anne de Bourgh. Anne my Mama, Mrs. Frances Bennet, my eldest sister, Jane, and the next younger after me, Mary." Elizabeth looked around and did not see Kitty and Lydia. "Are Kitty and Lydia in the nursery?"

"Nurse took them up for their rest," Jane informed her sister.

"Come, Lizzy, bring Anne with you to the drawing room, I think you have a story to relate to us," Fanny stated as she began to shoo the girls into the house.

"Mama, may we please hear what happened?" Mary requested as soon as everyone was seated in the drawing room. She was an inquisitive girl and at the age of eight, patience was not one of her strongest virtues.

Elizabeth related the story much as she had to her father earlier. When she made light of her life-saving actions, Anne filled in the information. The latter had to take deep breaths if she spoke too much.

"Lizzy, I am very proud of you for being so resourceful," Fanny praised. "You know it could have been very different had the horses objected to you being behind them when they were in a stressful situation, do you not?"

It was not to chastise her daughter Fanny pointed that out. She was giving voice to the worry she felt about what could have happened to her second daughter. And that was before considering if the tree had given way while Lizzy was on the side of the coach.

"Papa, Mr. de Bourgh, and their injured footman..." Elizabeth began to say before Anne tugged on her arm.

"Papa is not a...mister," Anne told Elizabeth softly.

Elizabeth arched an eyebrow. "What is his correct form of address?"

"He is a baronet, so...he is addressed as Sir Lewis," Anne shared.

"Our guests and Papa will be home soon," Elizabeth completed her thought.

"Anne dear, I assume you had a trunk on the carriage," Fanny enquired.

"Yes, Mrs. Bennet, I do...unless it is in the...bottom of the gully," Anne related.

"With five girls in the house, if we need it, I am sure we will have some clothing for you until yours arrives, when and if your trunk is retrieved," Fanny stated. "Would you like your own chamber, or would you and Lizzy like to share hers?"

"If you would like to share mine, I would welcome you to stay with me, Anne," Elizabeth stated keenly.

"As long as it is not…a bother, I would…like to share… with Lizzy," Anne replied.

"How old are you dear?" Fanny questioned. "Also, do you prefer to be addressed as Miss de Bourgh or Anne?"

"I much prefer Anne, unlike…" Anne stopped herself before she mentioned her mother, "I prefer informality." She shared when she was born, so it was learnt Anne was just a sennight shy of two months older than Elizabeth.

For her part, Anne could not believe that not only had she met Lizzy, who was practically her own age, but there were two more girls she was getting to know who were within two years of her age. Then there was Mrs. Bennet who was everything Anne could wish for in a warm and loving maternal figure.

"Jane, Lizzy, and Mary, please show Anne up to Lizzy's bedchamber. I am sure she would like to wash and change after her ordeal," Fanny suggested. The four girls had not long departed the drawing room when Fanny heard the sounds of horses and the distinctive noises the large cart made.

# CHAPTER 3

William Lucas was normally a very jovial and loquacious fellow. The exception was when he was called upon to discharge his duties as magistrate.

He and his wife Sarah—who was one of Fanny Bennet's best friends—lived in a nice sized house in Meryton right next to Hattie and Frank Philips' house and the latter's law practice. Lucas owned the general store in Meryton, the Lucas Emporium, the book store, and the milliners.

Sarah and William Lucas had been blessed with four children so far. The eldest, Franklin, was eighteen and would begin his studies at Oxford in September upcoming. Lucas was determined his boys would be provided a gentleman's education. The next eldest was Charlotte, who had just turned sixteen. Even though she was four years Jane's, and six years Elizabeth's senior, she was a very good friend to both of them.

The second Lucas son was John, called Johnny, who was thirteen. Like his older brother, rather than be sent to Eton or Harrow, Johnny was educated at home by tutors. The babe of the family, Maria, was but six. Just when the Lucases had thought their family was complete, Maria had arrived seven years after her next older sibling.

Kitty, who was about a year older than Maria, and Lydia, a little younger, spent much time with the youngest Lucas.

Bennet invited Lucas and his brother, Frank Philips to sit in chairs opposite from his guest. Mr. Jones had authorised Sir Lewis to come downstairs to sit as long as he felt no light headedness and he did not exert himself. The men were sitting in the parlour opposite the main drawing room at Longbourn.

After the introductions had been affected and Sir Lewis related what he remembered up to the point he awoke while Lizzy rode for help, Lucas asked the baronet if he was up to being questioned. Sir Lewis had nodded his agreement.

"The sabotage could not have happened too long before the axle broke," Lucas reasoned. "If it had, the accident would have occurred long before you were in our neighbourhood."

"I cannot but agree with you, Mr. Lucas," Sir Lewis nodded his head.

"You were travelling from London, if I understand correctly," Lucas verified. Sir Lewis nodded it had been so. "You and your daughter had sojourned at your home in Town for two days?" Again, Sir Lewis nodded. "That makes it certain the axle was tampered with in London or after," Lucas surmised.

"My coachman opined it could have occurred in London. Whoever did this only sawed about one-third of the way through the axle," Bennet explained. "As the roads are in good condition, there could not have been as much jarring as there normally would be, which accounts for your reaching here before it broke all the way."

"You stopped at the Bull and Spectacles Inn about two hours before here, did you not?" Lucas enquired.

"Yes, we did," Sir Lewis responded. "My late coachman along with the footman remained with the conveyance while Anne and I were inside. It would have been impossible for someone to meddle with the coach there, it was in a public courtyard."

"I assume you do not have the equipage watched overnight at your house in London, do you?" Lucas pondered.

"No, I have never felt the need, until now that is. I could not believe that not only myself but Anne too would be targeted," Sir Lewis shook his head sadly.

"Why would someone do this to you and your daughter?" Philips asked the question all three men wanted to hear the answer to.

"In a word, avarice," Sir Lewis spat out. "As I told Bennet yesterday, I am doubtful I will be able to prove it. What I did not say was I believe this is the handiwork of none other than agents of my wife."

All three men who were in happy and loving marriages had a hard time imagining a wife trying to murder her husband, and even worse, her daughter—her own flesh and blood.

"If you choose not to answer, I will understand," Bennet prefaced, "but why would you suspect your wife?"

Sir Lewis explained how his wife had been demanding more and more of late that he change his will and make her the beneficiary, citing their daughter's weakness as a reason Anne should not be the heir. As he spoke he remembered some pointed references to Bedfordshire.

"I believe she has discovered I own Oak Hollow in Bedfordshire as well. I purchased it so Anne and I would have a peaceful retreat away from Catherine," Sir Lewis elucidated.

"You have not amended your will per her demands, have you?" Philips enquired.

"No, I have not, and never will!" Sir Lewis insisted.

"Then her only hope would be a forgery," Philips opined. "I wonder if she is proficient at replicating your signature."

"She thinks she is, but the truth is my wife's abilities are all in her head," Sir Lewis shook his head. "Even if she could forge my signature, it would do her no good." The three men looked at him quizzically. Sir Lewis explained that not only were copies held by his solicitor and two brothers, but he had filed one with the courts with the stipulation that only a will held by the court would be deemed legitimate, regardless of the date being later than the one held.

"In that case, you have the right of it. She would never be able to substitute a forgery for your true last will and testament," Philips stated.

"If it cannot be proved your wife had a hand in this, will she try again?" Lucas wondered.

"Knowing her and her opinion she is never wrong and that anything she does is sanctioned, yes, I believe she will," Sir Lewis responded. He turned to Bennet. "Would you object if I were to ask my brothers to join me at your home? I need to speak to them before I take any action against Lady Catherine."

"Fanny and I would be happy to host them," Bennet assured his guest.

"If you want, I can have the information forwarded to the Bow Street Runners for them to investigate, but I am not hopeful anyone would have seen the man or men who sabotaged your coach," Lucas offered.

"The mews and carriage house are in the rear of my home in London, so I do not believe there will be any witnesses found. I appreciate your diligence Mr. Lucas, but there is no need to contact Bow Street," Sir Lewis decided.

Lucas and Philips took their leave. "Will you really go back and live in a house with the woman you suspect tried to murder you and your daughter—a person who succeeded in causing the death of your coachman?" Bennet questioned.

"No, I have no intention of putting myself, or more importantly, Anne, in such danger again," Sir Lewis stated stoically. "As I stated, I will involve my brothers in that conversation, and you as well, if you would be willing."

"Anything I can do to be of aid, I will do," Bennet affirmed. "If you feel up to moving, would you like to write your letters in the study?"

Getting up slowly was imperative. Sir Lewis had found out the hard way if he rose too quickly, his head would complain with pain, or he would come close to passing out.

Making sure he stood slowly enough to not cause him an issue, Sir Lewis then followed Bennet to his study.

An hour later, a groom was sent to Meryton to engage an express rider.

~~~~~~~/~~~~~~~

"Why have I not read about the death of my disobliging husband and my weak daughter yet?" Lady Catherine demanded when she read the morning papers which had arrived from London.

Clay Younge was standing in front of her, his cap in hand. "Me an' me cusin did wat ya told us. We cut the axle part way. 'E should have died as I be sure the carriage would ave turned over," Younge insisted.

"If it turns out he is not deceased, then you will return my money!" Lady Catherine demanded.

Younge pulled himself to his full height and took a few threatening steps towards the lady who had employed him and his cousin, Jake.

"We did wat yer tol us ta do, nothin' more, nothin' less. If your 'excellent' plan did not work, then that be your problem not mine," Younge growled menacingly. "Not one penny will yer get back!"

Her innate sense of superiority did not mean Lady Catherine did not believe in self-preservation. She was sure the man threatening her would have no compunction in slitting her throat and then cleaning the blade on her gown.

For once in her life, Catherine de Bourgh née Fitzwilliam knew when to retreat.

"You are correct Mr. Younge, as long as you did as I asked, I can have no complaint," Lady Catherine soothed. "I will allow some more time to pass and then if I need your services again, I will contact you."

The toff's words placated Younge, causing him to relax.

He stepped back to where he had been standing before intimidating the insane biddy. As long as she paid him, what cared he of her mental state.

"If that be all, Jake 'n' me will leave. 'E's 'olding me 'orse wif 'is in the drive." With that Clay Younge replaced his cap, turned, and walked out of the drawing room and house before the lady from the quality could protest.

~~~~~~~/~~~~~~~

The afternoon, the day after the two de Bourghs took up residence at Longbourn, the girls—five Bennets, two Lucases, and one de Bourgh—were playing in the park, taking turns being pushed while seated on the swing suspended from the thick bough of an ancient oak tree. The older girls were taking their turn pushing the younger ones under the watchful eye of Mrs. Annesley, a nursemaid, and a footman.

"Jenki!" Anne exclaimed.

The woman who arrived in front of the house was Anne's governess who was driving her pony-pulled phaeton from Oak Hollow. As much as she wanted to run to see her governess and pony, Anne knew her limitations and walked at a sedate pace while the three youngest girls scampered towards the low phaeton.

Charlotte, Jane, Elizabeth, and Mary accompanied Anne with far more dignity than their younger sisters.

Once everyone was standing around the phaeton, Anne introduced her new friends to her governess and she to them, emphasising that Lizzy had saved her and Papa's lives. Anne did not miss there was more than one trunk lashed to the phaeton.

"From the letters I received from you and Sir Lewis, I was not sure if your clothing had been recovered intact, and Miss Anne, your father requested I bring some for both of you, just in case," Mrs. Jenkinson explained. "Until I saw you now and could tell you were unharmed for myself, I could not rest easy." She turned to look at the second Miss Bennet. "I must thank you for your bravery Miss Elizabeth. I know not what I would have done had Miss Anne been hurt, or worse."

Uncomfortable with all the praise she had been receiving, Elizabeth blushed and downplayed what she had done, pointing out that without Anne's help, she would not have been able to do anything.

"Mrs. Jenkinson, this lady is our governess, Mrs. Annesley, and Sally is my younger sisters' nursemaid." Elizabeth made the introductions to divert the conversation from her actions. "Thankfully, Sir Lewis and Anne's trunks were fastened well enough to the coach so they did not fall into the gully."

"How is Peters, Miss Anne?" Mrs. Jenkinson enquired after the injured footman.

"Mr. Jones," Anne saw the questioning look from Jenki, "the local doctor, says...his arm will heal fully." Anne took a moment to regain her breath. "And thankfully Papa...is recovering as well."

The footman began to remove the trunks from the phaeton as Mrs. Jenkinson was led into the house by the older girls to greet her master as well as Mr. and Mrs. Bennet. The Bennet governess and nursemaid followed the three youngest girls back towards the swing.

~~~~~~~/~~~~~~~

The Darcys were visiting the Fitzwilliams at Snowhaven when the express rider arrived. He asked the butler for the quickest way to Pemberley and was pleased to learn Mr. Darcy of Pemberley was in residence at the castle which saved him an additional ten miles each way to ride.

When the butler entered the drawing room with letters on the silver salver, the two sets of Fitzwilliam and Darcy parents were the only ones present. The three boys were out riding and Gigi (as Georgiana was called by her family) was resting in the nursery.

"Why have I received a missive here?" Darcy asked the butler. The man explained what had occurred. "Then it was provident he asked for the direction to my estate."

The butler bowed and withdrew from the drawing room.

"This is from de Bourgh," Lord Matlock announced.

"As is mine," Darcy added.

Both men broke the seal they recognised as their brother-in-law's and began to read. There were dual and almost simultaneous exclamations of "My goodness!"

"Robert and Reggie, what has Lewis written to cause you both to react thusly?" Lady Anne asked concernedly. Lady Matlock nodded her agreement as she too wanted to know.

Before answering, the men exchanged their letters and confirmed they were almost identically worded. "I will read mine," Lord Matlock decided. He cleared his throat and began to read.

*19 June 1800*

*Longbourn, Hertfordshire*

*Matlock,*

*As I am sure you do not recognise the direction, both Anne and I are being hosted at the above estate owned by Mr. and Mrs. Thomas Bennet—and yes, he is the same one who holds so many records in chess at Cambridge. That is not the reason we are here.*

*After a short sojourn in London, we set out for Oak Hollow where Mrs. Jenkinson was to meet us. We took the same route through Hertfordshire as we always do. We stopped at the inn about 2 hours from Town and after an hour, we continued. We were close to the market town of Meryton, negotiating a rather sharp corner in the road when I heard the loud sound of wood rending. The next thing I knew, the coach tipped and we landed next to a sharp drop into a gully with rocks below.*

*As soon as I felt the aspect change, I dove to protect Anne and I must have hit my head, because when I was once again conscious, the carriage was level (except for one broken rear wheel) and on solid ground.*

*God must have been watching out for us because what I now know is the remnants of a tree stopped the conveyance from tipping over and crashing to the rocks below. Next, He guided the bravest 10-year-old girl I have ever met to find us.*

*Anne tells how she first calmed the team and then freed them. Then she took some sturdy rope she had with her (she was riding her pony which was pulling a small cart) and climbed up the raised side of the coach inserting it in one window and had Anne pass the end to her from another one.*

*If all of that was not enough, She somehow attached the rope to the team's tack, climbed on top of one of them, and then urged them forward in order to right the carriage.*

*I owe Anne's and my own life to Miss Elizabeth Bennet. The little tree trunk gave way just when she had the team pull the rope tight. If not for her...*

"Does Lewis say Anne is well?" Lady Anne called out worriedly.

"He does, I was about to read that little sister," Lord Matlock replied indulgently.

*Anne is unharmed. Other than an aching head, I too am well. Unfortunately, the coachman was thrown into the gully and lost his life. The footman on the rear bench hit his head and suffered a broken arm.*

*Brother, this was **no accident**! The rear axle was partially sawn through.*

*Given letters can get lost I will not mention the name of the one I suspect—I have no proof—but I am sure you will know who I mean.*

*Matlock, I ask you, and I am requesting the same of Darcy,*

37

*to come to Hertfordshire. We must talk of the future and the safeguards I will need to put in place. If I do nothing, I fully believe this will not be the only attempt.*

*Your brother,*

*De Bourgh*

For a few minutes after the letter was read there was disbelieving silence. They all knew Catherine was bad, but they never suspected she was this bad.

"There is no question; we must go," Darcy stated unequivocally. Lord Matlock nodded his agreement. "Anne, you, William, and Gigi should remain at Snowhaven. Matlock and I will return as soon as may be and report all to you and Elaine."

Within an hour the two men were headed south in a Matlock coach.

# CHAPTER 4

Each day they were together, Anne got closer and closer to Lizzy. It had begun with her saving her and her Papa, but it was so much more than that.

Lizzy had a *joie de vivre* of which Anne would have loved to have a fraction. It was not just her friend's health which made her so vibrant, but Lizzy embodied something she had heard Papa say once. His family was originally from France and on more than one occasion he had mentioned a French phrase: *deuil me carre*. It was an idiom roughly translated which meant that grief does not concern me. The more common meaning was devil may care, which in French was *le diable peut s'en soucier*.

Anne smiled to herself. Although Lizzy could be mischievous—she had heard stories from Jane and Mary, and even a few from Aunt Fanny—which is how she had been invited to address the Bennet matron.

From everything she had heard it was easy to tell Lizzy's mischief (almost all of it were things she was either physically unable to do or would not have enough daring) was never at the cost of others, she just liked to have fun, so she was, in fact, the furthest Anne could imagine from being devilish.

When Lizzy had saved her and Papa's lives, she had embodied the spirit of the idiom Anne felt fit Lizzy so well.

What touched Anne's heart deeply was as much as Lizzy loved to walk or ride her Hector, so far while Anne had been at Longbourn, Lizzy chose much less active pursuits and spent much of her time with Anne.

Her friend had begun to teach Anne to play chess. It was a game the three eldest Bennet sisters were taught by Uncle Thomas. Papa had shared about Uncle Thomas being some sort of unbeaten champion in the game at Cambridge University.

Anne was very comfortable with Lizzy's sisters as well as the Lucas sisters she had met twice so far. She had been told depending on how long it took the coach to be repaired, she would meet more girls who were around her age and lived in the neighbourhood.

That was something Anne was anticipating since before meeting Lizzy and her sisters, the only other girl she had spent time with was her cousin Gigi who was between Kitty and Lydia in age. Her cousin was an extremely sweet, if not somewhat shy girl—just like Anne—who she loved dearly. Her new friends would not replace Gigi in her heart, and she hoped Lizzy and her sisters would meet Gigi one day.

"Anne! Anne!" Elizabeth called.

Hearing Lizzy brought Anne out of her deep thoughts. "Sorry Lizzy, I was...deep in contemplation," Anne responded contritely.

"You have nothing to beg my pardon for, I am lost in my thoughts sometimes as well," Elizabeth waved Anne's concerns away. "Your phaeton and Hector are ready for us. You still want me to show you the estate, do you not?"

"Of course I...do," Anne stated excitedly. "Is Jenki ready?"

"Yes, *Mrs. Jenkinson* and a groom are waiting for us in the drive," Elizabeth confirmed.

"You know you may...call her Jenki too, do...you not?"

"No Anne, I do not. If and *when* Mrs. Jenkinson tells me to address her thusly, I will consider it."

With wide smiles, arms linked, the friends made their

way outside.

~~~~~~~/~~~~~~~

Not long after the two girls and their escorts departed for Anne's tour, a large, luxurious travelling coach came to a halt in the drive in front of Longbourn. One of the footmen from the back bench placed the step and opened the door.

Lord Reginald Fitzwilliam and Robert Darcy alighted. They were met at the front door by the butler who took their cards to his master in the study.

Much to their relief, de Bourgh was one of the two men who approached them. "De Bourgh, will you introduce us please," Lord Matlock requested.

"Matlock and Darcy, I present my friend and host, Mr. Thomas Bennet, the master of Longbourn. Bennet, these are my brothers-in-law, Lord Reginald Fitzwilliam, the Earl of Matlock, and Mr. Robert Darcy of Pemberley." Sir Lewis stood back and allowed the newly introduced men to shake hands.

"Let us adjourn to my study," Bennet suggested. He led the men into his sanctuary.

As soon as the door closed, Darcy who was from a long line of bibliophiles, and revered the written word, was impressed by the collection of books he saw. The quantity was not great, but the quality was.

"In your letter, you told us you were being hosted by the legendary unbeaten chess master, but not that he was a fellow bibliophile," Darcy said to his brother.

"Your library at Pemberley has been mentioned by de Bourgh," Bennet noted. "If I remember from the Cambridge record books you were no slouch at the game of chess."

"If we have time, I would enjoy challenging you to a game or two," Darcy responded.

"I do not see why not," Bennet inclined his head to Darcy.

"Where is this wonderous daughter of yours who saved both my brother and niece?" Lord Matlock enquired.

"Lizzy and Anne are touring the estate at present, your Lordship," Bennet averred.

"None of that, please call me Matlock," the Earl requested.

"And I am Darcy."

"In that case, please call me Bennet." He turned to de Bourgh, "Are you sure you want me to remain?"

"Positive," Sir Lewis returned.

"You think this was Catherine?" Lord Matlock confirmed.

"Yes, but as I wrote to you, there is no witness to the sabotage so we have no proof." Sir Lewis paused. "That being said, I cannot take the chance of her moving against Anne again."

"Are you sure there are none but your wife who would try to murder you?" Bennet enquired.

"No. My wife is under the impression she is due anything she wants simply because she wants it," Sir Lewis averred.

"What about an asylum?" Bennet pushed.

"When she wants to be, she can be quite rational," Sir Lewis told. "She is ignorant and uneducated, but as far as I know those are not reasons to consign one to an asylum."

"Catherine is ignorant but she is cunning," Darcy stated. "Unless we get her to confess, we will have no way of proving it was her doing."

"My thoughts exactly. But that does not mean she should not feel some consequences of her actions," Sir Lewis asserted.

"What do you intend?" Matlock queried.

"To remove her from Rosings Park and seriously curtail her access to funds," Sir Lewis replied.

"Where will you send her?" Darcy enquired.

"It is for that reason I requested your presence here," Sir Lewis looked from Matlock to Darcy. "I was thinking of sending her to my house in Bath. Do you think it is far enough? If it is not enough distance, Darcy, do you not have a satellite estate in Ireland?"

"Yes, it is west of Dublin, but I do not think it will be needed," Darcy responded. "Bath is a two-day carriage ride from London, and not much closer to Rosings Park. In my opinion, as long as she is well guarded, that should be sufficient.

"I do have another reason, the main one actually, as to why I requested your presence," Sir Lewis owned. His brothers looked at him with raised eyebrows. "If you two agree, would you go to Rosings Park to inform her of her impending move? If I see her so soon after her attempt on Anne's and my lives, I will surely say, or do, something I would rather not."

"I assume you will employ men to watch over her closely?" Bennet enquired.

"That is my intention. What think you all? I was considering twelve men. That way six will be guarding her at any time day or night," Sir Lewis proposed. "It is a pity none of Catherine's dowry remains. I would have given it to her victim's family, but they will still receive money to live on. Much of it, two hundred and ninety pounds a quarter, will be from my wife's reduced allowance. If she had sufficient funds to pay some scoundrel to do her dirty work, then I have been giving her too much."

"I will go to my sister, but I would send a letter to show her you are still very much in the mortal world," Matlock suggested.

"And I will join our brother," Darcy stated.

"It will be done before you depart," Sir Lewis agreed.

"If I may, this day is half over. Matlock and Darcy, please be our guests and then you will be refreshed to depart in the morning," Bennet invited.

Both Darcy and Matlock accepted the offered hospitality. It was not only the possibility of challenging Bennet to a game of chess, but both men wanted to meet the girl who had been so brave.

"How long will you be with the Bennets?" Darcy enquired.

"A new wheel is being fabricated in Hatfield, that will take about a sennight to be ready," Sir Lewis shared. "However, the man who can manufacture a new axle came from Hertford yester-morning. That will take between a fortnight to three weeks, so as long as Fanny and Bennet do not grow tired of us, we will be here until the coach is ready to be used again."

"While you write your letter, de Bourgh, I will introduce my wife to your brothers," Bennet stated.

Sir Lewis sat at the desk, pulling a fresh sheet of paper from the pile while Matlock and Darcy followed Bennet out of the study.

~~~~~~~/~~~~~~~

Elizabeth, Anne, and their escorts arrived back at the stables while the Matlock coach was being pushed into the coach house.

"That is my Uncle Reggie's...carriage," Anne pointed to the Matlock coat of arms. "Papa told me he had written to... my two uncles and requested they....come see him at...your estate."

"One of them is an earl, is he not?" Elizabeth verified, "and the other owns an estate in Derbyshire. I must ask him if his estate is close to Lambton."

"Do you know someone who...lives in that town?" Anne

queried.

"Yes, well she does not live there any longer," Elizabeth stated, confusing Anne somewhat. "Mama's brother is Uncle Edward, the one I told you lives in London." Anne nodded she remembered. "His wife, Aunt Maddie grew up in Derbyshire in the town of Lambton. She always tells me Derbyshire is the best of all shires."

"Uncle Reggie's estate of...Snowhaven is in Derbyshire as...well, but I think it is close...to the town of Matlock," Anne recalled. "Lizzy, I am sorry I could...not walk up to see the... summit of Oakham Mount."

"Anne de Bourgh, do not dare apologise for something you cannot control. You did not choose to get ill or the restrictions you have to live with afterwards!" Elizabeth stood with arms akimbo glaring at her friend.

"Thank you, Lizzy. You...did give a good description, and...we can ride out in the phaeton some mornings...to see the sunrise if you like," Anne smiled.

Elizabeth smiled to herself. She did not yet know when or how, but she would make sure Anne would see the view from the summit of Oakham Mount one day.

Once Anne's pony was unhitched from the phaeton and Hector was unsaddled, the girls made sure they would be brushed down and well fed before making their way back into the manor house.

~~~~~~~/~~~~~~~

Mary normally ate in the nursery with Kitty and Lydia. Much to her delight, since Anne had been in residence she had been eating in the dining parlour.

Everyone met in the drawing room before dinner. It was there the three eldest Bennet sisters were introduced to Lord Matlock and Mr. Darcy. Like Jane, Mary was awed when she was introduced to an earl. As would be expected, Lizzy treated him like anyone else she met.

"I can see what my brother told me is true, you are fearless and unintimidated, Miss Elizabeth," Matlock smiled at the young girl.

"There are times I wish my second daughter had a healthy fear," Fanny shook her head, "but then again, I suppose if she had hesitated the day she helped Lewis and Anne, things could have ended differently."

"You must have a way with horses if you were able to calm the team enough to be able to unhitch them. I would assume with the coach pulling against them they would have been much perturbed," Darcy stated.

"Thanks to my observations of John the coachman and our grooms, I learnt what they do to calm the horses when they are a little skittish," Elizabeth explained, "that was all I did."

"Humble too," Matlock shook his head. "I have been told how you like to downplay your role in saving my niece and her father, not to mention the footman."

"Because I did what any person who saw they were in need would have," Elizabeth said simply.

"No Lizzy," Sir Lewis disagreed. "You are only ten, yet you kept a cool head, saw what needed to be done and how to do it, and then you executed your plan. So as far as Anne and I are concerned you were the right person at the right place at the perfect time."

Further discussion of Elizabeth's actions was interrupted when Hill announced dinner.

~~~~~~~/~~~~~~~

Lady Catherine was furious. She had spent all of her saved funds and for what! It had been almost a week now and not a mention of a carriage accident killing her husband and daughter in any of the papers.

It was not to be borne. Her plan had been perfect so it must have been that simpleton Younge and his cousin who had erred.

All there was for it was to begin to plan again. If he was alive she would petition her husband for an increased allowance. As much as she hated having to ask him for anything, it was necessary to save money at a faster rate.

Rosings Park, his other estate in Bedfordshire, the houses in London and Bath, all of it should have been hers by now. She would not rest until she achieved her aim.

# CHAPTER 5

A feeling of excited anticipation shot through Lady Catherine's body when her two brothers, and not her husband, entered the drawing room at Rosings Park.

She schooled her features not wanting to give away her feeling of glee at the impending news that her flawless plan had in fact worked as she knew it would. "Reggie and Robert, it must be something extraordinary which brings you hither from your estates. It has been some years since you have deigned to visit me, but I will forgive you..." Lady Catherine began but faltered when her brother raised his hand.

"We are not here to see you Catherine, but to fulfil a promise. Before we proceed, read this letter." Lord Matlock extracted the letter from his inside jacket pocket and proffered it to his sister who did not look nearly as gleeful as she had when he and Darcy had entered the drawing room.

Neither man missed how her face fell when she identified the writing on the outside of the missive as belonging to her husband.

Hoping the letter was written before his demise, Lady Catherine opened it slowly and began to read.

*25 June 1800*

*An estate in Hertfordshire*

*Yes Catherine, Anne and I are very much alive, as sorry as I am to disappoint you.*

*You will claim, and I agree with you, there exists no proof of your culpability, so unless you choose to confess, I cannot have you prosecuted for murder and attempted murder.*

*The only one your plan killed was Mr. Jimmy Green, my coachman. As his family has lost a husband, father, and the earner of money all by your hand, your quarterly allowance is, with immediate effect, reduced to £10 per quarter.*

"How dare he, how am I to get by with such a paltry sum!" Lady Catherine exploded. Neither brother commented, so regardless of her simmering fury, she returned to the page.

*The difference of £290 I previously gave you each quarter will be paid to the Greens from now on. I will add to that sum as well, but I was determined that even if you cannot be arrested as you should be, you will help compensate the Greens for what you have done. Catherine, you can caterwaul until the end of your days but it will not sway me in this.*

*Had I proof, I would not only see you in gaol, but I would divorce you! If I was on my own it would be one thing, but Anne was with me! What turned you into the heartless, avaricious, envious, covetous woman you are?*

*There is none other in your family who is like you, so whatever it is inside of you did not come from them.*

*From now on, you will be guarded at all times. Also, if you think I will allow you to live at any of my estates, you are more delusional than I suspect. Matlock and Darcy will explain what is to occur now. I wanted to make sure you knew they are acting with my full authority.*

*As bad an error my marrying you was, I am not sorry for the product of that union—my daughter, Anne. Unlike you, she has a good character, and Catherine, she plays the pianoforte, and is gaining an education. She is proficient and does not have to lie to cover her deficiencies like you do. Do you really think no one knows the truth, that your inability to play is because you are tone deaf?*

*I will make sure neither Anne nor I are ever in your company again.*

*Sir Lewis de Bourgh*

Lady Catherine was flummoxed. How did her husband know it was she who had attempted to kill him and Anne?

She relaxed slightly as she remembered his words about no proof. At least she would not lose her freedom or have to face the hangman. She had a niggling feeling that had her husband had the proof needed, he would not have hesitated in having her tried. She also knew her brother Reggie would not have lifted a finger to stop it.

The letter was folded, placed on the table next to her chair, and then Lady Catherine folded her hands in her lap and looked at her brothers with an unworried mien. She was sure her brothers would believe anything she said.

"Surely you two do not believe this fiction my husband has written," Lady Catherine pronounced as evenly as she was able. "It is proof of his insanity. He needs to be consigned to Bedlam and the management of his estates and everything else should be given to me."

"Catherine, the only person who may end up in Bedlam is you," Lord Matlock barked. "Any more talk like the delusional nonsense you just uttered and I will be the one to ask for you to be committed! Your only action now is to listen. Do I make myself clear?"

Catherine de Bourgh would have hated to admit it, but her brother's tone of voice and the looks of pure disdain from both men was intimidating. She would think on it later, but it was perhaps, a time to change her tactics.

"Say what you must," Lady Catherine sniffed like she was unconcerned.

"You are to be sent to de Bourgh's house in Bath." Lord Matlock raised his hand seeing his sister was about to interject. "You will remain silent until we have completed what we need to tell you." Lady Catherine scowled with displeasure but gave a tight nod.

"If you would prefer, we can investigate until we discover who you paid to carry out your disgusting plan. If that is your choice, we will," Darcy threatened. "I am sure he or they would be more than willing to tell us all in return for transportation and not the noose."

Lady Catherine blanched. She was fully aware if they caught up with Clay Younge or the halfwit cousin, they would not hesitate to tell all so they could save their necks.

"As I was attempting to say, you are to be sent away, and you will not be allowed back at Rosings Park or any other de Bourgh property other than the house where you will be resident," Lord Matlock continued. "Your chambers and belongings are being searched while your trunks are being packed. You will not be allowed to take any of the funds you have squirreled away or jewellery to sell to raise more money, just to employ more brigands to try to carry out your murderous intent.

"All you will be given each quarter day is the money de Bourgh mentioned in his letter, not a single penny more. Writing to either my or Darcy's family begging for funds will not even be dignified with a reply.

"My question is the same as the one de Bourgh asked in his letter. Anne and I were raised by the same parents, in the same house as you. Not in our wildest dreams would we even think about wilfully harming another, not to mention our own flesh and blood. Darcy and I will not allow one like you around our families again either."

"As Matlock stated, you will be observed at all times," Darcy took over from his brother. "If de Bourgh receives a report which indicates, even in the smallest measure, you are causing trouble, you will be moved to my horse farm in Ireland. No, you would not be the mistress, but resident in a small pensioner's cottage. Your living arrangements can be far worse than residing in a comfortable house in Bath."

For now, all thoughts of her plan to remove her husband and daughter from the mortal world were forgotten. Now was the time for her to worry about her own survival. *'Thank goodness,'* Lady Catherine thought, *"The will I intended to use is with the solicitor I paid to create it. They will all pay for this indignation I am to suffer!'* She knew not how yet, but she was confident in her abilities, and she would prevail one day!

~~~~~~~/~~~~~~~

About three hours later, a very sullen Lady Catherine departed the estate for Bath in an old, nondescript, small carriage. Her funds and the de Bourgh jewels she had hidden had all been discovered and secured.

The only servant who accompanied her was her lady's maid. She had been informed there were staff and servants at the house, which much to her displeasure was only about half as large as the dower house at Rosings Park. She was escorted by a group of eight footmen who were from both the Fitzwilliam and Darcy households who would be her guards in the interim. As soon as Sir Lewis employed his own men for the purpose, the eight would return to their employers.

On her departure from the manor house, Lady Catherine had kept her nose in the air and put on as unaffected an air as she was able. There had been no goodbyes between her and her traitorous brothers.

~~~~~~~/~~~~~~~

"Your assistance is much appreciated," Sir Lewis told his brothers when they returned to Longbourn. "I have sent word I am looking for former soldiers, marines, or sailors, and as soon as I employ the contingent I need, they will replace and release your men. In addition, I will employ more men to act as personal guards for Anne and me."

"There is no hurry," Darcy assured his brother. "Is there any word on the progress of the fabrication of the axle?"

"It should be ready within a sennight," Sir Lewis

responded. "I asked to speak to you two privately as I want to make some changes to my will."

Both brothers listened intently as de Bourgh explained the changes he intended to make. When de Bourgh had completed his telling, there was silence for some minutes as his brothers absorbed the information.

"As long as this is what you truly want to do, we will support you completely," Darcy stated and Matlock agreed as well.

"When will you two depart for the north?" Sir Lewis enquired.

"There is no point beginning the journey on the morrow as it is Saturday. If the Bennets are willing to host us, we will remain here for the sabbath and then depart at first light on Monday," Matlock responded.

"That way you two can lose to Bennet at chess a few more times before your departure," Sir Lewis ribbed.

"I expected to lose to him, not to his daughter of ten!" Darcy exclaimed. "Not only is she brave, but highly intelligent as well."

"Darcy, would you and Anne allow Gigi to come keep Anne company at Oak Hollow?" Sir Lewis wondered. "As Anne was before she met Lizzy and her sisters, Gigi is shy. I am sure being in the Bennet sisters' company will do wonders for her like it has for my Annie." Sir Lewis got a sad, wistful look on his countenance. "If only her health could improve just like her shyness has."

Neither brother added anything. They were well aware Anne de Bourgh's life would be cut far too short thanks to her illness some years past. They worried about how their brother would continue if Anne passed away before him. She was the whole of his world.

Once Darcy saw the melancholy pass, he responded to de Bourgh's question. "If Gigi would like to come, and my Anne does not object, I will be happy to bring her," Darcy stated.

The news caused Sir Lewis to smile, if only a little.

~~~~~~~/~~~~~~~

The welcome for the Earl and Darcy to remain at Longbourn was extended without delay. When she did so, Fanny also insisted the men, and any members of their families, were welcome to stop at Longbourn whenever the family was present.

Anne was informed there was a good chance her young cousin would be joining her for part of the summer. "Thank you, Uncle Robert and Papa, I...would love to see Gigi again," Anne gushed before she needed to recover her breath. She turned to Elizabeth and Jane who were seated next to her on the settee. "You will love Gigi...and, I am sure, she will love all...of you. Mary," Anne addressed the middle Bennet daughter sitting on a chair next to where she was after some deep breaths, "even though she has only...begun to learn to play the pianoforte, Gigi loves playing...it as much as you do."

"If Miss Darcy comes to visit, it will be a pleasure to meet her," Jane spoke for her sisters.

"I can help her learn to play the pianoforte," Mary volunteered.

"She will enjoy that, I am sure," Fanny said indulgently. Mary began her lessons two years ago and certainly had an aptitude for the instrument. She was on par with Lizzy who was almost two years older. Lizzy would have been far more advanced had she enjoyed the hours of practice it took.

Jane had chosen to learn the harp. At twelve her eldest was quite proficient on that instrument already. As they had done with the older three, Fanny and her husband would not push Kitty or Lydia towards a particular instrument. It would soon be Kitty's turn to choose her instrument.

Fanny sat contentedly and watched the two groups in the drawing room. Her husband, Reggie, and Robert were in a deep discussion. The girls had their heads together, more than likely making plans regarding Georgiana Darcy's possible visit.

Her reverie was disturbed when Hill announced dinner.

That evening after dinner, Bennet and Matlock were combatants across the chess board, while Darcy challenged Lizzy to a game as well. Soon the former two were watching the game thanks to Bennet making short work of Matlock. It was a long game, Elizabeth eventually surrendering when neither player had too many pieces left, but Darcy had managed to drive her king into a corner with no option to escape.

As planned, on Monday morning, with the breaking of dawn, the Matlock coach departed to convey Matlock and Darcy back to their families.

~~~~~~~/~~~~~~~

Lady Catherine had spent a most unhappy few days in her new residence since her arrival Friday past. Rather than a house on the Royal Crescent, the house she was in was far from that most exclusive address in Bath.

Also, the structure was far smaller than she deserved. Lady Catherine conveniently forgot the alternative was a cottage on an Irish horse farm.

On top of her complaints about the house, the men her brothers had sent with her, would not follow her instructions. She had thought about writing a letter to Clay Younge to see if he was able to assist her, but thankfully her maid had mentioned how all incoming and outgoing post was to be inspected.

All she needed now was to arrive at another plan. Lady Catherine was determined this time it would be truly infallible. She would have to control everything herself; she could not allow some lowborn man like Younge to do things on his own out of her supervision.

The question was what to do, and how. An idea started

to form in her head. It would take much self-discipline, but that, she told herself was not something at which she would fail. It may take time, but in the end, she would be victorious!

# CHAPTER 6

It was a little beyond the first stop when Matlock decided to broach a subject for which he was aware his brother had a significant blind spot. Why Darcy, who was normally very perceptive and logical refused to see the truth in this case, was beyond Matlock's comprehension.

"Darcy, I would like to discuss the reasoning behind your ignoring William when he reports the mischief he is being blamed for is not by his hand, but by another and the blame being placed on him," Matlock began.

"Please Matlock, not you too," Darcy sighed. "Has William convinced you to plead his case for him?"

"Let me ask you this. Except in these cases when he denies his wrongdoing, have you *ever* known your son to dissemble? I know I have never seen it."

Darcy opened his mouth, but then closed it before he spoke. What his brother said was nothing but the truth. "Then why do you think in this case William will not be honest with me?"

"Come Darcy, are you so blinded by your friendship for your steward, and your sympathy for young George since his mother passed two years previously, you cannot see the fallacy in your question?" Darcy looked outraged at the assertion, but Matlock continued before he could interject. "Do you think both Andrew and Richard choose to prevaricate to me regarding George Wickham as well?"

~~~~~~~/~~~~~~~

Lucas Wickham was the third son of a gentleman.

When Darcy was in his final year at Cambridge, he had met the man. The men had struck up a friendship and once he graduated, Wickham had chosen to read the law. On his friend's recommendation, Wickham had been employed by the solicitor in Lambton.

There he had met Jenny Horton, the daughter of a tradesman. Wickham had thought himself in love and proposed to and then married Jenny. Six months after their wedding, in October 1785, a boy had been born. All evidence to the contrary, Jenny had sworn she had been a maiden when they wed and the babe was only born early.

Wickham had found out too late his wife was a spendthrift, which was one of her better traits. By the time George was three, Wickham could see a distinct similarity between his son and one of the men who worked at the stables at the Rose and Crown Inn in Lambton.

It was around this time Jenny had tried to seduce Wickham's employer and the outraged man had terminated his head clerk's employment.

Darcy had heard of his friend's woes—well the part about the employment at least. Wickham was too embarrassed to share he had been tricked into marrying a woman who was with child, so Darcy remained ignorant of George's true parentage.

Lucas Wickham was offered the position of under-steward at Pemberley, which he gratefully accepted. Even though his friend paid him wages which far exceeded what he had earned as a law clerk, thanks to his wife, there was nothing left to save.

For the first year or two, Jenny behaved at Pemberley. Her son was accepted as a playmate for the highborn Darcy son. Once a week, when the Darcys were in residence, they dined at the mansion with the family, and afterwards, she was able to spin stories that made her acquaintances in Lambton green with envy.

That all ended the day Jenny decided to try to seduce Mr. Darcy thinking he would find her irresistible and would reward her with his largess. She had been angrily rejected and from that day on, she was not allowed to enter the park around the house, never mind the manor house itself. Mr. Darcy had reported what she had attempted to his wife and Lady Anne had been livid. It had come close to the Wickhams having to leave Pemberley.

In July 1792, the master and his steward, Lucas Wickham—the position had become available a year previously—were riding the fields to discuss the fall harvest.

There had been a snake lying in the grass on which Darcy's horse almost trod. In turn, the snake tried to bite the horse, the horse reared and then bolted. He was not thrown off, but Darcy was hanging rather precariously on the side of the galloping beast.

Wickham gave chase and was able to catch the stallion and slow him down in the nick of time before his master fell off at full speed onto some rather rocky ground.

Knowing his steward had saved his life, Darcy was beyond grateful. As Wickham would accept nothing for himself, Darcy took his son, almost seven, on as his godson and pledged to provide a gentleman's education for the boy.

Soon George Wickham joined William for tutoring, and although Jenny was not allowed near the house, she revelled in the fact her son was there daily and had been so favoured by Mr. Darcy.

By the time George was twelve, unbeknownst to her husband, Jenny had begun to pour poison in his ear convincing him he was as entitled to what the Darcys had as they were. She taught him how to toady up to Mr. Darcy to earn his favour, and the last and biggest lie she told him was that Mr. Darcy was his true father. She convinced George it was why he showed him the favour he did. Eventually, George forgot the story about his father's heroics, just as his mother planned.

Before George could follow the Darcy heir and his cousin into Eton a year later, Jenny Wickham had an accident in Lambton when she was run over by a cart. That the wife of a man she had seduced was close to her when she fell, or that she may have been pushed, was never confirmed.

After his mother's death, George grew apart from his father who in his eyes did not mourn his wife as she deserved. He used the stratagems his late mother had taught him and got much closer to Mr. Darcy, playing on his sympathies in everything he did.

It was from that point George started his campaign to discredit William in his father's eyes thinking he would become the heir of Pemberley and fulfil one of his mother's dreams.

~~~~~~~/~~~~~~~

"They would do anything to support William, especially as he and Richard are more like brothers than cousins," Darcy rebuffed.

"So, you are telling me you believe William, who wants for nothing, has been going around Eton and Windsor opening accounts and not paying his debts? How is it that never happened the first year he and Richard were there before young Wickham joined them? Are you so convinced you have the right of it you do not accept what Richard has told you regarding William never frequenting most of the shops where he is supposed to have opened accounts? And why in heaven's name have you not done what William begged of you? To travel with him to each of the stores to verify if it was him who had been there? If he was guilty, would he ask that of you?"

Darcy felt like he was being pummelled. As he listened to Matlock he could see how any man of logic would question his reason. As his brother just pointed out, would William have begged him to take him to the area around Eton had he been guilty? Had he wilfully ignored the way George had looked nervous when William had made that request?

"Before you answer, I must tell you what my friend Colbath shared with me. His son heard your godson telling a story about how you were his true father and you were in the process of disinheriting William in his favour. We were too worried about the situation with de Bourgh for me to broach this on our journey into Hertfordshire."

His brother had just delivered the *coup de grâce*. It was impossible to ignore this. Had he, who was incorruptible in almost everything, been manipulated by George?

Robert Darcy felt as if he had been struck by a bolt of lightning. "I allowed my gratitude and feelings of sympathy to blind me to the fact George has been trying to turn me against William. I was a simpleton who permitted him to do it. When we arrive back at Pemberley, I will have a conversation with Wickham and George. I intend to invite William to join us and tell him that he, George, and I will depart for Eton to visit each and every merchant whom I made whole for William's supposed debts."

"I am no seer, but I think one will be keen to go while the other will use everything at his disposal to convince you not to do so." Matlock sank back into the squabs satisfied he was able to break through the wilful blindness Darcy had when it came to the young Wickham.

~~~~~~~/~~~~~~~

Sir Lewis had made an appointment to see Mr. Philips to assist him in drawing up a new last will and testament.

Before riding into Meryton on Bennet's stallion Plato, he met with Anne and explained what the changes to his will were going to be. When he had laid out everything, he asked his daughter, "What do you think, Annie?"

"Papa, that is perfect. I...could not be happier," Anne

responded before she had a coughing fit. "I am fully aware that most...girls of ten do not have to contemplate...their leaving the mortal...world too soon, but," she took some deep breaths, "it is something I cannot...ignore."

"How I wish it was not so my sweet girl," Sir Lewis said, his voice gruff and his eyes suspiciously moist. "But I will always give thanks in my prayers for the joy meeting Lizzy and her sisters has brought you. Never have I seen you happier. When we were alone at Oak Hollow, we were content, but I have always known you needed friends close to your age. Gigi has been your only friend to date, but no longer; you now have five new friends as well, not to mention the Lucas sisters and others you have met in the neighbourhood."

"When will Aunt Anne and...Uncle Robert inform us...if Gigi will be joining us at Oak Hollow?" Anne queried.

"Your uncles should arrive home on the morrow, so I would expect to see a Darcy courier by the end of the week."

"Papa, may I invite...Jane, Lizzy, and Mary to Oak Hollow...to reside with us?" Anne enthused.

"Of course, you may, Annie my dearest girl," Sir Lewis allowed. "Now I must away to see Mr. Philips."

He kissed his daughter on the crown of her head, collected his beaver and gloves from Mr. Hill, and made his way out to the drive where Plato was being held by a groom.

~~~~~~~/~~~~~~~

"My clerk will scribe your new last will and testament exactly as you desire, but are you sure this is how you want it written?" Philips verified. "This is an accurate listing of the bequests?" Philips pointed to the page on his desk.

"Positive, and yes, everything is in order regarding who receives what," Sir Lewis confirmed. "I have sent an express to my solicitor, Mr. Rumpole, in London. In the letter, I used a phrase he expects from me to know what I am instructing him is being done by my free will. When two copies of the signed will are delivered to him, he will keep one replacing the former will, and the other will be lodged with the courts."

"A very secure way of making sure a forgery can never be claimed to be legitimate. Not to mention all the copies which will be distributed to those on the list," Philips applauded as he lifted said list. "Each copy will be witnessed and certified as genuine, per your instructions."

"One of which will remain here with you," Sir Lewis reminded Philips. "Knowing my wife was willing to kill my daughter and me to gain what she desires; I will not chance her being able to try and use a forgery."

Philips clarified some points. As soon as he was certain of everything Sir Lewis required, the two men shook hands. The instructions were in the clerk's hands within moments of Sir Lewis exiting the office.

~~~~~~~/~~~~~~~

As soon as Matlock and Darcy washed and changed after arriving at Snowhaven, they met their wives in the private sitting room between the mistress's and master's chambers.

"Is there no doubt it was Catherine who was responsible?" Lady Anne questioned.

"If we had any doubts, as soon as we saw her reaction on identifying de Bourgh's script on the letter, that would have convinced us," Matlock asserted. "The anger she attempted to hide when she realised he and Anne were very much alive was easy to see."

"Catherine has always fancied herself able to fool everyone around her," Lady Matlock shook her head.

"And the family with whom our brother and niece are being hosted? How is the little heroine?" Lady Anne queried.

"A delightful family and such a girl Lizzy is," Matlock responded. "Not only is she brave, but very beautiful and intelligent in the extreme. Remember our brother mentioned Mr. Bennet's chess prowess?" Both ladies nodded. "Lizzy, who is the second of five daughters, started to learn the game when she was five or six. She beat Darcy once and he beat her the second time."

"Robert, a girl of ten bested you in chess?" Lady Anne's eyebrows shot up.

"Yes, and I played as I would against anyone else," Darcy admitted. "The best change is in Annie. She has made deep and genuine friends with all of the Bennet sisters, who range in age from twelve to four as well as some other girls in the neighbourhood. However, the bond between Lizzy and Anne is more like the one Richard and William share."

"Robert, you know William is still very hurt, do you not? You never believe him when young Wickham is involved," Lady Anne related sadly at her husband mentioning their son.

"I will address that soon. Allow us to tell you what has been done with Catherine," Darcy requested. Both ladies nodded.

The men explained the steps their brother had taken.

"My sister does not deserve to be in Bath, she should be in prison," Lady Anne stated.

"We do not disagree. She will not be allowed to harm de Bourgh or Anne again," Matlock reassured the two women.

"Before I inform you of our conversation regarding William and George, Gigi has been invited to join de Bourg and Annie at Oak Hollow," Darcy revealed. "If you agree, we can travel as a family to take her to Bedfordshire."

"Andrew, Richard, and William have been invited to spend the next month with the Huntingtons in Staffordshire. They departed yester-morning," Lady Anne reported. "I did not think you would object."

"I do not," Darcy agreed. "Now as to George…" Darcy, with Matlock's assistance, related their conversation in the coach.

"Thank goodness!" Lady Anne exclaimed. "It has been some time now I have known that boy was no good, but you chose not to see it or listen to anyone who pointed the facts out to you. I think we should go to Pemberley to see Mr. Wickham and his son before we take Gigi south."

Darcy did not disagree.

~~~~~~~/~~~~~~~

"You sent word for George and me to see you, Mr. Darcy?" Lucas Wickham stated once the door to the study was closed.

George had been feeling confident until he saw Lady Anne was with her husband, and unlike the latter, the former was not taken in by him.

"Thank you for coming so promptly, Wickham. My wife and I would like to discuss these debts which have been made in William's name around Eton." Now that he was looking for it, Darcy did not miss the sly smile of satisfaction that flitted across George's face. "I have decided to grant William's request. With your permission Wickham, as he is adamant the charges against my son and *heir* are all true, I would like George to join us when we go to see each merchant who was cheated."

None of the three adults could miss, even if they wanted to, the sudden change in George's pallor to the white of a sheet. "F-f-father I-I h-have t-t-t-too m-much w-work…" George tried to claim.

"What work? You have refused everything I have suggested," the older Wickham scratched his head.

"The reason George does not want to return to the area with us, I suspect, is that it was he who opened the accounts in William's name," Darcy stated firmly. "If not, he would be only too pleased to see me acquire proof against William, especially as George claims he is my *true son* who will *replace William as my heir*."

"That would be a physical impossibility! The months

65

when your mother would have had to become with child based on the date of your birth, we were in London," Lady Anne revealed.

"B-But Mama swore I was not of your blood," George said as he looked at his father.

"That is one of the few true things she told you. Your birthfather is Jed Hutchin who works in the stables at the inn in Lambton," Wickham stated as he shook his head sadly. "If you choose to see for yourself, go meet the man and you will see your face."

"You are no longer my godson, although I will pay for your final two years at Eton. After that Wickham, I am sorry, but I will not support George any longer. I know I owe you much for saving my life..." Darcy was cut off by his steward.

"I never thought you were in debt to me for that. I only accepted the offer for an education as my late wife had fritted away all the money I was saving for George's future." Wickham turned to his reeling son. "Yes, even though I knew I did not beget you, I have always treated you like a flesh and blood son."

"Will you admit the truth or do we need to make the journey to Eton?" Darcy questioned. "If we go there and we discover you are responsible, you will be sent to debtors prison to work off your debt."

"It was me, not William," George admitted softly, at a barely audible level.

"George Wickham, how could you," Wickham thundered at his son. "I will repay all..."

"No, Wickham, you will not. I told your son he would be liable if he did not tell the truth," Darcy insisted. "He is not yet fifteen and he did have his mother's lies in his ear. But that does not excuse all the times over the years he has blamed William for things I am now convinced George did himself. From now forward, George will not be allowed around my family, especially not my son and daughter."

"In light of my son's misdeeds, I will resign my position," Wickham offered.

"That would only punish you and me," Darcy objected. "I do not want to lose you, but George will not be able to roam freely around Pemberley as long as he is under your roof."

"In that case, I will not resign, but with all due respect, Mr. Darcy, you will not pay for anything more for George, including his final years at Eton," Wickham insisted. "Without my money being drained, I have begun to save. Whatever education George will have will be at my expense, not yours."

George Wickham was not happy. Mostly to discover not only was he not a son of Pemberley, but his true father was a man who laboured at the inn's stables. He was aware enough to know his position was precarious so he would have to be careful.

The Wickhams exited the study.

"When I see William again, I have many amends to make," Darcy acknowledged to his beloved wife.

"That you do. You never added a bequest for young Wickham in your will, did you?" Lady Anne queried.

"No, I had planned to next time we were in London. Do not concern yourself Anne, I will not add him to it." Darcy paused. "My eyes are open regarding young Wickham."

Husband and wife shared a languid kiss. The Darcy courier was on his way to Hertfordshire an hour later.

# CHAPTER 7

When Gigi returned from her two month sojourn in the south and until he departed for his and Richard's final year at Eton, all William heard from her was about the stay in Bedfordshire and Hertfordshire and the good friends she had made. His sister was particularly effusive when she spoke of one of her new friends, Lizzy, the one who had saved Uncle Lewis and Anne.

If his parents had not confirmed the veracity of the tale, William would have thought Gigi was exaggerating the wonder of the young girl.

He had been more than pleased Father had finally seen George Wickham for who he was. It was most gratifying to have had Father own his errors and apologise profusely for not believing him over the liar. Not having to worry about what Wickham would do to try and get him sent down, or otherwise look bad in Father's eyes, made William's enjoyment of his time at Eton as it had been the year before the blight began his studies.

All of this was forgotten when he was summoned home from Eton to arrive as expeditiously as possible in November of 1800, only days after his sixteenth birthday, and a month before the commencement of the Christmastide term holiday. His beloved mother had been taken seriously ill, and William had to arrive home with all speed if he was to be able to say goodbye to his mother while she still lived.

The whole way home to Pemberley, William felt a sense of dread. Shortly after the start of the new school year, Father had written that Mother was ill, but there had been no hint it was a serious malady or a life-threatening one.

William replayed his memories of the summer. Mother had seemed more lethargic than he remembered, and her face had slimmed down somewhat. With the dresses and gowns she wore it would have been difficult to see if his mother was losing weight. All he could do was to pray his mother would recover and not leave the mortal world.

Mr. Reynolds, not his father, was waiting when the coach came to a halt in the internal courtyard at Pemberley.

"The master refuses to leave Lady Anne's side," the butler explained when he saw Master William's questioning look.

"Is my mother truly so very ill?" William asked hoping it would not be the answer he dreaded.

"Unfortunately, there is not much hope, Master William," Reynolds related sadly.

As soon as he handed, more like threw, his outerwear to the waiting footman inside the courtyard door, William broke into a run and did not stop until he reached the hallway outside of the master suite.

He gave a perfunctory knock and opened the door to his mother's bedchamber before anyone could do so. The room was gloomy with not much light, but he could make out his father, tears streaming down his face and holding his mother's hand.

Aunt Elaine and Uncle Reggie were holding each other while both were crying silently as well.

"Anne dear, William is here," Darcy said softly to his ailing wife. His beloved wife had said her goodbyes to Gigi the previous day when she was able to speak more than she had since the morning. The girl was confused and did not quite understand why Mama was ill.

"William..." Lady Anne croaked.

"I am here Mother," William, who had walked around to the other side of the bed, responded as he took her other hand.

It was cold to the touch and William was shocked at how gaunt his vibrant mother was. She was a shell of her former self.

"I...love...you," Lady Anne managed before her laboured breathing became barely audible.

"Go be with Him, Anne, you have suffered enough," Darcy told his beloved as the tears fell freely.

Lady Anne Darcy took two rasping breaths, and then there was a long exhale and she moved no longer.

William had not seen Mr. Harrison, the older, the local physician, standing in a back corner of his mother's bedchamber. The doctor came forward now and checked his mother for signs of life. He simply shook his head.

Like his family members in the chamber, tears were streaming down William's cheeks.

~~~~~~~/~~~~~~~

By the time Lady Anne was interred, her nephews, brother-in-law, niece, and a sizable group of local friends were present at Pemberley.

Respecting his father's desire for solitude after the non-family guests had departed, William asked his uncle what had caused his mother's passing.

"It was a cancer, William," Lord Matlock reported sadly. "Anne had not felt well for some time and had hidden the fact from your father. He had begun to notice things shortly before you returned to school. She was examined by Harrison who informed your parents what my sister was suffering with."

He had heard enough about cancers to know those afflicted sometimes passed away soon after being diagnosed while others lived for some time, but they all came to the same end. William was angry with God for allowing his mother to suffer in that way.

More than that, he found himself growing furious at the world, at anything and everything, because his mother had been taken from them.

His faith, which ran deep, told him his mother was suffering no longer and was receiving her eternal reward in heaven. That belief did nothing for the fact William felt like a piece of his heart had been cut out.

William tamped down his feelings and knew he needed to do his duty as a Darcy. His sister needed comforting and he would assist his father in any way he could.

He sought solace in the company of his two Fitzwilliam cousins.

~~~~~~~/~~~~~~~

Over the subsequent five years, the friendship between the two de Bourghs and the Bennets deepened. The Bennets had been hosted at both Rosings Park and Oak Hollow multiple times.

Easter was at Rosings Park; Anne was hosted at Longbourn for at least two months each summer; and Christmas was either at Oak Hollow—where the Bennets, Gardiners, and the Philipses celebrated—or at Snowhaven.

The Fitzwilliams would visit Rosings Park for Easter, but even though the mourning for her mother was completed, the only Darcy who would join them most years was the youngest one.

~~~~~~~/~~~~~~~

Since his wife's death, Robert Darcy had withdrawn from society and did not leave Pemberley. William, when not at Cambridge, felt it was his duty to be with his father, so he did not attend either Easter in Kent or Christmastide in Bedfordshire. Unfortunately, he had become a much more serious and aloof young man.

Alongside the steward, Lucas Wickham, William was more or less running Pemberley as Darcy was not as conscientious regarding his estates as he had been before his great loss. He still participated in the management, but his son had to learn all there was about the Darcy holdings some years before he had expected it would be required of him.

In June 1804, William graduated from Cambridge before he turned twenty. He had accelerated the pace of his studies to graduate a year before Richard so he could turn his full attention to Pemberley and the other Darcy holdings.

His sister, when she turned nine, insisted Gigi was the name for a young girl, she had told her friends and family they were allowed to use either Georgiana or Giana. When she told him of her time with the de Bourghs and their friends, he would nod as if he was listening politely, but William's mind would be thinking of all of the duties he needed to fulfil.

~~~~~~~/~~~~~~~

Anne and Elizabeth had become more like sisters than friends over the years since they had first met. The former still rode her pony-pulled phaetons—one was still available to her at each of her father's estates—but when the latter turned thirteen, she had been gifted a mare who she named Penelope, for the wife of Odysseus in the Iliad.

Hector had been given to Lydia and whenever Lizzy went to ride Penny—as she was commonly called—she made sure to present Hector with a treat if he was not being ridden at that moment.

Bennet and Fanny decided regardless of the fact many of their neighbours brought their daughters out locally at the age of sixteen, their daughters would enter local society at seventeen and London's when they turned eighteen. Lady Matlock had pledged herself to sponsor the girls so they would be able to be presented at court.

One afternoon, not long after Jane turned sixteen in

February 1804, Bennet invited his wife to join him in his study. "Fanny, you know I began to invest with Gardiner right after our wedding, do you not?" Bennet reminded his wife.

"I do, why do you mention it now?" Fanny enquired.

"With Jane a year from her local come out, I felt it prudent to write to your brother and ask for a recent accounting," Bennet explained. "It was a rather big surprise as I have not had Gardiner send us annual reports."

"A good surprise, I trust?"

"If you think over eighty thousand pounds a positive, then yes, it is so."

"Such a sum! How Thomas?"

"Gardiner achieves excellent returns, and additionally Longbourn has been producing more than three thousand per annum income for some years now. Rather than blindly sending our brother one thousand pounds, I have been sending him anything above two thousand pounds each year."

"It should all go to dowries for our girls," Fanny insisted.

"No, my dearest wife. As much as the sentiment does you credit, twenty thousand pounds will be set aside for you if I leave the mortal world before you. As things stand today, each of our girls will have twelve thousand pounds as a dowry."

"Thomas, I am concerned such sums will attract fortune hunters."

"It pleases me to hear you say that. I propose the only thing which should be shared with those outside of the circle of our family is they only have one thousand on your passing and that Longbourn's income is not above two thousand pounds per annum."

Fanny had no opposition to her husband's suggestions. If men were to form an attachment to one of her daughters, she would know it was not for their dowries.

~~~~~~~/~~~~~~~

Lady Catherine de Bourgh was still languishing in Bath in her husband's unfashionable house.

She had begun a campaign of contrition to try to convince her family she had not planned to have her husband and daughter murdered. At the same time, she had done her best to appear contrite and demonstrate to her relatives she deserved to be among them again. So far, they had been unmoved. It had been more than four years since her banishment from the estate which should have been her own.

About a month after her arrival in Bath, the man in charge of her gaolers had informed Lady Catherine he and his men would depart on the morrow. She had celebrated prematurely.

The next day she was introduced to twelve men who had been employed by her husband to replace those returning to the Darcy and Fitzwilliam estates and houses. She had quickly learnt these men were less pliable—and not more like she had hoped—than the men they had replaced.

Even had she money to bribe them, it did not take long for Lady Catherine to learn these men, like those before them, were not interested in her orders or demands unless it was something their master had authorised.

When she had finally received a notice regarding her sister's passing, it had been weeks past the interment. Add to that, those guarding her had refused to take her to Derbyshire when she had demanded they do so.

She had seen Anne's death as a way to escape the confines of her imprisonment. She had intended to go to Pemberley to *console* Robert Darcy and take over the running of his estates and houses. The Darcys were far richer and owned much more property than the de Bourghs after all.

But no, the men had ignored her orders. She had not known, but her husband had sent instructions to the men to make sure she did not get close to Derbyshire.

From Anne's eleventh birthday on, Lady Catherine had written warm letters of congratulations, well, with as much good cheer as she was capable. If she could not pull the wool over her husband's eyes, surely, she would succeed with her daughter.

To date, Anne had not replied to any of her letters.

~~~~~~~/~~~~~~~

In his final year at Cambridge, Richard Fitzwilliam had reached a decision. He had chosen to become an officer in the Royal Dragoons when he graduated in May 1805.

Those plans were thrown out with the bathwater when his mother informed him a great-aunt of hers had passed away leaving her estate to her great-niece, the only family member who spent time with her; she had no children.

On their way to Rosings Park for Easter in 1804, the Fitzwilliams made a stop at the estate of Cloverdell in Northamptonshire. There, Richard was informed his mother had signed the estate over to him, thereby negating his need to take a profession.

The estate was large. It was not as large as Snowhaven or Pemberley, but more on a par with Andrew's estate, Hilldale. The large manor house was built in the Tudor style, and the estate had an income above seven thousand pounds per annum. Best of all for a lover of horses like Richard, there was a well-established horse breeding programme in place at his estate.

His estate! He needed to familiarise himself with that concept. His spirit of adventure would have enjoyed being an officer, but he knew his family, especially William who was still suffering from the loss of his mother, would be far happier he was not going into the army, particularly as the little tyrant had dragged France into a war with England, as well as other countries.

He was keen to return to Cambridge to share the news of

his good fortune with his new friend, who was a year behind him but had only begun that year after transferring from Oxford, Charles Bingley.

# CHAPTER 8

**August 1805**

Anne and Sir Lewis were visiting their friends at Longbourn and had been for more than a fortnight.

As he always did when the visit was planned, Sir Lewis had one of his grooms from Oak Hollow drive Anne's phaeton to Longbourn so she would have the freedom of being mobile.

Sir Lewis and Bennet were seated in the latter's study, a chess board between them and glasses of port within reach. Neither man had sipped his port yet, they were too engrossed in their game. To date, the former had never beaten the latter, but this game was the closest Sir Lewis had come to, if not winning, playing Bennet to a draw, which in and of itself would be an accomplishment.

Some ten minutes later, after both men were repeating the same back and forth moves over and over, they looked at one another. "If you agree, I would call this a draw, de Bourgh," Bennet suggested.

"A draw it is," Sir Lewis responded happily. "It is the best game I have played against you."

"I concur, my friend," Bennet agreed, "and based on your steadily improving play, it seems you can teach an old dog new tricks."

"Thank you, Bennet...I think. I am not that many years older than you," Sir Lewis ribbed. The truth was there was more than fifteen years separating the men in age.

"On a more serious subject, is it just me, or does Anne have to take more rests at smaller distances when she walks?"

"As much as I wish it were not so, I am afraid you are not mistaken," Sir Lewis replied mournfully. "You know Bennet, the day Lizzy saved us, she did not only stop us from falling to our deaths, I believe her friendship has given Anne a new lease on life."

"Of what do you speak?"

"Lizzy has never treated Anne like a delicate flower. Yes, she makes allowances for Anne's reduced abilities, but it never stops her from including Anne in everything she does. Your other daughters, the Lucas girls, and some of the others Anne has met in the neighbourhood have been good for her too. They, however, are more careful around her." Sir Lewis stared off into the distance for a few moments while he thought about Anne and her life. "Lizzy will never do anything to hurt Anne, but she pushes Anne further than any of the others. I believe Anne will fight to live and be in Lizzy's company as long as, and as much, as she is able."

Bennet was somewhat uncomfortable with the heavy emotions expressed by his friend, regardless of how much he understood them. Each man took a sip of his port. "Where did you find those enormous guards who watch over Anne?" Bennet wondered to change the subject.

"They had both been five years in the navy. They had served on the same frigate and not long after I employed the men who make sure my wife does not step out of line, they came to my notice. My man of business had found the men who are in Bath. When I told him in addition to them, I needed some of the best guards for Anne possible, he recommended Biggs and Johns without reservation."

"*Biggs* is an appropriate name." Bennet swirled the dark amber liquid around in his glass. "How do Darcy and his son do? Is Darcy still a hermit at that estate of his?"

"He is and the way he is living has rubbed off on his son which has resulted in aloof, taciturn, and sometimes downright arrogant behaviour by William. In my opinion, if Anne is watching from heaven, as I think she is, she is neither too happy at the way Darcy has withdrawn from life, nor at the way her son is following his father's example."

"I only met her that one time when she and Darcy escorted Giana, or Gigi as she was known then, to come spend time at Oak Hollow. From what I remember, she was a little shy, but she was happy, and once she got to know you, an outgoing lady."

"You have summed up my late sister's character rather well. This past Christmastide when we were all at Snowhaven, William did attend for two or three days, but Darcy did not come, not even to spend Christmas day with us."

"I know if, goodness forbid, my Fanny was called home to God before me, my heart would be rendered from my chest. However, I am well aware she would see it as a betrayal if I did not give my life its all. She would haunt me if I was not the father I should be to my girls."

"That is something I can well believe of your Fanny. If only I had found a woman who I could have loved and respected. One who returned the sentiments with full measure."

Bennet said nothing in response. It was a similar sentiment his friend had expressed many times over the years since they had met and become close.

After a few moments, Bennet grinned. "Should we set up the chessboard again?"

"We will play this evening perhaps. Allow me to savour what for me is a victory."

The friends lifted the glasses of port and saluted one another before each taking a small sip.

~~~~~~~/~~~~~~~

"Why are we stopped at...Oakham Mount, Lizzy?" Anne enquired as she watched her friends hand the reins of their mounts to the grooms who had accompanied them.

"You remember I promised you that you would join us on the summit one day?" Elizabeth smiled.

Anne nodded. "But Lizzy, you know...I cannot walk up and...down, unless you have a few...days available for each way."

"That is why I made a plan." Elizabeth nodded to Anne's huge guards.

John Biggs smiled to the vivacious miss and retrieved the seat and back they had removed from an old, discarded chair. With aid from Longbourn's carpenter, a piece of lumber was attached to the bottom front of the seat with wood extending either side allowing for someone to hold onto it.

There was a second piece of lumber, of similar shape, thickness, and length attached near the top of the backrest on the rear side.

Brian Johns stood across from Biggs, each man held the protruding wood on his side, keeping the seat at the height of a normal chair. That way Anne would be able to sit without any bending.

"Anne, please sit," Elizabeth requested.

Knowing how strong the two men were, or certainly they looked it, Anne lowered herself into the makeshift chair slowly. As soon as she was seated, Jane looped a belt around Anne to help secure her.

With the belt buckled, in one swift move, Biggs took hold of the two front pieces of protruding wood, while at the same time Johns had his hands on both rear pieces. As soon as both men were happy, Biggs released his one hand, twisted until he gripped it with his hand behind him and soon was standing, his face to the path. He lifted the front a little and Johns lowered his hands by the same amount. The effect was

Anne was reclining, her back leaning to the rear, and her legs raised at an angle to the ground, but felt quite comfortable.

With Jane and Elizabeth in the lead, the two men carrying Anne on her *throne,* they were followed by two Lucas and three Bennet sisters.

To make sure Anne would be safe, the walk was slower than normal. The group of girls and the two guards reached the summit in about double the time it would normally take, but no one had any complaints.

Biggs and Johns righted the angle so Anne felt like she was seated on a normal chair. The men switched their hands so they were standing either side of the makeshift sedan chair. Mary unfastened the belt and Anne stepped down onto the summit.

"Lizzy, this is...wonderful, many...thanks," Anne stated gratefully.

She had never thought she would ever see the top of the hill. It was exactly as Lizzy had explained it would be, not that she doubted Lizzy's word. The summit was more or less flat. There was a stand of oak trees—no doubt the ones which leant themselves to the name of the eminence. Although the leaves had not started to fall from the trees yet, they were already starting to change colour. After all, it would be autumn in but a few short weeks. Anne noted the two benches under the trees Lizzy had told her about. There were boulders, some larger than others, at various points around the summit.

Elizabeth pointed to a large one near the one side of the hill's summit. "That is the one facing the east where I sit to welcome the sunrise when I come early in the mornings," Elizabeth explained. "Come, Anne." Elizabeth took one of Anne's hands and slowly led her under the trees to the one side of the hill.

From there they were looking down on Meryton. They were standing close to the boulder Lizzy indicated before.

Elizabeth pointed out Netherfield Park beyond the town. She led Anne to the northern side of the hill while pointing out various estates and the lush rolling farmland dotted with tenant and manor houses. To the west was more of Longbourn and estates beyond it. As they walked more to the southern side, Mary pointed out the Bennets' house. As they continued the slow walk—making sure to stop and allow Anne to rest and breathe whenever she needed to—around the summit, they moved to a position that looked southeasterly.

"You can see Lucas Lodge between Longbourn and Meryton," Charlotte pointed out her home.

Some two years previously the King and Queen had been travelling back to London when they had made an impromptu stop in Meryton. It had been Bennet's turn to take over the mayorship, but he had asked his friend Lucas to add a year to his term before Bennet would be able to fulfil his duty. Lucas had agreed with alacrity as he enjoyed the tasks.

Thus, when the Monarchs stopped in Meryton and word of who was present reached the mayor, he made a flowery speech of welcome which impressed King George III to such an extent, His Majesty knighted the mayor. A month later, now Sir William and Lady Lucas attended the latter's investiture at St. James.

On his return, Sir William decided he would like to join the ranks of the gentry. He however never forgot what had provided for his family for so many years. Hence, he sold the general store, but not the bookstore or millinery shop. With the proceeds from the sale of his largest concern, Sir William purchased the small estate between Longbourn and Meryton. Thanks to keeping the two concerns—Bennet was well pleased there would be no changes to the running of the bookstore— Sir William's income remained essentially the same.

The eldest Lucas son would inherit the estate while his younger brother would one day own the two remaining businesses.

"Do you prefer the...estate to your house...in Meryton?" Anne enquired.

"Yes, it means we are able to keep horses and a pony for Maria, although she has been asking Papa for a full size horse since she turned eleven," Charlotte stated as she looked at her sister indulgently. Maria was talking to Kitty and Lydia. "She will have to exercise some patience. Papa will wait until she is at least thirteen like Mary was before he considers a gelding or mare for her."

"Anne, would you like to sit on a bench, or can the *small* men carry you back down to where Jenki is waiting for you in the phaeton?" Elizabeth enquired.

That first time Anne and Uncle Lewis had been hosted at Longbourn, Anne had asked Jenki to inform Lizzy she was allowed to address Anne's governess thusly. Since then, it was the way Elizabeth, and her sisters, addressed her.

It was not difficult for Elizabeth to see Anne was tiring fast. Over the years of their friendship, she had become much attuned to her best friend's physical needs.

"I think it will be good...to return to the...phaeton, as long as John and...Brian are able to bear...my weight," Anne jested drolly.

There were giggles from all of the girls while Biggs and Johns grinned at Miss Anne's teasing. It was quick work before the young mistress was safely belted in the chair once again and she was being carried down the hill in her specially constructed sedan chair.

~~~~~~~/~~~~~~~

Lady Catherine was not well pleased. She had sent a letter to Clay Younge using her lady's maid to carry the missive and post it at the nearest posting inn.

It was his impertinent and disrespectful reply, her maid had collected from the same post stop and then delivered to her, which had disturbed her equanimity. The letter was too well written to have been scribed by that brainless piece of brawn. It was then Lady Catherine remembered Younge had a younger sister, one who—according to the brother—had been educated so she would have more employment opportunities.

It was definitely a woman's script. Lady Catherine read the letter again.

*14 August, 1805*

*8 Worthing Road*

*Margate, Kent*

*Lady Catherine,*

*No, I will not do anything for you on the promise of future money to which you are* sure *you will have access.*

*You know my fee to assist you and unless and until you are able to provide me the required amount (£600) before I do anything, you will not be seeing me. The paltry £30 you say you have would not even convince me to hobble someone's horse, never mind any of the things you list in your letter.*

*I wonder how much your husband would pay me if I sold him that letter and what would happen to you?*

*Unless you have funds, do not contact me again. And no, I will not provide you with the name of another.*

*Clay Younge*

The letter did not improve after the second reading.

How dare that nobody speak to her, Lady Catherine de Bourgh, in that fashion! Did he not know who she was. She was seriously displeased. The way he had threatened her five years ago had been pushed out of her consciousness.

# CHAPTER 9

Cloverdell was everything Richard could have hoped for. After almost a year and a half that he had been the master of the estate, Richard was quite proficient in his duties— thanks to lessons in estate management from his father, Andrew, Uncle Lewis, Mr. Bennet, and to a lesser extent William.

Even while still at university, when he had any available time, he used it to make sure he learnt everything he could. In fact, since moving to his estate once he had completed his final year at Cambridge, Richard had not ventured to London to partake in the season at all.

Even the invitation from his friend Bingley to be hosted at his London home on Curzon Street had not convinced Richard to go to Town. The fact Bingley's older and younger sisters had both decided he should pick them as his future wife, was another deterrent to attending Bingley in London. The only respite he took from his diligent oversight were a few days at Oak Hollow with his family (sans William), Christmastide past, and four days at Rosings Park in April of the current year. Since his graduation in May 1805, Richard had been at his estate constantly. The only major change he had made was to employ a new steward.

The steward he had inherited along with the estate had been well into his seventh decade and had informed the new master he intended to retire by the end of 1804. With more than sufficient forewarning, Richard looked for men who had prior experience with estates that had a horse breeding programme.

He had employed Mr. Victor Mercer who had managed a large breeding programme for more than ten years at an estate in Wales. Both he and his wife were from Northamptonshire so he had been on the lookout for a position in the shire of their birth.

Cloverdell was barely ten miles from the town where their parents and family lived.

The one thing which saddened Richard greatly were the changes in William since Aunt Anne's passing more than four years past. His cousin had withdrawn into himself and hardly ever left Pemberly and his father.

The only time William went anywhere other than one of the satellite estates was when the family celebrated Christmastide at Snowhaven. The last time Christmastide had been celebrated there was in 1803, so it would be there again this year, but Richard knew not if William would attend.

Poor Giana would have felt completely abandoned had it not been for her friendship with Anne and the Bennet sisters. She spent very little time in the depressing home which was Pemberley; she spent most of the year between his own parents' home and Uncle Lewis's homes.

Richard had come close to blows with William when he had wanted to introduce him to his friend Bingley. His cousin had refused, claiming he had no interest in meeting the son of a tradesman.

It was hard not to remember that conversation without feeling anger at William all over again.

~~~~~~~/~~~~~~~

*Pemberley July 1805*

*Two months after graduation and with William refusing an invitation to Cloverdell, Richard had mounted his stallion, Invictus, and made the day and a half ride to Pemberley.*

*On arriving he had made his way to his normal chambers,*

washed, and changed before going to pay his respects to Uncle Robert. His uncle and cousin had been in the master's study pouring over a ledger when Richard had knocked and entered.

It had been the best part of a year since he had seen Uncle Robert and Richard had to fight to school his features. His uncle was a shell of his former self. His clothing hung off his body and his skin was pallid, almost grey. It seemed his uncle had not been in the sun or on horseback for a long time.

"Richard, I did not know to expect you," Darcy stated, "William did you forget to tell me my nephew was coming to visit?"

"William did not mention anything because I spontaneously decided to arrive and had not told him of my intentions," Richard informed his uncle. "It has been some time since I have seen both of you and as there are no imminent foalings at Cloverdell, I was able to take some days away."

"We have completed what we needed to review. William, go spend some time with your cousin," Darcy instructed.

The two made their way to the billiards room. William rang for some refreshments and then the cousins began their game.

"I am to hold a harvest ball in October, can I count on you to attend?" Richard invited.

"Richard, you are fully aware I do not dance, not since Mother passed away," William refused.

"Do you really think Aunt Anne would be happy that Uncle Robert and you have stopped living and locked yourselves away at Pemberley the way you have?" Richard prodded.

"Do not overstep," William growled. "Besides, I will not know anyone who will attend and you know how I hate being among those with whom I am not acquainted."

"And of course, it is impossible to be introduced and meet new people at such an event." Richard took the warning in William's scowl and raised his hands in supplication. "Peace William. You will know several of those attending. My parents, Andrew, Uncle Lewis, Anne, and what is the name of the other *young lady you are familiar with...oh yes, Georgiana Darcy. You will be able to meet the Bennets and my friend Bingley and his sisters as well."*

*"Bingley, the son of a tradesman you met after I graduated from Cambridge?" William noted.*

*"Yes, but when he completes his studies, he intends to carry out his late parents' charge and purchase an estate."*

*"Even then, he would have the stink of trade attached to him—a member of the* nouveau riche. *I will not associate with one so far below me!"*

*"When did you become such an arrogant, proud, horse's arse?" Richard barked as he threw his cue stick slamming down onto the billiards table sending the balls every which way. "I remember when you used to count character above all else! Please tell me you are not ascribing to our criminal aunt's theories about maintaining the distinction of rank!"*

*"I must uphold the honour of the Darcy name," William claimed haughtily.*

*"You do know I am the son of an earl, do you not." Richard had a burning desire to plant a facer into his cousin's arrogant mien. He took a step back before he did.*

*William did not miss the way Richard had balled up his fists and was fully aware his cousin was much stronger and more proficient with his fists than he was. Richard had been a champion pugilist at university.*

*He knew he was out of line, but for some reason, William could not bring himself to own his errors.*

*"I will say my farewells to my uncle and then be on my way." Richard turned on his heel leaving William staring at his retreating back.*

*Rather than stay at Pemberley, Richard rode into Lambton and took a room at the Rose and Crown Inn for the night. He would begin his ride home in the morning.*

*He was fully aware both his uncle and cousin were in pain, and had been so since Aunt Anne was called home. Richard realised part of William's reaction earlier had been because he had not wanted to hear what Richard had said about what Aunt Anne would have thought of the way her husband and son were mourning her.*

*All he could pray for was at some point someone would be able to break down the walls William had constructed around his heart and strip away the mask he wore.*

~~~~~~~/~~~~~~~

As he remembered the conversation, Richard was saddened he had not been in William's company since their almost physical fight that day. He wondered if his relating the behaviour of Miss Louisa Bingley, who was two years her brother's senior, and Miss Caroline, three years younger than Bingley, had contributed to William's reticence to meet them.

Miss Bingley was, as far as Richard remembered, two and twenty while Miss Caroline was seventeen. Both acted as if they were the daughters of a duke, not a tradesman, thinking their dowries of twenty thousand pounds somehow elevated them.

Of course, it did not. Although they had previously dismissed Richard as a *mere* second son, as soon as they had learnt he had become the owner of Cloverdell, they set their caps for him. The truth was, he could only imagine the sisters' reaction if they were to meet William and discover the information regarding all to which he was heir.

If they were ever to meet William, Richard knew he would have to make sure Bingley kept his sisters under good regulation. His cousin would not do well with their fawning and pretentions they were anything but the daughters of a tradesman.

~~~~~~~/~~~~~~~

The subject of his cousin's rumination was sitting at

his father's desk in the study at Pemberley contemplating yet again Richard's words from a month past.

The more William cogitated on the words, the more he had to admit his mother would not be happy with the way either he or Father had reacted to her passing. That Giana spent most of her time with others, made William feel a deep shame.

Mayhap he should write to Richard and accept his invitation, that is if his cousin still desired his company. He had heard so much of the Bennets from Giana when she had been home for brief periods. Truth be told, he really did not object to meeting Richard's friend. His cousin had the right of it, character was much more important.

That Richard had compared his attitude to that of their banished, murderous aunt had stung terribly. With time and distance, William had come to accept there was truth in Richard's words.

He was about to write a letter of apology when there was an urgent knocking on the study door. "Come," William called out.

Reynolds opened the door, his face, which was usually a stoic mask, showed grave concern. "Master William, the master's valet asks you to come urgently and he thinks we need to summon Mr. Harrison."

"I will go see what Hodges wants. Please send for the doctor and tell him it is urgent," William barked before running out of the study and up the stairs.

Since his father had stopped riding and spending time in the fields, he had lost much of his colour, but in the last few days William had noticed his father's pallor had become almost grey. The one time he had seen his father climbing the stairs, William had noticed it seemed to be a great effort to reach the family floor. It had been the last time—two days ago —he had seen his father downstairs.

Without knocking, he burst into his father's bedchamber. The valet, Hodges was trying to have his master sip some water. Most of it was dribbling down Mr. Darcy's chin.

"Leave...us," Darcy rasped to his valet.

The man did as he was bade and disappeared into the servant's hallway.

"Father, what is it, you do not look well," William stated worriedly.

"Soon...be with...your...mother. William...sorry to...leave you...and Giana."

"No, Father, you cannot leave us as well," William wailed.

Was he to be an orphan before he reached his majority? It seemed so. As much as he did not want his father to die, he could hear a crackling sound with each breath he took and when he felt his father's pulse, he could tell the heartbeat was far slower and weaker than it should be.

Was this punishment for his wanting to start living again?

William did not consider the illogical nature of the thought. However, at that moment it was all that made sense to him.

Mr. Jackson Harrison, accompanied by his son Benjamin, entered the bed chamber. The latter had recently graduated from the Edinburgh Medical School. Now he was working with his father as a second physician in the neighbourhood.

"This is what I feared," the older Mr. Harrison shook his head.

"You were aware Father was ill?" William accused.

"I was, his heart had begun to weaken about two years past," Mr. Harrison the older replied. "He ignored my counsel that you and your uncles be informed. It was your father's choice not to do so. As much as I disagreed with his decision, it was not my place to gainsay him."

"Can anything be done for him?" William questioned.

The younger doctor listened to Mr. Darcy's breathing and took his pulse. "I believe there is fluid in the lungs and his heart is barely beating," Mr. Harrison the younger announced.

"May I have some time with my father," William requested as the tears began to prick his eyes.

"We will be right outside Master William," the older man stated. He and his son exited the chamber pulling the door closed behind them.

"Father, you should have told me," William lamented.

"Sorry...William. Not...repeat...my...mistakes. Love... you...and...Giana..." Nothing further was said.

William watched helplessly as his father's eyes closed and the crackling sound of his breathing was heard no more. He allowed the emotional dam to burst as he lay across his father's chest and wailed.

~~~~~~~/~~~~~~~

As August was one of the warmest months of that year, in order to wait for his uncles, aunt, and cousins to arrive, his father's body had to be kept in the icehouse.

In William's opinion, it was an indignity, however, he knew he could not inter his father without his family in attendance. He was the new Mr. Darcy. Even though he had been effectively running everything for some years now, Father had been there when William had needed him.

Father was with Mother in heaven and Pemberley, and all of her dependants, was his responsibility.

Within three days of Robert Darcy's passing, the family was assembled. The Fitzwilliams had been visiting Richard's estate and the de Bourgh's had been at Rosings Park with Giana and the Bennet sisters.

Sir Lewis had considered sparing Anne the long and gruelling coach ride by leaving her at Longbourn with her friends. Anne had refused saying she needed to be with Giana.

Richard had written to those who were to join him for the celebration, to let them know that in light of his uncle's death, the upcoming harvest festival had been cancelled at Cloverdell.

While the men, which included many masters of the surrounding estates, the senior male staff, and male servants, watched the coffin of Robert Darcy placed into the family crypt alongside his beloved Anne, Lady Matlock was hosting the ladies of the area at the manor house in the largest drawing room.

Anne kept Giana company in the suite they shared. "I am sad Papa no longer lives, but I hardly knew him since Mama passed away. Am I a bad daughter that I am not sadder?" Georgiana, who had turned ten in March past, asked her older cousin.

"No, Giana, you are not...a bad anything," Anne insisted as hard as she was able to without causing a coughing fit. "Each of us mourn...in his or her...own way."

"Do you think I will be William's ward?" Georgiana wondered. "Since he always remained here with Papa, I am not as close to him as I used to be. I still love my brother, but I hardly know him."

"In a few days, your late...father's will should...be read. Until then, we...will not know." Anne smiled reassuringly at her cousin and friend.

"I wish Lizzy, and the rest of the Bennet sisters could have accompanied us," Georgiana repined.

"Remember what Aunt Fanny...and Uncle Thomas... said? It is not a time...for them to visit," Anne pointed out.

The truth was Anne would have loved to have Lizzy with them, but she understood why it could not be at this time.

Giana lay face down on her bed while Anne rubbed her cousin's back soothingly.

# CHAPTER 10

George Wickham was sure Mr. Darcy had left him something substantial in his will. He had chosen to ignore his father's admonitions that there would be nothing for him.

Yes, the late master of Pemberley had caught him out in his scheme to discredit the prig. That, however, had not dimmed his hope the old man had remembered all the times George had entertained him and made him laugh, even though it had been some years since Mr. Darcy had seen him.

Thanks to the talk among the servants, namely the maid he had seduced, George knew the will was to be read two days after the interment. Rather than arrive at the manor that same day, George decided to wait one more day. He would go claim his due—he hoped it was one of the satellite estates—on the morrow.

~~~~~~~/~~~~~~~

Mr. Rumpole, the same solicitor both Lord Matlock and Sir Lewis used for their legal work in London, arrived at Pemberley the day prior to the reading of the will. He requested the new Mr. Darcy meet with him in the study before the will was to be read.

"As you now know, your father was aware he was ill for some time," Rumpole began. Darcy nodded it was so. "Not long before his passing, with the aid of his secretary, he wrote this letter and sent it to me with the final version of his will. He charged me to allow you to read this before the will is read."

The solicitor withdrew a letter from his inside coat

pocket. He proffered it to his late client's son and then slipped out of the study, softly drawing the door closed behind him.

Darcy stared at the letter in his hands. Rather than being scribed with his father's strong pen strokes, it was written in Simmons's hand. How he wished his father was still with him, as he was before he was taken ill, not as he saw him the day he left the mortal world.

Looking at the letter would not solve the mystery of what Father wanted him to know before the reading of his final will. Darcy broke the familiar seal, the one from the signet ring he now wore on his right hand. Before beginning to read, William Darcy took a deep breath to prepare himself for the words on the paper before him.

*30 July 1805*

*My dearest, one and only son, William,*

*If you are reading this, then I am no longer alive and am finally again with your mother, my beloved Anne.*

*Let me begin by sincerely apologising for not telling you about my malady ahead of time. I should have done so, William. I, more than most, know knowledge is power. It does not pardon my not telling you, but after seeing the way you reacted to the death of your mother, I did not want to burden you with my impending demise.*

"If you had confided in me I would have been prepared!" Darcy lamented to his study. He then stopped himself and realised it was hypocritical of him to take his father to task for something he would have done too. He would have thought it his duty to protect someone by not revealing distressing information to them. He shook his head and allowed his eyes to return to the page before him.

*Both Mr. Harrisons (father and son) and my solicitor, who I am sure handed you this letter, strongly advised me to share the truth about my health with all of my family, not just you. If I did not talk to you before the end and tell you all, please accept my abject apologies. I have been debating relating all to you. If I find the words, I will do so before I leave the mortal world.*

*In the case you were unaware, to my regret, I did not have that conversation with you, one I should have had the day the Mr. Harrisons told me what my fate would be.*

*Like my choice to withdraw from everyone after my beloved wife's death was a gross error, so was my choice not to share all with you before it became too late to do so. Not only with you, but I should have spoken to Gigi (she will always be Gigi to me as it is the name your mother gave her) and the rest of the family.*

*Before I explain a term in my will you may question, I must charge you to live your life and not lock yourself away at Pemberley or any of our other estates like I did.*

*You have Richard who is as close to you as any brother can be. Do not repeat what I did and push everyone away, especially not Richard. I am not telling you not to mourn, but I am instructing you to not mourn me for more than a year complete. I want you to live.*

*It has come to my attention based on some comments you have made that you believe marrying for love causes too much pain. If my behaviour since your mother passed has taught you that, then it is my greatest regret. Do not let the self-indulgent and selfish example of my erring cause you to give up on what would be the most wonderful thing in the world—to marry for true love and respect. And no William, I am not telling you to marry a certain rank or class, your mother and I would be happy as long as she is a gentleman's daughter.*

*I did not marry your mother because she was the daughter of an earl. I did so for one reason, and one reason only. Love! We fell in love, and it was an unbreakable bond (as your wayward Aunt Catherine discovered when she tried to turn me from your mother to herself). Even with the pain I have felt since my Anne was taken from us, I would not have traded our love for anything.*

*Had I been offered a choice of never experiencing the pain of her loss or never sharing the love and respect we did, I would choose the latter, over and over, and over again.*

*Please tell Gigi (Giana I know) I apologise for pushing her away. The older she became, the more she looked like my dear Anne. It was selfish, but it pained me to see her looking so much like your mother.*

*Now to the will. There are no surprises regarding the disposition of all the Darcy holdings. They are yours, save some small bequests to others. I will mention only this one: I have left Hodges £2,500. He is no longer a young man and I do not want him to work any longer if he chooses not to do so. Please tell him he was the best valet I could have ever wanted to have.*

*What I want to tell you regards Georgiana. I gave serious consideration to making you the lone guardian of your sister. Then I was going to designate you and Richard as co-guardians. In the end, I chose your Aunt Elaine and Uncle Reggie as her guardians.*

*Before you allow your equanimity to be disturbed think of this: Since your mother's passing and I, and to a large extent you did as well, withdrew into myself, Elaine and Reggie have been Gigi's* de facto *parents. When not with them, she spends time with your Uncle Lewis and Anne. You know better than any that in the last almost five years she has been very little in our company.*

*Do not allow your pride and indignation to cloud your judgment. If you, as objectively as possible, think about what will be best for your sister, you will know I have made the right choice for her wellbeing. What would you do if the choice was between you, a young man who is not yet 21, (unless I have passed after your birthday—but I doubt I will live to see you reach your majority), or those who have been like parents to her for some years now.*

Darcy stared at his father's words and the more he did, the more his momentary anger dissipated. "You have the right of it, Father," he said to the heavens before returning to read the rest of the letter.

*In the event my brother Matlock predeceases Elaine, then his sons and you will be Gigi's guardians until she is 21. I am however confident Matlock is in fine fettle.*

*The reason I wanted you to know about this ahead of time is because like I used to, you sometimes, rather clearly, show disapproval on your countenance when you see or hear something with which you are not sanguine. I did not want your aunt and uncle to think you question their fitness to be my daughter's guardians. You will need them and all of your family to lean on so it will not do to alienate them.*

*One more thing, William. Duty is important, but it is not, and should not be, the be all and end all of your life. You MUST find the balance that eluded me towards the end. Do not sacrifice the living, and enjoying of your life, using duty as your excuse.*

*You are a highly intelligent, moral, Godly, and diligent son. I know I am leaving all of those who are dependent on the Darcys in good and fair hands.*

*As much as I wish I had more time with you, I must say my goodbyes.*

*Even when I suffered what I can only call my temporary madness and blindly believed young Wickham over you, I never stopped loving you. I am now, and have always been, proud of you, William.*

*With much love and apologies for no longer being with you,*

*Father*

Darcy sat and stared at the letter for some minutes before he moved.

His father had been wise to inform him of his choice of guardians for Giana and his reasons for them. Now that he was able to cogitate further on his father's words, he determined his father had made the only choice he could for Giana's wellbeing. He had learnt all about managing the estates and holdings since his mother had passed away, but that came at the expense of time with his sister and other family members.

As his father told him he could, he would mourn for a year, half in deep mourning and the rest in half mourning, then he would begin to follow Father's advice.

William Darcy stood, straightened his jacket, and made his way towards the parlour where his aunt, uncles, sister, and cousins were awaiting him.

~~~~~~~/~~~~~~~

Elaine and Reginald Fitzwilliam were not surprised they had been named guardians of Giana given they were also presented with a letter which expressed their late brother's thinking about them, and not William being Giana's guardians. This letter too was in Simmons's hand but dictated and signed by their late brother.

During the reading of the will, Georgiana sat holding Anne's hands for support.

As the letter had laid out, there were no other surprises in the will, save one small one. Like Hodges, he left Simmons a sum so he could retire. If was obvious he did not feel comfortable having his secretary write about a bequest to himself. One thing Darcy had not been aware of, but applauded his father for, were the restrictions placed on Giana's dowry of thirty thousand pounds if she married without her guardian's permission.

With everyone agreeing they had no questions for him, the solicitor withdrew.

Once the door closed a timid Georgiana approached her brother. "William, I am happy to be Aunt Elaine and Uncle Reggie's ward, but did you not want me to live with you?" she asked tearfully.

Darcy went down onto one knee so he was able to look his sister in the eyes. "No sweetling, never think that, because it is not at all true," Darcy assured his sister. "Do you remember

I told you I was unaware Father was ill?" Georgiana gave a watery nod. "It was only in a letter Mr. Rumpole presented to me before the reading of the will, I was informed why Father chose Aunt Elaine and Uncle Reggie as your guardians. My first reaction was hurt pride, but the more I read his words regarding his choice, the more I could see the logic behind it. It has nothing to do with you not being wanted. It is simply what serves your best interests, and in that, I agree with our father's wishes. Aunt and Uncle are the perfect guardians for you." He paused. "Had Father named me guardian, I would have happily filled that role."

"Thank you for telling me that," Georgiana responded. Knowing William was not rejecting her made her feel infinitely better. She threw her arms around her brother's shoulders and kissed his cheeks.

He stood up and looked at those in the room. "This I promise you before all of our family who is present," Darcy turned his hand palm up and swept it around the room indicating all who were there, "you will see me as much as you desire. We must all mourn in our own ways, but thereafter I intend to re-enter society."

There were nods of approval from all in the room.

~~~~~~~/~~~~~~~

The following morning, subsequent to his meeting with his father's secretary who did in fact choose to retire, Darcy was seated at his desk studying a ledger when there was a knock at the door. Responding to the master's summons to enter, Reynolds did so and stopped in front of the desk.

"Mr. Wickham is asking to see you," the butler intoned.

"Although I am unaware of a planned meeting with the steward, please have him come see me," Darcy stated.

"It is the younger Mr. Wickham," Reynolds reported with obvious distaste.

"Please inform *that* man my father's rules about him

entering the park and the house have not changed," Darcy shot back.

"He stated he expected you would say that and claims he only wants to condole with you, Sir," the butler reported.

As much as he did not want to see his former friend, Darcy knew it would be churlish of him to deny the man the ability to deliver his sympathies in person. Then again knowing the younger Wickham's penchant for bending the truth, he did not trust the man's motives.

"Reynolds, please have my uncles join me here. Once they are present, you may show George Wickham into the study," Darcy instructed. The butler bowed and left the room to carry out his charge.

Not long after, Darcy was joined by his two uncles. Seeing the questioning looks he explained why he had requested their presence. Uncle Reggie took a seat on the settee between the windows, while Uncle Lewis sat on a wingback chair opposite. A minute later George Wickham was shown into the new master of Pemberley's study.

Until he saw Lord Matlock and Sir Lewis seated in the study with the prig, George had felt confident he would be able to manipulate his erstwhile friend in case he had been omitted from the old man's will.

"Wickham, say what you came to say and then leave," Darcy commanded. "After today, if you contravene the rules of not approaching the park or our house as my father instituted, and I am continuing, you will be arrested for trespassing."

"Is that a way to welcome an old friend who has come to condole with you?" Wickham drawled.

"Young Wickham, you sound as delusional as ever. Did you forget you were trying to undermine William's position with his father," Lord Matlock barked.

"That was but a youthful indiscretion," George hedged.

"You wanted to convey your sympathies. Say what you

came to say and then please leave," Darcy stated.

"Yes, that. I was sorry to hear about my godfather's passing. I also wanted to know what I was bequeathed in his will," George stated nonchalantly.

He had expected much, but not the derisive laughter from the prig and his two uncles.

"For one of around twenty, it is sad your memory is so poor," Sir Lewis mocked. "You know full well my late brother withdrew as your godfather once your perfidy came to light. My brother Matlock has the right of it, you are delusional." Sir Lewis turned to his brother and nephew. "Do you think we should send him to bedlam? He is clearly insane."

"My uncles can attest to the fact your name was not so much as mentioned in the will. Now please leave," Darcy related.

George Wickham could see he would get nowhere in his quest for easy wealth, well certainly not in this room.

With a scowl on his face, he turned and stomped to the door, pulled it open, and with two footmen following close behind, headed towards the main doors. Once outside, he stopped and looked back at the house, in the direction of where he knew the study was.

"You will be sorry you crossed me," he threatened towards where Darcy sat.

Seeing the two large footmen starting to move towards him, Wickham turned and walked as fast as he could back towards his father's cottage.

# CHAPTER 11

Elizabeth was keen to welcome her friends back the day they arrived from Derbyshire after having to travel there due to the death of Mr. Darcy, Giana's father. There was no missing how drained Anne looked from travelling. Elizabeth was aware Uncle Lewis had added an extra two days of travel—each way—to make the journey a little easier for Anne.

When she exited the de Bourgh coach, Anne was leaning on Jenki's arm for support while the big guard Biggs was giving her support on the other side. "Anne, what do you need?" Elizabeth enquired worriedly.

"I think Miss Anne only needs good and uninterrupted rest and then she will regain her energy," Mrs. Jenkinson stated.

Whether it was what Mrs. Jenkinson desired or factual, Elizabeth did not know, all she knew was she prayed it was what would occur. Before Elizabeth could say another word, she heard her mother begin to direct things.

"Mrs. Jenkinson, allow Biggs to assist you in taking dear Anne up to the chamber she uses at Longbourn so she may have as much rest as she needs to recover," Fanny ordered. Next, she pulled Georgiana into a hug. "Giana you poor thing. We are all so very sorry your father has been called home to God. He was such a good man. I am very regretful we only met the late Lady Anne that first time when we were introduced to you."

"I especially miss Mama. I love my late Papa, but I had

hardly seen him since Mama passed away," Georgiana stated sadly.

Georgiana was dressed in a black muslin gown. Before she departed Pemberley with Uncle Lewis and Anne, two mourning dresses had been made up and three of her older gowns had been dyed black.

Aunt Elaine and Uncle Reggie were to remain at Pemberley for a few more weeks. She was to remain with Uncle Lewis, Anne, and her friends for now. In a fortnight they would make for Rosings Park where she would reside until her guardians came to join them. Giana would discover what the plans after Rosings Park were once her aunt and uncle arrived.

Elizabeth waited back to speak to Uncle Lewis. She was very concerned about Anne. In the years they had been friends, never had she seen Anne looking so very haggard.

Sir Lewis did not miss the look of concern on Lizzy's face. "It was the journey, nothing more Lizzy, I promise you," Sir Lewis stated guessing what she was about to ask.

"That will allow me to rest a little easier," Elizabeth visibly relaxed, although she still felt some worry for Anne. "Do you still want Jane, Mary, and me to accompany you to Rosings Park when you depart?"

"Yes, we do. Unless your parents have changed their minds," Sir Lewis confirmed. "I assume you will be bringing Penelope so you are able to ride in the groves again. I know you like to walk there as well."

"Mama and Papa have not rescinded their permission, and yes, you know me well enough to know how much I enjoy walking and riding in the groves, and visiting the glade," Elizabeth smiled widely.

She loved taking her exercise on the paths at Longbourn, especially going up to the top of Oakham Mount, but she had become enamoured with Rosings Park. Especially the groves, glade, and the replica Greek temple on the hill overlooking the mansion.

When she entered the house, Elizabeth was shaken from her reverie by Jane. "Lizzy, what did Uncle Lewis say about Anne?" Jane enquired. Their three younger sisters were listening intently.

She related what she had been told. "We should wait until Jenki tells us we may visit Anne and then we can see for ourselves all is well with her," Elizabeth suggested.

"In the meanwhile, we will spend some time with Giana," Kitty decided. She and Lydia made for the stairs to go to their friend.

~~~~~~~/~~~~~~~

By the next day, much to everyone's relief, not least of all Sir Lewis's, Anne was back to her normal—such as that was—self. Mrs. Jenkinson still wanted her to rest for another day to be safe, so after a short visit she began to herd the visiting girls from her charge's bedchamber.

"Jenki, if you will allow it, I...would like Jane and...Lizzy to remain," Anne requested.

The two eldest Bennet sisters looked at Mrs. Jenkinson expectantly. With a wide smile, a nod of permission was received. "No more than a half hour, then you need to rest more, Miss Anne," Mrs. Jenkinson allowed.

"Thank you, Jenki," the three young ladies chorused.

The nurse and now companion in one inclined her head and then exited the bedchamber.

"Jane, what happened to...that man who wrote the hideous...poetry for you? Lizzy...wrote about him," Anne clarified.

Jane had come out locally in March of the current year, a few weeks after she turned seventeen. Her first assembly had been at the end of May. The son of the tenant of Netherfield Park had become smitten with Jane. He was thirty years old.

The age did not bother her very much, but Jane had found him boring. All he could talk about was his horse and hunting. Any other subject was beyond his limited knowledge. Also, the only thing he seemed to admire about Jane was her looks. The quickest way to turn Jane's attention away from a man was for him to objectify her and not see past her external shell. She was too used to the respectful way her father, and other men in her life related to her, to ever accept one who objectified her.

At the mid-July assembly, he had presented Jane with the worst attempt at poetry she had ever seen. As he had not taken her hints, Jane spoke to Papa about not wanting the man to continue to attempt to court her. Her father had spoken to both the father and son at Netherfield Park the next day.

A fortnight later, they moved out of the area, giving up their lease. Uncle Philips was the agent for the owner, Sir Morris Samuels, and he had attempted to sell the remaining one year in the lease, but to date, it had not occurred.

"Did Lizzy not write and tell you after Papa warned him off? The family left Netherfield Park," Jane replied.

"I forgot to write about that, and then Mr. Darcy passed away and you and Uncle Lewis had to travel north," Elizabeth explained.

"There is a more serious...subject I want to discuss with...both of you, but Jenki will return...soon," Anne related.

"Hopefully on the morrow, you will be allowed to join us, then we three may find somewhere to sit and talk," Jane suggested.

"Did Jane write to you that Aunt Elaine has a date for her presentation and come out in London?" Elizabeth questioned. Anne shook her head. "It is on the penultimate Friday of February, only six days after Janey turns eighteen."

Before there could be more discussion, Mrs. Jenkinson entered the chamber. Jane and Elizabeth exited before they were asked to do so.

~~~~~~~/~~~~~~~

"Bennet, losing Darcy like this reminded me of my own mortality. I would like to make another change to my will," Sir Lewis related. "As Darcy will not be able to do so if I predecease Annie, will you agree to be her other guardian, and my executor alongside Matlock?"

"Although I pray that never comes to pass, it would be both an honour and a pleasure," Bennet agreed. "You are aware Fanny and I see Anne as another daughter already, do you not?"

Sir Lewis nodded it was so. "You know I had Philips redraw my will for me not long after the attempt was made on our lives, do you not?"

"I remember you telling me you requested my brother do some legal work for you, I did not know the specifics. Why do you mention that now de Bourgh? Surely Rumpole in London can make the changes you are speaking of now?"

"That is not why I mentioned that at this time." Sir Lewis removed a thick document from inside of the leather bag he carried with him. "This is the will as it is now, the only change will be substituting your name for Darcy's."

"Why do you need me to see this at this point?" Bennet raised an eyebrow in question.

"As one of my executors, you will need to keep a copy, and you should know I have taken some extraordinary steps to make sure a forgery can never..." Sir Lewis explained what he had done to ensure his wishes would be the only ones that governed the distribution of his property after his death.

"Keep a copy, yes, but that will only be after the changes you have enumerated."

"Bennet, read the document."

Still not sure why, Bennet read. The more he read the

closer his eyebrows approached his hairline. "Surely you jest!" Bennet exclaimed.

"No, I do not, and before you ask the question, I was of entirely sound mind when I made the relevant decisions. My actions were driven by reality. I know Anne will not survive me, or if she does, it will not be by many years. Yes, I spoke to Matlock and Darcy before I made these changes and neither man objected."

"I am dumbstruck." Bennet, who was normally very articulate was at a loss for words.

"There is nothing to discuss at this point. Even if we did, it would not change my mind," Sir Lewis insisted.

Bennet raised his hands in surrender. "All I can do is pray it will be many years before any of this," Bennet picked up the documents, "needs to be executed."

Sir Lewis lifted his glass of port to the heavens. "Amen to that."

~~~~~~~/~~~~~~~

Just like the girls had hoped, by the next day Anne was allowed out of her chamber and felt and looked like her normal self. It was a hot day, so they were told to keep to the house and not take Anne out into the heat.

The three sat on a settee in the small parlour. Anne was in the middle between Jane and Elizabeth.

"About what did you need to speak to us?" Elizabeth enquired of her best friend. "You know there is nothing we would not do for you."

"It is about my...mother, you remember what...she was accused of?" Anne revealed.

"We do," Jane confirmed, "but what has she done?"

"Nothing, yet. It is what she...is asking of me..." Anne, with frequent breaths to take enough air into her lungs, explained how her mother had first begun to write to her on her birthdays, and then of late more frequently. "This letter," Anne reached into the pocket of her dress, "is the most…recent one. It arrived at Rosings Park…shortly before we made…for Derbyshire."

Anne unfolded the letter. "You want us to read it?" Elizabeth verified.

"Yes, and then give…me your advice. I need to decide…if I should speak…to Papa," Anne explained.

Jane and Elizabeth each leaned a little towards Anne so they were able to easily read the writing.

*1 August 1805*

*12 Littlefield Street*

*Bath*

*My dear Anne,*

*That you have not responded to any of my letters has cut me to the quick, but it will not stop me in my determination to repair the rift between us which is due to my being accused of that which I did not do.*

"Uncle Lewis did say there was no proof to connect Lady Catherine to the attempt on his and your life," Elizabeth recalled. "And she never admitted to any involvement, did she?"

"Yes, that is…all correct," Anne confirmed.

"Let us read on," Jane advised. "We need to see what this is about before we are able to make an informed recommendation."

Anne and Elizabeth nodded. Jane and Elizabeth continued to read.

*How do I prove I did not do something? How can anyone believe I would want to harm my own daughter, the only one I have?*

*We have been cruelly separated these almost five years.*

*I know not how much you have grown or what additional accomplishments you have gained. It is unnatural for a mother and daughter to be kept apart in this fashion.*

*What can I do to prove myself to you, my dear daughter? Tell me and it will be done.*

*I am always watched, even when I go to sleep there are 2 men in the hall outside my door and another on guard under my window. I am sure the guards have sent their reports to your father which will show I have done nothing I am not allowed to do.*

*I beg your pardon for whatever I did to make you believe me capable of the heinous thing of which I have been accused. I know I was not the warmest of mothers, but the time away from you has shown me what I am risking if I do not repair the relationship between us.*

*Is it too much to hope I will be forgiven one day? Is that not why our Lord and Saviour died on the cross? To redeem and forgive us mere mortals? Am I judged beyond redemption?*

*All I can do is continue my daily prayers that God will soften your and your father's hearts.*

*Your loving mother.*

"Has Uncle Lewis seen this or any of the other letters your mother has sent you?" Elizabeth queried. Anne shook her head. "My first suggestion is no matter what Janey and I recommend; you need to show your father all of the letters. He knows your mother far better than even you, and he will be a better judge of her sincerity than we are."

"I agree with Lizzy about Uncle Lewis needing to know about the letters," Jane added. "However, regardless of what she has, or has not, done in the past, to me at least, her pleas for forgiveness sound genuine."

"The truth is, that it is our Christian duty to forgive the trespasses of those who have trespassed against us," Elizabeth used some of the words and imagery from the Lord's prayer.

"Do you want to forgive and see your mother again?" Jane questioned.

"My life will not...be long. Yes, I suppose...I would like that," Anne decided.

"Then you know you need to speak to your father," Elizabeth stated.

Anne knew what had to be done. She could only hope Papa would not be angry at her for the omission of not revealing the letters to him before.

~~~~~~~/~~~~~~~

"Annie, I have known since the first letter your mother sent you that she has been doing so. My guards report everything to me, remember?" Sir Lewis told his daughter with a smile. "I am not upset in the least. I am aware you have never responded to any of the letters and I knew you would come to me when you felt the time was right. Let me assure you, I know not what the contents are. That is your private business."

Anne handed her father the twelve letters in date order. "Here they...are, Papa," Anne stated simply. Sir Lewis read from the first one to the most recent one.

"She certainly sounds contrite," Sir Lewis stated. "If I am to consider a change where she would be allowed in your company again, I will meet with her in Bath first, and I must be convinced of her sincerity. That is why it needs to be face-to-face." Not for one second did Sir Lewis believe his wife had changed, or even had the capacity to do so. However, his love for his daughter was so great, he would see if there was a way for Anne to get to know her mother.

"When will you...go see her, Papa?"

"After we return to Rosings Park and once your aunt and uncle have arrived."

"Should I write to...her?" Anne wondered.

"If you want. I will take the letter with me when I go to see her."

With that decided, Anne went to join her cousin and friends and Sir Lewis went to inform Fanny and Bennet of his decision.

# CHAPTER 12

Lady Catherine knew not what to make of her husband calling on her at the house to where he had banished her. Had he not written in his letter she would never see him again?

She schooled her features. Was it possible her campaign to convince her simple-minded daughter she had changed was about to succeed? *'I will have to show deference to my dunderheaded husband during this meeting,'* Lady Catherine told herself. *'If he suspects anything, I am sure he will leave me to languish here.'*

Plastering a smile on her face, she tried to look as welcoming as possible when Sir Lewis entered the room.

"Catherine," Sir Lewis greeted his wife curtly.

"Lewis how good of you to come see me," Lady Catherine simpered.

"Let us plainly understand one another," Sir Lewis bit back as he sat in an armchair opposite his wife. "Like it is referred to in Jeremiah 13:23, a leopard is unable to change its spots. I am not fooled by your act Catherine; you always did think yourself so much more intelligent than you are. The only reason I am here is for Anne. She believes in redemption and so far I have chosen not to disillusion her by sharing my opinions on the matter with her."

As he spoke, Sir Lewis noted the way his wife's face got a more and more pinched look with every word. He shook his head, she really believed she was able to pull the wool over everyone's eyes.

He agreed with Elaine and Matlock her words rang false. They too concurred if he could have safeguards in place, and as long as she behaved, it would not hurt for Anne to come to know her mother in whatever time was left to her in the mortal world.

"If you believe I am dissembling to my daughter," Lady Catherine responded imperiously, "why are you here?"

"Because unlike you, I love Anne and will do anything to facilitate her enjoying whatever time God grants her before He calls her home." Sir Lewis went silent for a few moments. "Read this, and then I will tell you my plans."

He slid Anne's letter across the low table between himself and his wife.

Lady Catherine retrieved the letter, broke the seal, and began to read.

*26 August 1805*

*Mother,*

*I truly want to believe you have the capacity to change. In addition, it is my Christian duty to forgive.*

*As I am not sure how many more years I will have before the damage to my heart and lungs claims my life, I would like to know you.*

*Mother, please do not think I will ever forget what happened to me those years ago, when, if it was not you, someone tried to murder Papa and me. It was bad enough that poor, faithful Jimmy Green's life was taken that day.*

*I am well aware of your strictures regarding maintaining the distinctions of rank. I say this because Mother, I have many friends, from various strata of society. If you cannot accept that, then tell Papa now and he will depart and leave things as they are.*

She had to fight to appear outwardly unaffected while she struggled to maintain an air of equanimity. How was this to be borne? Then Lady Catherine reread the last sentence. She

115

would have to appear to be accepting of these lowborn friends until she was in a position of power, as she fully intended to be. She went back to the letter trying to keep a neutral visage.

*It is my hope you are the person who has been writing to me over the years, that is a person I would be able to like.*

*Respectfully,*

*Anne*

Sir Lewis saw his wife had completed reading. "Before we continue, it is my sad duty to inform you that our brother Robert Darcy passed away some weeks ago," Sir Lewis related.

Her first instinct was to be gleeful one of the men who had removed her from Rosings Park was dead and that she needed to go to Derbyshire to make sure Pemberley was well run. Lady Catherine stopped herself before saying anything. One thing at a time. She needed to achieve her overall plan before looking elsewhere.

"That is very sad," was all Lady Catherine commented about the death of her late sister's husband. "Why was I not informed before now?"

"Given your reaction in trying to make for Derbyshire after Anne's death, and had I not come now, you would not have been told." Sir Lewis did not miss his wife's look of outrage. "Do not delude yourself that I do not know *all* which occurs here." Sir Lewis paused and took a deep breath. "You may return to Rosings Park so Anne may come to know you."

"At last I am to see my home again," Lady Catherine enthused.

"Before that occurs, there are some things you need to know." Lady Catherine gave a tight nod. "Here is a list, read it and then I will require you to sign at the bottom of the page so you will never be able to claim you were unaware of the expectations of yourself." Sir Lewis handed his wife the document.

Not well pleased she was being treated like an errant child, and with no good cheer, Lady Catherine retrieved the sheet of paper from the table between them. With a sniff, she began to read. She knew she needed to hold her peace until all was read.

### Terms for the return of Catherine de Bourgh to Rosings Park

1. *You will not be the mistress of the estate. To wit, you will not reside in the mistress's chambers.*
2. *Your lady's maid will be released from your service, with a character.*
3. *All of your incoming letters will be read before being given to you and all of your outgoing will also be read before being posted.*
4. *If you do anything which is judged as harmful to either Sir Lewis de Bourgh or Miss Anne de Bourgh, (including trying to have secret letters posted on your behalf) the Bow Street Runners will investigate everything, including to whom you had your maid post the secret letter from the post stop in Bath.*
5. *Your allowance will remain as it is now.*
6. *You will be guarded at all times.*
7. *When you have contact with them at Rosings Park, both Anne's and your husband's friends will be treated with respect by you.*
8. *You will treat all staff and servants with kindness and striking of anyone, like you have in the past, will not be tolerated.*
9. *You are to have no contact with the tenants.*
10. *You will refrain from trying to advise Mr. Jamison regarding his sermons or any other parish business and you will not impose on his wife at the Hunsford parsonage, or anywhere else for that matter, to give her your sage advice.*

*Contravene any single one of the above points, and you will find yourself on your way to Ireland to live in a cottage.*

It took Lady Catherine some time to tamp down her fury at what she had just read. She would still be gaoled. She was seriously displeased. Then she reminded herself that Anne was not long for this world and when she was gone, her husband would have to leave everything to her.

He was much older than she was, so there was the possibility he would pass away in not too many years. If he did not leave all to her in his will, she still had the will, the one she had written and was being held by the man she had paid while she still had funds. She would simply date it a few days before his death, submit it, and then all would be hers anyway.

The first step was getting back to Rosings Park so she would act in the way that would be expected of her. She would prevail in the end.

"It is unfair you should deprive me of my maid," she objected.

"You may remain here and retain her," Sir Lewis replied evenly. "It is your choice. If you are to come back to one of *my* estates, then I will have every servant who has interactions with you be ones I know are loyal to me and cannot be manipulated by you."

Lady Catherine knew it would be futile to push the point any further.

At least she understood why there was an inkpot with a quill in it on the table. Without a word, she removed the quill and signed her name below the insulting list of terms for her return to Kent.

~~~~~~~/~~~~~~~

On arriving at Rosings Park a few days after her husband departed Bath, escorted by the men who had guarded her up to now, she relaxed somewhat as soon as she saw the mansion before her.

Lady Catherine could tell by the lack of respect she garnered that the staff and servants were aware of her husband's strictures. Once the estate was hers, she would sack every single one of them without a character.

Although the chambers she was placed in were much larger than the one in Bath, they were still far smaller than the suite that should have rightfully been hers. Her new lady's maid, Masterton, who she was sure would spy on her for her husband, was waiting for her in the bedchamber. Just as her husband had written, the guard dogs followed her wherever she went, and some were stationed outside of her suite when she was within.

Once she had washed and changed, Lady Catherine made her way down to the drawing room where she was surprised that besides her husband and daughter, her brother and sister-in-law were present. Then, sitting near Anne, she noticed four girls of varying ages, all pretty, and one of the blondes, dressed in mourning garb, who looked suspiciously like her late sister.

"Catherine," Matlock inclined his head, as did his wife without saying anything.

"Mother, allow me...to introduce those...you do not know, or in one...case, mayhap you do...not remember," Anne began to say.

"Annie, save your breath," Sir Lewis interceded.

"As you may have noted, Giana looks very much like her late mother," Sir Lewis took over the introductions. "That very pretty young lady is your niece, Georgiana Darcy who we all call Giana. The three beauties are sisters. Miss Jane Bennet, Miss Elizabeth—the one who saved us all those years ago," Sir Lewis looked at his wife pointedly when he stated the last, "and Miss Mary of Longbourn in Hertfordshire. They are close friends to both Annie and Giana."

At first Lady Catherine only glared at the one named

Elizabeth. She had foiled her plans, which had led to her banishment. She was seriously displeased. Then she schooled her features and reminded herself it was critical to maintain the outward façade of cooperation. It would not do to be sent to Ireland before the patience she had exercised for so very long, bore fruit. The dark haired pretty one would receive her just rewards for her unwarranted interference when the time came.

"It is a pleasure to meet any of Anne's friends," Lady Catherine forced herself to say with good cheer.

Her husband, brother, and sister-in-law were not fooled by the performance. Neither was Elizabeth. '*As long as Lady Catherine does nothing to try and harm Anne, I will keep my observations from her. I will ask Jane and Mary if they noted anything,*' Elizabeth thought as she watched Anne's mother suspiciously. While Anne wanted to allow her mother to prove she had changed, Elizabeth decided all she could do was be vigilant.

The girls excused themselves to go ride, Anne would be in her phaeton of course. "How come our niece is with you and not with Fitzwilliam at Pemberley? Would she not want to mourn with her brother?" Lady Catherine enquired.

"Elaine and I are Giana's guardians," Matlock stated. "*William* will only be one and twenty in November, he is too young to care for a girl of ten."

"Such an unrefined name for Fitzwilliam," Lady Catherine sniffed.

"Would you like to inform the royals that the three King Williams have had unrefined names?" Sir Lewis derided. "William is the name he wants to be called, the same name his parents used, as do all of us. *If and when* he ever chooses not to be addressed by that name, we too will cease using it for him."

Lady Catherine took a deep breath and reminded herself she needed to show no outward signs of displeasure. If she had to, she would call Fitzwilliam by that name. What cared she if it was the name of three past kings. In her opinion, there was no more noble name than Fitzwilliam.

~~~~~~~/~~~~~~~

That evening after they wished Anne and Giana goodnight, the three Bennet sisters met in Jane's chamber. Jane, Elizabeth, and Mary were sharing a suite with a sitting room between the two chambers. With Giana in the second bedchamber in Anne's suite, Elizabeth had opted to share a bedchamber with Jane rather than one of them being on her own.

"What did you think of Lady Catherine?" Elizabeth asked as neutrally as she was able.

"I do not trust her," Mary responded.

"Is it not too soon to judge?" Jane, who liked to give people the benefit of the doubt, questioned.

Jane did not see the world through rose-coloured glasses, but she was careful in her judgements and always hoped a person's better angels would win out in the end. At the same time, she was aware it did not always happen that way.

"My feelings align with Mary's," Elizabeth stated. "However, Jane has a point, and we may be allowing our prejudices based on what we knew she was suspected of doing in the past to cloud our judgement." Elizabeth looked at her older and younger sister. "In my opinion, we need to keep an eye on Lady Catherine when she is around Anne. Do not forget, per Uncle Lewis's orders, she is watched at all times. Neither Uncle Lewis nor Aunt Elaine and Uncle Reggie trust her, so she will not be allowed to cause any harm."

The other two Bennet sisters agreed with Lizzy. Soon thereafter, Mary went to her bedchamber and was soon asleep. Not long after, Jane and Elizabeth were in Morphius's arms.

~~~~~~~/~~~~~~~

The first thing Lady Catherine did as soon as her new

maid left her was scream into a pillow, which thankfully muffled the noise.

Not only did she have to go against her character —which had always been celebrated for its frankness—and constantly bite her tongue and show a *happy* face to her family, but she had to put up with Anne being friends with these nothing Bennets.

She had picked up enough to understand the father's estate was entailed to some distant cousin. They had no wealth, and she may have heard there was at least one uncle in trade. Lady Catherine ignored the fact the Bennets' connections were essentially the same as her own.

Once she was screamed out, Lady Catherine blew out the final candle, climbed under the coverlet, and fought to fall asleep.

# CHAPTER 13

## November 1806

Richard Fitzwilliam was beyond pleased William had accepted his invitation to join him at Cloverdell where he would meet Bingley. Unfortunately, he would also be exposed to the sisters.

At least the number of Bingley huntresses had been cut in half. The older sister was now Mrs. Louisa Hurst. Just after his six weeks of deep mourning for Uncle Robert, Richard had taken the extraordinary step of being blunt with the then Miss Bingley.

He had noticed Harold Hurst, the heir to a small to medium-sized estate, Winsdale in Surrey, was interested in Louisa Bingley while she was lavishing her attentions on himself. Rather than allow her to waste her time, she was the sister of a friend after all, Richard had told her in no uncertain terms he would never marry either her or her younger sister.

The fact she was the daughter of a tradesman (something she and her younger sister did everything they could to hide) had not been the reason he had no interest in either Bingley sister. They just would not suit and he had no feelings for her or Miss Caroline as anything but the sisters of his friend.

He knew he had bordered on being rude when he had spoken to the now Mrs. Hurst. It had to be done to save both Miss Bingleys much heartache in the future. However, Richard had informed his friend of his intentions before speaking to Miss Bingley. Bingley had attempted to have his sisters see reason many times, but they simply ignored him. Therefore, he gave his full-throated blessing to Fitzwilliam to do what he had to do.

A month after Richard's speech, Miss Bingley had accepted an offer from Harold Hurst, ignoring her younger sister's lamentation that Hurst was only a member of the lower second circles, if that, and could not raise the Bingley family to the heights of society, as she required.

Over the youngest sister's vociferous objections, the eldest Bingley had married Hurst in early February 1806. Richard had attended the wedding. His friendship with Bingley had won over his personal preference not to be anywhere near the sisters.

The Hurst-Bingley wedding had occurred at the same time Miss Jane Bennet had been brought out by his mother. Over the years both Richard and his older brother had become close to the Bennet sisters. They were all beauties, the eldest was of the exact look Bingley would fall in love with as soon as he saw her—blonde, blue eyes, and willowy.

Richard had no tender feelings for any of the Bennet sisters—none he would admit to until the one who had truly caught his eye came out that is. He enjoyed being in their company and was sorry to miss the ball his mother had hosted at Matlock House for Miss Bennet. William had not even been invited as he was still in deep mourning at that stage.

With his thoughts returning to the subject of his slightly younger cousin, Richard grinned as he thought about his cousin's reaction when he had forewarned him about Miss Caroline Bingley's fortune hunting and social climbing ambitions. He had also informed his cousin of her pretentions and she would more than likely set her cap for him as soon as she met him.

If Caroline Bingley's cloying attention became too much for William, Richard intended to speak to Bingley to have him warn her off. If that did not work, he would suggest Charles allow his cousin to speak plainly to the youngest Bingley.

Richard was willing to take the situation into his own hands if things became too much for William and his fastidious nature would not allow him to tell Miss Bingley the truth of his feelings for her. His cousin had just begun to venture away from Pemberley, and he would not stand for any harpy driving him back into the solitude in which he had been living. Seeing William willing to be away from Pemberley was too valuable to allow anything—or anyone—to make him return to his hermitage, even his friendship with Bingley.

The Bingleys and Hursts would arrive at Cloverdell in two days, on the second Wednesday of November, and William was to arrive two days later, on Friday.

~~~~~~~/~~~~~~~

As he often did when he sat in his study with a steaming mug of coffee in his hand, Darcy spoke to his parents the morning he was preparing to begin the two day coach journey to Richard's estate.

"Well Father, I am honouring your wishes. I pray it pleases both you and Mother. I will no longer lock myself away at Pemberley. As I am sure you and Mother noted, I mourned you no more than the one year as you instructed." Darcy had his eyes lifted to the heavens as he spoke. "My first step is a small one. I will be spending time at Cloverdell with Richard and I will finally meet his friend by the name of Bingley. I know neither of you would have been proud of me when I used the fact his friend's father was a tradesman as a reason not to meet him before.

"I have been a selfish being all my life, in practice, though not in principle. As a child, you and mother taught me what was right, and how to correct my temper. You gave me good principles, but at times I have followed them in pride and conceit, only looking inward. Unfortunately as an only son and until Giana was born, an only child, in some ways I was spoilt by you. I know that is not what you intended, you who were goodness personified. You were both all that was benevolent and amiable, and you never allowed, encouraged, nor taught me to be selfish and overbearing; to care for none beyond my family circle; to think meanly of all the rest of the world; to wish at least to think meanly of their sense and worth compared with my own. That was all my own sense of superiority. I know it is not a value either of you ever shared. Such I was, from eight to one and twenty; and such I might still have been but for Richard's admonition followed by your letter, Father.

"I will try not to be aloof and arrogant with Richard's friend. You know it takes me a while to become comfortable with those I am unfamiliar with. I cannot make the same promise with his younger sister. I read you the description Richard wrote in the letter a fortnight ago so I do not have to tell you what she is like again. I will try to be polite.

"However, if she or any other lady—once I begin to make forays into London society—tries to entrap me I will not allow anyone to force me into marriage. I will follow your directions regarding the person I should marry.

"Yes, I have seen the wisdom of your advice regarding marrying one I love and who loves me for myself and not my connections and possessions. I was going to do exactly what you suspected, use your pain after Mother passed away as an excuse never to marry for love. I have come to realise had I done that, I would have been miserable for all of my days.

"You know Mother, when Father first named Aunt Elaine and Uncle Reggie as Giana's guardians, I was very resentful. It did not take me long to see the wisdom in Father's choice. My sister flourishes with them. It has been some years now since she has exhibited any shyness, and Mother, I am sure I do not have to tell you that at eleven she is more proficient on the pianoforte than young ladies four and five years her senior. This coming Christmastide will be at Snowhaven, and I will be there every single day and I will spend as much time with my sister as she will allow.

"I love you both and miss you all the time, but I will not allow that to stop me from living. I must away now. Carstens is waiting for me in the coach. I love you both."

Darcy drained his cooling coffee, stood, and lifted his eyes to the heavens for some moments. Thereafter, he made his way to the interior courtyard to say his goodbyes to the Reynolds and Wickham.

A few minutes later, the Darcy coach was on its way south.

~~~~~~~/~~~~~~~

Even though her mother had done nothing overt to rouse suspicion, Sir Lewis would not leave Anne in Lady Catherine's care. When he had to travel, Anne would be at either Longbourn or Matlock House. Sir Lewis and Anne still spent time at Oak Hollow. To date, Lady Catherine had not been included on a visit to that estate. He had decided he would never sully their retreat with her presence.

After her first season in London, Jane had returned for part of the little season. Uncle Lewis was away on business, and she was missing her sisters and Anne. Anne was at Longbourn, so Jane chose to return home in the middle of November rather than mid-December.

One man had caught Jane's attention, but as yet, other than dance with her, one set only, at the balls they had attended in common, he had not requested to call on her. Given he was from a family who were friends of the Bennets, she did see him more often than just at the occasional ball.

As her family members had not been able to accompany Jane to London, and Aunt Elaine had not been available as much as needed, Mrs. Annesley had been with Jane as her companion.

When Jane came out, it was decided she needed a companion. Given Mrs. Annesley's familiarity with London society and its mores, she was offered the position. The former governess was keen to take the new position, especially with the increased wages. The only issue was finding a new governess for the two youngest Bennets. Elizabeth, who turned sixteen in March, and Mary, fifteen in August, no longer needed a governess and only studied with masters or their father.

Kitty and Lydia, thirteen and ten respectively, still needed the services of a governess. The problem had been solved by employing Miss Anita Jones, sister to Meryton's apothecary and doctor in one person.

Jane enjoyed having Mrs. Annesley as her companion. The lady was ever watchful, but knew when to remain in the background and allow Jane to speak to those she desired to. It was not just the two of them in London, Uncle Lewis had, after conferring with Bennet, sent Brian Johns to watch over the two ladies when they were out in public.

When Aunt Elaine, Uncle Reggie, and Giana were not at Matlock House, Jane, her companion, and her temporary personal guard would be hosted by the Gardiners at their house on Gracechurch Street.

That morning Jane and Mrs. Annesley were riding in the old Bennet carriage with Johns seated on the box next to the coachman. Bennet had purchased a larger coach and two matched pairs of greys in January of the current year, a month before Jane came out. When his neighbours enquired how he could afford such a conveyance, he told them he had one very good year which gave him some additional funds. It was true— he just did not reveal all the years had been like that.

A little more than four hours passed since departing Town before the coachman guided the team through the gateposts which marked the entrance of Longbourn.

Even though it was windy and chilly, the Bennet parents and four younger sisters were waiting for Jane in the drive by the time the carriage door had been opened. As soon as she was hugged and kissed by her parents, Jane was surrounded by four excited sisters.

There was no need to ask about Anne. Cold days were not good for her, even more so when it was windy as well.

Given the falling temperatures, with Mrs. Annesley—who also had been welcomed warmly—trailing, the Bennets entered the warm house. "Anne?" Jane enquired while she was divesting herself of her outerwear.

"In the drawing room," Elizabeth cocked her head to the closed door, "with Jenki."

Each year that passed Anne became more and more sensitive to the elements, especially the cold. Once the days became too cold, as much as Anne loved to drive one of her phaetons, she no longer did so. Jane entered the room where Anne was.

"Jane, it is good...to see you," Anne managed before she began to cough.

Mrs. Jenkinson administered a spoonful of tonic Mr. Jones had provided which seemed to diminish Anne's coughing fits.

"As it is to see you," Jane responded. Not wanting Anne to talk too much after her coughing, Jane looked to Mrs. Jenkinson. "Jenki, how long will Anne be with us?"

"Until the first week in December, Miss Bennet," Mrs. Jenkinson stated. "Miss Anne and Sir Lewis will be at Rosings Park for the season."

What went unsaid was they would also be with Lady Catherine.

She had never said anything outright to tell the Bennets they were unwelcome the times they had visited since her return to Rosings Park, but it was not hard to read in the surreptitious looks she shot at them as well as her body language when she thought no one was observing her.

Knowing Anne was building a relationship with her mother, no matter how strained it was, none of the Bennets said a word to Sir Lewis, and especially not to Anne. The past Easter had been the first year the Bennets had made the excuse they were to be with the Gardiners and Philipses for the holiday. There was no doubt Sir Lewis knew the reason for the change in plans, but he too did not want Anne to suffer for her mother's actions.

"Janey you should see how much Anne has improved at playing chess," Elizabeth said to distract any maudlin thoughts about them not spending Christmastide with Anne. "She played me to a draw last time we played; she, in fact, almost beat me."

"Uncle Thomas has...been teaching me...some of his strategies," Anne managed.

"Ones he has not taught his own daughter yet," Elizabeth gave her father a mock glare.

The truth was Elizabeth had begun to win against her father occasionally. He had not told her yet, but he believed she would ultimately be even better at the game than he was. It had been almost a year since Matlock or his sons had been able to best Lizzy at the game.

Not long before dinner, Fanny knocked on her husband's study door and entered when he called out. "Thomas, are we doing the right thing not telling Lewis how his wife makes sure we know she does not welcome us at Rosings Park?"

"The woman has no power. Do not forget she is not even the mistress there," Bennet replied. "If she did anything overt, I would speak to de Bourgh, but I will not do anything to upset Anne unless there is no choice."

A tear slid down Fanny's cheek. "How I wish it was not

a certainty that Anne's life will be cut short." Fanny wiped the tear and others that had followed it with her husband's proffered handkerchief. "I love her as well as any of our daughters."

"It is how we all feel. Remember we have promised de Bourgh we will never make Anne feel like all she has to do is to prepare to pass away. He wants her to live as full a life as possible until the time comes."

Fanny straightened her spine as she heard Hill announcing dinner. "Then that is exactly what we will continue to do!"

After sharing a warm hug and a rather languid kiss, Fanny and Bennet left the study heading for the dining parlour.

# CHAPTER 14

Darcy arrived at his cousin's estate as planned; he was met in the drive by Richard.

"William! Welcome back to Cloverdell. Do not make it obvious you are looking, but I am sure you can see the redheaded lady staring at you from the window of the drawing room," Richard said in greeting as he barely inclined his head towards the window behind him.

There was no missing the shock of red hair in the direction Richard indicated. "That colour is hard to miss. Miss Bingley, I assume?" Darcy responded.

"One and the same. Bingley and I have each warned her off, but we doubt that will sink into her consciousness," Richard explained. "She has heard the rumours of ten thousand per annum. Even though it is far below reality, being an inveterate fortune hunter and social climber combined, all she sees is wealth and you being her entrée to the *Ton* after I became unattainable to her."

"What do you advise?" Darcy enquired.

"Be blunt when it gets too much for you. I spoke to Bingley when we saw nothing we said was dimming his sister's desire to make you her husband. He agrees. If she is as relentless as I know she can be, then you must be as direct as you need to be." Richard held up his hand to forestall William's protest. "As the honourable gentleman you are, I know it would irk you to be anything less than polite. However, sometimes, with someone like Miss Bingley, allowing her delusions of a future with you to grow is much crueller than what you would consider rude by shattering her illusions now."

"I will think on your advice and act accordingly if I see it is needed. You told me your friend is an affable fellow. What of his older sister and brother-in-law?"

"Now that Mrs. Hurst is married she is tolerable, although she placates her sister rather than point out her deficiencies. Hurst is more interested in food and drink than anything else, except when hunting is mentioned. It is the one sport he loves." Richard paused. "Yes, Bingley is a jovial man, but do not be fooled by his easy going façade. He is firm with his sister, is resolute, and not easily led."

"Do you think we have been examining the coach and the team long enough?" Darcy asked with a grin. "I will make directly for my chambers and join you and your guests in the drawing room after changing and some ablutions."

"You are lucky the family chambers are not on the same floor where the Bingleys and Hursts are being housed." Richard grinned and his cousin nodded his agreement.

The two men headed towards the house.

~~~~~~~/~~~~~~~

Bingley shook his head and asked, "Caroline, do you not know what ill-breeding you display when you stand at the window and stare at Fitzwilliam and his cousin?"

Not one word he and Fitzwilliam had said to her had pierced the fog of Caroline's desire to be the next mistress of Pemberley. He greatly regretted he had not confirmed his study door closed properly at his house in London, the day he and Fitzwilliam had discussed his cousin and his estate.

Evidently, she had heard parts of their discussion. He had heard something in the hallway, opened the door, and run her off. The door had been shut correctly at that point. Since that day, a footman was stationed outside of his study anytime he was in it whether he was alone or with others.

Bingley thanked his lucky stars all she had heard about the cousin's income was what it was *purported* to be, not the real, far larger, number Fitzwilliam had shared later in the conversation.

"What do you know of breeding," Miss Bingley sneered. "You were not the one who attended the exclusive seminary in London. I did."

"So they teach social climbing, fortune hunting, eavesdropping, and chasing a man not interested in you there? That being the case, Father wasted his hard earned money," Bingley derided.

Miss Bingley was about to respond with vitriol when she heard the sound of boots approaching the drawing room. The pinched look disappeared from her face replaced with a simpering one. Much to her distaste, it was their host who entered the drawing room, without his very rich cousin.

"My cousin will join us after he has washed and changed," Richard informed those within the room. Seeing the look on Miss Bingley's face, he decided to make sport of her—indirectly of course. "He did wonder if I had a new dog in the house."

Bingley understood what his friend was about. "New dog? Are not all your hounds in the kennels?"

"He noticed something which looked like red hair against the window. He knew no one was so classless as to stare at us in that fashion, so he assumed I had an Irish Setter in the house," Richard related with a perfectly deadpan expression.

"That was, unfortunately, my sister displaying her inadequate knowledge of etiquette," Bingley responded.

Caroline Bingley spluttered but could not seem to form a coherent sentence.

The cousin thought she was a dog at the window! Ignoring the parts about bad manners, she decided she would have to do everything she could to impress the man.

~~~~~~~/~~~~~~~

This was not how things were supposed to be! The only positive change Lady Catherine de Bourgh could find in her situation was that she was at Rosings Park, and not in Bath.

She had tried to push the limits of her restrictions, only to discover the guards, staff, and servants at the estate were not intimidated by her in the least. Not only that, but the first time she had tried to have the housekeeper follow her orders, Sir Lewis had reminded her what would occur if she kept on in that fashion.

At least those low born, no consequence, and no wealth Bennets had taken her hints they were not welcome at Rosings Park. It irked her no end her daughter was being hosted by the Bennets while her husband was travelling for business.

Thankfully she had stopped herself from questioning her husband when he had told her where Anne would be while he was away. Lady Catherine was sure doing so would have caused her husband to send her to Ireland. Each time her ire boiled over, she had to regulate it. She would not be exiled!

When Anne was in Kent, one of her massive, intimidating guards was always in her company when she was around the house or riding in her phaeton. How was she to exert her influence and manipulate her daughter if she was never alone with her?

The only positive was she had noticed her much older husband had begun to wheeze at times. When he did, he would sweat and his complexion would become pallid. She hoped it would lead to his end.

~~~~~~~/~~~~~~~

George Wickham remained with his father at Pemberley for about six months after his failed attempt to gain a fortune from his former friend. His father had begun to demand he work if he remained under his roof. Working, especially the type of work his father would have him perform, was not at all palatable to George.

He had told his father he wanted to seek his fortune in the South and asked for whatever legacy he intended for him to be given to him then. His adoptive father had given him a paltry five hundred pounds and admonished him there would be no more. Writing and begging more from him, would not produce any results.

The next day George was on the post headed to London. It did not take him very long in London to learn two things; he was not good at games of chance—over four hundred pounds was gone in short order—and he had the ability to charm both sexes.

With a few sweet words, he was able to open accounts with tradesmen in his own name, or any other name he invented, allowing him to acquire what he needed without having to pay for it thus saving most of the balance of his funds. He discarded the idea of blackening the Darcy name by using it as he did not want to come to their notice.

He would remain in a boarding house or inn for about a month at a time until the landlord became insistent on payment before moving on. After about four months in London, there were too many creditors seeking him, even in a city that large, so Wickham decided to move south.

He eventually reached Margate in Kent, and there he met Miss Karen Younge. Needing a place to stay, he charmed Miss Younge and soon they were paramours, and he was residing in the house she shared with her brother Clay, and at times, their dim-witted cousin, Jake.

Thankfully, for self-preservation, George learnt it would not be good if he tried to cheat the Younges, especially if he wanted to continue living. In return for living with them, the brother expected George to assist him when he robbed the toffs, as he called them. As Wickham had been educated to a certain extent, and could speak like one of the toffs and could charm people, while making them relax and divulge information, Younge found his sister's lover rather useful. As such, George would receive a small cut of whatever he assisted Clay in gaining.

~~~~~~~/~~~~~~~

When Darcy entered the drawing room, he was well pleased Richard stepped in front of the red-headed woman who was advancing towards him, more than likely to introduce herself.

"Richard would you introduce me to your friends, please," Darcy requested before the woman attempted to approach him again.

"William allow me to present Mr. and Mrs. Harold Hurst of Winsdale in Surrey, Mr. Charles Bingley of Scarborough where his late father's businesses are located, and Mr. Bingley's sister, Miss Caroline Bingley." He ignored Miss Bingley who, as he was sure she would, turned purple at his allusion to her family's roots in trade. Hurst, Mrs. Hurst, Bingley, and Miss Bingley, my cousin, Mr. Fitzwilliam Darcy of Pemberley in Derbyshire."

While the rest of those introduced were offering a curtsy and bows, Miss Bingley was stymied. How could Mr. Fitzwilliam mention her father's business in front of his cousin? Now she would have to work even harder to induce the extremely handsome man to offer for her.

"Richard has told me much about you, Mr. Bingley; it is good to finally meet you," Darcy stated as he extended his hand towards the amiable man.

Darcy had to fight to keep his face from showing the shame of his remembered words to Richard when his cousin had first suggested meeting Mr. Bingley. Darcy could tell from the grip of the handshake this man possessed an inner strength.

"As he has about you," Bingley responded.

"Some of it was even positive," Richard jested.

Caroline Bingley was not sanguine with being left out of the conversation between the three men. After being introduced, her matrimonial target had not looked at her. She had her maid dress her in her newest orange ensemble with the dyed-to-match turban and matching ostrich feathers. She had sprayed her preferred perfume on liberally and made sure she was wearing an impressive amount of jewels. She needed to be noticed.

How could her brother and his friend direct Mr. Darcy's attention away from her in such an infamous manner? Even though her sister was furiously signalling her not to do so, Miss Bingley moved to stand between her brother and the man who she had decided would marry her—even before she met him.

"Mr. Darcy, it is so good to be among more of our circle," Miss Bingley purred as seductively as she was able, all the while batting her eyes at Mr. Darcy coquettishly.

"Excuse me, Madam," Darcy barked. "Did you not observe we were conversing? For those who grew up being part of the *landed gentry,* it is well known how rude it is to insert oneself into a conversation without invitation."

"Among those of us who were raised in the house of a tradesman, my sister's behaviour is just as unacceptable," Bingley interjected. "I can only think her excuse is she is awed to be in the presence of another one from the first circles, as other than your cousin, she has not had that experience previously."

Caroline Bingley felt her fury building. She had not missed the inference. Mr. Darcy and then her brother alluded to them being raised in the house of a tradesman. Charles spoke as if he was proud of his roots. It was not to be borne.

The woman turned a deep shade of purple after her

brother mentioned their roots. Darcy had to fight to stop himself from bursting into laughter. Her current complexion clashed with her hair almost as much as her hideous orange outfit and mismatched jewels did. The odour of her over applied scent made Darcy want to sneeze.

Thankfully before he started a fit of sneezing, the woman turned and without a word to anyone, stomped out of the drawing room and up the stairs.

Mrs. Hurst stood, her face burning red with embarrassment—both for her sister's behaviour, and their hated roots being pointed out so clearly. "If you will excuse me, I need to make sure my sister is well." The lady made a quick curtsy and took off after her younger sister.

While his wife went to see to her sister, her husband reclined on a chaise lounge not paying attention to, or not caring, what was occurring in the room.

"Mr. Bingley, I apologise if I was harsh..." Darcy began but ceased talking when the brother held up his hand.

"First, please address me as Bingley. Next, what did you say or do that my sister did not deserve?" Bingley questioned. "From the time we arrived, Fitzwilliam and I have tried to counter her delusions about marrying you, which stem from..." Bingley explained about his sister's propensity to eavesdrop. "I am only pleased she did not hear the real amount, which was mentioned after I closed the door securely, otherwise she would compromise you if that is what it took."

"Entrapment would get her nothing, other than self-ruin. I will not be forced into marriage under any circumstances..." Darcy explained what his father had instructed him on the subject and his determination to only marry when, and if, his heart was well and truly engaged. "Please call me Darcy."

"I will attempt to make her understand, but I am afraid my sister has the affliction of only hearing that which fits the narrative in her head," Bingley explained. "In fact, I believe she takes anything she deems negative and makes the words over until they are what she wants them to be. It may be time to send her to live with our aunt in Scarborough. Nothing I have attempted has worked on her."

"I do not envy your task in managing her," Darcy responded.

~~~~~~~/~~~~~~~

Mrs. Hurst followed her sister into her bedchamber on the guest floor. Caroline was standing with a vase in hand ready to hurl it against a wall. "Caro, that will not make anything better. Besides, you are a guest in Mr. Fitzwilliam's house and you cannot take your frustrations out on his possessions." Mrs. Hurst soothed as she pried the *jardinière* from her sister's shaking hand.

"How dare Charles embarrass me in such a fashion, to mention we are the children of a tradesman!" Miss Bingley screeched.

"Caro, do you really think Mr. Darcy did not know of our roots before Charles mentioned it? As much as I too do not like being reminded, it is not a secret. His cousin referred to it in his introduction, and I would wager Mr. Darcy was aware of our antecedents before he arrived here today," Mrs. Hurst reasoned. "Mayhap it is time to set your sights lower. Both you and I were warned off Mr. Fitzwilliam and he told you, more than once, before his cousin arrived he would not appreciate being hunted."

"Just because you married that lout of a husband of yours and settled for much less than you should have, does not mean I will ever accept the same!" Miss Bingley stamped her foot to emphasise her point. "It seems I will have to be a little more patient and allow Mr. Darcy to see all of the advantages I bring to a match. How many women can say they have twenty thousand pounds for their dowry?"

Louisa Hurst knew full well that among the upper ten thousand such a dowry was nothing exceptional. She was also aware her sister's dowry would be seen as having the stink of trade attached to it, making it far less attractive unless a man was desperate for funds, something Mr. Darcy was not.

"Even so, Caro, if you push our brother too far he will send you to live with Aunt Hildebrand, and then where will you be?"

"I cannot allow that to occur! I will have to be more circumspect, will I not?" Mrs. Hurst nodded her head emphatically. "As soon as I compose myself, I will make my apologies. In the meanwhile, I will bide my time, but Mrs. Darcy I shall be, even if I have to affect a compromise!"

~~~~~~~/~~~~~~~

None were more surprised than Bingley when a calm and collected Caroline rejoined them before dinner and apologised for her behaviour from earlier. Richard and Darcy, being gentlemen, could do nothing else but accept her contrition as genuine even if they would not relax their vigilance.

For the remainder of Darcy's visit, although she always watched him and made sure she was in his company as much as possible, Miss Bingley did nothing which could be construed as misbehaving.

Bingley decided as long as she behaved reasonably, he would not send his sister north to their aunt.

# CHAPTER 15

## April 1808

Elizabeth had just been presented to Her Majesty at the Queen's Drawing Room. Hate was too mild a word, as far as Elizabeth was concerned, for the hooped dress and the rest of the ensemble she had to wear in which to offer her curtsy to Her Majesty.

Thankfully they were on the way back to Matlock House in one of the Earl's comfortable coaches. Elizabeth was seated next to Jane on the rear facing bench sitting opposite Aunt Elaine and their mother! That had been a massive surprise to Elizabeth. She had not been aware her mother had been prepared to be presented as well this day. It seemed everyone knew about the fact her mother was to take her curtsy, except for Elizabeth.

"Jane, how could you have not told me," Elizabeth asked softly in an accusatory tone.

It was her mother who responded, she had not spoken as softly as she thought she had. "Lizzy, if you are to be upset at anyone, then aim it at me," Fanny stated in a conciliatory tone. "I wanted it to be something we shared. The ball this evening, however, will be for you alone."

"Mama I am not upset because you were presented. It is quite the opposite, I am well pleased," Elizabeth replied as she reached across the space between the benches to take her mother's hand. "If I am agitated, it is with myself. I was so caught up in my preparations I did not see all the clues, which in hindsight, were rather clear."

"You have nought for which to be disquieted," Fanny assured her second daughter. "I know from Jane's preparations —not to mention my own—how all-consuming it can be before one takes her curtsy. Of course, there are concerns over your coming out ball, which I did not have to worry about for myself."

"You know Lizzy, your propensity to be so hard on yourself is similar to my nephew, Giana's brother," Lady Elaine related. "Just like you do, he berates himself about things over which he has no control."

"It would be nice to finally meet this Mr. Darcy we have heard so much about," Elizabeth observed without commenting on what Aunt Elaine had said.

"William shies away from London and the huntresses of the *Ton*. He actually would have attended your ball, but his steward who served at Pemberley since before his father's passing, was called home to God less than a month ago," Lady Elaine responded. "My nephew will not mourn him officially, but he will remain at Pemberley until the end of the summer. The late Mr. Wickham was a link to William's father which is now broken."

"Did Giana not say the steward had a son?" Jane remembered.

"He did, named George, and he turned out very wild..." Lady Elaine related what she knew about George Wickham's propensities and lascivious lifestyle.

"To try and sow discord between father and son!" Jane exclaimed. "That shows a very black heart."

"Brava, Jane. That is the most unforgiving speech I have ever heard you utter," Fanny stated proudly. "Good girl! It would vex me, indeed, to see you be the dupe of one like this Mr. Wickham about whom Elaine has told us."

"Where is this libertine now?" Elizabeth enquired.

"From what we know he was traced to Town, and then

from there we know not," Lady Elaine shared. "If you ever have the unfortunate luck to meet the man, it will be easy to tell when he is dissembling." Lady Elaine smiled as she saw the questioning looks from Jane and Lizzy. "His lips will be moving."

All four ladies in the coach descended into laughter.

Lady Elaine looked at the young ladies opposite her. Even if their reputed dowries were almost non-existent, she would not mind if one or both of them became her daughters-in-law.

~~~~~~~/~~~~~~~

"Anne, how I wish you would be able to dance at the ball tonight. My deepest desire would be for it to be a ball for both of us," Elizabeth told her best friend after she had changed out of the hideous hooped gown she had worn to the Queen's Drawing Room.

"As would...I, Lizzy," Anne managed.

With each year that passed, it became harder and harder for Anne to speak and more difficult for her to move about under her own power. It was the reason it had been impossible for her to be presented.

"In that case, I will have to dance for the both of us," Elizabeth insisted. "You will allow Biggs and Johns to assist you to the ballroom so you can at least be present at the ball, will you not?"

"Yes, I...will," Anne confirmed.

John Biggs and Brian Johns were not only Anne's guards, but they would carry her up and down stairs, or anywhere else she needed to go which would have been too difficult for her to achieve using her legs.

Sir Lewis had a special bath chair constructed for Anne —it was based on the modified sedan chair which had been used to take Anne up and down Oakham Mount—which the two men would carry when Anne needed to go somewhere which was not on the floor she happened to be on at the time. Most of the time, one of the men would push Anne to wherever she needed to go. They would only give way to Mrs. Jenkinson, a close friend, or family member.

Miss Lizzy had their loyalty almost as much as Miss Anne. The two men saw and understood the unbreakable bond of friendship and sisterhood between the two.

Elizabeth looked at the two guards who were standing at the back of the room. "No scaring any of my potential dance partners away tonight," she admonished in jest.

"Me an' Johns will be watchin' Miss Lizzy," Biggs responded with a glint in his eye.

She was fully aware they would not step in unless they saw some form of danger, which Elizabeth did not expect with a ball held at Matlock House.

~~~~~~~/~~~~~~~

The three patriarchs were sitting in the master's study later that afternoon so they could escape the madness of the last minute arrangements for Lizzy's ball.

"Even though I know there is no hope of a cure, I had Anne examined by two recent additions to the medical field in London," Sir Lewis shared. "They are both men who subscribe to the modern treatments and belong to the school of thought starting to question the efficacy of bleeding patients. They are in a minority, but the two men I took Anne to see believe it is more harmful than helpful." Sir Lewis paused as he shook his head. "That is not what you asked. No, they were not able to offer me any new hope for some new and miraculous cure for Annie."

"I wish it were otherwise," Bennet stated sympathetically.

"As do I," Matlock added. Matlock looked over at Bennet. Both men tried to hide their concern for de Bourgh.

They had had a conversation more than once regarding

how his whole life was caring for Anne. They were convinced de Bourgh would not live much longer than Anne. Both men were storing the most recent official copy of de Bourgh's will in their studies, and as the two executors, they were ready for any possible machinations Lady Catherine would attempt to finally gain that which she had long coveted.

"How is Catherine behaving herself?" Matlock enquired.

"When she is in company with Anne and me, reasonably well," Sir Lewis responded. "She truly thinks she has fooled all of us. I think she believes I did not notice how she treated the Bennets at Rosings Park." He turned his head towards his friend. "Had you not begged me to leave things as they are for Annie's benefit, I may have sent her packing to Ireland."

"Has Anne derived some peace from knowing her mother?" Bennet verified.

"She has. Anne is never left alone with Catherine so she has no choice but to behave as she should in her company," Sir Lewis explained. "If I had proof she was behind the attempt on our lives, I would not hesitate to have her tried. We know she had her maid post a letter for her, and the same girl collected a response from the post stop. Unfortunately, Catherine burnt the reply before my guards could retrieve it, so we know not who the missive was sent to or from."

"And even if the maid were interrogated, there is no guarantee she read the direction," Bennet opined.

"Speaking of daughters, are you ready to lead Lizzy to the floor for her first dance tonight?" Sir Lewis queried his friend.

"Very much so," Bennet replied without hesitation.

Sir Lewis knew what his brother-in-law and friend were both thinking when they looked at him as soon as Bennet spoke of his desire to squire Lizzy for the first set at her ball.

"Just because I am not able to do the same with Annie

does not mean I am not well pleased for Lizzy," Sir Lewis assured them. "This will be the second of your daughters I get to dance with at her coming out ball."

"Do you think now she is twenty, Andrew will stop looking at Jane longingly and finally request a courtship," Bennet questioned Matlock. "What is the boy waiting for?"

"For some reason, Andrew does not want to marry before he is seven and twenty. I have pointed out to him some artificial date is meaningless. What if she falls in love with another while he waits for his next birthday?" Matlock shook his head. "The boy did say he would consider requesting a courtship and explaining that if they become engaged he would like to wait until after his birthday in September to marry."

"That way if Jane agrees, he will not have to worry about her affections being engaged elsewhere," Bennet stated.

From that point, the conversation between the three turned to more general topics.

~~~~~~~/~~~~~~~

"Why has Mr. Darcy never introduced us to his Fitzwilliam relations, or for that matter his younger sister?" Miss Bingley whined.

"Caroline, do I need to remind you what both he and Fitzwilliam told us?" Bingley responded exasperatedly.

It was just the two of them at the house on Curzon Street. Bingley had laid down the law that he would no longer fund the Hursts' lives since they felt if they lived with Bingley, they would not need to expend their funds. He loved his older sister, but she was her husband's responsibility, not his. Hence the Hursts were at Winsdale, the Hurst estate. Unfortunately, his younger sister was still with him and had not given him a reason to pack her off to their aunt—yet.

In the almost one and one-half years since Bingley had been introduced to Darcy at Cloverdell, they had become good friends. Not like he and Fitzwilliam were, but they often met at White's when both were in London. The club was an option which precluded any ladies—namely Caroline—from inserting themselves into their conversations.

His sister had kept her behaviour under moderation since the visit to Fitzwilliam's estate. However, it was as plain as the nose on her face she had not given up her dream of being the mistress of Pemberley and Darcy House. That it was a dream which would never be realised did not seem to sway her.

As far as being introduced to Fitzwilliam's parents, she had been informed in no uncertain terms the Earl, Countess, and Viscount had no interest in meeting Miss Caroline Bingley. Caroline was also aware that her desire to become Miss Darcy's friend would never occur. She was a ward of the Fitzwilliam parents, which therefore precluded an introduction.

"I read the Fitzwilliams are holding a ball tonight," Miss Bingley stated ignoring the inference her brother made. "Had we been introduced; we would have been invited."

"How long have I been Fitzwilliam's friend? For many years, is that not so?" Bingley answered his own question.

"I suppose so," Miss Bingley sniffed.

"If in all those years he has not introduced you to his parents, why would you think Mr. Darcy, their nephew who is not their son, would do so?" Bingley demanded. "It is a coming out ball for a young lady the Countess sponsored. Unlike you, I have been introduced and I will attend tonight, and I will not be late, fashionably or any other reason."

"Then you must bring me with you!" Miss Bingley screeched. "You are a terrible brother not to have your sister introduced to a peer of the realm."

"Did you introduce me to every friend of yours from that seminary you attended—if, in fact, you made any?"

"Well, no, but that is not the same thing."

"It is. Thank you for making my point for me. I am warning you now, attempt to push your way into Matlock House and you will be on your way to Scarborough faster than you think."

By now Caroline Bingley knew her brother did not make empty threats. As soon as he had told her of his invitation, showing up uninvited was exactly what she had intended to do. She had been sure when she explained she was supposed to be there with her brother she would have gained entrance.

The plan was discarded with alacrity. With a scowl on her face, she began to stomp out of the drawing room, all the while thinking of another option to have her brother take her with him.

Bingley, knowing what his sister did when she was upset and or angry, stopped her. "Caroline, you had better control your temper. As I have warned you before, I will deduct the value three times from your allowance, and if needs be, from your dowry, for each item you destroy in a snit." For the second time in minutes, Miss Bingley had to change her planned actions.

~~~~~~~/~~~~~~~

"Miss Bennet, may I have a private interview with you?" Andrew Fitzwilliam, Viscount Hilldale, requested.

Jane looked to her mother and the countess who were in the drawing room with her and Mary. "I will allow it without disturbing the men in the study," Fanny granted. "The door will remain open, and you will have no more than ten minutes. And Andrew," Fanny looked at him slyly, "do not forget, Johns will be in the hallway close to the door.

"He will have no cause to act," Andrew promised.

"In that case, I will allow Andrew to address me," Jane agreed.

Their mothers and Mary stood and exited the room. Lady Elaine may not have intended her voice to be heard, but both in the drawing room did not miss her comment: "It is about time that boy began the process of making Jane my daughter."

"Jane, it has been since before your come out I have known you are the only woman for me. However, I promised myself I would not marry before my birthday in September upcoming," Andrew began. "I know, as my father pointed out, there is no magical age when one is ready to marry, but I have seen so many of my friends marry too young, making unwise choices, and then have miserable marriages. For myself, I wanted to reach a certain level of maturity and be as sure as I could be I had found the right woman to be the partner of my future life.

"Of course, I may not be the one for you, but I can tell you it has been a long time since I have known I am in love with you and there is no woman I could respect more than I do you. You are so much more than your outward beauty, which is second to none, but it is your mind, kindness, compassion, and intelligence which were the main attractions for me. Jane, will you allow me to court you?"

"Andrew, I have a question," Jane responded. Andrew nodded for her to ask it. "What is the purpose of a courtship?"

"Ahem, ehrm, well to find out if the couple is compatible, to get to know one another as well as possible, and to discover if they desire to spend the rest of their lives together," Andrew answered in a state of confusion.

"And do you need any of those questions answered regarding myself?"

"No, I know you are the one for me, but I wanted to give you as much time as you may need."

"Have we not known one another for many years now?" Andrew nodded. Jane went further. "Was it not obvious to you my feelings match your own, and have since before I came out?"

As he processed Jane's words he ended up with a face-splitting grin. "You love me?" Andrew verified hopefully.

"Most ardently," Jane confirmed. "As such, there is no need for a courtship."

Andrew sunk to one knee. "Jane Eloise Bennet, will you agree to be my wife?"

"Yes, Andrew Reginald Fitzwilliam, I most certainly will." As Andrew stood, Jane looked at him slyly. "If you still think we need to wait until September, six months distant, to marry, I will not object. However, if you do not want us to ever have to part sooner than that..."

"I agree a six month engagement will be too long. We can examine a calendar on the morrow." Andrew lowered his head towards his fiancée after seeing permission in her eyes.

Given the door was open and Johns was right outside, before their mothers and Mary returned, they enjoyed just a few chaste kisses, with the definite promise of more when the situation allowed.

As soon as the others returned, Andrew went to speak to Bennet.

# CHAPTER 16

Although they all felt like they were already family, news that the two families would be connected with the marriage of Jane and Andrew, once Fanny and Bennet had bestowed their permission and blessing, was met with much joy by the Fitzwilliams, de Bourghs, Bennets, and the one member of the Darcy family who were present.

"It seems everyone anticipated this happening and were only waiting for me to speak," Andrew shook his head as he smiled at his fiancée.

"I was one of those waiting as well," Jane teased.

"It is with much pleasure I have rewarded your patience," Andrew jested back.

"Are you not the one being rewarded with our Janey's hand?" Elizabeth bantered with her brother-to-be. "After all, she is a jewel of the first water."

"Lizzy!" Jane blushed.

"Your sister does have the right of it, you know," Andrew agreed. "I will thank my lucky stars for the rest of my life that you accepted me."

"As will I." Jane rested her hand on her fiancé's forearm and gave it an affectionate squeeze.

"Mother and Father, have you written to William with the news yet?" Andrew enquired. "I will have the pleasure of informing Richard when he returns from meeting his friend at White's"

"A letter will be on the way to Pemberley in an hour, well

before Lizzy's ball," Lady Elaine informed her eldest son. She turned to her brother. "Lewis I assume you will share the news with Anne when she wakes from her rest?" Sir Lewis nodded he would do so.

"Do you not mean my coming out ball and Jane and Andrew's engagement ball?" Elizabeth suggested with an arched eyebrow.

"But Lizzy this is your..." Jane began and stopped when she saw Lizzy shaking her head.

"The announcement will only enhance my ball," Elizabeth insisted. "Although I am sure she would if needs be, but why should Aunt Elaine have to plan another ball in a week or two when it can be accomplished with so little trouble today?"

"What announcement?" Richard asked as he sauntered into the drawing room.

He was informed in short order and was soon being effusive in his congratulations to Jane and his brother. "Poor Bingley," Richard shook his head.

"What has your friend's sister done now?" Lord Matlock enquired.

"This time it is not the shrewish harpy," Richard clarified. "After lunch, I described Jane to him." Richard did not miss his brother's scowl. "Andy, do not look at me so. How was I to know you would finally act today? I thought if Bingley, who as I have told you would find our Jane to be his ideal woman, started to pay her attention, it may have finally spurred you to speak."

"In that case, I will forgive you," Andrew said magnanimously with a *royal* wave of his hand and a heavy dose of mock hauteur.

"How could Mr. Bingley decide to admire Jane before he even met her?" Mary asked.

"Because Mary, my friend looks for certain physical

attributes, all of which your eldest sister possesses in abundance," Richard responded. '*Woe betide if he is attracted to Mary who is similar in looks to Jane. Luckily she is not out yet. Oh my, Mary gets more and more beautiful with each year. She will be seventeen in August and then there will be only one year until she comes out in London,*' Richard told himself. '*After her birthday I will have to make sure I am in Meryton for the assemblies so I can dance with her before her debut in Town.*'

As she usually did when she noticed Richard looking at her intently, Mary blushed rather deeply.

"I for one agree with Lizzy regarding celebrating the engagement at the ball," Fanny stated. "However, it is now time for us all to go rest a little before we dress for tonight's entertainment."

Except for the three youngest Bennets and Giana who would not be attending, everyone else made their way upstairs to rest. Sir Lewis made for his daughter's chambers to inform her of the engagement between Jane and Andrew.

~~~~~~~/~~~~~~~

"Caroline, why are you dressed for a ball and waiting at the door?" Bingley asked as he took his overcoat, hat, gloves, and cane from the butler.

"Did you not take pity on me having to remain here alone?" Miss Bingley stated trying her best to look wretched.

"No Caroline, I did not!" Bingley exclaimed. "Even had I changed my mind, you still would not be admitted, the invitation was for me, and me *alone*."

Miss Bingley was about to unleash a tantrum when her brother's promise regarding her being sent north pierced her consciousness. As much as she wanted to release her vitriol, she did not want to be sent away. Instead, she bit the inside of her mouth and held her peace. She turned on her heel and flounced back towards the stairs to go up and change out of her ball gown.

She needed to remain with her brother until she succeeded in capturing Mr. Darcy. The additional reason Miss Bingley so wanted to attend the ball was she was aware the unmarried Viscount Hilldale would be present. As far as she knew, Lord Hilldale was as rich as Mr. Darcy, and being a viscountess and a future countess would have done nicely.

Bingley shook his head at his sister's temerity as his coach carried him towards Grosvenor Square. For her to think he would take her with him after the conversation earlier in the day was incomprehensible.

He had much more pleasant things to think about. Fitzwilliam had described the sister of the debutante. She was an angel based on his description, and was unattached. If only she had multiple sets still open, he would be daring and request a second one. Bingley's friend had informed him Miss Bennet and her sisters had no dowries to speak of, but with the wealth his father left him, Bingley's angel, when he selected one, would not be required to possess a large dowry.

Thinking about the dowry made him shake his head as he thought about Caroline's wrongheaded opinions regarding their wealth, and the effect it had on their position in society. His sister believed it raised them to the heights, when he well knew, as did anyone with even a slight education, it was birth and connections, not wealth which determined one's rank. As he had told her, his father had wasted his money having Caroline educated as she had learnt nothing.

Soon enough his coach joined the line of conveyances waiting to allow the occupants to alight at Matlock House.

~~~~~~~/~~~~~~~

Richard was pleased he had caught Bingley before he approached Jane. The drop in his friend's face when he was informed of the engagement had made him feel contrite for ever mentioning her to his friend. But at least when the announcement was made at supper, Bingley would not be unprepared. There was no missing the look of longing the man had when he watched Jane dancing the first with Andrew.

For his part, the disappointment that the veritable angel on earth had been proposed to that very day did not stop Bingley from enjoying himself at the ball. Not one built for sadness, Bingley enjoyed himself immensely regardless of the disappointment. He had danced the third with Miss Bennet and would dance the second set after supper with the debutante.

It was well Fitzwilliam had prepared him for the lightning-fast wit and intelligence of Miss Elizabeth. Besides her colouring, hair colour, eye colour, and stature all being wrong for him, his friend had been correct in his assessment few men would be able to keep pace with her intellectually.

Elizabeth was enjoying the ball, doubly so whenever she saw her Janey glowing when in Andrew's company. She had danced the first—as would be expected—with Papa, and then the following sets with Uncles Reggie, Lewis, Edward, and Frank.

Richard had partnered with her for the supper set. He was one of the big brother's she never had, and she felt no romantic inclination towards him at all. Even if she had, she would never have allowed it to blossom. There was no missing the furtive glances passing between Mary and Richard. After Jane and Andrew married Richard would then become her brother indeed. However, in her opinion, he would become her brother again sometime after Mary came out into society.

As Elizabeth was only eighteen, she was not looking for her life partner yet. When and if she met him, she was sure she would know. In the meantime, Jane and Andrew had said they would discuss a wedding date on the morrow once they had slept after the ball.

At supper, Charlotte and her partner along with Jane and Andrew were among the couples seated at the table.

Elizabeth was well pleased the Lucases had been able to join them as they had for Jane's ball some two years ago.

After supper she was to dance with Sir William, then Richard's friend, Mr. Bingley—the one who had been looking longingly at Jane since they were introduced—and then the next sets with each of the two Lucas brothers. Her final two sets were with men she had not met before she had been introduced to them at the ball. One of them was a marquess, Lord Archibald Chamberlain, the Marquess of Hertford Heights. He was a friend of Andrew's.

Every experience, the décor of the room, the people, and dances, were all being filed away in her memories. On the morrow, or later the same day, she would be making a full report to Anne.

Uncle Lewis had told her during their dances how pleased Anne had been when he had shared the news about the engagement. Elizabeth had just listened and not reacted to the wistful way Uncle Lewis spoke of his time with Anne before the ball. She was used to the periods of melancholy which would grip him when he thought about all the things Anne would never be able to do in her short life.

Elizabeth had been one of the members of the family who farewelled the guests and was ready to just drop into her bed when she finally reached her chambers.

The maid Aunt Elaine had assigned her made short work of helping her change. She washed her face, rubbed some tooth powder on her teeth, and then fell into bed. She fell asleep with a smile on her face within seconds of her head resting on the pillows.

~~~~~~~/~~~~~~~

As late as it was when Elizabeth had gone to sleep, she was up earlier than anyone else. She had slept an hour or two longer than normal but was still awake with little more than four hours of sleep. After enjoying a steaming cup of hot chocolate, Elizabeth made her way to Anne's chambers.

John Biggs was standing outside her friend's door dutifully. "Is Miss Anne awake?" Elizabeth asked the gentle giant—gentle to anyone but those who meant harm to the one he was protecting.

"Aye, Miss Lizzy. I seen Missus Jenki bring 'er sum tea 'alf 'our ago," Biggs responded.

Elizabeth thanked the huge man and knocked on the door. It was opened by Mrs. Jenkinson who stood back when she saw who was there. "Did Anne have a good night?" Elizabeth queried quietly.

"She did. All the rest she has had of late has caused her to recuperate, if only a little," Mrs. Jenkinson shared.

There were no secrets between Miss Anne and Miss Lizzy, so Mrs. Jenkinson knew she was allowed to tell Miss Lizzy anything, regardless of how personal it may be.

"Lizzy," Anne greeted with more power in her voice than Elizabeth had heard for some time. "Come tell me...all" Anne patted a spot near her on the bed.

"Rather than us sit indoors, what say you we have Biggs and some of the men carry you downstairs in your bath chair and we take a ramble in Hyde Park?" Elizabeth suggested. "It is a warm day already so you will have no issue with the cold."

Biggs was consulted, and as Elizabeth surmised, Johns was sleeping having been on duty the night before. While her maid and Jenki assisted her to dress, Biggs rounded up two brawny footmen to assist in carrying the young mistress and her bath chair to the first floor.

With Jenki pushing Anne in the bath chair, they headed towards the park—after informing the butler where they intended to walk and for how long they would be away—escorted by Biggs and two additional men.

They found a nice, shaded spot along the Serpentine. With Anne's chair next to her, Elizabeth sat at the end of the bench and related everything she was able to remember about the ball. Thankfully her memory was like a steel trap and she was able to retain all of the information she wanted to relate to Anne.

"Richard's friend is a very affable fellow," Elizabeth told after describing the rest of the ball. She saw her best friend raise her eyebrows. "No Anne, we would not suit. I think he is too young to think of marrying, and quite frankly, I am too. Truly, we would not do well together. He is a nice fellow but interested in more frivolous pursuits than I am."

"In other words...he is not...intelligent enough...for you," Anne managed.

"You may have the right of it," Elizabeth owned. "That however does not change the fact he is pleasant to dance and hold a conversation with." She shook her head. "You have heard Richard talk about the younger sister, have you not?"

Anne nodded.

"Richard informed me even with her brother categorically refusing to bring her to the ball when she asked yester-morning, she tried to insert herself before he departed his house."

Anne just shook her head in wonder.

"Yes, she seems very delusional. Mayhap Mr. Bingley needs to have her committed to an asylum."

"You danced the...final set with a...marquess?" Anne verified as she changed the subject.

"I did. Anne he asked to call on me," Elizabeth admitted. "I will have to put him off as I am not ready to think of a serious relationship yet, and although he is a pleasant man, I do not believe we would suit. Of course it is a great compliment to be singled out by him, but unless I loved him, that would be of no matter."

"You would be...the Duchess of...Hertfordshire," Anne pointed out.

"You know as well as anyone that is not important to me. I will allow him to call once and then inform him of my disinterest—as respectfully as I am able."

Anne shook her head. Other than Elizabeth and her sisters, Anne could not imagine any young ladies in the *Ton* not jumping at the chance to become a marchioness and one day a duchess.

With Elizabeth doing almost all of the talking the friends chatted for a while longer as they walked—Elizabeth pushing Anne—for a little after leaving the area around the shaded bench. When Mrs. Jenkinson pointed out they were approaching the time for the belated morning meal, they made their way back towards the Grosvenor gate.

~~~~~~~/~~~~~~~

When Andrew—who was residing at Hilldale House on Portman Square now that he and Jane were engaged—arrived at Matlock House in time to join everyone in breaking their fasts, Jane could not have been happier to see her fiancé again. The fact they had been parted for little more than six hours was immaterial.

After the meal, Andrew led Jane into his father's study. The door was wide open and the maid who had been assigned to Jane at Matlock House was seated on a chair in the hallway.

The engaged couple examined a calendar. They decided to marry on the third Wednesday of June, the fifteenth day of the month, a little more than three months from the date of their betrothal. The fact the date was about two months shy of his birthday caused no objection to be raised by Andrew.

They would, of course, marry from Longbourn.

~~~~~~~/~~~~~~~

Two days after the ball her brother had refused to take her to, Miss Bingley was reading the only part of the paper which bore any interest for her—the society pages.

Much to her chagrin she read the announcement of the engagement of Lord Andrew Fitzwilliam to a Miss Jane Bennet of Longbourn in Hertfordshire. The lady was an unknown—to Caroline at least—in society.

She threw the paper down in disgust. A marriage option had been removed, so it would have to be Mr. Darcy. If he would not come to the point on his own, she would force the issue.

~~~~~~~/~~~~~~~

There had already been a few callers the second day after the ball when The Marquess of Holder Heights was shown into Matlock House's drawing room. Elizabeth was present with her mother, Jane, and Aunt Elaine. The ladies all curtsied to his bow.

He congratulated Jane on her engagement to his friend before he addressed Elizabeth. They spoke on inconsequential subjects for some minutes before tea was offered.

"I must away, but may I call on you again, Miss Elizabeth?" Lord Archibald requested as he refused the tea.

"It would not be a good idea, your Lordship," Elizabeth stated as gently as she was able.

"If you are concerned about the disparity in our stations and wealth, do not be. My mother and father have no concerns..." The Marquess stopped when he saw Miss Elizabeth hold up her hand.

"While I appreciate the Duke and Duchess's condescension, my reason is twofold. I am not ready to begin an official relationship yet, and much more importantly, I do not think we would suit," she related. "I know you to be a good and honourable man, so it is not that which sways my decision."

Although he was sorry not to be able to pursue the vivacious, intelligent beauty, the Marquess appreciated she would not accept him for the wrong reasons.

"Thank you for being candid, Miss Elizabeth." Lord Archibald stood, bowed over her hand, then bowed to the other three ladies, and took his leave.

There was much for Elizabeth to tell Anne that day.

~~~~~~~/~~~~~~~

The same day the notice appeared in the London papers; Darcy was reading his aunt's letter. Although he had never met them, the name Bennet was known to him.

One named Bennet had saved Anne and Uncle Lewis and they had been friends ever since then. He remembered Aunt Elaine telling how she would sponsor each daughter to be presented to Her Majesty.

He realised he should have paid more attention to his sister when she had related information when they were together. He was sure Giana had mentioned being very close to...four or five Bennet sisters. He could not remember the exact number.

He knew nothing of the lady's fortune or connections and hoped she was not a Caroline Bingley, hunting for wealth and advancement in society.

No sooner had that uncharitable thought reared its ugly head when he discounted it. The Bennets had been known to members of his family since before Mother had passed away. If they had been anything but Godly, upstanding, and honourable people, the connection would not have been maintained.

~~~~~~~/~~~~~~~

When Andrew and Matlock presented Bennet with a draft settlement, they had left the space for Jane's dowry open. To say that both men were flabbergasted when Bennet revealed that each of his daughters had a dowry approaching twenty thousand pounds was an understatement.

# CHAPTER 17

George Wickham had made his way to London on behalf of the Younges.

They owned a boarding house, if one could call the dilapidated dwelling on Edward Street in St. Giles by that name. It had only three rooms for guests, and that was when the so-called master chamber was rented out as well.

It was run by their cousin, Jake. The truth was his wife was the one who managed the house as Jake did not have enough intelligence to keep even a boarding house as bad as the Younges' concern running competently. With nothing to keep him occupied, Jake spent most of his time soused. It was only when Clay Younge needed him for a job, he was reasonably sober.

Jake's wife, Glenda, was not happy having to do all of the work while her husband was invariably deep in his cups. Her disappointment had made her susceptible to Wickham's charms and he had been tupping her since his second visit to Edward Street.

Wickham had just left Glenda at the boarding house after a session of love making, and was on his way to the closest tap room when he remembered he had asked the landlord of the last inn where he had a room during his short stay in London before ending up in Margate—one he actually paid for—to hold any letters for him.

It had been many months since Wickham had called at the Grey Goose Inn, but as he always paid the postage and a fee for holding his letters, if there were any, the landlord kept anything addressed to George Wickham for him.

"Do you have any letters for me?" George asked after he had greeted the landlord.

"Yeah, this 'ere black-edged one arrived in early April. You owes me a shilling and tuppence," The man stated as he reached below the counter to find the letter to which he referred.

He handed over the coins and the landlord handed the letter to Wickham. After all the time it had been sitting, it was now stained, dirty, and dusty. He found himself a table in the corner of the taproom, not close to any other patrons who were frequenting the dingy place in the middle of the day.

First, he stared at the letter. Although he had not seen the prig's handwriting for some time, he recognised the script which had scribed the direction. How Darcy knew he had resided at this inn for a fortnight, Wickham could only guess.

There was no point in procrastinating. He broke the seal and began to read.

*31 March 1808*

*Pemberley*

*It is with great sorrow I write to inform you that your honoured father passed away on the 29th day of this month. The Mr. Harrisons both agree the signs point to an issue with his heart which was heretofore unknown.*

*If you by some miracle receive this and are able to reach Pemberley before the interment, you will be allowed to attend. However, thereafter, the same rules regarding you and Darcy land or property will be enforced.*

*Regardless of the disagreements which have passed between us, I am deeply sorry your father has been called home and I convey my heartfelt sympathy to you.*

*As you are aware, your father gave you your legacy of £500 before you departed my estate. He had told you, I am informed, there would be nothing more after that. On cleaning his house after his death, a sum of £675 was discovered. Your father did not leave instructions for what was to be done with the funds, hence, as far as I and my solicitor are concerned, they belong to you. They have been sent to my London solicitor, Mr. Horace Rumpole.*

*If you make your way to 221 Baker Street, office suite B, he will turn the funds over to you.*

*With my condolences,*

*FD*

Wickham was in a state of shock. Not so much that his adoptive father had passed away, but that Darcy had taken the trouble to not only find out where to send a letter and write to him but was willing to turn over the blunt.

As he hailed a hackney cab to take him to Baker Street, he told himself it was no more than his due that the money should be his.

It was an uneventful ride to Baker Street where the small carriage stopped at 221. Office B was up the stairs. He was shown into Mr. Rumpole's office without delay as the lawyer had no client with him at that time. Mr. Rumpole asked him three questions only the son of Lucas Wickham would know. Satisfied the man before him was in fact George Wickham, he rang for his clerk who handed Wickham a pouch of banknotes.

He was soon on his way to the nearest gambling hell, evidently having forgotten, or not caring, about having lost four hundred pounds so quickly the last time he had tried his hand at cards for serious money.

~~~~~~~/~~~~~~~

A few weeks after he received notification from his solicitor's office that Wickham had collected his money, Darcy received a letter from his Aunt Elaine informing him of the date of Andrew and his fiancée's wedding.

Although he had told everyone he would remain at Pemberley for the summer, he would make his way to Hertfordshire in June.

His new steward, Edwin Chalmers, had been an under-steward trained by the late Mr. Wickham. Thanks to the excellent education he had received from his predecessor he was far further along than Darcy had suspected he would be. That took his last excuse to remain at Pemberley away.

If it had been anything other than his cousin's wedding, Darcy would have found a reason to remain in Derbyshire for the remainder of the summer. No, he was not slipping back into his hermit-like ways. It was simply Mr. Wickham's passing had stirred many unresolved emotions regarding his father's death which Darcy had thought had been permanently tamped down.

He admitted to himself he bore a little resentment towards his father for leaving him when he did. While Lucas Wickham had been alive, Darcy had not allowed himself to indulge those feelings. However, it was now something he had been doing since Mr. Wickham's death.

~~~~~~~/~~~~~~~

Lady Catherine was furious that one of her nephews she had wanted to engage to Anne, but had been refused, was to marry a lowborn nobody.

As much as she wanted to write to her brother and his wife and deliver her opinions along with orders to have her noble nephew break the engagement, no matter how much it irked her to hold her peace, she did.

It galled her that with the upcoming marriage, she would be related to the Bennets. Not only had the one daughter interfered and spoiled her plans in 1800 but now one of the upstarts was to be her niece. It was not to be borne, but she knew not how to prevent it without causing herself to be sent away.

She was sure if she expressed her righteous indignation, her husband would use it as a pretext to banish her to Ireland. She could not risk that, there was too much at stake. She had been able to save up fifty pounds which was intended to be paid to the man who had created the will she would use when her husband passed away.

At least it was safe with him so even had her chambers been searched no one would discover the document which would be her salvation.

All she had to do was to find a way of getting the new information to him. She needed him to add the estate in Bedfordshire to her documents he was keeping safe for her. She would not allow an additional estate to be excluded from her future property.

Her problem was the watchdogs her husband had assigned to her. Not only that, but she could not take a chance of trying to bribe any of the servants at Rosings Park. She was sure her attempt would be reported to her husband. It was a quandary but she was confident in her exceptional intelligence, she would solve it soon enough. It was possible she would have to wait until her useless husband shuffled off the mortal coil.

As soon as he did, she would be released from her prison. It would take a ride into Westerham and for her to call on the man, get the codicil regarding the estate added, and then present it.

Dreaming of everything being hers was the one thing which caused her to smile.

~~~~~~~/~~~~~~~

As the month of June, and Jane's wedding approached, her younger sisters spent as much time with her as possible before she left Longbourn.

After the amount of her true dowry had been revealed to the Earl and Andrew, Bennet and Fanny had informed their daughters regarding the true extent of the family's wealth and their fortunes. They had, however, made it clear the facts were not to be broadcast to keep the knowledge from fortune hunters. At the same time, Bennet had explained the restrictions on the dowries if one of them either eloped or married without permission.

Thankfully, misbehaviour of that kind was not something the sisters would ever contemplate. Their parents and those who had educated them had instilled values which would not allow them to behave in such a fashion.

In early May, notwithstanding the growing heat and odours in London, Jane, accompanied by her mother, Mrs. Annesley, and Lizzy, travelled to London to purchase Jane's trousseau. The youngest three had remained at Longbourn with their father and Miss Jones. Bennet avoided London as much as he was able.

The three Bennets and the companion were hosted at Matlock House. For propriety's sake, Andrew remained resident at his own house in Portman Square.

Much to the engaged couple's delight, other than visits to the modiste and sleeping, they were in company one with the other most of the time. One of the days was dedicated to Jane being given a tour of Hilldale House.

Except for making over the mistress's chambers, which had not been redone in well over thirty years, Jane had not asked for any redecorating.

Elizabeth did not mind being usurped in Jane's affections by Andrew; it was as it should be. She spent much of her time in Giana's company when Jane was occupied and lost in Andrew's eyes.

One afternoon Elizabeth and Georgiana were taking a stroll on the green in the centre of Grosvenor Square escorted by a pair of Matlock House footmen. "That is Darcy House," Georgiana pointed to the house on the opposite side of the square.

Other than a slight difference in the colours of the façade, Elizabeth could see the house Giana was showing her was very similar to Matlock House's exterior.

"Do you have chambers there?" Elizabeth enquired of the girl who was thirteen.

"No, when Papa passed away I was still in the nursery so I had never been assigned a set of chambers," Georgiana replied. "When I was old enough Mama Elaine placed me in a suite both here and at Snowhaven. You have not visited Snowhaven have you?"

"No, we have not, but I have heard Andrew and Richard describe the castle and the wildness of Derbyshire and I think I would love to see it one day," Elizabeth responded. As she thought about her future and where she would like to travel, Elizabeth felt a little melancholy, as she always did, when contemplating the future without Anne in it.

"Lizzy, did I say something to upset you?" Georgiana enquired concernedly.

"No Giana, not at all. I was only thinking of how sorry I am Anne is not able to join us. I am sure you are aware it has been since after my coming out that Anne has not been able to come to London."

"Yes, Papa Reggie explained the reasons why to me," Georgiana averred. "He told me even in the winter the smells and vapours in Town are now harmful to Anne and her weakened lungs."

"Aunt Elaine remarked your brother is to join us for Jane and Andrew's wedding. We will finally get to meet the elusive Mr. Fitzwilliam Darcy."

"I am looking forward to seeing William again. It has been far too long since I have seen him, and Pemberley as well." Georgiana changed the subject back to Anne. "Is it not sad Anne is not able to sit and play at the pianoforte for very long?

I used to enjoy when the three of us, or just she and I, would sit and play together."

"As did I, Giana. At least we still get to play duets together. When Mary is present then we can have three on the bench again. As you know, Mary is far more proficient than me."

"But you have the voice of an angel, and your playing is as good as mine and almost as Mary's."

"You are very kind to me Giana, but you know I do not practice as faithfully as I should, not like you or Mary. Lyddie has taken up the harp like Jane, and Kitty plays the pianoforte, but prefers her artwork above all else."

"I am very happy that in a little more than a month, we will be cousins. It has felt like we are family for some years already though."

"That is how all of my sisters and I feel about you." Elizabeth paused as her mind returned to her sister of the heart and best friend in the world. "I am pleased that Uncle Lewis and Anne will be at the wedding, without the dragon lady."

"We all are," Georgiana agreed. "I am not sorry I have hardly ever been in my Aunt Catherine's company. From everything I know of her, she is nothing like my dear late mama."

"It is time to return to the house. We are to leave for my aunt's and uncle's house for dinner so we need to change."

"I like Mrs. Gardiner very much, especially when she tells me of times she met my late mother and speaks of her love of Derbyshire."

"Yes, the Gardiners are wonderful people. Now, enough dallying, it is time for us to return." Elizabeth smiled as she took Georgiana's hand and with the two footmen following, they made their way back to the house.

~~~~~~~/~~~~~~~

Darcy was looking forward to his journey to the South. He remembered all the good he had heard about the Bennets, especially the heroic miss who had saved Anne and Uncle Lewis and was rather keen to finally meet them. Fate it seemed had other plans.

He was out riding Zeus one morning a few days before he was to begin his journey south. He planned to stop at Cloverdell for about a sennight and then he and Richard, who was of course standing up for Andrew, would travel to Hertfordshire together.

A fox had been hiding in the underbrush and it seemed it was asleep when one of the forehooves came down next to its head. It caused the vermin to nip at Zeus's legs, which in turn led to the normally placid, obedient mount to rear.

Darcy, who rode like he had been born in the saddle, was not prepared for what occurred and fell off, landing on his left leg which led to a cracking sound and explosive pain.

He knew there was no possibility of his remounting his stallion. "Zeus!" The horse looked at his master, almost apologetically. "Home!" Darcy repeated the command when the horse looked at him. As he had been trained to do, Zeus took off towards the stables.

As Darcy had known it would, his stallion returning without his rider triggered a search, which discovered the master less than an hour later.

Thankfully, according to the younger Mr. Harrison, it was a clean break of a bone called the fibula, which was the thinnest of the leg bones. He would heal, but it would be the work of two to three months so there would be no travelling anywhere.

While the master dictated, his valet, Carstens, wrote the letters he needed to send to apprise his family of his accident and his eventual, and full, recovery.

# CHAPTER 18

"You know Giana, if your brother does not want to meet us he does not need to break his leg in order not to attend Janey's wedding," Elizabeth teased.

"Lizzy!" Jane admonished playfully.

"I was well aware Lizzy was jesting," Georgiana assured her soon-to-be cousin. "I have learnt to look into her eyes, when she is teasing they are laughing, just like Anne's do."

Anne was sitting on the swing under the oak tree at Longbourn being gently pushed by Elizabeth. Mrs. Jenkinson was seated on a nearby bench while Biggs stood in the background watching over the young mistress and her friends. It was June, mere days before Jane and Andrew would marry. The de Bourghs, sans Lady Catherine of course, had arrived in Hertfordshire a few days previously.

Although it was well known she would not recover from her affliction, Anne was looking better than she had for a while. She was still moved in her bath chair more often than not, but on this visit, she seemed to be able to walk, unassisted, a little farther than she had the last time she had been in company with the Bennets. It also seemed—perhaps it was wishful thinking—she was able to speak more words before taking a deep breath than before.

Her eyes sparkled with mirth as Anne nodded her agreement regarding her younger cousin's statement.

"Giana, you wound me," Elizabeth responded as she placed her hand over her heart rather dramatically. "You will make it that no one ever believes I am serious again."

"Lizzy is auditioning to be…the new court jester," Anne stated drolly.

"Enough funning at my expense," Elizabeth huffed with mock indignation. "Will your brother make a full recovery?" she asked seriously.

Based on what she had heard from his sister and cousins, the truth was Elizabeth had been looking forward to meeting William Darcy. He was a bibliophile like Papa, Mary, and herself, and loved to play chess based on information gleaned in conversations with Uncles Reggie and Lewis, as well as with Andrew and Richard. Given how much her playing had improved over the years, where she routinely beat all of the aforementioned men at the game, and even beat her father occasionally, she had been keen to play Mr. Darcy as from what she had been told, he was as good, if not a better, player than his late father.

"Richard received a letter from him just before he departed Cloverdell," Georgiana shared. "In it, William told him the Mr. Harrisons," Georgiana saw the raised eyebrows of Jane and Lizzy, so she explained who the Harrisons were. "As I was saying, the doctors opined he is making good progress and will be able to attempt to use a crutch in the next few weeks."

"That is good news," Jane responded. "Andrew told me Hilldale is only about five hours southeast of Pemberley."

"Your future home is an estate where I would love to ride Penny," Elizabeth sighed.

"I am sorry due to…my restrictions on travel…and the cold, we will not be able…to travel north…for Christmastide," Anne stated.

"Anne, do not dare apologise for something for which you are not responsible!" Elizabeth admonished her friend. "I would much rather spend as much time with you as I am able and I care not where it is. When it is time, I will travel and see the north."

"You will come visit me at Hilldale as planned next summer, will you not Lizzy?" Jane verified.

"I would not miss it, you know I would do anything for you," Elizabeth confirmed as she took and squeezed one of Jane's hands.

Anne was Elizabeth's best friend in the world, but Jane occupied, and always would, a very special place in her heart. Jane and Elizabeth had been the closest of sisters and friends since Lizzy had been old enough to play with her older sister. The bond between them was of such a strength neither of them ever saw the other's friends as competition for her sister's love.

In fact, Elizabeth was standing up with her older sister as her maid of honour. When, or if, Elizabeth married, Jane would be her first choice to support her on that day.

Jane would have asked Anne to be a bridesmaid, but she knew Anne would not be able to walk up the aisle unassisted and standing during the ceremony would have been an issue.

When Jane and Lizzy had discussed asking Anne, they had agreed it would have placed a burden on their friend. Knowing Anne as they did, she would have overexerted herself to try and fulfil her duties and then she would have suffered for it later. Besides they were sure Uncle Lewis would not have agreed knowing how much of a strain Anne would have placed on herself. Thus, in the end, Jane had asked no one else to be a bridesmaid.

"As I told Lizzy, if...she did not go visit you...because I am unable to, she...would have seriously displeased me," Anne smiled.

The girls giggled recognizing the well-loved phrase from Anne's mother.

"Miss Anne," Mrs. Jenkinson called her charge's attention to herself as she approached the swing. "It is time to take a rest."

Knowing she was flagging, Anne did not object. Biggs pushed the bath chair next to the swing. Anne stood and stepped over to her chair and with her companion and the guard's assistance, she sat. Mrs. Jenkinson placed a light cover over Anne's legs and soon they were on their way back towards the house.

"Should we take a ride while Anne is resting?" Elizabeth suggested. "We can see if Mary, Kitty, and Lydia want to join us. I think we should ride across the fields and stop at Lucas Lodge on our return to see Charlotte and Maria."

Jane and Giana agreed, as did the three younger Bennet sisters who had completed their lessons for the day. They all retired to their chambers to change into their riding habits.

~~~~~~~/~~~~~~~

As was her wont, when Elizabeth entered the stables, she went to visit Hector as these days he was only ridden on occasions when the younger Gardiner cousins were visiting.

As Lydia was to be thirteen in December of that year, and she was physically larger than any of her sisters had been at the same age, she had been introduced to her mare. She had named her Titania for the Queen of the Fairies in A Midsummer Night's Dream, Lydia's favourite work by the Bard.

Hector nickered when he detected his former mistress's scent and was rewarded with an apple. Once she had rubbed Hector's neck, Elizabeth made her way to where Penny was being saddled by a groom. As she had been by Hector, Penny welcomed Elizabeth and was especially happy when she too was rewarded with an apple.

Soon all six horses were ready and with a footman and groom attending them the Bennet sisters set off in the direction of Lucas Lodge. On the way there, the three eldest sisters rode abreast while Kitty, Georgiana, and Lydia followed a little behind them.

As much as Elizabeth wanted to give Penny her head, she did not, knowing a leisurely ride on side saddle was not the time to go galloping across the fields.

Jane was in the middle with Elizabeth to her right and Mary to her left. "When will Andrew return from London?" Mary enquired.

Jane's fiancé had departed for Town the previous day to see to some business interests. "On the morrow," Jane responded dreamily, as she always did whenever she contemplated her Andrew. "What he had to accomplish will be completed today."

"And you Mary, it is less than three months until your local come out, are you in anticipation of dancing at the September assembly?" Elizabeth asked.

"Methinks Mary will enjoy her first assembly much better if my future brother will be present," Jane, who had recovered from her dreaming of Andrew, stated slyly. "Is that not so, Mary?"

Mary blushed scarlet from the roots of her hair to to the lace edge of the neckline of her riding habit.

"Jane, do not tease our poor Mary so...even if it is nothing but the truth," Elizabeth added as she allowed one of her tinkling laughs to escape.

"Humph," was Mary's only comment as she spurred her mare forward so she would be riding ahead of her two older sisters and their accurate comments regarding the state of her feelings about Richard Fitzwilliam.

"We should not tease poor Mary so," Jane opined.

"Probably not," Elizabeth agreed. "Are you looking forward to being married to Andrew?"

"You know I would never have accepted him had that not been the case," Jane responded. "I will miss all of you, especially you Lizzy, and Longbourn, but I would be dissembling if I told you anything other than I cannot wait until we are married and never have to part again."

"Mayhap after you are married you will be able to introduce Charlotte to some men who would appreciate her for the gem she is," Elizabeth changed the subject.

At four and twenty their friend was considered all but on the shelf. She and Maria had dowries of one thousand pounds each which, as far as was known, was like the Bennets sisters, the largest dowry in the neighbourhood. Per their parents' instructions, none of the sisters had ever breathed a word about the true extent of their wealth and dowries.

There were some in the area who called Charlotte plain; the truth was she did not have a classical look like Jane, Mary, Kitty, and Lydia. She was however pretty and like Elizabeth her looks were not those considered traditionally beautiful.

"Andrew and I plan to invite her to spend the little season with us this year. If she chooses, she will be welcome for the full season as well," Jane revealed.

"I am happy for her. With the greater variety of men in London I am sure she will catch someone's eye," Elizabeth replied happily.

Since she had come out in London, and her rejection of the Marquess, Elizabeth had not been back to partake of a season in Town. She decided she would do so when Charlotte visited Jane and Andrew, as long as things were well, as well as they could be, with Anne.

~~~~~~~/~~~~~~~

Thanks to Lizzy's ball turning into their engagement ball as well, Jane and Andrew eschewed having another ball before their wedding. Netherfield Park had been rented for the months straddling the wedding. As it had been leased by the Bennets, if they had desired one, there could have been a ball held there, or failing that, at the assembly hall in Meryton.

Having access to Netherfield Park's manor house meant

there was no shortage of chambers for the wedding guests who were not locals.

The fact was the neighbouring estate had not been leased out again, other than the one month the Bennets had it, since the family with the son who had written the atrocious poetry, and then been warned away from Jane by Bennet, had left the place.

"You know Fanny, as much as I would not like to take advantage of another's misfortune, I think we should ask Gardiner if he will join us in purchasing Netherfield Park," Bennet told his wife as they sat in the study at Longbourn.

"Is Sir Morris willing to sell? I thought he only wanted to lease it to people?" Fanny asked.

"He wrote to me recently." Bennet lifted a letter from his pile of incoming correspondence. "He has offered me the right of first refusal. He needs to sell as not having tenants these last years combined with some bad investments has put him in a position where he needs capital. The sale price is below the actual value as he wants to sell sooner rather than later."

"Can we afford to without taking a mortgage?"

"That is why I want to ask Gardiner if he will provide about fifteen percent of the needed capital. Until I buy him out he would receive the same percentage of the profits. We would not have to agree on a future price. When we are ready to purchase Gardiner's share, he will set a price."

"He arrives on the morrow; you will be able to discuss this with Edward then." Fanny paused. "If we are not able to lease out the estate, will that not put a strain on us like it did Sir Morris?"

"No, it will not. I will work with the steward to fill the empty tenant farms and bring the income back to, or more than, the five thousand pounds per annum it should be earning. I will not make the same mistakes Sir Morris made by neglecting the estate. If we can find people to lease it, then it will only increase our earnings."

"Will you use Frank as our agent like Sir Morris does?"

"That is my intention, yes."

"Thomas, how does this affect the entail, or the entail affect the estate if we purchase it?"

"The entail documents are specific. Only the land and chattels listed in the entailment contracts belong to the estate and the heir. Fanny, do you remember all those years ago I explained the Collinses could not touch any money I have earned before they inherit?"

"I think so. So even if you merged the estates the heir presumptive would not be able to claim the additional land?"

"You have the right of it wife of mine. As I cannot be sure the son will not be as miserly, avaricious, and grasping as the father, I will keep the two estates as they are." Bennet cogitated for a second. "That is if we do this."

"I assume like the girl's dowries; our ownership of Netherfield Park will not be broadcast abroad?"

Bennet nodded.

"You have told me all about..." Bennet raised his hand.

"I know what you were about to say, Fanny dearest, but I will not count unhatched eggs. If and when that comes to pass, then we will address it."

Fanny agreed. Before she exited his study Fanny kissed her husband deeply. An action he returned in full measure.

~~~~~~~/~~~~~~~

Gardiner agreed to assist in the purchase of the estate on one condition. The Bennets would buy him out for the same amount as he was investing. He tried to refuse his percentage of the annual profits until he was bought out, but on this Bennet was intractable.

No sooner had agreement between the brothers been reached than an express was on its way to Sir Morris.

# CHAPTER 19

Jane was not a bride who feared her wedding night. It was just the opposite—she anticipated it greatly.

The previous night her mother and then Aunt Maddie had spoken to her about that component of her upcoming marriage that no one would ever share with a maiden—at least, not before just prior to her wedding. Unlike mothers who spoke of duty, lying still, enduring her husband's attentions, and pain, her mother had told Jane of the wonders of the marriage bed when it was shared by a couple who had made a love match.

Before her mother had spoken to her, Jane had felt a certain level of apprehension. Mama had made sure she knew to expect some pain during the first coupling when her maidenly barrier was pierced. She also spoke of the time before the coupling which, when it was a giving and caring relationship, would make her ready to receive her husband.

When Mama had left her, Aunt Maddie had come to make sure Jane had no more questions. Other than asking her aunt about having marital relations during a time she was with child; she felt her mother had covered the subject more than adequately.

Once Mama and then Aunt Maddie had left her chamber, there was a soft knock on the door and Lizzy slipped into the room.

"I do not suppose you will share anything you were told, will you," Elizabeth asked as she blushed deeply.

"If you were marrying on the morrow, then yes, I would

have shared all with you," Jane responded.

"If I was getting married in the same ceremony with you, Mama and Aunt Maddie would have told me what they told you, so I would not have needed to come ask you," Elizabeth reasoned.

"Exactly," Jane stated smugly. "When it is your time my inquisitive sister, you too will gain the knowledge you seek."

Elizabeth had not thought Jane would repeat what she had been told, but she knew she would never be certain until she queried Jane on the subject. She was well aware no amount of cajoling, had she been inclined to try, would have succeeded in having Jane lessen her determination not to say anything about what she had been told.

"I will miss you every day you know," Elizabeth stated as she changed the subject. "I know, I know, it is the way of things. We girls live in our childhood homes and one day, we marry and leave the home of our youth behind, and cleave unto our husbands."

"After the wedding trip and some time at Hilldale for me to familiarise myself with the estate and my new home, we will be stopping in Meryton to collect Charlotte on our way to London," Jane related. "There is no reason you cannot join us in Town."

"You know Anne will be here with us from the end of November. I would not, could not, abandon her," Elizabeth shook her head.

"How many times has Anne told you how she does not want you to change what you would normally do because of her health?" Jane asked her younger sister.

"That she has. Although I am no misanthrope, you know I like the intrigues of the Ton no more than Papa does. I enjoy the theatre and other such activities, and you know I love to dance, but I dislike being among those who will smile at you while they are stabbing you in the back."

"Not everyone in polite society is like that, you know that Lizzy," Jane disagreed.

"I suppose I do, but I am still not enamoured with the way many of those of the upper ten thousand behave." Elizabeth paused as she looked at her sister. "To be with you and Andrew, I would brave the sharks of the Ton. As such, as long as Mama and Papa allow it, I will consider joining Charlotte and come to Town for the little season."

"That is wonderful, Lizzy!" Jane hugged her sister. "Do not worry, we will not invite the Marquess of Hertford Heights to our house when you are in residence."

"Jane, you well know we parted on good terms," Elizabeth admonished, and then changed the subject. "I envy you spending your wedding trip in the Lake District."

"In that case, when you come visit us next summer, I will suggest to Andrew we visit Lakeside Cottage for a fortnight so you may see the lakes too."

Elizabeth threw her arms around her sister as she expressed her gratitude.

Both sisters were aware of the fact that come the morrow after Jane was married their relationship would would fundamentally change. They also knew that neither time nor distance would ever dim the sisterly love they shared.

~~~~~~~/~~~~~~~

The Wednesday morning of the wedding of Jane Bennet to Andrew Fitzwilliam promised to be a warm day if the temperature at half after nine in the morning was any indicator. The sun was already climbing in the sky, well above the horizon. The sun's rays were mitigated by the fact it was a partly cloudy day. There was no threat of rain as the clouds were white, high up, and rather wispy. There was a light breeze moving the small branches and leaves of the verdant trees and the birds were serenading the bride with their sweet song.

Jane was ready, standing in the hallway which led to

the front door. She was in her pure white silk, empire waisted wedding gown which had a fine Belgium lace overlay. Given the season, there was no need for a pelisse for the walk from the house to the church in the Longbourn Village.

The sleeves ended just below her shoulders. Her bouquet, which Lizzy as her maid of honour was holding, was made up mainly of roses. Uncle Lewis had some of his famous rose blossoms delivered yester-afternoon.

The jewels she was wearing were an engagement gift from her Andrew. It was a set which had been in the Fitzwilliam family for many decades. The necklace was a triple strand of pearls, a matching bracelet with dual strands of pearls, which had some sapphires mixed in between, and earrings which each had three pearls hanging, each one a little lower than the previous one, ending with a sapphire hanging at the lowest point.

In her hair were some pearl and some sapphire tipped pins which held the transparent gossamer veil in place. Jane's hair was swept up and placed atop her head with a few of the curls the maid had created hanging down her neck and the sides of her head.

As she stood and admired her eldest daughter, Fanny had to fight to keep her emotions in check. One of her girls would be leaving home in a few short hours. To distract herself, in her head, she went over the lists of things she had had to organise. The wedding breakfast would be a veritable feast, and she knew Cook and Hill had that well in hand. They did not have a ball room at Longbourn, and the purchase of Netherfield Park had just become official, but given the numbers of expected guests, she had chosen not to organise the festive meal there.

Thankfully, some years ago, Thomas had the first floor renovated and enlarged. Some of the principal rooms like the dining parlour, the large and small drawing rooms, the music room, and the largest parlour all had walls which could be opened, as they were now, to make one large contiguous room.

It took no time at all for Fanny to mentally tick off each item and realise there was nothing which had not been done. She told herself she now understood the apprehension her mother had when Hattie married, even though she only moved a few doors down from the Gardiner House. Sadly, by the time she married her Thomas her mother had not been alive for a few years.

'This is not a day for maudlin thoughts!' Fanny admonished herself silently as she watched Lizzy verify everything was as it should be with Jane's gown.

The three youngest Bennets and Georgiana conveyed their congratulations to Jane. Next it was Fanny's turn. She wanted nothing more than to hug and kiss her daughter, but she knew that would crease the gown and negate all of the maid's careful work on Jane's coiffure.

Instead Fanny took both of her daughter's hands in her own. "Never has a more beautiful bride been seen." She looked to her other daughters. "I will tell you the same on the day of your weddings." Fanny shooed the four young girls out of the house, and then followed them. That left Bennet, Jane, and Elizabeth.

"Jane, I am sure you will be a very happy woman," Bennet told his eldest daughter. "I have no doubt he will be a good husband to you."

There was no missing the moisture in their father's eyes, but neither of his daughters commented on that fact. "It is time, Papa," Elizabeth prompted. She handed Jane her bouquet of roses.

Bennet nodded his head and offered Jane his arm. Elizabeth lifted the train of Jane's gown with one hand while she held her nosegay of roses in her other.

There was no conversation as they made the short walk to the church in the village. When they arrived in the vestibule, the inner double doors leading into the nave of the church were closed. The four younger girls had already entered, and Fanny and Madeline were waiting for them. The latter was holding May's hand. The second youngest Gardiner had turned four a few months previously and was the flower girl.

"I am so sorry Janey, but May is too nervous to perform her role today," Madeline stated contritely.

"As I will not be the first, nor I dare say, the last bride to marry without a flower girl, there is no harm done." Jane looked at her young cousin who was hiding her face in the folds of her mother's gown. "May dear, I am not upset with you at all. At four it was very brave of you to even consider doing this today."

"Fankyou Janey," May whispered. "I wuv you."

"As I love you May," Jane smiled one of her beatific smiles.

"Come Fanny, we will see them inside," Madeline urged her sister. She could see Fanny was fighting tears of joy so she refocused Fanny on May and them taking their seats.

~~~~~~~/~~~~~~~

Richard was fighting to keep his brother's nervous energy from spilling over. They were in a retiring room just off the altar and Andrew was pacing back and forth like a caged big cat at the menagerie in London.

Just before Andrew was about to ask if it was time for perhaps the tenth time, Mr. Pierce, the clergyman who was about to perform the marriage rites of the Church of England which would unite him and Jane in holy matrimony, put his head into the room.

"It is time my Lord," the pastor informed Andrew.

Andrew felt like he wanted to run to his place until Richard placed a restraining hand on his arm.

"Andy, Jane will soon be standing next to you, all you

need to do now is relax," Richard urged his brother.

He would have preferred to have waited off to the side of the altar. That way he would have been able to watch Mary Bennet as she entered the church. Richard was sure that his feelings for her were not one sided, but until she came out officially in London next year and he could declare himself, he would not know for sure. He was there to support Andy. Once his brother was calm, Richard removed his hand from his brother's arm and followed him to where he was to stand.

As soon as they were in position, Andrew's eyes locked onto the double doors at the rear of the packed church where his bride would appear on her father's arm while Richard sought Mary. Just before one of the inner vestibule doors opened, he found her in the front pew between her mother and Kitty. Their eyes locked for an instant. She gave him a shy smile.

As soon as the one door opened, Elizabeth began her walk up the aisle. The door she entered through was closed and remained so until she reached her place opposite Richard. Mr. Pierce signalled the congregation to stand as soon as Elizabeth reached her position. Elizabeth noted that Anne stood, but with the aid of Uncle Lewis. She smiled to her best friend who smiled back at her. All Elizabeth hoped was that Anne would not overexert herself. She was sure Uncle Lewis would make sure his daughter did not.

Mr. Pierce then nodded to two men standing at the rear of the nave. In concert, they opened the inner vestibule doors allowing Bennet, with Jane on his right arm, to begin their walk up the aisle.

Seeing Jane and her looking just like what Bingley would have called her—an angel—Andrew's mouth almost fell open. He was extremely grateful he had been so blessed to have been given the gift of Jane's love. He would cherish that love and her person until he drew his final breath in the mortal world.

As she walked, Jane was also marvelling at the fact she had won this fine, upstanding, godly, and honourable man's love.

Bennet led Jane to where Andrew had, with a little nudge from Richard, come to wait for them at the base of the four steps leading up to the altar. He lifted the lace veil and kissed his eldest daughter on both cheeks. After allowing the veil to fall into place, Bennet placed Jane's one hand on Andrew's forearm. With that, Bennet joined his wife and family in the first pew on the right.

Jane and Andrew smiled at each other and would have lost themselves in one another's eyes had Mr. Pierce not cleared his throat as he had done to indicate the congregants could sit.

"Dearly beloved..." The reverend followed the ceremony as found in *The Book of Common Prayer*. Bennet answered he was the one giving the bride away at the relevant time, there were no objections, and bride and groom recited their vows flawlessly. As they did, their blue eyes were locked on each other's.

All too soon for the parents, and not soon enough for the bride and groom, they were pronounced man and wife.

Richard and Elizabeth joined them in the vestry to witness the newlyweds' signatures in the parish register. Richard allowed Elizabeth to proceed him out of the room and then, per his brother's request before the ceremony, he pulled the door closed giving Jane and Andrew some much desired privacy.

During the time of their engagement, the chaperones had been too good which meant they were only able to steal the occasional kiss, and they had to be quick.

Alone in the registry, the newly married Fitzwilliams made up for lost time. It was almost ten minutes later when both exited, quite unabashed at their swollen lips and Jane being quite out of breath.

# CHAPTER 20

Seeing how much weaker Anne had become since Jane's wedding, Elizabeth chose to spend as much time as she could with her sister of the heart. Due to this fact she had cried off joining Jane and Andrew in London for the little or full season and had foregone—regardless of how much Anne entreated with her to go—visiting Jane in Staffordshire at Hilldale during the summer months.

In the two years since Jane and Andrew married, there had been many events of note in Elizabeth's life, as well as those of the loved ones around her.

The most momentous occasion of all had been first Jane reporting she was in the family way when she felt the quickening that led to the birth of Elizabeth's first nephew and grandson for two pairs of extremely happy grandparents. Born at the end of July 1809, Thomas Reginald Richard Fitzwilliam, called Tommy, joined the family. Jane had been attended to by her mother, mother-in-law, and two aunts. At the time, Elizabeth and her younger sisters had been with Anne and Giana at Oak Hollow.

They had been under the watchful eyes of Sir Lewis, ably assisted by their companions and guards, led by John Biggs and Brian Johns. As it had become much more taxing for Anne to speak, when she wanted to communicate more than a word here and there, she would write what she wanted to say. Walking was not something she did for more than a few steps now and again. Anne was either carried where she needed to go or pushed in her bath chair.

The melancholy in Uncle Lewis and Jenki's visages whenever they thought they were being unobserved was obvious but not mentioned. Elizabeth was aware Anne would not live too much longer, which is why she was taking every opportunity possible to be in her best friend's company.

Thankfully for all, Anne's imperious mother was not at the estate in Bedfordshire and never would be. Uncle Lewis kept his wife at Rosings Park and she was never allowed to travel anywhere else.

Ignoring the blowhard, which was Lady Catherine de Bourgh, the Bennets had once again begun to spend Easter at the estate in Kent with the de Bourghs. The first time Lady Catherine had made a cutting remark aimed at the Bennets; Uncle Lewis had been unseen by her in the room. He had let her know, in no uncertain terms, she was teetering on being exiled. Since then, when any of the Bennets were present, other than disdainful sniffs or looks aimed to convey her opinion of them, all of which were ignored by the Bennets they were aimed at, she said not a word to any of them.

Elizabeth, her sisters, and any others who had not met Tommy, had the pleasure over Christmastide 1809. That year it was held at Longbourn, with Netherfield Park being utilised for those who would not have chambers at the Bennets' primary estate. The Fitzwilliam grandparents had missed the celebration thanks to Uncle Reggie having suffered a bad case of influenza. Aunt Elaine, Giana, and her brother, who Elizabeth had not met yet thanks to her not making her visits to London or Hilldale, had been together for the festive season.

Richard had not missed the opportunity to be in Mary's company, as he had not since she had first come out locally in August 1808, then in Town the following August. He had claimed he did not want to miss spending time with his nephew, of whom he was one of the godfathers, but everyone knew his true motivation.

Elizabeth was fully aware Papa had asked Richard to wait until Mary was at least nineteen, as she would be soon, before he declare himself. Richard was secure in Mary's regard for him, as she was in his. Hence he had not put up more than a token objection when he had been informed he would have to wait another year before a courtship—which seemed superfluous for them—or an engagement was permitted.

Elizabeth was not in any way envious her older sister and next younger sister had found the other half of their hearts. She knew when it was her time, she would meet the man who would be her perfect match.

Thinking about matches led her thoughts to her friend, the former Charlotte Lucas, now Mrs. Smythe.

She had met the Honourable Ernest Smythe, the younger brother of the Earl of Granville, Lord Harry Smythe, during the first little season Charlotte had attended. He had not officially called on her during that first foray into London's society, but he had asked for a courtship on her return to Town just after Twelfth Night 1809. A month later they were engaged.

The two had married from St. Alfred's in Meryton at the end of March of the same year. Thanks to Mr. Smythe owning his own estate in Lincolnshire, a little north of the meeting point of the borders of that county, Leicestershire, and Nottinghamshire, Charlotte's husband had not needed to shift for himself and choose a profession. She was less than seven hours away from Jane's and Andrew's estate by carriage. Elizabeth knew her friend was very happy, but to date she had received no news of Charlotte being with child. To go visit Charlotte at her husband's estate was another invitation she had felt she needed to refuse in order to remain near Anne.

Now she was at Longbourn, Uncle Lewis and Anne were present. Elizabeth knew she should have been thinking of Mary's approaching birthday and the proposal from Richard she was sure would be forthcoming, but she was as concerned for Anne as she ever was.

In January of the current year Anne had turned twenty, Elizabeth had joined her, reaching the same age in March.

She had heard Uncle Lewis confide in Mama and Papa that he had not expected Anne to reach that milestone given the deterioration in her health. As much as she wanted to believe it was otherwise, Elizabeth was not so myopic as to ignore the facts she could see before her eyes.

Anne was beginning to fight for every breath and her pallor had taken on an off-white, almost grey tinge.

Elizabeth banished the mounting maudlin thoughts regarding Anne's health, or lack thereof—at least for a short while. She needed to be with Anne who would be able to detect her mood and that would do her friend no good.

~~~~~~~/~~~~~~~

Even though the break in his leg had been in the thinnest of the bones, it had taken more than four months before Darcy felt he was back at full strength.

Since then, he had spent time at Richard's estate a few times and Richard had visited Pemberley in return. When Richard visited in July 1808, Darcy had recently begun to use his crutches to be independently mobile. His cousin had requested that he be allowed to bring Bingley, and only Bingley, with him.

Without Miss Bingley as part of the party, William had agreed without reservation. During the three weeks Richard and Bingley had been at Pemberley, the bonds of friendship had been furthered between Darcy and Bingley.

The latter had told of the tantrum his younger sister had unleashed when rather than joining him at Cloverdell and then possibly at Darcy's estate, she was sent to visit their aunt in Scarborough for the summer. According to her, the master of Pemberley would be greatly angered by her absence. Even when she had been informed—in no uncertain terms—the exact opposite was true, she had insisted she had the right of it.

Richard had extolled the virtues of his new sisters. So far Darcy had met only one of the fabled Bennet sisters, his new cousin, Lady Hilldale, Jane Fitzwilliam. In May 1809, a little more than two months before Andrew's son was born, Darcy had accepted an invitation to Hilldale. Any of his former uncharitable thoughts, which he had briefly had when he had read Aunt Elaine's letter, were banished.

Lady Hilldale—Jane, as he had been invited to address her, and she addressed him as William—was everything that was proper and good. If he were blind he still would have been able to see the love which flowed between the two. Andrew was beyond besotted with his wife and she with him.

It had been a disappointment he would not meet any of the younger Bennet sisters, and specifically not Anne's best friend, Miss Bennet, who had shown such bravery those years ago when she had saved the lives of his uncle and cousin. All Jane and Andrew had related was their sister had a prior invitation she had to honour.

From Hilldale, Darcy had journeyed to Cloverdell and spent more time with Richard. He was greatly impressed at the improvements he saw each time he visited Richard's estate. Word of the quality of the Cloverdell horses was well known in the country. That led to a long waiting list for Richard's horses. The steward, Mercer, had been given charge of the stables and the breeding programme, so another steward had been employed for the remainder of the estate.

There were four trainers, any one of which Darcy would have tried to entice away to come work at Pemberley had Richard not been his relation. In addition to the trainers, there were a large number of grooms and stable hands.

On this visit to the estate, Richard revealed plans to double the size of the stables. The owner of the neighbouring estate had passed away some six months previously. His heir was not interested in an estate in Northamptonshire, so with some help from his father and Andrew, Richard had purchased the estate which had many acres of prime pasture land. The acquisition had led to him being able to begin to expand the operation according to his plans.

Once all the additions were complete and with the additional income generated from the new breeding stock and stallions, Richard's income would be close to Pemberley's.

It was on that visit Darcy had noticed the faraway look Richard got whenever he discussed a certain Bennet sister, Miss Mary, and how he was looking forward to dancing at her coming out ball in October of that year. The ball had been deferred to allow the heat of summer to give way to the cooler autumn. Not only did Darcy learn Richard's heart was lost, but he discovered his aunt sponsored each Bennet sister who had so far come out, and he had missed two balls in their honours at Matlock House. When he listened carefully to Richard talk about the family, he had a feeling they did what he did. He surmised that they disguised the true extent of their wealth. He hoped he would meet them one day and be able to challenge both the famous Thomas Bennet, and from what his uncle and cousins had related, his second daughter, to a chess match.

The next visit Richard made to Pemberley was around Easter, 1810, and with him came Bingley. This time, much to Darcy's chagrin, he had reluctantly agreed to Miss Bingley being with her brother. Evidently no one in her family wanted her as a guest, not her aunt in Scarborough nor the Hursts. Bingley had written to request permission for her to accompany him, due to him not having managed to set up her own establishment yet. It was something he told Darcy he was determined to do as soon as they returned to London.

More than once while the shrew was in residence, did Darcy hear someone trying to open the doors leading to the master's suite, in an attempt to enter his chambers at night.

Even though he would never give in to a compromise, he kept all doors leading into his chambers locked whether he was away or present in his suite. Ever since the first occurrence, Darcy had Carstens sleep on a pallet near the main door in his bedchamber.

When Bingley confronted her, she had vehemently denied she was the guilty party. From that point on, two large footmen were posted in the hallway outside the master suite. They reported not two nights later, Miss Bingley, dressed in a rather inappropriate outfit, had approached the door.

As soon as she saw them she had attempted to dissemble about having begun to sleep walk and then she had become lost upon '*waking*.' Much to her dismay, and ignored vitriolic complaints, she was moved to the Rose and Crown Inn the very next day.

Before he departed with Richard, and after profuse apologies for his sister's unconscionable behaviour, Bingley had shared he intended to lease an estate near London. Richard suggested one only twenty miles from Town, called Netherfield Park in Hertfordshire. Both Richard and Darcy agreed to assist Bingley in his first foray into the world of landed gentry.

~~~~~~~/~~~~~~~

## September 1810

As their ward, Giana, was now fifteen, Lord and Lady Matlock decided it was time to employ a companion for her. Had Mrs. Annesley, who was companion to Lizzy and Mary for now, been available they would have employed her without delay. Sadly, she was not.

Lady Matlock placed advertisements for the position of companion to their ward in April, not long after Easter. Four ladies had been selected based on the letters they wrote combined with their characters. Interviews had been set to start that afternoon. The first lady to be seen was a Mrs. Karen

Younge.

When Miss Younge, Mrs. Karen Younge for the purposes of gaining the position she was confident would be offered to her, was shown into the drawing room at Matlock house, she was a little disconcerted to be faced with not only one lady, but with an additional six ladies.

"Thank you for taking your time to meet with me, Mrs. Younge." Lady Matlock indicated a chair opposite herself in the centre of the room.

"It is my pleasure your Ladyship," Miss Younge responded carefully. She was a little nervous as the Countess had not introduced any of the other ladies in the room. *'George said it would be simple to pull the wool over their eyes, he had better not be mistaken!'* she thought to herself.

"Your characters were the most impressive I have seen from any of the applicants. I am tempted to employ you before I see any of the other ladies…" Lady Matlock began to say.

Miss Younge felt far more confident. The forgeries had done their job.

"…however…" Lady Elaine did not miss the way the momentary confidence disappeared from the woman's face. "However, I would be remiss if I did not contact each of those who wrote the most stellar characters for you."

"Y-y-you m-m-must e-e-excuse m-me…" Miss Younge began to stammer seeing that George had been absolutely wrong in his assurances.

Before she could bolt for the door, it was blocked by two large footmen who had appeared when Miss Younge was talking to the Countess.

"You will not be leaving before we know why you sent this work of fiction to try and gain a position as my niece's companion. Now sit!" Lady Matlock commanded.

She looked around the room for a possible avenue of escape, but there were none. Karen Younge now noted there were men in the room, and by the fine clothing they wore, she knew they were not servants.

"You sent me four forged characters, one each from Lady Jersey, the Duchess of Bedford, Lady Granville, and Lady Cowper. Those four ladies are sitting to my left. They all happen to be friends of mine, and none have ever employed a Mrs. Younge, as you claimed." Lady Elaine turned to her friends. "You have never seen this woman before, have you."

The three countesses and one duchess all shook their heads vehemently.

"Unless you would like to be transported for trying to defraud a peer of the realm, I suggest you tell us the truth, and now," Lady Elaine demanded.

"George Wickham sent me," Karen Younge admitted.

"Why?" Lord Matlock insisted on knowing.

"One day before he was cheated out of his inheritance by the lies told to his true father, he saw a document which listed Miss Darcy's dowry," Miss Younge related. "I was to convince you to send her with me to Margate or Ramsgate once I was employed. He would have played on her tender feelings from her youth and then have her agree to elope. That would gain him her fortune and gain revenge on those who cheated him."

"I see he is still as bad a liar today as he was when his father was alive," Lord Matlock scoffed. "Did it not give you pause he wanted to elope with one, who he *purports*, is his sister?" Miss Younge blanched; she had never considered that. "Here is the truth about your man..." The earl told her all. "Before the late Robert Darcy turned him out, George signed a statement attesting to the truth of the facts I laid out for you. Is your name even Younge?"

"Yes, your Lordship, Miss Karen Younge," she admitted. She knew her only hope was to be truthful now.

"As my wife told you, I will not order you transported as you told the truth. I will honour what she promised," Lord

Matlock decided. "You will never come near any of us again and tell George Wickham if he ever tries anything to harm any member of my family, he will rue the day he was born. If I see you, him, or any connected to you, transportation will be the least of your worries!"

With her tail between her legs, Karen Younge was escorted from Matlock House via the servants' entrance.

~~~~~~~/~~~~~~~

After interviews—assisted by Mrs. Annesley and Fanny Bennet, who had been the other two in the room when the imposter was unmasked—with actual candidates, a Mrs. Hermione Mayers was employed for the position of Georgiana's companion. She had in fact been the companion of Lady Cowper's daughter before that young lady married.

~~~~~~~/~~~~~~~

Clay Younge was so angry Wickham had sent his sister on a fool's errand which had almost got her transported, he first beat Wickham with his fists and then threw the man out of his house warning him to leave Margate as soon as may be.

Nursing his wounds, which included a broken nose, Wickham thanked his lucky stars he still had a few banknotes squirrelled away and made for London.

# CHAPTER 21

**M**ary Bennet felt as if she was floating on air when she thought about her fiancé. A few days after her birthday—her nineteenth—Richard declared his love for her, which she told him, in no uncertain terms, she returned in full measure.

Like Jane and Andrew before them, they decided an official courtship would accomplish nothing that had not already been accomplished. Hence, Richard had dropped onto one knee and proposed. It had been ever so romantic and Mary had accepted him with alacrity, then when Richard spoke to Mama and Papa, permission and blessings were conveyed without delay.

It had not pleased her to learn Richard had been forced to wait a year before declaring himself, however much she understood her parents' reasoning for imposing that particular restriction. There were no more parental restrictions, but there was a reason Mary and Richard had not set a date yet.

Thinking of Anne made Mary very sad. There was no doubt their cousin was nearing the end of her all too short life. As happy as they were, they were not so insensitive as to have the most joyous day of their lives when Anne was so close to leaving the mortal world.

The main worry Mary had was when Anne passed how Lizzy would react. She would need all of their support which was another reason for them not to choose a date yet. All of the Bennet sisters had become very close to Anne over the years, but none of them shared a bond similar to the one between

Anne and Lizzy. The two of them could not have felt closer had they been sisters by blood.

Each night Mary prayed for a miracle. She begged Him to heal Anne so rather than mourn her, Anne would be at her wedding and live a long and full life. So far, God had not granted her prayer. Nevertheless, Mary still kept asking every day.

~~~~~~~/~~~~~~~

Fanny and Bennet were seated in the study to discuss the report Philips had provided regarding the potential lessee of Netherfield Park. For a few months now the estate had been solely owned by Bennet thanks to a few years of exceptionally good profits at both estates. Even though he had tried to insist Gardiner be paid more than he had invested, his brother had flatly refused.

"Thomas, is there anything in the report which would disqualify Mr. Bingley?" Fanny asked.

"No Fanny, I see nothing of concern," Bennet averred. "Even had Richard not assured me regarding his friend's character, I would have accepted him as a tenant."

"What of the sister?"

"She is no longer a weight around his neck since Mr. Bingley set her up in her own establishment. Richard has told many stories about the woman and her unswerving hunt of his cousin."

"Did Richard not say his elusive cousin will be one of the party at Netherfield Park if Mr. Bingley is awarded the lease?"

"Yes Fanny, he most certainly did. Like his late father, the current Mr. Darcy is an avid chess player and bibliophile. I look forward to finally meeting him."

"Jane did report although he is reserved, he is a good sort." Fanny paused as she thought of their grandson. "I cannot wait to see Tommy again. I am sorry we missed his first birthday in July, especially as he had begun to walk and talk just before the celebration."

While worry for de Bourgh and Anne had kept the Bennets at home, they did not regret remaining near their friends.

"You will see him soon enough; Jane and Andrew arrive in less than a sennight." Speaking of Tommy's young life which was stretched out before him caused Bennet's thoughts to drift onto a much less pleasant path. "Is it just me, or have you noticed de Bourgh looks like he has aged many years in the last few months as Anne has moved closer to being called home to God?"

"It is not you alone. Elaine and I spoke of it before Mary's ball after she sent that imposter on her way. Like we do, Elaine does not believe Lewis will long survive Anne's passing. He is fighting to remain alive for her."

~~~~~~~/~~~~~~~

Lady Catherine had to fight to contain her glee. She was almost free! Her daughter, who had lived more years than she had believed possible was near her end, and if she was any judge, and with her unmatched intelligence she was, her damned husband would not be long for the world once Anne was dead.

The best thing was no one would be able to accuse her of wrongdoing. Yes, it was many years past the date she had intended before that girl had interfered, but all of her patience was about to be rewarded. She smiled to herself as she thought about the will that would give everything to her.

A few months past, her simpleton of a husband had agreed to permit her to go into Westerham and Hunsford no more than once a week to either town. Thankfully when she entered a shop, the guards would stand at the entrance and back doors, but leave her unmolested in the establishment.

Using her vast intellect, she had paid one of the lowly tradesmen in Hunsford to post a letter to the solicitor who had created her will.

In the letter, she had provided instructions for the changes she desired and sent him fifty pounds. She had written she would be in a certain shop in Westerham in a sennight and for him to leave a package for her which included the completed will.

The fifty pounds had been sufficient and when she had gone to the shop, her package was waiting for her.

For the last three months, she had the document that would give her everything she both desired and deserved. It was worded exactly as she had instructed her solicitor. He had tried to tell her the clauses were irregular, but she had ignored his advice and commanded him to do exactly what she instructed.

All she needed was for her daughter and husband to hurry up and die.

She had tried to take her rightful place as the leader of local society, but so far, it had not gone according to her plan. It vexed her greatly that she had no visitors from the neighbourhood, or from anywhere for that matter. Even Lady Metcalf, who she had considered a friend at one point, never called nor responded to her notes.

At least she was left alone at Rosings Park, except for the guards, whom she would sack, along with all of the rest of the staff and servants as soon as everything was hers.

That useless man had taken Anne to be at Oak Hollow for her final days more than three months past. She had objected to them going, or she had made a show of doing the same as she was supposed to be a caring mother, after all. It would give her the utmost pleasure to sell that estate as soon as may be after his death. She knew how much he and Anne liked the estate so it would give her a measure of revenge to be rid of it. Even better, she would have it divided into smaller farms and sell each one so the name of the estate would be wiped from the face of the earth!

To make sure he did not write a will recently, she would date her substitute will the day before he died.

One of the things she would do, even before she broke up and sold his precious estate in Bedfordshire, would be to cease all payments to the Greens and have them evicted fromhe rent free cottage her dunderheaded husband had allowed them.

Thinking about all of her soon-to-be wealth led her to thoughts of all who had wronged her and would be dealt with. She would keep Clay Younge, very busy and, once he had done her bidding, she would find someone to dispose of him and the impertinent sister who had written that letter for him.

Yes, exacting her vengeance would be most satisfying.

~~~~~~~/~~~~~~~

To say Caroline Bingley was furious her brother had practically labeled her an on-the-shelf spinster by forcing her into her own establishment was no understatement. How was she supposed to be in Mr. Darcy's company? She had tried begging Charles's forgiveness, pleading that what occurred at Pemberley was all a big misunderstanding.

Her letters to Charles and Louisa for the most part went unanswered when she berated them for abandoning her. If she wrote of her life in London and enquired how they were, they would deign to reply to her letters. It was in this way she kept abreast of news regarding her siblings. Louisa had borne a brat, named Isaac Arthur for her useless brother-in-law's father and her late father. In her mind, Arthur should have been first as the Bingleys were far more wealthy than the Hursts.

The apartments she lived in were of a standard far below what she felt she deserved. Not only that, they were near to *Cheapside*. Not daring to share her address, Miss Bingley had broken contact with her former friends. She could imagine what Miss Grantly would do if she knew the truth!

There were two bedchambers, one for her and one for the companion. The room she was currently seated in was a sitting room and dining parlour in one. Thanks to the deductions Charles had made for overspending—as he called it —and breakages, all that remained of her dowry was a paltry fifteen thousand pounds which meant she had only fifty pounds a month to live on. Due to her paucity, she no longer had a lady's maid. There was a housekeeper and cook in one and a maid of all work. All of her expenses, including wages to the servants and the rent on the hovel she was forced to live in, were paid before she was given the balance of her money each quarter day.

She had written one of her bland letters to Charles recently and a reply had just been received. She broke the seal and began to read.

*12 September 1810*

*Bingley House*

*54 Curzon Street*

*Caroline,*

*From the 1st of October onwards, please direct all letters to me at Netherfield Park, Hertfordshire.*

*I am taking my first step to becoming a member of the landed gentry. I am not purchasing this estate, but I have recently signed a lease for one year. Both Fitzwilliam and Darcy recommended I rent first so I can truly know if being a member of the gentry is for me.*

*Before you ask what I know about selecting an estate, both of my friends looked over the estate with me and agreed it is a fine one, well run, and very well maintained. The house is of similar size to the one at Fitzwilliam's estate, but is a newer structure than his.*

*Given I am very new to all of this, both of my friends have agreed to join me at the estate when I take possession of it in October. They will be with me for a few months. It is perfect for Fitzwilliam because his fiancée and her family live at the neighbouring estate.*

Miss Bingley pulled up her nose in disgust. Not only was the Viscount married to one of these unknown Bennets, but now the second son had been entrapped by a sister. Suddenly she became alarmed. "What if there is another sister who uses her arts and allurements on my Mr. Darcy?" she asked the walls of the room. She had to make sure it did not occur, she returned to her brother's letter.

*Before you waste your time writing to me to* volunteer *your services as my hostess, Aunt Hildebrand has agreed to act as such and will arrive here before I make for Hertfordshire.*

*I trust you are well and have finally reconciled yourself to your situation.*

*Charles.*

Had she not heard a conversation regarding the fact there were five Bennet sisters? The eldest was the one married to the Viscount and if memory served, Mr. Fitzwilliam was engaged to the middle one. That meant there was one of marriageable age between them.

All Miss Bingley could do was hope the woman was homely and had some serious defects if her next younger sister was engaged before her.

However, she could not, *would* not, leave that to chance. She had to scheme and find a way to be one of the party in Hertfordshire. As soon as possible she would compromise Mr. Darcy and then she would have the life she deserved.

~~~~~~~/~~~~~~~

It had taken Wickham more than a monthfor the evidence of Younge's beating to fade enough to be in public, though nothing would fix his nose which had healed at an awkward angle.

If only he had not lost so much of the money Darcy had sent to him from his adoptive father. As he was not flush, Wickham had taken a room in a rather rundown inn in Seven Dials. His room in Younges' boarding house on Edward Street now seemed palatial by comparison.

One evening he was drinking in the taproom of an inn outside of Seven Dials. He noticed two men wearing the scarlet coats of the army who were seated at the counter drinking ale.

A snippet of their conversation revealed them to be officers in the militia, not regular army that might be called to combat on the continent, who were looking for men to join their ranks as officers. Given his situation, Wickham could not imagine things getting much worse. It would not be long before he was out of funds. On a whim, he approached the two and was pleased to hear his native Derbyshire accent.

"Did I overhear you are looking for officers to join you in service of King and country?" Wickham drawled emphasising his accent.

"You did. I am Lieutenant Denny and this," Denny inclined his head to the other man, "is Captain Carter."

The three men shook hands and Wickham was invited to sit.

"By your accent, I can tell you are from our county," the Captain stated. "We are members of a regiment of the Derbyshire Militia and we are looking for officers from that county. Do you have a gentleman's education?"

"I do," Wickham dissembled.

"In that case, if you are interested, you are entitled to a free Lieutenant's commission with us. Colonel Forster is looking for good and honourable men," Carter related.

The two officers proceeded to tell Wickham about their duties, wages—only two pounds a month, but meals were included—and the regiment.

"Our encampment is just outside of Oxford in Oxfordshire, but we are moving to winter quarters in Hertfordshire at the beginning of November," Denny revealed. "At the end of March, we make for Brighton."

"I have always wanted to serve, so I would like to accept a commission in your regiment," Wickham stated as sincerely as he was able.

"Meet us here in two days at midday. We will be making for our encampment," the Captain instructed.

To make a good impression, Wickham, using his dwindling cash reserves, paid for a few rounds of grog before he took his leave.

# CHAPTER 22

Elizabeth looked at the letter Anne had handed to her. She had been at her best friend's side since after Mary's birthday, refusing any entreaties to be anywhere else.

Anne was appreciative Lizzy was willing to dedicate all of her time to her. At the same time, she knew it was not healthy for her best friend, which had led her to write the letter. Other than a word here or there, Anne no longer spoke as it cost her too much effort to do so. Writing was about the only activity she could accomplish without getting too tired.

"Read!" Anne managed before she had to gasp for air.

Not wanting to be the cause of any more pain for Anne, Elizabeth followed the command and opened the folded paper.

*13 September 1810*

*My dearest, sister of my heart, Lizzy,*

*I love that you want to be at my side at all times, but you are causing me concern that you have stopped living your own life and are living for me now.*

*I need the girl who saw me and not my malady. Where is the girl who made sure I was able to climb Oakham Mount, the one who is never intimidated? I want the Lizzy back who treated me like any other, not an invalid.*

*Lizzy, I have passed the age of 20, an age I never thought I would attain, and if it was not for you, I would have gone to God 10 years ago. Although my life will be a short one, it has been made infinitely better because you are in it.*

*As much as I love you being here every day, I need you to live your own life. I am much concerned you will forget how to live without me, and I need to know you will be able to carry on and live your life fully after I am gone. Remember, I will always be with you. By you going on and making the most of your life, being that vivacious, impertinent, and* le diable peut s'en soucier *(devil may care) girl I love as well as anyone could love her sister, I will experience it along with you even though you will not see me.*

*If I am not being clear, I want you to return home, and live! Go ride Penny, walk, sit on Oakham Mount and watch the sunrise, find a man who you love and respect, and marry. My only demand (hope) is that you will name one of your daughters Anne.*

*Please understand, I am not saying I do not want you to visit. You are welcome, but no more than two days a week here with me. And you are to attend the assembly in October if I am still alive —I would not ask you to dance if I have just passed away. Do not forget you can write and I will reply to your letters as I always have in the past.*

*Now, I need to ask a favour of you, of you, and all of your family. When I am called home, please make sure Papa does not give up—if you are able. The truth is I think Papa is not well and he is fighting with all he is to make sure he does not pass away before me. If I have the right of it, he will not long survive me.*

*Lizzy, be careful of my mother once Papa and I are in heaven. As much as I wanted, hoped, and believed my mother had changed, I know now she has not. She thinks she has fooled all of us, especially me, but she has not.*

'Why would I have to be careful?' *Elizabeth asked herself silently.* 'It is not like I have anything she wants?' *Elizabeth shook her head and returned her eyes to the letter.*

*Lizzy, I need you to promise me you will do what I ask. Please do not allow my death to destroy your* joie de vivre.

*Yes, I will allow you to mourn me, but no more than a total of 6 weeks!*

*Now if you look up you will see I have been watching you while you read. I need your promise.*

*I love you, my sister,*

*Anne*

Elizabeth had tears streaming down her cheeks when she looked up into Anne's blue eyes. Anne's eyebrows were arched waiting for the promise.

"I swear," Elizabeth managed with a watery smile.

"Everything?" Anne rasped.

"Yes Anne, everything, I would not try to obfuscate," Elizabeth promised.

Anne wrote another quick note which Elizabeth read:

*Thank you, Lizzy, I can be at peace now.*

There was no missing the way Anne was looking at Elizabeth as if she was waiting for something. "You mean starting now?" Elizabeth verified as she dried the remaining tears from her cheeks.

Anne nodded in confirmation.

She stood and then Elizabeth leaned forward and gently hugged Anne. It was then she observed the half smile on Jenki's face. Elizabeth stopped next to the companion as she made her way towards the door.

"You know what Anne wrote to me, do you not, Jenki?" Elizabeth asked with one of her eyebrows raised.

"Yes, Miss Lizzy, I do," Mrs. Jenkinson confirmed. "It may be hard for you to accept, but I agree with Miss Anne. Remember, it is ultimately for her own peace of mind so she will not feel guilt at you giving up everything she knows you love to do."

"It will take me some time to reconcile to what Anne has asked, but I believe I will see the wisdom of her request when I allow myself to," Elizabeth averred.

Mrs. Jenkinson reached out and took Elizabeth's hands in each of her own and gave a motherly squeeze. "I always knew you could not be so intelligent for nothing."

"You will send a note if Anne takes a turn for the worse when I am not here, will you not?" Elizabeth requested.

"Of that you can be certain, Miss Lizzy," Mrs. Jenkinson assured her.

When Elizabeth reached the drive, Penny was saddled and waiting for her, as were Uncle Lewis, John Biggs, and Brian Johns.

"It seems my Annie made her wishes known," Sir Lewis smiled—for the first time in a long while.

"Her wishes seem to be the worst kept secret, except to myself," Elizabeth shook her head. "Jenki will send for me if there is a change and I am not here."

A look of deep pain crossed Sir Lewis's countenance. "Lizzy, before you go, I must tell you something," Sir Lewis said in a gentle tone. "It is my belief your friendship has kept my Anne living much longer than she may have otherwise. I am not referring to your saving of both our lives. It is since then, the way you gave of yourself and made Annie feel like she was a true sister of yours and your sisters. You may not understand it yet, but Lizzy you gave her a reason to keep fighting, a will to live. For that, you will have my undying gratitude."

"You give me far too much credit," Elizabeth stated modestly. "Never forget I received as much sisterly love and friendship from Anne as I gave."

Sir Lewis knew Lizzy well enough to know she was not comfortable with all of this praise, so he did not press his point or tell her any more. "Biggs and Johns will ride to Longbourn with you. They will return after they and the horses have rested sufficiently."

With that, Sir Lewis kissed his honorary daughter on her forehead and nodded to Biggs who then assisted Miss Lizzy into her saddle.

~~~~~~~/~~~~~~~

For the first three days she was back at Longbourn, Elizabeth kept to herself when not eating a meal. When at the table, she pushed her food around her plate more than she actually ate.

Having visited Oak Hollow the day after Lizzy returned, Fanny and Bennet were aware of what Anne had made Lizzy promise to do.

Neither were upset Anne had taken the bull by the horns in that fashion. Lizzy's reaction to Anne's worsening health was a great worry to them. They had decided to keep their peace on the subject for now as they both had confidence Elizabeth would work through everything on her own and arrive at the correct conclusions. If her introverted behaviour continued for too many more days, then they would step in.

The night of her third day home from Oak Hollow, Elizabeth dreamt she was with Anne who was admonishing her for not keeping the vow she had sworn to her.

*"Elizabeth Rose Bennet! How dare you make me a promise and then return home and mope around the way you have been? Is that what you promised me? Is this the way you live your life fully?"* Anne demanded; her arms akimbo as she stood outside of the smashed coach.

*The carriage looked the same, but rather than their ten-year-old selves, they were both the age they were now. It was just the two of them standing next to the coach, no team of four bays, no Hector and his cart, no Sir Lewis, and no injured footman.*

*"Anne, how can I do everything you asked of me when I know you are close to the end of your life in the mortal world?"* Elizabeth protested. *"How am I to continue without you?"*

*"Lizzy, did we not discuss this very thing when you made me your promises? When you live, I live. My body is broken and will soon not be able to carry on, but as I told you in my letter, I will live*

*within you. I will always be in your heart! I will be with Aunt Anne and Uncle Robert in heaven and we will all watch over you. When Papa joins us, he will be another who will keep an eye on you."* Anne approached Elizabeth and held her hands.

*Her touch was warm, not cold and clammy as Elizabeth remembered from the times she held Anne's hands in her chamber at Oak Hollow.*

*"The only way you will betray me and my memory is if you ever give up! I do not want you to do that. If you do I will haunt your dreams every night!"*

*"I am so sorry Anne; I promise you; I will begin to honour my word to you in deed and spirit as well as word. Before you go, what did you mean for me to be careful of your mother?"*

*As soon as Elizabeth made that promise, and before she could answer the last question, Anne disappeared.*

Elizabeth woke up in a cold sweat, every moment and word of the vivid dream emblazoned in her memory.

"You win, Anne, I will not sit and *mope* any longer.

~~~~~~~/~~~~~~~

Elizabeth woke again before the dawn.

The dream was still replaying in her head. "I heard you, Annie. If you took the time to come see me in my dream in addition to your letter, I will not fight it any longer," Elizabeth said to her chamber.

She dressed herself in her hunter green riding habit, with the special split skirt for riding astride, and made her way down to the stables after a detour through the kitchens where Cook presented her with a freshly baked muffin and roll wrapped in a cloth.

On arriving at the stables, once she fed Hector and Penny a carrot each, the groom and stableboy who had begun their day not too long before she arrived, saddled the mare with a men's saddle. At this time of the morning, her father allowed her to ride astride on Longbourn's land.

By the time Elizabeth was mounted the groom was waiting on a gelding to escort her for her ride.

Once into the fields, Elizabeth allowed Penny her head as they thundered across the ground. The groom and his gelding fought, and failed, to keep pace with them. A mile from Oakham Mount she slowed Penny to a canter, then a trot, and finally a walk. At the base of the hill, once the groom had assisted her to dismount, Elizabeth handed her mare's reins to the lad and made her way up to the summit.

She made directly for the rock facing the east in time to see some of the sun's rays fighting to be seen above the horizon. It was an almost clear day with only a few clouds moving from north to south. The closer the sun came to breaching the horizon, the more colours were reflected off the sparse clouds. It started with reds and purples, but soon it was silvers, golds, and yellows. As the sun broke above the horizon, Elizabeth extracted the cloth with her treats wrapped in it from the habit's jacket pocket.

She broke the roll into three and popped a piece into her mouth and savoured the taste. Once it was chewed and swallowed, she repeated the same with the other two pieces.

Next was the muffin, except she divided it into quarters.

With the sun beginning to climb above the horizon and the freedom she felt sitting on the hill watching it, she finally understood why Anne had given her the charge she had—twice.

"I know you are with me Annie," Elizabeth placed one of her hands over her heart, "and you always will be." In that instant she renewed her promise, not only to Anne but to herself, that she would live her best life for both of them.

~~~~~~~/~~~~~~~

Two days later Elizabeth was at Oak Hollow for the *allowed* days. She related her dream and the change in her demeanour since it would amuse Anne.

With a wide smile on her face, Anne wrote her a note:

*I told you I would be with you!*

Elizabeth knew Anne was funning with her and laughed. Anne just gave her an unreadable look with a knowing smile.

# CHAPTER 23

O f the three men who were on their way to Netherfield Park on Monday morning the first day of October, two were very keen to arrive while the third was reserving his judgement.

Bingley was much in anticipation of being master of his own, albeit leased, estate. His aunt had arrived in London as scheduled and she sat across from him now as his coach travelled the final miles before they reached Meryton. Aunt Hildebrand was a lady who was efficient and would not allow anyone to push her around. She was his father's youngest sister and had never been inclined to marry. She was one of the few people who intimidated Caroline.

Thoughts of his younger sister were the only thing which could spoil his good mood. He shook his head as he thought about all of her entreaties to be the mistress of his leased estate, or at least one of the party. He had roundly refused her. There was no doubt her reasons related to her hopes for a future as Mrs Darcy. Bingley shook his head. Caroline was the only one who refused to see her pursuit of Darcy was pointless. The object of his thoughts was riding in his own coach with Fitzwilliam.

Darcy did not want to be reliant on only one carriage in case he had to travel to London for business which had made him choose to bring his own conveyance along.

Richard had last seen his fiancée more than a fortnight previously. As much as he wanted to be in Hertfordshire with Mary, his duties to his estate could not be pushed aside. Besides, his Mary would not be impressed if he placed his personal enjoyment ahead of taking care of his duties which included his estate, tenants, and servants. As such, Richard Fitzwilliam was willing the miles to pass as speedily as humanly possible. Invictus, his stallion, was being led by one of the grooms while another led Darcy's Zeus.

Richard had not shared who owned the estate, just like he had not mentioned Mary's actual dowry; Bennet had not authorised him to do so. As soon as they arrived at the leased estate, he intended to wash, change, and then borrow William's coach to head to Longbourn. Soon enough he would be in his beloved's company once again. Without realising it, thoughts of seeing Mary caused him to display a wide grin.

Darcy was seated on the forward facing bench amazed at the mooncalf looks Richard was displaying. As far as Darcy knew, the Bennets had no fortune of which to speak, but after having met Cousin Jane, he extrapolated if she was an example of the Bennet sisters then he could not argue Richard's falling in love with one of them.

Yes, he was doing what his father had urged him and was not closeted at Pemberley. But that had not changed the fact Darcy did not enjoy being in crowds, especially those made up of persons unknown to him.

One he was looking forward to finally meeting was Miss Elizabeth Bennet. Jane Fitzwilliam had nothing but positive accolades for her next younger sister while the members of his family—not the least Giana—praised her to the skies.

Thinking of Giana, Darcy was beyond pleased he had rebuilt his relationship with her. It had taken a while for her to trust him, but now they were once again as brother and sister should be. He spent time with her when she was at Snowhaven, or in London during the season, and she spent a few months each spring and summer with him at Pemberley.

His sister would arrive with his aunt and uncle in about a sennight. Anne's deteriorating health necessitated all of the family, save her mother, be present in the area. His aunt, uncle, and sister were to be hosted at Netherfield Park. They would be joined within days of their arrival by Jane, Andrew, and little Tommy. In fact, he and Richard would be spending a good part of the day at his Uncle Lewis's estate on the morrow.

On the approach to Meryton, Darcy's coachman negotiated a rather sharp turn.

"This is where Lizzy rescued Uncle Lewis and Anne," Richard drawled as he inclined his head towards the window on his left. "The Bennets' estate is on our right."

Darcy looked out of the window on the left. He saw the drop into the gully and the rocks below. Now that he saw the place, the actions of the girl who was but ten at the time were all the more impressive.

"Did I remember your relating something about Miss Bennet turning down some suitors in London after she came out?" Darcy asked.

"Yes, in fact, one was a marquess, heir to the Duke of Hertfordshire," Richard averred.

"But, other than the connections they have, they have no fortune. Would not that have been a prudent match for her?" Darcy wondered.

"If Lizzy cared about such considerations, yes it would have been a brilliant match. She wants to marry for the same reasons your late father urged and will not compromise her values."

"So she will only marry for love?"

"Yes William, that and respect. Even had I not known Mary was the only woman for me, Lizzy and I would have never suited." At his cousin's raised eyebrows, Richard explained. "It is not her intelligence, because Mary has that in spades, but we are too much alike in personality. Mary on the other hand is my foil and balances me perfectly. Now that I think on it..."

"What are you scheming in that *little* brain of yours?"

"Nothing. Only that just like Mary is for me, I believe if you come to know Lizzy, she will be the same for you."

"Do not try any harebrained matchmaking schemes. If you do I will kick your arse!" Darcy growled.

Richard lifted his hands in surrender. "Peace, William. I will do nothing. All I am suggesting is that you be open to the possibilities when you meet her. A man could do far worse than to win Lizzy's love. I am sure you have heard how loyal she is to those she loves. Ask Giana and wait until you see her with Anne."

"I have heard all about their friendships," William acknowledged.

"One thing I will warn you of though. It is possible Lizzy will not be her normal self. She has taken the changes in Anne's health almost as hard as Uncle Lewis has."

"I have not seen Anne for some years, not since she and Uncle Lewis were at Pemberley after Father passed. Is she truly so close to the end?"

"As much as I would like to refute that, I cannot. After I returned to my estate about a fortnight ago, I would not have been surprised to have been summoned back from Cloverdell to attend Anne's funeral." Richard paused as he looked at nothing in particular. "As much as I wish it were otherwise, it is not."

After such a maudlin subject, the cousins remained silent for the rest of the journey. Darcy looked out of the window as they entered the market town and traversed it. At the end of the main street they turned to the left and, followed the road for about two miles, Darcy guessed.

Still following Bingley's coach, they turned past the estate's gate posts and onto the drive.

~~~~~~~/~~~~~~~

The next day while the cousins took Darcy's coach to make the journey to Oak Hollow, Bingley was at home to receive the gentlemen of the neighbourhood.

The fourth man to call was Mr. Thomas Bennet of Longbourn. "Welcome Mr. Bennet," Bingley bowed. "I do not know if you remember, we were introduced by Fitzwilliam at Miss Elizabeth's...Miss Bennet's coming out ball."

"Now that you mention it, yes, I do recall," Bennet returned. "Will you introduce me to the lady please?"

"This is my aunt, Miss Hildebrand Bingley, who will act as my hostess and mistress of the estate. Aunt Hildebrand, Mr. Thomas Bennet of Longbourn."

"Richard told us he and his Darcy cousin were to visit Oak Hollow today." He turned to Miss Bingley. "My wife sent me with an invitation to a dinner at our estate four days hence, on Saturday." Bennet handed the note to the lady.

After a nod from her nephew, Miss Bingley accepted the invite on behalf of the whole party.

"That would be the day after the assembly in Meryton," Bingley verified.

"I saw Sir William departing as I arrived, I assume he informed you about the ball?" Bennet surmised. "He is the master of ceremonies at such events."

"Yes, he did. My aunt will not attend, but the rest of the party will." Bingley knew Darcy may not be pleased he was committed to attend the assembly, but with support from Fitzwilliam he was sure—at least he hoped—Darcy would not be too put out.

Soon after Bennet took his leave, Spencer Goulding and Johnathan Long arrived together to meet the new tenant of the estate.

~~~~~~~/~~~~~~~

"Is he as affable as the report stated?" Fanny asked about

their tenant after her husband had kissed her on his return from Netherfield Park.

"Yes, he is indeed. But as it stated, he has an iron will. The younger sister is not present, instead his spinster aunt is the mistress," Bennet averred. "Before I forget, they will attend the dinner on Saturday."

"I suppose we will finally meet Giana's brother at the assembly on Friday," Fanny guessed.

"Yes, young Bingley stated all except the aunt will attend. You know Richard will not miss a chance to dance with Mary."

"I wonder why Mary insisted she was to also go visit Anne and Lewis today. It has nought to do with Richard visiting there, I am sure." Fanny smiled widely.

All she cared about was that Mary was happy with her choice, which Fanny knew beyond a shadow of a doubt her middle daughter was. She already considered Richard an honorary son, so the wedding would only make it official.

"After what the Fitzwilliams and Giana have told us about William Darcy, it will be interesting to see how he does in the company of strangers, and at a ball as well."

"I am sure he will behave in public," Fanny opined, "How can he not with his education and the parents he had?"

~~~~~~~/~~~~~~~

Elizabeth had spent the morning with Anne and now that Mary had come, she had Penny made ready and she was soon on her way home with Anne's two guards escorting her.

She had not long departed Oak Hollow when she and her escorts moved to the one side of the road to allow a large travelling coach to pass them by. Elizabeth thought she noted Richard as one of the occupants, but she could not be sure.

Darcy was looking out of the window closest to him at nothing in particular when he saw a lady atop a black and white horse. She was being escorted by two giant men. If he did not know better he would have said they were the same guards who had accompanied Uncle Lewis and Anne to Pemberley for his late father's funeral.

He told Richard what he had seen. His cousin snapped out of his reverie and stuck his head out of the window looking back at the horses and riders. He would have called out but there was too much distance between them already.

"That was Lizzy being guarded by Biggs and Johns," Richard revealed after he sat down once again. "We must have just missed her. She is riding Penny, that is another thing she has in common with you."

"What has a 'Penny' to do with me?" Darcy quizzed.

"Her mare is named for a character from the Iliad."

"Then her horse's name is Penelope?" Richard nodded. "Odysseus's wife."

"You name your stallion for a Greek god and she names her horses from the Iliad. Her pony she was riding the day she saved our uncle and cousin is named Hector."

"She sounds like an interesting lady," Darcy owned.

"Not to mention she will beat you at chess," Richard grinned.

"That is something I would like to see," Darcy stated sceptically as the coach slowed due to their arrival at their Uncle Lewis's estate.

~~~~~~~/~~~~~~~

On the journey back to Netherfield Park, Darcy had much over which to cogitate. He rode alone as his cousin was in the Bennet carriage with his fiancée and her companion on the way back to Longbourn.

There was no doubt Anne was not long for this world. She seemed to make the best of her remaining time. He was shocked at his first view of Anne when he and Richard followed Uncle Lewis into her sitting room. She was gaunt, her skin was pallid, and her breathing was laboured. At least when he had seen Anne at Pemberley, even though he had spent no time with her, Darcy had heard her speak. Now, other than a single word here or there, she did not talk at all. Instead, if and when Anne needed to communicate, she would write a note to make herself understood. Uncle Lewis did not look well at all either and there was no mistaking the accuracy of Richard's assessment, that their uncle would not long survive his daughter, was accurate. There was a great sadness in his uncle's eyes.

As soon as he had seen Mary Bennet he had known who she was before the introduction was effected by Richard. She looked like a younger version of Jane. Speaking to her briefly he could easily discern her intelligence and dry wit. If Miss Bennet was the most intelligent of the five sisters then he could only imagine the level of her intellect. Miss Mary, or as he now called her, Cousin Mary, had informed Darcy her older sister was another bibliophile in their family.

When she had mentioned that, a memory had stirred in Darcy's consciousness. He remembered his father mentioning that fact on his return from Hertfordshire ten years past. He also recalled how impressed his father had been with the little heroine.

As much as he wanted Anne to live for many years, he knew it would not be. He only hoped her suffering—no matter the brave face she showed—would not be of long duration.

His thoughts returned to Richard's fiancée. There was no mistaking the genuine love and affection shared by the engaged couple. Thinking of his father's final missive, Darcy hoped he too would find the same thing.

~~~~~~~/~~~~~~~

All of her efforts to garner an invitation to her brother's leased estate in the backwater had been rebuffed so Caroline

Bingley had no choice.

She rented a carriage and planned to depart early (for her it was early) on Friday morning. Miss Bingley was sure her brother would not turn her away once she arrived. To that end, she planned to have the conveyance return to London as soon as she alighted and her trunks were off-loaded.

Charles would make her mistress as Aunt Hildebrand knew nothing of the ways of society.

That same night she planned to compromise Mr. Darcy. She had waited long enough. If that failed, her second option was Mr. Fitzwilliam. The slight inconvenience of his engagement would not get in her way, she would do what was required to achieve her aims.

# CHAPTER 24

Penny galloped across the fields with gay abandon on Friday morning. A groom and footman were doing their best, while rapidly falling behind, to keep up with Miss Lizzy as she allowed her mare to run. As was her wont early in the morning on her father's land, Elizabeth was riding astride wearing one of her special split skirt habits. She eschewed the hat which went with the outfit knowing—from experience—it would not remain on her head once she allowed Penny her head.

Elizabeth was unaware she was being observed as Penny's hooves thundered across the field kicking up clumps of dirt and grass behind her.

Looking at the horse—he had a very good eye regarding horseflesh—Darcy could tell it was a thoroughbred. That puzzled him exceedingly. Had he not heard the family's income was barely two thousand per annum and the daughters had no fortune to speak of? It was a quandary for another day.

Darcy recognised the horse as the one he had briefly seen pass his coach the day he and Richard had called on Uncle Lewis and Anne. That meant the lady riding in a most unladylike fashion was none other than the elusive Miss Bennet he had yet to meet. Pushing aside his disdain for her flouting society's conventions as she was, from what he could see of her figure from behind, she was a rather comely woman. As her head was uncovered, he could see her hair was raven-coloured, not blonde like her other two sisters he had met. Also, he could tell she was more petite than Jane and Cousin Mary. She was headed away from him so he could not see her face. It also accounted for the fact he had not been noticed. At least she was not so improper as to roam about without escorts.

He had to admit to himself he was the one who was intruding on her father's land. It was not like she was riding in that fashion in a public place. He remembered too when he had seen her and the giant men escorting her, she had been on a side-saddle like any proper lady. If he had not jumped the fence marking the border between the two estates, then he would not have been in a position to observe her. As he was the trespasser, Darcy felt shame for his former opinions.

He wheeled Zeus and pointed him back towards Netherfield Park, jumping the fence into one of Bingley's fields.

As he rode, he wondered if she would be at the assembly Bingley had committed him to attend. Thinking of the dance upcoming brought up his anger at his host for volunteering him to attend without first asking him.

Not long after he and Zeus were back on Netherfield Park's land, Darcy heard the conversation he had with Richard playing in his head. It had been right after Bingley had informed them of the assembly on their return from Oak Hollow.

*Richard had cocked his head indicating Darcy should follow him out of the study before he was able to tell Bingley he refused to attend.*

*They had walked into the library and Richard had pushed the door closed.*

*"My following you into this room has only delayed the inevitable refusal I intend to deliver to Bingley. How could he obligate me to attend a dance without my permission?" Darcy had barked.*

*"William, calm yourself. Bingley did nothing malicious!" Richard had responded evenly. "You are no longer a pup wet behind the ears who needs to hide himself from those he does not yet know.*

*Would you truly refuse to be introduced to my future parents-in-law?"*

*"You know I would not refuse the introduction. That does not mitigate the fact Bingley accepted in all of our names when he should have spoken to us first."*

*"What is done is done. If you refuse now after he has accepted on your behalf you will cause him embarrassment in the eyes of his new neighbours and you will be seen as a misanthrope." Richard had paused and grinned. "Besides you will get to meet Lizzy...Miss Bennet, and Kitty...Miss Catherine, who is recently out locally."*

*With no good cheer, Darcy agreed he would attend and the two had returned to join Bingley in the study.*

Having seen Miss Bennet tearing across the fields, riding with no fear, Darcy admitted to himself that being introduced to her would not be a bad thing.

~~~~~~~/~~~~~~~

Thanks to her indecision as to which of her gowns to pack, it was past noon by the time Miss Bingley exited her benighted dwelling and made her way down to the rented carriage.

So her companion would not forewarn her brother, Miss Bingley had given the lady some days off to go visit her sister. Since she would be alone in the conveyance, she paid the maid of all work five pounds to be her escort to her destination. The girl would ride back to London once Miss Bingley had alighted at Netherfield Park.

About two hours out of London, the coachman had stopped at the Bull and Spectacles Inn. Miss Bingley had demanded a private parlour where she and the maid had taken refreshment.

She heard a knock on the door thinking the driver was about to tell her they were on their way. "Beggin' yer pardon, Miss Bingley," the Coachman stated, hat in hand. "One o' the 'orses be lame. The inn 'as an 'orse fir me to rent, but 'e just come back an must rest two ta four 'ours 'afore we can depart."

Even though she was annoyed by the delay, as long as she got there, Miss Bingley cared not. "Just come inform us when it is time to depart," she said and waved the man away dismissively.

The coachman would have asked the annoying and rude lady to pay the cost of the rental of the horse, but he had taken three times his usual rate from her already.

~~~~~~~/~~~~~~~

Had Elizabeth not promised Anne she would attend the assembly, she would have been at Oak Hollow with her friend and not in the new Bennet coach being used to convey her parents, Mary, Kitty, and herself to the assembly hall in Meryton.

Lydia was at home with Mrs. Annesley and Miss Jones. At fourteen she still had another two years plus before she came out locally.

At least she would finally meet Giana's brother. It was well known in the neighbourhood the three gentlemen resident at Netherfield Park would attend, two of them eligible, which excited many of the mothers and daughters in the area. Several local young ladies were imagining being paired with one of the wealthy men.

With Jane married to Andrew and Mary engaged to Richard, some thought it was their turn now. Elizabeth could not but help smile at the thought of the machinations of some of her neighbours.

She could not imagine wanting to connect herself to a man unknown just because he happened to be wealthy. She would marry for love and respect, or not at all.

"Mama, did you hear about a regiment of militia being stationed in Meryton next month?" Kitty asked.

"Yes, both my sister and Lady Lucas have informed me."

Fanny looked at her two unattached daughters. "I know wealth is not your main concern, but please know that there are many unscrupulous men who join the militia. If they knew you girls have twenty thousand pounds each, they would swarm like honeybees do when they detect pollen."

"Take heed of your mother's words," Bennet reinforced. "We are not saying all men in the militia are dishonourable. However, most are very poor, and their wages are only two or three pounds per month. There are men in these regiments who would seduce a girl without the intention of ever marrying her."

"Lizzy, we know you are not easily worked on, but Kitty dear, you are too trusting at times. Please promise me you will never be alone with any of the soldiers or officers once they arrive," Fanny beseeched.

"You know I am a good girl, Mama and Papa," Kitty insisted. "Besides, I do not find men in scarlet coats to my liking."

"Once they arrive there will always be more than one of us when we walk into Meryton and we will have at least one footman with us," Elizabeth assured her parents.

"It is good Lyddie is not out," Kitty stated, "she has opined how she would enjoy being courted by an officer."

The Bennet coach stopped at the entrance to the hall and the footman placed the step and then opened the door. Bennet stepped out and handed his wife and three daughters out.

The Darcy conveyance arrived just as the Bennet one was being driven to the back where the equipages for those who came in one were held.

Darcy noticed the coach which had been ahead of his own. It was a large, comfortable looking one, similar to his own. It was not a conveyance he expected to see in this neighbourhood of medium to small estates. He was about to ask Richard how someone hereabout could afford a coach and four like he had seen when the footman opened the door and the three men alighted.

By the time the three entered the hall, it was only a few minutes until the first set was to be called.

~~~~~~~/~~~~~~~

It was well after eight by the time Miss Bingley's rented carriage arrived at her brother's leased estate.

As planned, she had the coachman and his man offload her trunks and depart as soon as may be. She pointedly ignored the footman who had approached. Once the conveyance was well on its way, Miss Bingley climbed the stairs to the small stone veranda where the double front doors were.

Her brother's footman followed her, still not understanding why the woman had arrived without notice and left a heap of trunks in the drive.

Miss Bingley used the knocker to make her presence known.

Mr. Nichols, the butler opened the one door partially. "May I be of assistance, madam?" he enquired.

"Stand aside, I am to be mistress here," Miss Bingley blustered.

Without a word, the butler closed the door. Miss Bingley used the knocker, combined with her screeches, to keep demanding the door be opened and was thinking what pleasure she would have by sacking the rude man with no character.

The door opened. Before Miss Bingley could release her vitriol, her aunt spoke. "**Caroline Maleficent Bingley**! What is the meaning of this behaviour more akin to one who frequents the fish market than one who holds herself out to be a sophisticated lady?" Hildebrand Bingley demanded, arms akimbo, all the while skewering her niece with a disdainful look.

"Charles invited me..." Caroline Bingley began to prevaricate.

"Do not dare stand here before me and lie!" her aunt responded with asperity. "Is that why you made sure to send your carriage away before you were returned to your home in it?" The older Miss Bingley turned to the butler. "Mr. Nichols, allow her entry and then have your wife assign my niece a chamber, on a floor where no one else is residing. Her room is to be guarded at all times. When my nephew returns he will decide what to do with his wayward sister."

After instructing some of his footmen to collect the trunks in the drive, Mr. Nichols stood back to allow the lady entrance.

"How can you treat me in this way?" Caroline Bingley screeched before the door was closed fully.

"Do not take that tone with me!" Miss Hildebrand Bingley stated as she delivered her niece a slap to her cheek. "You arrive here uninvited and unwanted, and you expect to be welcomed with open arms. I am sure you are here for Mr. Darcy. You, Niece, are delusional!"

By now Mrs. Nichols arrived in the entrance hall, her husband having conveyed the mistress's instructions to her.

Caroline Bingley was still reeling from the combination of the slap and her aunt's anger. She followed the housekeeper without a word. She was placed in a corner room on the fourth floor, two floors above where the others in residence were situated.

~~~~~~~/~~~~~~~

Not long after entering the assembly hall, Elizabeth joined a group with the Long sisters, the Goulding daughter, and the two Lucas sons.

Johnny Lucas who knew his crush on Eliza was unrequited, still made sure he requested her first set. If he did not know she would have denied him more than one, he would have requested two more.

The eldest Lucas offspring, Franklin, who was engaged to Jennifer Goulding, requested Eliza's fifth set. He felt badly for his little brother, but there was no missing Eliza did not return his feelings; she was far too intelligent for Johnny. While they waited for the first set to be called, Franklin shared Charlotte's news that she was in the family way.

~~~~~~~/~~~~~~~

When the visiting men joined those in the hall, they were approached by Sir William. As he was most familiar with Miss Mary's fiancé, he requested that Richard introduce him to the one man he had not met.

Darcy looked around the hall as he was introduced to the jovial and ebullient knight. People were dressed in the quality of clothing he would expect to see at an assembly in Lambton. That was until he spied Richard's fiancée who was smiling at his cousin. She was standing with an older couple and one young lady. He assumed they were some of the Bennets. The other young lady looked even more like Jane Fitzwilliam than Miss Mary, so she had to be the sister who was out locally.

They were all dressed in clothing as fine as he would expect to see in London. When combined with his questions about the quality of Miss Bennet's mount, seeing the way they were clothed only added to his wondering about their supposed lack of wealth.

Darcy was frustrated the one he really wanted to meet, Miss Bennet, was not with them. He looked around the room but before he spied her, Sir William led them over to introduce him and Bingley to his wife and youngest. Richard had placed himself at his betrothed's side and was not aware of any others around him.

Next, Bingley and Darcy were presented to the Bennets. Seeing Mrs. Bennet up close he could see where Jane and the two daughters with her got their looks. Darcy heard a tinkling laugh and looked up to notice Miss Bennet in a group of two men and three other ladies.

He could only see her from behind, as he had seen her when she was flying across the field.

His inspection of Miss Bennet's back was interrupted by Bingley's voice. "Miss Kitty, if you are available, may I dance this set with you?" Bingley requested, "and if it is not yet claimed, may I have the next, Miss Mary?"

Kitty looked to her parents who nodded. "I am not engaged for the first, thank you Mr. Bingley," Kitty accepted.

She looked like an angel to Bingley but he remembered Fitzwilliam's admonitions. These ladies were his sisters and he would not take kindly to anyone who trifled with their emotions. Fitzwilliam had secured the next older while the Viscount was married to the eldest one. He took his friend's warnings to heart and would be very careful.

As the ladies were technically his cousins, Darcy knew he must do his duty. "Miss Kitty, may I have your second and Miss Mary, your third?" Darcy requested. Miss Mary accepted as did Miss Kitty once her parents nodded to her.

The line for the first set formed leaving Darcy alone with the Bennet parents.

"We were very sorry to hear of first your mother and then your father's passing," Fanny stated sympathetically. "We are only sorry we did not get to know them better than we did."

"Yes, they were excellent people, thank you, Mrs. Bennet," Darcy averred, his voice thick with emotion.

Darcy looked up as the dance began and his breath hitched as he saw Miss Bennet's face for the first time. Her emerald-green eyes were shining with mirth at something either she or her partner said. In beauty, she outshone her sisters. Darcy wanted nothing more than to be introduced to her.

As they watched Mr. Darcy's eyes lock on to Lizzy, Fanny and Bennet smiled at one another. It was not the first time they had seen a man react in that fashion on seeing their second daughter. Whether he would be acceptable or not to Lizzy was yet to be determined.

# CHAPTER 25

Anne smiled to herself while she reclined in her bed imagining Lizzy dancing at the assembly. She was sure Lizzy and William would meet. For some time now she had believed the two would be each other's perfect match. That is if they would allow themselves to be open to the possibility.

From speaking to the Fitzwilliams, Giana, and even her papa, Anne was aware when William was uncomfortable, he would sometimes engage his mouth before his brain had a chance to filter his words. There were times he would appear rude, condescending, and arrogant. Richard had related a time or two when William had been so discomforted, he had insulted people he had hardly even met.

On the other hand, there were few who could be more stubborn than Lizzy. Anne loved her sister of the heart but was not unaware of her faults. She was ill, not blind. Her mind was as sharp as ever and there was very little which escaped Anne's notice. If one wanted to excite Lizzy's prejudices, all one had to do was hurt, or even intimate you would hurt, someone dear to her. If William made the error of insulting her, Lizzy would let it wash over her like water off a duck's back. However, if he made the *faux pas* of insulting someone she loved, then it would take much hard work on his part to recover her good regard.

Sometimes when Anne was left alone with her thoughts, she contemplated the unfairness of her life coming to an end at such a young age. In the past, she had railed against God for allowing her life to be truncated as it would be. As she got older, she admitted she had no way of understanding His plan, so questioning Him was not only wrong but rather arrogant.

As much as she did not want to leave Papa, Lizzy, and the rest of her family and friends, Anne was ready to be called home to God. She knew she had no way of knowing when, but she suspected Papa would not be long in joining her in heaven. She of course did not wish it on Papa to pass out of the mortal world soon after her; like her own illness, it was not something over which she had control.

Anne had spoken to Lizzy about her mother. She realised Lady Catherine had never loved her, only pretended to so she could return to Rosings Park. For so long Anne had wanted to believe her mother was better than that. Papa, Lizzy, and everyone else had seen the truth but had not wanted to disillusion her if there was a sliver of hope she would get some iota of affection from Lady Catherine. Finally seeing her mother cared for nothing except her own twisted, selfish desires was a bitter pill to swallow, but swallow it Anne had.

When she admitted seeing the truth about her mother to Lizzy, not even once had Anne's best friend hinted or intimated she knew it would be the end result. Lizzy had commiserated with her and said she was sorry Anne's faith in her mother had been in vain. Since her realisation, she had not asked Papa for them to return to Rosings Park. Deciding she had wasted more than enough of her precious time thinking about her mother, Anne engaged her mind in much more pleasant thoughts. She imagined she was at the assembly dancing in the line near Lizzy and her partner.

Lizzy's partner in Anne's mind's eye, was none other than William.

~~~~~~~/~~~~~~~

During the first set she danced with Johnny Lucas, Elizabeth had been aware of the tall, extremely handsome,

235

dark-haired man watching her intently as he stood next to her parents. She had noticed him enter with Richard and Mr. Bingley, who she had met at her coming out ball. Mr. Bingley was also reasonably handsome, but of slighter build and stature, and had an unruly mop of strawberry blond hair. By process of elimination, Elizabeth assumed the dark-haired man was Giana's brother, the enigmatic Mr. Darcy.

At the end of the set, Elizabeth was delivered to her parents by the second Lucas son. Up close the man was even more handsome than what she had noted while dancing. He had the most piercing, intent slate blue eyes.

Darcy was frozen where he stood. Miss Bennet stood before him, one of her eyebrows arched in question, intelligence and mirth shining in her fine, no the finest, eyes he had ever seen on any woman, ever. Had Richard not arrived and seen his quandary, Darcy was sure he would have stood there, staring at her like a fool for who knows how much longer.

"Lizzy, have you met my mute cousin yet? I know you have met Bingley here," Richard cocked his head to his friend who was returning Kitty to the family party.

"Not yet," Elizabeth averred after she greeted Mr. Bingley. "At least he did not break his leg to avoid meeting us this time."

The beauty's tease helped to relax Darcy which led to the corners of his mouth turning up. Now with a grin, he looked at his cousin. "Will you introduce me to your sister, or should we have Bingley do the honours?"

"Lizzy, this great, big, tall, rather *homely* fellow is my cousin, Fitzwilliam Darcy of Pemberley in Derbyshire," Richard jested causing the Bennet sisters to giggle and Darcy to smile, revealing one of his dimples. "William, my sister Miss Elizabeth Bennet, the second of my five Bennet sisters. Now all that remains is for you to meet Lydia who is not yet out."

Seeing the dimple when he smiled, which if it was possible, made the tall man even more handsome, almost made Elizabeth go weak at the knees. *'Elizabeth Rose Bennet, control yourself. You have met handsome men in London before!'* Elizabeth admonished herself silently.

"Miss Bennet." Darcy bowed over her hand.

"Mr. Darcy," Elizabeth managed a creditable curtsy after she collected herself.

"I am to dance the following two sets with your sisters, but if your fourth set is open, I would beg that one from you," Darcy requested.

"A man who knows when to beg..." Elizabeth teased. It had the desired effect, the man smiled even wider than before and revealed *both* of his dimples. "Yes, Mr. Darcy, that set is yours."

Richard shook his head. What happened to his cousin who was not able to perform like a gentleman when he was not familiar with people? Somehow Lizzy seemed to cast a spell over him and turn him into an affable man.

When their daughters had been led to the floor by their respective partners, Fanny and Bennet simply stared at one another.

"Thomas, what just happened?" Fanny asked in wonder. "They just met and the electricity between them was palpable."

"Never have I seen Lizzy react like that to any man. Not even the prospect of being a duchess has caught her interest so far. We will have to watch and see what develops between them—if anything at all," Bennet averred.

"We will just have to determine if the chemistry between them was only at their meeting or something which will last for a longer duration," Fanny stated. "Selfishly, if Mr. Darcy is the one for Lizzy, I hope it will be some time before anything is decided between them. Jane has been married for more than two years, and soon enough it will be Mary. I do not know if I am ready for the prospect of two more daughters married and leaving our home."

"As long as we have each other, all will be well," Bennet responded as he tenderly kissed his wife's hand. Just then he remembered a letter lying unopened on his desk. "A missive arrived from one William Collins earlier. I forgot about it. We will read it on the morrow."

"Is he not the heir presumptive? It has been some years since he wrote and told us his father had passed away," Fanny recalled.

"The very one. All I can hope is the son is not like the father," Bennet mused. "Let us talk of more pleasant things. Our three daughters seem to be enjoying themselves."

"Very much so." Fanny paused as she too remembered something. "Sarah Lucas is very excited. Charlotte is with child. She felt the quickening recently."

Bennet steered his wife towards where Sir William and Lady Lucas were receiving congratulations for the good news.

~~~~~~~/~~~~~~~

For some reason she could not explain, Elizabeth was in great anticipation of her two dances in the set with Mr. Darcy. The moment he had taken her hand and bowed over it; she had felt a frisson of pleasure shoot from her hand throughout her body, even though they both wore gloves.

When he led her to the floor and the forming line for the set they were to dance, Elizabeth felt like it was the first dance she had ever danced. His cologne of sandalwood and spice pricked her sense of smell, and when mixed with his masculine odour, Elizabeth felt it was the best smell she had ever experienced from a man.

Darcy was no less affected by her than she was by him. As they touched, he felt a tingling throughout his body. When he had bowed over her hand, he had come within hair's breadth of kissing her hand! Never had he been enchanted, as he was now, by any woman before. Just as she had cast her spell over his parents, his sister, the de Bourghs—at least the good ones—and the Fitzwilliams, now he was under her power. What he would not have given to be able to go back in time and watch her ten-year-old self charm a nervous team of four, and then use the same team to stop Uncle Lewis and Anne from crashing to their deaths in the gully below.

There was one word for her—magnificent. Darcy looked to the heavens. *'Mother and Father, you have brought me to this place at this time to meet Miss Bennet when I was ready to do so. Richard told me I should be open to the possibility; how prophetic he was! I know it is very early and my rational side rejects the concept of love at first sight, but I will be open to it. If Miss Bennet —Elizabeth—is the one, I will endeavour to make it work,'* Darcy promised silently.

"Mr. Darcy...Mr. Darcy the dance is about to commence," Elizabeth shook him out of his reverie. "I thought I was a more interesting dance partner." She arched her one eyebrow in challenge.

"Please pardon me, Miss Bennet, I was thinking of my late parents," Darcy explained.

"I met both of them and liked them very well," Elizabeth stated as the dance commenced.

He felt somewhat embarrassed Miss Bennet had thought him inattentive to her. Darcy promised himself to give her his full attention for the duration of the dance. "I was riding this morning and I could swear I saw a wood nymph riding her beautiful thoroughbred astride," Darcy teased right back when they came back together. "Mayhap it was in my imagination."

Now it was Elizabeth's turn to be embarrassed and blush. "You saw me?" she verified. He nodded. Thankfully the dance separated them. She had regained her composure when they came back together. "My father permits me to ride thusly on *our* land at times when I will not be observed."

There was no mistaking her defensiveness. "I must admit at first…" The dance took them in opposite directions, they were across from one another soon enough. "…I was judgemental of a young gentlewoman riding in that fashion…" They entered a pattern with a second couple. After a few minutes, they were together again. "…however, I soon realised I was the one who was not where he should have been. You had no expectation of being observed by a stranger so I apologise for spoiling your solitary time."

Elizabeth had not expected him to be either so understanding or to be the one to apologise to her for being on Longbourn's land at that time of the morning. Her defensiveness flowed out of her posture as she relaxed.

"Her name is Penelope, but I call her Penny. What is your horse's name?" Elizabeth enquired before they were separated once again.

"Zeus," Darcy replied when they came back together. "My father named his horse Poseidon because he loved being in water."

"If you see me riding one morning and you are not too scandalised, we should see if Zeus can keep up with Penny." Elizabeth shocked herself with the forwardness of the rather inappropriate invitation. Thankfully they went down opposite sides of the line so she would not have to hear his refusal right away.

"I think I would enjoy that," Darcy stated as soon as they came back together. "I must correct one thing though." Miss Bennet gave him a questioning look. "It will be Penny following Zeus."

"We will just have to see now, will we not," Elizabeth responded pertly.

For most of the remainder of their set, neither spoke, just revelling in being close to one another. At the end of the set, Darcy stopped as he was leading Miss Bennet back to her parents.

"I thank you, Miss Bennet. I cannot remember a time I enjoyed any dances so much before the two we danced." Darcy returned the smile she gifted him. "Do I ask too much if I were to enquire of you whether you have another set available for me this evening?"

Since her come out, Elizabeth had always declined to dance the final set with anyone. She had started this practice as a way to express solidarity with Anne who could not dance. Anne was the one who commanded she attend the assembly this night, therefore, it stood to reason she should award that set, the only one she had open, to Mr. Darcy.

She was rewarded with a dimple revealing grin when she informed him her final set was his.

~~~~~~~/~~~~~~~

Fanny watched the tableau which unfolded between her second daughter and William Darcy. She did not miss the way Lizzy reacted to him, as she had never reacted that way to any man before.

She would be pleased if Lizzy found the other half of her heart, though she was sad at the prospect of parting with another daughter.

# CHAPTER 26

All five Bennets were well pleased with the assembly as they rode back to Longbourn.

"Mary, you seemed to greatly enjoy your three sets with Richard," Elizabeth observed with a smile.

"I most certainly did. My fiancé is light afoot and dances very well." Mary looked to her older and younger sisters. "You two were not required to sit out at all, and Lizzy I am not the only Bennet who danced more than one set with a man."

"To whatever are you referring?" Elizabeth hedged as her cheeks turned a deep pink.

"Richard told me he has never seen his cousin so keen to dance with any lady, and until tonight, he had never seen him dance more than once with anyone."

"He did seem to single you out for his attention," Kitty added.

"You mean as Mr. Bingley did with you," Elizabeth responded to take the attention from herself.

"He only danced with me once," Kitty deflected.

"True," Elizabeth said with a sly look. "However, he did *request* another, and I heard you explaining our parents' stricture regarding not dancing more than one set with any man until you come out in London."

Now it was Kitty's turn to blush.

"Kitty did exactly what she should have," Fanny interjected to settle things. "Your sister cannot control who asks for how many sets, and with Mr. Bingley being new to the area he was not aware of the rules we have imposed regarding dances with Kitty until next year."

Elizabeth decided to hold her peace and not mention their tenant at Netherfield Park had not requested a second set of any other dance partner.

"Thankfully all five of you are very good girls and know how to behave with decorum and propriety." Bennet looked at his wife and took one of her hands in his own, and added, "I, no we, could not be more proud of all of you."

"Regarding the future, none of us know what it holds, so que sera sera. When and if there is something to decide, it will be done at that time." Fanny smiled at her girls.

Fanny and Bennet had noted Mr. Darcy's marked attention to Elizabeth before he had requested and danced the final set with her. If he continued to pay exclusive attention to his second daughter, Bennet would ask him about his intentions towards Lizzy.

As much as she wanted Lizzy to be happy, Fanny was selfishly hoping if that was where things led, there would be a lengthy courtship and engagement period.

~~~~~~~/~~~~~~~

The three men on their way back to Netherfield Park were all in very good spirits. In fact, Darcy felt downright jubilant.

His eyes pointed to the heavens. *'Mother and Father, I think I have found the other half of my heart,'* Darcy told his late parents silently. *'I know, I know, it is far too early to be sure, but I feel it in my heart that Miss Bennet is the one. Yes, I will take my time and get to know her before I do anything precipitous. I can already tell how intelligent and witty she is, and she is one of the most beautiful women I have ever met. Her eyes! I was lost as soon as I looked into the finest eyes in the world, at least in my opinion. She is so very much more than her looks.'*

His silent communication with his late parents was

disturbed when Richard, who was sitting next to Bingley on the forward-facing bench opposite his cousin, kicked his foot. "William, where were you? I called you three times."

"Please pardon my inattention, Richard," Darcy requested contritely. "What did you say?"

"Never have you singled out any lady before as you did with Lizzy tonight," Richard pointed out. "As one of her brothers, I must ask you what your intentions are towards my sister." He then turned to the smug-looking man sitting next to him. "Bingley, my sister Kitty had better not be another one of your *fall in and out of love with* ladies."

Bingley's smug look faded in an instant. "I-I d-do not do that...any longer," Bingley spluttered.

"Do not forget, Kitty is only out locally and will come out in London next year, which is why she could not dance a second set with you," Richard warned.

"Miss Kitty did explain that," Bingley responded.

"William, did you forget about my question?" Richard reminded him with raised eyebrows.

Darcy had rather hoped his cousin had forgotten about him once he had focused on Bingley. No such luck. How could he explain the feelings roiling within himself to Richard? He could hardly understand them himself.

"All I will tell you is that my intentions towards your sister are completely honourable," Darcy assured his cousin as the coach began to slow for their arrival at Netherfield Park.

"All jesting aside, I know you would never trifle with a lady's affections," Richard slapped William's back after they alighted from the coach. "What say you two, a nightcap is in order, is it not?"

Neither of the other men disagreed.

~~~~~~~/~~~~~~~

Caroline Bingley heard the coach arriving.

After the way her aunt had dealt with her, she was not confident the reception from her brother would be very warm. She cared not for his approbation. All that was important was Mr. Darcy being in the same house, and she would compromise him this night. She was aware the door leading into the hallway was locked and being guarded, but as much as she abhorred having to use it, the servants' door and corridor would enable her to escape her chambers. Once out, she would discover where Mr. Darcy was sleeping.

When he woke up next to her naked form, he would have no choice but to marry her. Caroline was sure she was about to get her due.

~~~~~~~/~~~~~~~

As soon as Bingley saw the six trunks against the wall in the entrance hall, he had no doubt his wayward sister was in his home—uninvited and unwelcome! Before he exploded with anger, Bingley needed to know everything.

Bingley looked at the trunks and then at Nichols. "Miss Bingley, your aunt, is in the drawing room awaiting your return home," the butler informed the master.

"This is private family business, William and I will take ourselves to our chambers," Richard drawled.

"Nonsense," Bingley retorted. "Besides, it will assist me to hear your opinions of what needs to be done about her."

The three men entered the drawing room to find an agitated Aunt Hildebrand. She quickly related the facts of her niece's arrival and how speedily the rented carriage had been dispatched.

"If she thinks sending her rented conveyance back to Town will somehow keep her here past the morning, then she is far more delusional than I thought her to be," Bingley shook his head.

"You are aware, are you not, that your sister still believes Mr. Darcy will marry her?" Aunt Hildebrand enquired of her nephew.

"Surely not, she has been told more times than I care to remember he will never offer for her," Bingley whistled in disbelief. It was not that he was fooled about his sister's ambitions, Bingley was fully aware of her social climbing and fortune hunting desires, he just could not, perhaps did not want to, believe she had slipped the bounds of reason to such an extent.

"Charles, she has failed to attain that which she desires through, what she thinks are, means fair. Now, it is my belief she will try to compromise Mr. Darcy to get her way," Aunt Hildebrand opined.

"It will gain her nothing," Darcy stated firmly. "As I have said in the past, I will not allow her or any other woman to force me to marry where I have no inclination."

"I have a suggestion," Richard spoke up. He had been listening up to now and formulating a strategy to try to stop his friend's sister from ruining herself.

"Well, what is it young man?" Aunt Hildebrand questioned.

"We go speak to her plainly, like I did with the now Mrs. Hurst," Richard proposed.

"It may turn her away from her ruinous path," Bingley averred. It was more of a wish than an expectation.

"As much as you do not want to contemplate it," Aunt Hildebrand placed a calming hand on one of her nephew's forearms, "you must be prepared that she will see nothing but her delusions. In that case, I am afraid she is too far gone and…"

"Yes Aunt, you do not need to say it. If I see no other way, I will take that step," Bingley said resignedly.

"There is no time like the present," Darcy suggested. He wanted the delusional shrewish harpy dealt with. When he thought of his future, he conjured a pair of emerald-green eyes in his mind's eye.

There were nods from the other three in the drawing room.

~~~~~~~/~~~~~~~

While in the middle of contemplating all she would do and purchase as Mrs. Darcy once she was married after successfully compromising him, Caroline was snapped out of her imaginings as she heard the key being turned in the chamber door. She scowled when she saw her aunt enter, followed by her brother. She was expecting a dressing-down, which she would of course ignore.

Her visage brightened up and she began batting her eyelids coquettishly when she saw the object of her matrimonial designs enter the chamber with his cousin. She stood and straightened her gown while directing her most alluring look at Mr. Darcy.

"Miss Bingley, are you well?" Darcy enquired.

"I have been treated infamously, but I am much better for seeing you," Miss Bingley averred as she batted her eyelids furiously.

"You must have something in your eye which is causing you to do...well, I do not know what to call it. Should we summon a doctor?" Darcy asked all the while keeping his expression deadpanned.

Miss Bingley froze her facial expressions. How was it Mr. Darcy was not attracted by her actions? He thought her ill!

"As for the way you are being treated, you are most fortunate it was our aunt who was home and not me when you arrived uninvited. I would have had you under guard at the inn and on the post first thing in the morning!" Bingley barked at his wayward sister. "What did you think you would achieve by coming here? Have I not told you over, and over, and yet over again Darcy will *never* offer for you? He is here before you, why do you not ask the man himself if you will not believe me?"

"Why would I bother dear Mr. Darcy with such..." Miss Bingley began to reply when Mr. Darcy raised his hand. She stopped, thinking surely he was about to put Charles in his place.

"Miss Bingley, you will not call me your *dear* anything," Darcy bellowed. Miss Bingley shrank back, her confident look wiped from her smug face. "You are not now, nor will you ever be, more than the sister of a friend. You are one who I do not find even close to tolerable enough to tempt me! I am in no humour at present, or ever, to give consequence to a supposed *lady* who deserves to be slighted by all men. You had better give up this impossible delusion of yours. You are wasting your time with me."

Caroline Bingley heard the words but did not process the meaning. It could not be! She would never accept the death of her dreams.

Darcy and the others with him noted the instant Miss Bingley got a predatory gleam in her eyes and was obviously preparing herself to jump at Darcy to attempt a compromise. Darcy glared at the virago with his most stern, disdainful look. It seemed to give her pause, if only for some moments.

"If you think I will ever submit to a compromise, you are sorely mistaken. The only one who will be compromised, if you lower yourself to make such an attempt, is yourself. You are the *last* woman in the world who I would agree to marry, under any circumstances! In fact, if we were the only two people left on earth and the fate of humanity depended on our marrying, I still would not marry you." Darcy glared at the woman.

Leaving her standing in the middle of the bedchamber, her aunt, brother, and the two cousins turned and filed out of her room. Miss Bingley heard the lock click as the key was turned once the door had been pulled closed.

Within an hour she had erased the words from her

consciousness and was again planning to find a way to compromise Mr. Darcy that night.

It would be after one in the morning, when she was sure the footmen would be tired, and not vigilant enough. They would never suspect her of using the servants' door and hallway to escape her chambers, of that she was certain.

She would be engaged to Mr. Darcy by the morning, or her name was not Caroline Maleficent Bingley.

~~~~~~~/~~~~~~~

Wickham sat in the taproom of an inn near the university in Oxford.

If it were not for bad luck, he would have no luck at all. He had selected this inn for its proximity to the university, thinking he would be able to win easy money from the young toffs who attended. So far he had lost much more than he had won.

He would keep using his charm to tell the young men he would pay them as soon as his inheritance, which was tied up in probate, was released. It was the same thing he was telling the merchants who were beginning to demand payment. Thankfully Oxford was large enough so he did not have a balance so much at any single shop that they would contact Colonel Forster.

He had hoped to be away from Oxford for a few weeks by joining the group of officers to travel to the town in Hertfordshire to scout locations for the encampment. His bad luck had struck again. The Colonel had thanked him for being willing to volunteer, but he would take more experienced officers with him. Denny was one of those who had been chosen. They would depart on the morrow.

Damn stupid Karen for failing to attain the position of companion to Miss Darcy. He had, of course, intended to double cross the Younges and keep all the dowry of thirty thousand pounds for himself. He would have been on his way

SHANA GRANDERSON A LADY

to the Americas before they realised he had gone. More bad luck! It should have worked.

Thankfully when they moved to Hertfordshire, he was going to a place where he would be unknown, and no Darcys or Fitzwilliams would be close to him.

# CHAPTER 27

Caroline Bingley waited until she heard a clock somewhere in the bowels of the house strike one in the morning. Wearing nothing but her sheerest nightgown, candle in hand, she slowly opened the door the servants used.

Knowing she was in a corner room told her the direction she was walking was the right way. She walked until she found the stairs. She could have entered one of the unoccupied chambers on the same floor as the room in which she had been imprisoned, but she was well aware if the footman on guard was awake, she would be seen and then everything would be for nought. Her brother was sure to send her back to London later that morning, so she had to succeed!

She gingerly walked down one flight of stairs to reach the floor below. She knew there was one level between where she was currently standing, and where everyone else was sleeping, including Mr. Darcy.

Miss Bingley entered the first chamber she reached. As she was sure it would be, it was quite empty. The furniture in the suite was not even uncovered. Reaching the door which would allow her to exit the room, she cracked it and slowly stuck her head out a little. The moonlit hallway was deserted.

Leaving the now extinguished candle on a table in the suite's sitting room, Caroline slid out of the door into the hallway. Just to be extra vigilant, she looked both ways to verify she was alone and saw not a living soul.

Feeling secure, she padded over to the grand staircase.

As silently as she was able, using the light from the moon, Miss Bingley descended the stairs cautiously one at a time. With each step, she halted and listened. On hearing no sounds or footfalls anywhere in the house, she continued to the next step and repeated the process. She was too close to her goal not to be as careful as possible. It would not do to get caught at this juncture.

Eventually, Miss Bingley arrived on the second floor. Now her problem was to determine which suite was Mr. Darcy's. She had to admit the lack of that knowledge was a flaw in her plan. She stood in the hallway which was lighted by the pale glow of moonlight which streamed through the windows on the side of the hallway facing the park.

Then it hit her, of course! The servants' doors!

Slowly she padded in her soft slippers to the last chamber in the hallway. She had to hope she had not gone the wrong way and was about to open the master suite's door. Gingerly and as slowly as possible to mitigate any possible creak or squeak, Miss Bingley slowly turned the handle and opened the door. To her relief the chambers were empty, and the furniture was covered in the same manner as in the suite one floor above. She entered the rooms with speed and carefully pushed the door closed.

She breathed a sigh of relief. Luckily she had turned towards the guest chambers, not the family suites.

Safe inside the rooms, she walked quickly to the servants' door and pulled it open. On entering the hallway beyond the door, Caroline had to stand for some minutes so her eyes would adjust to the reduced light. There were some small windows, high up on the wall opposite which allowed some moonlight to permeate the blackness of the dingy hallway.

With her eyes adjusted to the low amount of light, Miss Bingley made for the door closest to her leading into a bedchamber in the direction of the stairs. As slowly as she could, she pushed the door open. She slipped inside and found it was another unused chamber, but this one was prepared as if more guests were expected. Everything was uncovered and had been thoroughly cleaned.

The next two doors she entered led to empty suites as well which were also prepared for future occupants.

The fourth room she entered was occupied. Caroline felt the thrill of her desires about to be realised as she crept into the room. There was enough light for her to see the back of the person lying in the bed had dark hair, not lighter hair like Mr. Fitzwilliam.

Providence had guided her into her future husband's chamber. Miss Bingley shrugged out of her thin nightrail. She calmed herself and then slipped under the covers. She draped her arm over her victim seductively, and fit her body to Mr. Darcy's so they were touching on every plane. She knew she was successful when she felt the man next to her tense up.

As soon as she was ready, she started to screech. "But Mr. Darcy, we are not yet married."

The man next to her jumped out of the bed as if scalded by hot water. Next, rather than the door being thrown open to discover her in Mr. Darcy's bed, came the sound of derisive laughter. Candles were lit and there sitting across from the bed, all fully clothed, and laughing uproariously at her were her brother, Mr. Fitzwilliam, and Mr. Darcy.

Darcy turned to his dressed, scandalised valet who was standing where he had landed on springing out of the bed. "Well Carstens, it seems you have been compromised, do you want to marry Miss Bingley?"

"No Sir! I most certainly do not," Carstens shot back indignantly.

"Not even her dowry of around fifteen thousand pounds is an inducement?" Bingley enquired amusedly.

Miss Bingley wished she could disappear into thin air. Here she was lying naked in a bed with four men in the room, and the one she had pressed her nude body against was a servant! All her brother and his friends could do was laugh while they tried to convince a servant to have her.

"I am afraid not Mr. Bingley, I would rather remain in service than attach myself to such a termagant." There was no missing the look of disdain on the valet's face.

"It seems Caroline, even Darcy's valet wants nothing to do with you, That is as close as you would have ever come to being connected to Darcy," Bingley shook his head. His mien became rather stern as he looked at his sister. He was devoid of mirth when he barked at her. "What part of '*even a compromise will not induce me to marry you*' did you not understand?"

"Did you think I did not mean what I said when I stated…" Darcy stopped as the crazed woman tossed the covers aside and made to charge at him.

Before Miss Bingley was halfway across the room towards her intended target, she was knocked to the floor by Mr. Darcy's valet. Carstens pulled the coverlet from the bed and covered the lady's nakedness with it.

"**Unhand me! I must reach my fiancé,**" Miss Bingley yelled at the top of her voice.

By now the elder Miss Bingley, wrapped in her robe, had entered the chamber. She shook her head sadly at the sight of her screeching niece, now being held down by two footmen who had entered the suite, and relieved Carstens of his need to restrain the insane woman.

"Charles, you have no choice now. You allowed her the rope she needed to hang herself, and she took it, and then some," Aunt Hildebrand stated sadly.

"As much as I wish it was otherwise, I know you have the right of it, Aunt," Bingley shook his head sorrowfully.

His younger sister used to be a sweet girl until she began

to fill her head with gaining a fortune and the need to reach the pinnacle of English society. He had tried to counsel his late father that no good would come of sending his sisters to a seminary to rub shoulders with daughters of the *Ton*, but his late mother had insisted.

His sisters had taken the way they were treated by others as a way to treat those they felt below them. The way Caroline had been derided at the seminary had lit the flame of her desire to rise above all her naysayers. Now her delusion, which had taken over her life, would end with her committed to an asylum for the rest of her days.

Some time ago he had made enquiries and found an asylum on the Isle of Arran off the west coast of Scotland. Those committed to the institution were treated with kindness and dignity. Bingley knew he should not feel guilty since he had given his sister every chance to reform and change her course. She had either chosen not to, or she was incapable of doing so.

A footman looked to the master who nodded. The man applied a gag to cut off the stream of invective and expletives issuing forth from his youngest sister's mouth. Once it was securely in place, making sure she was covered for modesty's sake, the two men lifted the squirming Caroline Bingley to return her to her chamber and a maid who would dress her. Their aunt followed her niece back to her chamber. For her protection, a straightjacket would be placed on her after she was once again decently dressed.

"This is one time I wish I had been wrong Bingley," Richard stated mournfully. "I think you made the correct decision to allow things to go where she desired. That way you know you were left with no more choices."

All Bingley could do was nod his agreement. "My aunt and I will transport her to London to be evaluated by a doctor later this morning. Once she is committed, I will have her on the first ship headed to the Isle of Arran," Bingley informed his friends. "Will you two be sanguine remaining here with no hostess?"

"We will, you do what you need to do," Richard stated. Darcy nodded his agreement. "Do not forget, my mother and new sister will both arrive in the neighbourhood on Tuesday upcoming, so we will not long be without a hostess. As far as meals go, we are to dine at Longbourn on the morrow, and I am sure, we will be able to survive for a few days shifting for ourselves."

"Your mother will not object to filling the role of hostess until my aunt and I return, will she?" Bingley verified.

Richard confirmed it would not be any trouble for her. Not long after, the men made for their bedchambers. This time Darcy headed to his actual suite.

~~~~~~~/~~~~~~~

In the morning, Miss Bingley was gagged once again and placed in the coach with her aunt and brother.

It was painfully obvious even a night spent in the straightjacket had not dimmed the delusions. As soon as she saw the two cousins waiting to say farewell, she tried to break free from the footmen and run to where Darcy was standing.

He had no need to fend off the insane woman thanks to the footmen being more than able to restrain her. Whatever she attempted to scream would never be known by any who watched her placed in the coach on the front facing bench. One of the footmen sat next to her to make sure she behaved in the conveyance while the other took up station on the rear facing bench. As soon as he was sure his sister was secure, Bingley approached his friends.

"It is time for my aunt and me to be on our way. I have sent a letter to Louisa…Mrs. Hurst…by courier to inform her of the happenings here," Bingley told his friends.

Both men shook Bingley's hand and said nothing. What could one say in such a situation? They bowed to his aunt.

Following his aunt, Bingley entered the carriage; a footman closed the door and slid the step into place. Richard and Darcy stood and watched until the coach made a turn taking it from their field of vision.

Richard looked up and saw a groom had led Zeus to stand a few yards from where he and Darcy stood. "You did not invite me to ride with you," Richard observed.

"My feeling was you would want to join the Bennets at their estate as soon as possible," Darcy stated. It was the truth—mostly. "However, if I am in error, then I will wait for Invictus to be readied."

"You are not wrong in your assumption. I intend to ride out in about an hour," Richard informed his cousin. "Do you not want to join me at Longbourn? We are to have dinner there tonight after all."

"I need a nice long, punishing ride. After my bath, I have some correspondence to review. When I have completed my business I will be happy to join you at the Bennets' estate." Darcy mounted Zeus and doffed his beaver to his cousin who gave him a jaunty salute in return. He wheeled Zeus and was soon trotting towards the fields. Once he passed the stables, he brought his stallion to a canter and soon thereafter a gallop.

As he had on his previous ride, horse and rider cleared the fence that separated Longbourn and Netherfield Park with feet to spare. Darcy had been riding for about ten minutes on Bennet's land when he saw a flash of movement in an adjoining field. There on Penny, riding astride at full gallop unapologetically, was his Helen of Troy. Like Menelaus, if any other suitors emerged for her, he would be victorious.

A little before he spied her on her black and white mare, Darcy had slowed to a trot. He spurred Zeus into a full gallop as he pointed him to a point where the two riders would intersect.

He had to grin when he spied the groom and footman on their geldings fighting to keep up with their mistress.

Luckily for the escorts, Miss Bennet must have seen him because she gradually slowed her horse. By the time he reached them, she had stopped the mare and was looking at him expectantly with an arched eyebrow.

If it was possible in the early morning light, she looked even more beautiful than she had the previous night at the assembly.

When Darcy pulled Zeus to a stop next to her, Miss Bennet was smiling. "Good morning, Mr. Darcy. Is this not too late for you to be riding? I have been at it for some time now." Elizabeth smiled at the handsome man on his large stallion. She estimated his horse was one to two hands higher than Penny.

"It is good to see you again, Miss Bennet," Darcy stated as he doffed his hat and gave a half bow while seated in his saddle. "Thanks to a rather *eventful* night, we did not get as much sleep as normal."

Elizabeth did not feel like she could ask what he was referring to unless he volunteered more information. "I was about to return to the stables," Elizabeth related. "As I intimated, I am at the tail end of my ride."

"I see what you are doing," Darcy stated with a broad grin.

"And what pray tell would that be?" Elizabeth challenged.

"Rather than lose a race to Zeus and me, you and your Penny have an excuse to retire from the field," Darcy stated as he removed some imaginary lint from his riding jacket.

"Even though my Penelope has been running for some time, I am sure she will still best that enormous beast of yours," Elizabeth responded. She got a determined glint in her eye. The handsome Mr. Darcy could not possibly have known she never backed down from a challenge—as long as it was safe.

"If that be the case, shall we," Darcy prodded.

"Elizabeth turned to the groom. "Jim ride out to the tree," she inclined her head towards the tree a little more than a half mile from them. "Signal me with your arm when you are in position."

"Aye Miss Lizzy," the groom averred with an inscrutable grin, and took off towards where his mistress had instructed.

In a few minutes, he was in place and waved his arm at them. "When you are ready, Mr. Darcy," Elizabeth offered him the advantage of deciding when to begin. "Do not think about *allowing* me to win!" Darcy nodded he would not do that.

The two horses were side by side with about three feet separating them. Darcy looked at the magnificent woman next to him. Then he looked towards the distant tree where the groom waited. He took up any slack on the reins and as soon as he felt he was ready, he dug his heels into Zeus's flanks and they were off. His stallion was at full gallop within seconds.

Elizabeth spurred Penny about a second after Mr. Darcy took off. A quarter of the way there she was riding next to him.

Darcy was rather shocked, he had not for an instant thought Penny and Miss Bennet would be able to catch up to him, never mind maintain the same pace as Zeus. Each time he urged his stallion to increase his pace, Miss Bennet and her mare kept the same position never falling back.

When they reached what Darcy guessed was the three-quarter mark, He heard the most alluring tinkling laugh above the thundering of the hooves. Miss Bennet looked at him knowingly, gave him an impertinent wave, and then lowered her upper body until she was almost lying on her mare's neck.

At that moment, Miss Bennet and Penny increased their speed, and Zeus was unable to match it. By the time she reached the tree, there was close to two horse lengths between them.

When a roundly defeated Darcy pulled his horse up to

stand next to hers, she was giving him an impish smile. "Did I mention Penny is one of the fastest horses to come out of Richard's estate?"

"No, I was unaware of that," Darcy remembered Richard speaking of a bloodline which had been bred for speed. He had always thought stamina would have to have been sacrificed in those horses, evidently he had erred.

"One of Penny's sisters and two of her brothers have won at Ascot," Elizabeth revealed.

"Poor Zeus will have a rather bruised ego to lose to a mare, and one smaller than himself," Darcy lamented playfully.

"I am sure he will recover, all the others I beat have done so," Elizabeth stated. "Now if you will excuse me, I am on my way home. After I break my fast I am going to visit Anne. She is due a report from the assembly."

"Richard will soon be at Longbourn and I will join him later." Darcy maneuvered his horse until there was barely any distance between Zeus and Penny. He took Elizabeth's hand closest to him and impetuously leaned down and kissed it. "I look forward to seeing you when you return from Oak Hollow."

Darcy wheeled his stallion and began to canter back towards Netherfield Park.

Elizabeth sat for some time watching him go before she snapped herself out of her stupor. Her hand was still burning where he kissed it, even though she was wearing her gloves.

'Oh my,' she thought. 'Come now Lizzy, you are no schoolgirl! Pull yourself together.'

As she rode back towards the stables she had a feeling there may develop something special between her and the handsome man from Derbyshire.

# CHAPTER 28

While Elizabeth related all from the assembly and her surprise company for her morning ride, Anne's smile grew wider and wider.

Anne knew her end in the mortal world was fast approaching. One of her biggest worries was how would Lizzy carry on. She had a feeling once her best friend was through her mourning, she would have matters of the heart to deal with. If only she could have lived to see Lizzy wed, but she knew that was an impossible dream. Lizzy and William had only just met and Anne was certain nothing would change in the next few days. Although she understood why Mary and Richard had deferred their wedding for now, she would not have minded seeing them marry.

She was aware the rest of the family, including little Tommy, would arrive on Tuesday. It was only another three days so her fervent prayer was God would allow her to say goodbye to them before she was called home.

There was another thing Anne was almost certain about. Papa would not remain in the mortal world for many days after she departed it. Papa was not well, even though he refused to speak of it to her. His lack of healthy colour in his face, it was in fact pallid, was almost as bad as hers. Additionally, his breathing was also rather laboured. It was obvious to Anne that Papa was fighting to remain alive as long as she was, but as soon as she passed away, he would cease battling.

"I assume you are happy your cousin, William Darcy, and I seem to get along well?" Elizabeth asked snapping Anne out of her reverie.

Anne nodded and wrote something. She turned the paper and showed Elizabeth:

*I had a feeling you two would enjoy each other's company. He is one of the few men who can challenge you intellectually.*

"Richard has said something similar," Elizabeth noted. "According to what Richard related, until Aunt Elaine arrives they have no hostess at Netherfield Park," Elizabeth reported. She related what Richard had told of Miss Caroline Bingley's behaviour. Anne was as scandalised as everyone at Longbourn had been. "I am so pleased we will see Janey, Andrew, and especially Tommy on Tuesday. I will enjoy seeing my nephew each day I am at Longbourn thanks to his parents staying with us."

When Anne turned her page towards Elizabeth the latter read:

*I am sure Aunt Elaine and Uncle Reggie will be there daily to spend time with Tommy as well.*

"You have the right of it," Elizabeth agreed. "In her last letter, Jane said Tommy loves to run everywhere he goes, and greatly enjoys making everyone chase him." Elizabeth saw Anne's raised eyebrows and understood exactly what she meant. "Yes, Annie my dear friend, you have heard Mama and Papa tell you of my similar exploits when I was Tommy's age."

Anne nodded with a smile before she began a coughing fit.

"Miss Anne needs to rest Miss Lizzy," Mrs. Jenkinson told her charge's best friend.

"Be well, Annie, I will return on Tuesday when the arriving family members come to see you." Fighting to control the tears that threatened to fall, Elizabeth left Anne's bedchamber.

She stopped in the hallway outside of the chamber and

allowed her tears to fall freely as she cried silently. Elizabeth had no doubt it was not many days before Anne would be called home to heaven.

Mrs. Jenkinson who had seen Miss Lizzy's distress, exited the bedchamber and enfolded the younger lady in a warm hug. "You can see it is near the end, can you not Miss Lizzy?" Mrs. Jenkinson verified. Elizabeth gave a watery nod. "Never forget you have made her life, which could have been lonely and sad, one full of sisterhood and laughter. Thanks to you, Miss Anne has lived a fulfilled life. Never forget that."

Anne's companion said nothing more, she just allowed Miss Lizzy to quietly cry until it had passed. Elizabeth dried her eyes and straightened up when she was ready. "Thank you, Jenki. It is time for me to return to Longbourn. Before I depart, where is Uncle Lewis?"

"In the study, I believe," Mrs. Jenkinson averred.

Elizabeth made her way to the study and knocked on the door. She opened the door on hearing a weak "enter."

When she pushed the door open, a wave of heat hit Elizabeth from the roaring fire in the grate. Uncle Lewis was seated in a wingback chair before the fire, his legs covered with a thick blanket.

After her last call at Oak Hollow, she had asked Papa why Uncle Lewis always needed to be close to heat lately. He had explained that according to Mr. Jones, with certain ailments of the heart, the body was not able to keep as warm as it should. Armed with this knowledge, Elizabeth understood why her uncle's study was as hot as it was.

"Are you returning to Longbourn?" Sir Lewis queried.

"Yes, the carriage is being brought around as we speak," Elizabeth responded.

After the strenuous ride and race earlier that morning, Elizabeth had travelled to Oak Hollow in the old Bennet carriage. She had been escorted by Mrs. Annesley and two footmen.

"You are too intelligent not to know neither Anne nor I will remain in the mortal world too much longer." There was no missing the distressed look on Lizzy's face. "I mention this to prepare you. When the will is read…" Sir Lewis stopped as Elizabeth vehemently shook her head.

"Both you and Annie are still alive. I will hear *no talk* of wills and what comes after yet!" Elizabeth insisted.

Knowing how stubborn his adopted niece and daughter in one person could be, Sir Lewis did not drive his point home. With Matlock and Bennet as his executors, he knew that his wishes would be be carried out to the letter.

"Have a good journey back to Longbourn. We will see all of you on Tuesday." Sir Lewis beckoned to Lizzy who bent so he could kiss her on her forehead.

After the butler assisted her into her outerwear, Elizabeth and Mrs. Annesley entered the carriage for the relatively short ride home.

~~~~~~~/~~~~~~~

Fanny joined Bennet in the study as had been planned. He lifted the letter from the incoming tray and broke the seal. Bennet seated himself next to his wife so they would both have a clear view of the words on the page.

*2 October 1810*

*Thornburg's Theological Seminary, Wiltshire*

*Dear Sir,*

*The disagreement subsisting between yourself and my late honoured father always gave me much uneasiness, and since I have had the misfortune to lose him, I have frequently wished to heal the breach, but for some time I was kept back by my doubts, fearing lest it might seem disrespectful to his memory for me to be on good terms with anyone with whom it had always pleased him to be at variance.*

*My mind, however, is now made up on the subject. Although I received ordination at Easter, I have not been so fortunate as to be distinguished by the patronage of one who can prefer me to the living in their parish. If I gain a living it shall be my earnest endeavour to demean myself with grateful respect towards my patron and be ever ready to perform those rites and ceremonies which are instituted by the Church of England.*

*It is my understanding you hold the gift of the living of Longbourn Village. My hope is that you would be able to have the holder understand you wish to prefer the living on one of your bloodline. I think it natural and just that I, the next master of Longbourn, be the holder of the living, which I would continue to hold even after the unfortunate event of your demise.*

*As a clergyman, moreover, I feel it my duty to promote and establish the blessing of peace in all families within the reach of my influence, and on these grounds, I flatter myself, my present overtures are highly commendable, and the circumstance of my being next in the entail of Longbourn estate will be kindly overlooked on your side, and not lead you to reject the offered olive branch.*

*I cannot be otherwise than concerned at being the means of injuring your amiable unmarried daughters, and beg leave to apologise for it, as well as to assure you of my readiness to make them every possible amends, but of this hereafter.*

*I believe I read that your eldest daughter made a most advantageous match to one who is a viscount. I look forward to meeting her and my new cousins.*

*If you should have no objection to receiving me into your house, I propose myself the satisfaction of waiting on you and your family, Tuesday the 25th day of October, by four o'clock, and shall probably trespass on your hospitality till the Saturday sennight following, which I can do without any inconvenience.*

*Mr. Thornburg, is far from objecting to my occasional absence on a Sunday, provided one of the other curates is engaged to do the duty of the day.*

*I remain, dear sir, with respectful compliments to your lady and daughters, your well-wisher and friend,*

*William Collins*

"Is the man insensible?" Fanny asked after reading the drivel contained within the missive.

"Based on his letter, I must believe he is," Bennet opined. "What a mixture of servility and pomposity. If he meets the Fitzwilliams, de Bourghs, and Darcys I could see him bowing and scraping before them. Thankfully Lady Catherine is not allowed to appoint anyone to the Hunsford living when it becomes vacant far in the future. Mr. Jamison is still a relatively young man."

"I suspect his *olive branch* is his desire to marry himself to one of our daughters. I would rather starve in the hedgerows than allow such a man to pay court to any of our girls." Fanny paused to allow her ire to drain from her. "Thomas, what can be done? I know we have an estate if we need it, but how can we allow a man such as this one," she pointed to the letter disdainfully, "to inherit this estate and run it into the ground?"

"There is the option of a simple recovery, which I have discussed with Philips. Before I take that irrevocable action, I would like to speak to Mr. Collins and determine if he is amenable to some other possibility."

"You have my support in that, husband. With Anne and Lewis's health the way it is, we cannot welcome him into our home at this time. On that subject, what temerity to invite himself to our home. It seems he has no understanding of social niceties. I suppose that is his pompous side."

That I believe it is, Fanny dearest," Bennet leaned over and kissed his beloved wife.

Before they could discuss any more regarding Bennet's Collins cousin, they heard the sound of a conveyance in the drive. On the way to see if it was Lizzy who had come back, the

Bennets passed the open drawing room door.

Mary and Richard were seated on a settee, heads close together. Besides the door being wide open, Miss Jones and the two youngest Bennets were all within.

~~~~~~~/~~~~~~~

When Elizabeth shared her observation regarding Anne and Uncle Lewis's health, she was not able to stem the tears which fell again.

"It is not like I have not known this day would come from the first time Anne and I met. Knowing it was to happen has not assisted me in accepting what is to come," Elizabeth lamented. Fanny pulled her second daughter into a warm, secure hug.

"Knowledge and acceptance are not the same thing," Bennet told his daughter as he sat on the settee on Elizabeth's other side. "Just think, had you not been riding Hector that day ten years past, not only would you and Anne not have become friends, but she and de Bourgh would not be alive." Bennet gently lifted Lizzy's chin so she was looking at him. "Every day since the day you rescued them has been a day they would not have had without your actions. Your Uncle Lewis has told me at every opportunity what light and joy you have brought into their lives." Bennet kissed his daughter's cheek. "Do not forget the promises you made to Anne after you read her letter to you."

"Never did I promise not to be sad, but I will honour my word to Anne," Elizabeth affirmed.

Both her mother and father hugged her. Elizabeth kissed each of her parents on a cheek and made sure her eyes and cheeks were dry. That done, she made her way out of the study and back towards the drawing room. On passing the entrance hall, Elizabeth noticed Mr. Darcy dismounting from his great big stallion.

She waited while Hill divested him of his outerwear.

"Miss Bennet, I was not aware I warranted a welcoming committee," Darcy jested.

"I was on my way back to the drawing room when I noticed the horse Penny ran away from this morning," Elizabeth responded pertly. "It was out of sympathy for his drubbing and I was watching to make sure his ego had recovered."

"*Touché* Miss Bennet," Darcy bowed over her hand. How he wanted to kiss her ungloved hand. He stopped himself. The feeling of touching her hand with his uncovered one would suffice for now.

Elizabeth thought—was almost hoping—Mr. Darcy was about to kiss her hand, like he had earlier that morning. She had felt she was losing herself in his slate blue eyes. When his hand took hers as he greeted her, she felt a frisson of pleasure radiate to all corners of her body from the point where his hand had taken hold of hers.

In possession of her hand once again, Elizabeth shook her head. With Anne so close to the end of her life, now was not the time to begin considering her romantic future.

Once she felt she had regulated herself, Elizabeth led Mr. Darcy to the study to greet her parents. With that done, they made for the drawing room.

As they walked, Darcy evaluated what he had seen so far, and what he was currently seeing. Everything confirmed his suspicion—the Bennets were much wealthier than they let be known. He supposed they had reasons to do so and it was not his place to question them on the subject. He had long accepted the most important thing in people was character and from what he could see the Bennets had extremely admirable ones.

On entering the drawing room, Darcy greeted his cousin and Miss Mary. Miss Bennet introduced him to the two youngest Bennets, Mrs. Annesley, who had come sit on her return with Elizabeth, and Miss Jones.

It did not take Darcy long before he challenged Miss Bennet to a game of chess. He needed to soothe his bruised senses after being so easily trounced in the race that morning. Darcy did not miss the way Richard was smirking at him as he sat across the board from Miss Bennet.

In all of his years playing the game, even against his late father who was one of the few he had played who could beat him, Darcy had never seen a player move his—or in this case her—pieces at the lightning speed she did. Within seconds of his removing his hand from his piece, she had moved. It took her less than twenty moves before Darcy tipped his king. Horsemanship was not her only accomplishment.

"Lizzy, next time do not go easy on my *young* cousin," Richard ribbed Darcy.

"You applied a sound strategy, Mr. Darcy," Elizabeth allowed.

"Just not good enough." Darcy shook his head. His uncles and cousins had not been exaggerating Miss Bennet's prowess at the game.

Soon the two were debating a history they had both read. In this, they were far more evenly matched.

Each moment he spent in Miss Bennet's company only confirmed what Darcy had told his parents the last time he had spoken to them. Miss Elizabeth Bennet was the one he had not known he was looking for.

Now all he had to do was win her heart.

# CHAPTER 29

"Janey!" Elizabeth exclaimed before her sister and brother-in-law's coach's door had been fully opened.

Andrew stepped out first. "My apologies for disappointing you, Lizzy, but Jane will be next to alight," Andrew jested before he leaned in and handed out his wife.

Before any of her younger sisters could move, Elizabeth flew into Jane's arms. "I have missed you too, Lizzy," Jane told her next younger sister and then looked at the other three all waiting impatiently. "Just as I have missed all of you. The letters do not replace seeing you."

"It is all well and good that you are here, Jane and Andrew, but where is my grandson?" Fanny trilled.

At that moment, Andrew turned around with said grandson in his arms. Tommy had just been woken from a deep sleep so he was not his exuberant self as he tried to wake himself and take in all of the faces of those waiting expectantly to see him.

Tommy, who was not quite one and one half years old had his mother's colouring, insofar as he sported the same hair and eye colour. His face and ears were smaller versions of his proud father's.

His eyes settled on the two people he knew far better than the rest. "Gwanmama, Gwanpapa!" he squealed as he began to squirm in his father's arms demanding to be free.

"It seems our son is fully awake now," Jane smiled.

Andrew set the toddler on the ground and Tommy ran

into his Grandmamma's arms with all of his might. From his perch in her arms, he hugged his Grandpapa and bestowed rather wet kisses on both grandparents.

He looked at the four ladies surrounding his mother. "Mama, dees my Awnties?" Tommy asked.

"Yes my darling boy, this is Aunt Lizzy, Aunt Mary, Aunt Kitty, and Aunt Lydia," Jane reminded her son who had not seen his Bennet aunts since the last time he had been at Longbourn before he was walking and talking.

"No teaching him to climb trees yet, Lizzy," Andrew stated playfully.

"I will make no such promise," Elizabeth teased earning herself a playful slap on her arm from Jane.

"Did Elaine, Reggie, and Giana head directly for Netherfield Park?" Fanny enquired as she ruffled Tommy's golden blond hair. She led everyone into the house past Mr. and Mrs. Hill who were standing near the door to see Miss Jane's son.

"Yes, Mother Fanny. My parents and Giana decided they wanted to wash and change before we all meet at Oak Hollow," Andrew reported. His face lost much of the joviality it had displayed on arriving. "Is it truly so close to the end?"

"It seems so. I would have been with Anne had she not commanded in writing I be here to greet you three," Elizabeth averred. "It is a miracle Annie has lived this long. Both she and Uncle Lewis asked you do not leave Tommy in the nursery when we make for Oak Hollow later. They would like to see him."

"It will be so." Jane turned to her mother and the nursemaid who had followed them into the house. "Mama, do you want to keep Tommy with you or would you prefer Leticia amuse him until we depart?"

"What a question Jane, allow him to remain with us. He has to become familiar with his aunts after all," Fanny insisted.

"Leticia will be on hand if he needs anything we are unable to provide."

Jane and Andrew proceeded up to their chambers to wash and change. Tommy was so engrossed with his grandparents and aunts he did not notice their absence.

~~~~~~~/~~~~~~~

Every breath Anne was drawing had become a fight. She was aware Lizzy and her family would arrive at the estate very soon. She hated having to leave all of them, but especially Lizzy. She had meant what she said in her letter to Lizzy. If her best friend took her death as a reason to withdraw from living a full life, then Anne would haunt her until Lizzy did as she had promised to do.

William had come to visit the previous day and Anne had exacted a promise he would look out for Lizzy for her. He had shared it was an easy promise to make as he aimed, after mourning periods were over, to request permission to call on Lizzy. For Anne, it was one of the final things she needed to hear to be completely at peace with her fast approaching departure from the mortal world.

Yester-evening her papa had come to sit with her. He had dismissed Jenki. She could hear his words as if he had just spoken them to her as they had banished her very last worry.

*"Annie my darling daughter, even though we have had far too few years together in the mortal world, I know we will be together for all of eternity."* Anne had shaken her head trying to deny she would not be the only one to pass away soon. *"You are too vigilant not to know it is true Annie. I have known for more than two years that my heart is ailing. And I do not mean just because of my feeling of your impending loss.*

*"Like you fought to remain alive for as long as possible to be with Lizzy, me, and the rest of our friends and family, I have fought tooth and nail not to be called home before you.*

*"We have both reached the end of our fight my Annie. I*

*know how hard it is for you to breathe while feeling almost like you are underwater." Anne had reached for her paper, although even that was becoming much more difficult now. Sir Lewis placed one of his hands on her arm to stay her. "Do not be angry with Jenki for telling me. She has always shared any information she thought was pertinent with me. You know she sees you much more as a daughter than someone she serves."*

*Anne nodded. She was not angry with Jenki, she just had not wanted to worry Papa when he was fighting his own illness.*

*"As much as I disliked being married to your mother, even before she tried to have us murdered, at least I gained you from the union. That is something I thank God for each and every day, and I have done so since you were born.*

*"I know you are worried Lizzy will be in danger from her for the crime of saving us, and others, but do not." Anne had looked at her father quizzically. "Your mother thinks on our deaths she will be free..." Papa had explained the steps in place to make sure she would not be a danger to anyone. "As an additional layer of security, Biggs, Johns, and their men will become Lizzy's personal guards as soon as they are no longer yours."*

*All Papa had told her assisted Anne in relaxing and lifting that particular weight from her shoulders.*

*Once she realised her mother had never changed, but had only been acting a part, Anne knew it was she who tried to murder her and Papa. It was not an opinion, but a certainty. The knowledge of what plans were in place and that Lizzy would have John and Brian to look after her was a great relief.*

*"Knowing everything you do now, if you choose to cease fighting, know that you will go with my blessing, and Annie, we will be together soon. In His kingdom you will have no physical restrictions, you will be as you were before scarlet fever took hold of you."*

*Papa had kissed her on both cheeks and her forehead. He stood slowly and made his way, as best as he could, out of her chambers.*

Soon the people she was waiting to see would be with her. Once she was able to say her goodbyes, Anne would stop fighting.

~~~~~~~/~~~~~~~

The Bennet, Fitzwilliam, and Darcy coaches came to a halt in the drive outside of Oak Hollow's manor house. Those residing at Longbourn had stopped at Netherfield Park first. There they had all spread out between three carriages, rather than four. Andrew's conveyance remained at that estate.

Other than Tommy, who was in his grandmother Elaine's arms, everyone else was sombre.

Those who had arrived that day had been fully apprised of the health situation of both de Bourghs at Oak Hollow. That way there would be no surprises when they saw Lewis and Anne.

The five men made for the study while the ladies, save Lizzy who would go see Anne last and on her own, were on their way to Anne's chambers. For those who had not seen her for some time, seeing Anne was rather shocking.

Her face had lost all of its colour, was beyond pallid, and her breathing, such as it was, almost sounded like bubbles escaping from below water.

The two youngest Bennet sisters and Giana said their final goodbyes first, and then departed the room in tears

Mary replaced her sisters. "How I would have enjoyed having you attend my wedding like you were at Janey's," Mary told Anne as she fought a losing battle with her tears. "I love you, Anne." Mary took one of Anne's hands and gave it a squeeze. There was no missing how cold her hand was regardless of the fire which made the chamber rather hot.

"We could not deny you when your request for us to bring Tommy was conveyed to us. We are so pleased he is to meet his wonderful Cousin Anne," Jane stated with a smile. Anne nodded.

Jane took Mary's place with Tommy in her arms. As if he understood the gravity of the situation, Tommy was much more subdued than was his wont. Anne gave a wan smile when she saw the toddler. With a nod from Anne, Jane placed Tommy on the bed and he lay down next to her. Seeing a tear slide down Anne's cheek, Jane picked up her unnaturally quiet son and after saying goodbye to Anne, she left the chamber.

No sooner had Jane left than the five men entered Anne's chamber to join the two matrons.

Fanny and Bennet said their final goodbyes first, Fanny speaking for them both. Fanny sat close to Anne. "We will miss you every day Annie. You have been like another daughter to us. As sorry as we will be not to see you, we know you will no longer be suffering." Fanny leaned forward and kissed both of Anne's cold cheeks. After she did, Bennet leaned down and kissed Anne's forehead.

It was the three cousins next. After Andrew and Richard stood aside, Darcy took the seat next to Anne's bed. He took one of her small hands in his large one and rubbed it to try to warm it. He leaned close to Anne's ear so only she would be able to hear him.

"You have my word of honour that I will do everything in my power to make Miss Bennet...Elizabeth happy. When you see my father, please tell him I took all of his words to heart. Be at peace, Annie." Darcy kissed her hand and then gently put it back at her side.

The three cousins departed the room leaving Anne's aunt and uncle alone with her. "Annie, you will be missed our dear niece," Lady Elaine spoke for her husband and herself.

As strong a man as he was, Lord Matlock was too overcome with emotion to speak. He had just said his farewells to his only remaining brother and now it was time to do the same again with his niece. As he had for many years, he felt powerless to stop what was happening, and for a man of supposed power, it was not a feeling he enjoyed.

~~~~~~~/~~~~~~~

When the men had come from the study, they had told Elizabeth that her presence was requested by Uncle Lewis.

She entered rather gingerly steeling herself for how Uncle Lewis would look. The previous time she had visited he had not looked at all healthy. It had been quite some time since he had looked so.

"Lizzy," Sir Lewis croaked on seeing her.

"I am here Uncle Lewis." She hoped he did not want to talk about his will or what would be after as he had the previous time she had been in the study.

"Just want to…thank you…for the extra ten years…your bravery gave us," Sir Lewis managed. Then he pointed to a letter on his desk. "Read this…we are gone."

Elizabeth held up her hand. "Have it delivered to my Papa. I am not ready to take it from you yet. I gained as much from our friendship as Annie did," she asserted.

Sir Lewis smiled. He was used to Lizzy downplaying her role in their lives from the time she rescued them onward. He beckoned her to him and took each of her hands in his own cold ones. "Thank you…Lizzy." He waved her away as he took some wheezing breaths.

From the study, Elizabeth walked up the stairs on her way to Anne's chambers. She arrived in time to see Aunt Elaine and Uncle Reggie exit. Both had tears in their eyes.

Elizabeth entered the room and sat next to Anne, taking the hand nearest to her in one of her own. She was used to Anne's hands not being warm, but this was far colder than she had experienced before.

Anne smiled at Elizabeth and then forced two words

from her throat. "Thank...you." Just the two words led to a round of coughing and fighting for breath.

"I have as much to thank you for as you do me," Elizabeth claimed. "I cannot be selfish any longer. You have suffered enough and as much as I will miss you, it is time for your anguish to end. It is obvious we will lose both you and Uncle Lewis and that is a tragedy. In a way, it is as it should be. Your father has lived for you and now you will soon be together forever." By now tears were streaming down Elizabeth's cheeks as she said her goodbyes.

It broke Mrs. Jenkinson's heart to hear the misery in Miss Lizzy's voice as she said goodbye to Miss Anne. She was sitting in a darkened corner of the bedchamber to be of use as needed.

"Annie, I will sit with you until you are sleeping," Elizabeth sobbed.

She was somewhat hurt when she saw Anne shake her head slightly. "Miss Lizzy," Elizabeth had not seen Jenki sitting unobtrusively in the corner. "Miss Anne does not want you to watch her pass from this world into the next. She wants your last memory of her to be of her living, as she will always be alive in your heart."

As Elizabeth tried to stand her legs almost gave way but Mrs. Jenkinson was there to support her.

"Goodbye Annie. I love you as much as I love any of my other sisters." With that, Elizabeth kissed her best friend on her forehead and then ran out of the chamber.

~~~~~~~/~~~~~~~

According to Sir Lewis and Anne's wishes, the family did not sit and wait for them to be called home. Within minutes of their departure, Sir Lewis was assisted to his daughter's bedchamber by Biggs and Johns. He lay down on the bed next to his daughter, taking one of her hands in one of his own.

Mrs. Jenkinson and the two guards withdrew from the room and quietly pulled the door closed behind them. Biggs supported the sobbing Mrs. Jenkinson until she reached her bedchamber. Once she was inside, the two men took up station in the hall.

Anne turned her head to look at her beloved father as he turned to look at her. Her breathing became less frequent and more shallow until she breathed no more. Sir Lewis breathed his last seconds after he was sure Anne was with God.

# CHAPTER 30

John Biggs and Brian Johns arrived at Longbourn a few scant hours after the master and mistress passed away. Their mission was twofold. To deliver the letters they had been charged with making sure reached the Bennet estate, and to begin their new post guarding Miss Lizzy and her family. Miss Lizzy was as yet unaware of the fact they and the men who worked with them were now her guards.

As sad as they were Miss Anne and the master were in heaven, they would perform their duties and fulfil their promises to the two de Bourghs. The other four men would transfer to Longbourn after the interments. Both men were wearing black armbands on their left arms.

Bennet and Elizabeth had been engaged in a half-hearted battle across the chessboard when Hill informed the master the two guards from Oak Hollow were asking to see him. Bennet nodded his permission as Elizabeth began to cry. She knew there would be only one reason John and Brian would be at Longbourn now—Anne and very likely Uncle Lewis were not living any longer.

The two huge men were shown into the master's study without delay. As soon as Elizabeth saw the black armbands her weeping intensified exponentially. The sound of Elizabeth's mournful sobbing brought her mother, Jane, Andrew, and Mary from the drawing room.

Knowing what the tableau before them signified, Fanny, Jane, and Mary began to cry quietly. Fanny urged her second daughter out of the chair where she had sat playing chess with her father and gently led her sobbing daughter to the settee between the two windows looking out onto the park.

Mary sat on Elizabeth's other side while Andrew comforted his wife as best he could.

"Are they both…?" Bennet began but the words died in his throat as the emotion hit him like a punch to the gut.

"Aye, Mr. Bennet, they be wif' God," Biggs averred simply. "We 'ave to deliver these 'ere letters." Biggs withdrew three letters from his pocket and proffered them to Bennet.

"Thank you Biggs," Bennet managed as he fought for composure. "I am sure you need to return to Oak Hollow. Are your men watching over Sir Lewis and Anne?"

"Aye, them an' Missus Jenki," Biggs responded. "Them letters will explain why we are to stay 'ere at Longbourn."

Bennet nodded. He remembered the reasons his late friend would want the guards at Longbourn. The two men exited the study and stationed themselves in the hallway on either side of the door.

"I must send a note to Netherfield Park," Bennet realised, still very much in a daze.

"Come, let us return to the drawing room and wait for your father there," Fanny gently led Elizabeth and the rest of the other family members out of the study. It broke her heart to hear the anguish in Lizzy's crying.

Fanny guided Elizabeth to a settee. She pulled her to herself as soon as she sat next to her second daughter. "Lizzy, knowing Anne's and Lewis's passing was imminent does not make it easier to bear," Fanny stated gently as she dried her daughter's tears with her silk handkerchief. "Think about the fact neither Anne nor Lewis is suffering any longer and are together in God's Kingdom where they will watch over us."

"I know…Mama," Elizabeth managed between sobs, "but it does…not make the pain…any less."

"Of course not dear girl," Fanny comforted. She pushed her own pain and mourning aside for now so she would be able to take care of her daughter. "Over time the hurt will lessen and you will slowly begin to feel better."

~~~~~~~/~~~~~~~

Bennet sent one of his grooms to Netherfield Park with a black edged note. Then he sat back and looked at the letter addressed to himself, and the others below it, which remained untouched on his desk. He chastised himself that he was procrastinating as if seeing who they were addressed to, or reading one to himself would somehow make everything more final than they were.

He carefully lifted the missives. There was one for Lizzy, another for Matlock—he remonstrated with himself for delaying looking at the letters until after he sent the note to Netherfield Park. When the groom returned he would have to have Hill send the man back. The third missive, the one which had been on the top of the other two, was for himself. Bennet was well aware Lizzy was in no state to read the letter addressed to her so he would keep it until she was in a state of mind where she could digest the words.

He lifted his letter and after staring at it for some moments, he cracked the de Bourgh seal. He took a sip of cognac to help steady his nerves, feeling it burn as it coursed down his throat, and then began to read.

*7 October 1810*

*Oak Hollow*

*Bennet my friend,*

*If you are reading this then Anne and I are no longer in the mortal world. That Anne passed before me portends I have had enough strength to wait until she has begun her eternal slumber before beginning my own.*

*Biggs and Johns would have carried out my instructions and delivered this letter to you, along with others. You are well aware as one of my executors why I have arranged for them and the rest of their men to join your household.*

*Before I say anything else, you must allow me to tell you how much your friendship has meant to me and Anne. I refer to all of you, especially Lizzy.*

*I was always sad Anne had no siblings, but in Lizzy, she had a sister. Even though she was not quite as close to your other four daughters, they too were thought of as sisters by Anne. We were family long before Jane married Andrew.*

*You objected to the way I structured my will, but I expect you to honour my wishes. There are no more living de Bourghs (I have never counted Catherine as a true de Bourgh) and as you well know, the rest of my family through marriage is very well taken care of. Do not forget both Matlock and my late brother Darcy agreed with and gave their blessing to the way I structured my last will and testament once Richard was master of his own profitable estate.*

*The one thing I did not stipulate in my will, and I have stated in my letter to Matlock, is where Anne and I are to be interred. I debated for a long time vacillating between Rosings Park and Oak Hollow.*

*As I discussed with you, it is not only Catherine's presence in Kent which gave me pause regarding being laid to rest at that estate but also the fact my dishonourable and degenerate father is resting there. In the end, I decided Anne and I need to be placed into the de Bourgh family crypt. My mother and all other de Bourgh ancestors (from the time they came to England) are slumbering there and I will not disrespect them because of my wife or father.*

*You must promise me if Catherine is still at the estate when we are interred, she will be restricted to her rooms. I do not want her present to make a mockery of the proceedings, and neither would Anne. It surely would be if the woman who tried to have us murdered is permitted to attend anything connected with our deaths.*

*One last request my friend. If she chooses to continue to be in service, would you take Mrs. Jenkinson on as Lizzy's companion? It would help lessen the blow of Anne's death to both of them. You well know Mrs. Jenkinson was so much more than a paid companion to my daughter and she and Lizzy already have a good rapport between them. As you also know, due to the bequest I have made her, if she chooses not to, she will have no need to continue to serve.*

*In closing, please send my warmest regards to Fanny and your daughters. You and your family have been a bright shining light in Anne's and my lives.*

*Your friend,*

*L de B*

Bennet sat staring at the words on the pages for some time after he completed reading them. He could see from the shaky script compared to the firm handwriting de Bourgh used to have in letters past how weak he had been towards the end.

He stood and made his way to the drawing room.

~~~~~~~/~~~~~~~

"What is it Reggie?" Lady Matlock asked concernedly when she saw how her husband's face fell on reading the letter. It was then she noted the black edging to the page.

"This just came from Longbourn," Lord Matlock responded half-heartedly.

He and his wife had been sitting in their private sitting room. As far as they knew Richard, William, and Giana were in Richard's sitting room reflecting on the closeness of Anne's and Uncle Lewis's ends.

"Anne?" she asked tremulously.

"And de Bourgh," Lord Matlock replied. "We need to tell the rest."

The Earl stood and pulled his wife into his comforting arms as she cried into his chest quietly. It took some minutes for her to compose herself. She dried her eyes with her husband's large handkerchief he had offered her.

Once they felt ready, they exited their sitting room and walked to the next door suite.

Three pairs of eyes swung to the Fitzwilliam parents as soon as they entered the room. Even before any of them noticed the edging on the note, they knew what they were about to be told based on the sorrowful looks on the faces of the two who entered.

Giana was sobbing in her brother's arms before their aunt and uncle said a word. The crying only increased when the news of both deaths was shared.

As sad as he was about the passing of his cousin and uncle, Darcy's thoughts were for Miss Bennet and how she was suffering with the death of her best friend. As much as he wanted to jump on Zeus's back, saddled or not, and go to her, Darcy knew now was not the time to dash to her side. He would exercise some patience and wait until they were all together.

"When are we to Longbourn? I must be with Mary," Richard insisted.

"According to Bennet's note, we will all meet at Oak Hollow in the morning," Lord Matlock averred.

"Poor Annie," Georgiana bemoaned.

"She and Uncle Lewis are at peace now, Giana dearest," Lady Matlock told her ward.

"I know that," Georgiana responded. "It does not mean I will miss Anne or Uncle Lewis any less."

"Of course not, Sweetling," Lord Matlock agreed.

Lady Matlock had sent for Georgiana's companion who knocked and entered the sitting room. "Giana, go with Mrs.

Mayers. I will come to your chambers to look in on you soon."

The three Fitzwilliams and her brother gave Georgiana warm hugs and then her companion escorted her out of the room.

Moments after Georgiana's exit, there was a knock, which when the door was opened, revealed the butler holding a silver salver with a letter on it. He proffered it to the Earl.

Matlock read the accompanying note.

*Please forgive my omitting this with the first note, I only saw the letter from de Bourgh addressed to you after the groom was already away.*

*Bennet*

He broke his late brother's seal and sat reading while the other three in the room waited for him silently.

"He and Annie are to be buried at Rosings Park. Catherine will be restricted to her rooms and will not be allowed to act as the grieving widow and mother," Lord Matlock reported. "As Bennet is the other executor of de Bourgh's will, we will discuss all on the morrow."

~~~~~~~/~~~~~~~

Elizabeth lay in her bed late into the night not being able to find sleep. Life could seem so arbitrary and at times unfair. On the other hand she, like all Christians, believed God had a plan. It was hard to think on that at this moment, but thankfully her faith was strong.

"It has been mere hours, Annie and how I miss you already," Elizabeth said aloud as she looked to the heavens. "If only you had not been sick and there had been no need for God to call you home now... I know, I know, it is a dream and not the reality. How am I to go on without you?"

As she said the last, she could see Anne's face when she had extracted the promises to live on and have a good life for both of them. As much as she missed Anne, she did not want to give her a reason to haunt her.

She had to fight her inclination to mourn Anne for the rest of her life. Rather she knew she had to live up to the promises she had made to Anne when she had read the letter, a letter she kept in her memory box, and then reiterated verbally when she had visited her, the day she had dreamt Anne had taken her to task for not living up to her promises.

It hit Elizabeth that not sticking to her promises would be a betrayal of Anne and she could never allow that to occur. She really had no choice.

"You win Annie, I will mourn you for six weeks, like you allowed, and then I will live my life. I never promised to stop missing you and that is something I will do until I join you in heaven. Sleep peacefully, my sister."

Once she had spoken to Anne, Elizabeth felt somewhat easier and was able to fall asleep, even if it was a fitful slumber.

# CHAPTER 31

Elizabeth would not be able to explain how she kept her equanimity and remained calm on their arrival at Oak Hollow knowing Anne was no longer in her bedchamber and Uncle Lewis was not in his study. She supposed it was part of her determination not to disappoint Anne and fall apart even though her stomach was tied in tight knots.

Elizabeth had ridden with her parents, Jane, and Andrew in the lead coach. The remaining three sisters were in one of the two following conveyances. Mary, of course, rode in the same equipage as Richard.

All the ladies wore black bombazine dresses. Sadly, as Anne's and Uncle Lewis's health deteriorated, black gowns had been ordered in preparation. The men wore black arm bands on their left arms at the point closest to their hearts.

Bennet handed his wife out before his second daughter. They were followed by Andrew who handed out Jane. The men who had been in the other two coaches were handing out the ladies who had ridden with them. No one left it to the footmen waiting on the sides of each carriage in case they were needed to assist.

Elizabeth looked back towards the second conveyance and watched as the exceedingly handsome Mr. Darcy alit, and stood aside for his uncle. Uncle Reggie reached in for Aunt Elaine and then Mr. Darcy did the honours for Giana.

The last equipage held Richard and the three youngest Bennets. The former handed Kitty and Lydia out before he helped his fiancée.

While she was watching everyone alight, Elizabeth's eyes kept on returning to the person of Mr. Darcy. She looked down at the gravel as she berated herself for indulging her attraction to him the day after Anne and Uncle Lewis had passed away.

At that instant, Elizabeth could swear she could hear her best friend's voice whispering to her. '*If you think looking at William is disrespectful to me, then you did not know me very well!*'

Elizabeth shook her head; she was sure the wind and the situation were playing tricks on her brain.

Soon enough everyone entered the house where the butler and footmen were ready to relieve them of their heavier outerwear. Thanks to the cold snap they were experiencing, autumn wear had been replaced with winterwear.

They all made for the drawing room where the housekeeper had hot drinks waiting for them. "Mrs. Ashton, where is Jenki...Mrs. Jenkinson?" Elizabeth enquired of the housekeeper.

"She is watching over the master and Miss Anne, Miss Lizzy," the housekeeper averred.

It was decided that the Fitzwilliams—the parents first and then the younger three—would go spend some time with the earthly remains lying in repose in the parlour. The two Darcys would be next, and then the Bennets, sans Lizzy, would go pay their respects. Elizabeth would take her turn last, and alone, having as much time as she desired.

No sooner had the Earl and Countess entered the parlour than Mrs. Jenkinson exited it to give them private time with their late family members.

The instant Elizabeth spied her passing the drawing room door, she ran out and threw herself into Mrs. Jenkinson's arms. Being with the one who had been as close, if not closer to Anne than she was, cracked Elizabeth's determination to regulate her emotions as she cried freely in the circle of Jenki's arms. Just when she did not think she could cry for the young mistress any more, Mrs. Jenkinson joined in the crying.

Fanny guided the two into the small parlour and then returned to the drawing room.

"Jenki, I miss her every second of every minute," Elizabeth admitted when she was able to speak again.

"As do I Miss Lizzy," Mrs. Jenkinson agreed as she dried her tears. "You know what Miss Anne asked of you, do you not?" Even had she not been the one to scribe the letter for her charge, Miss Anne would have told her about the contents as, like Miss Lizzy and Miss Anne, there were no secrets between them.

"I have not been able to read the letter from Anne yet," Elizabeth admitted. "Yes, and I will keep my word to Annie."

"As far as the letter goes, I would suggest you read it after the reading of the will. Mr. Rumpole will be here on the morrow and it will answer many questions I am sure you may have. I always told Miss Anne you would never go back on your word."

"Was she at peace in the end?" Elizabeth wondered.

"Yes, I believe both she and the master were," Mrs. Jenkinson opined. "After everyone departed, the master entered Miss Anne's bedchamber. I said my goodbyes and left them. When I checked on them a little while later, they were lying on the bed, next to one another, hand in hand, both smiling. They will deny it if you ask them, but it was the only time I have seen either Biggs or Johns shed a tear."

"Do you know why they remained at Longbourn and accompanied us here today?" Elizabeth queried.

"When the master's will is read your questions will be answered, Miss Lizzy, and any that are not, the letter will." Mrs. Jenkinson hugged Elizabeth again.

"I have no expectation for myself, but I did hear my father and Lord Matlock state that Uncle Lewis told them not to inform Lady Catherine of his and Anne's death until his last will and testament is read," Elizabeth puzzled.

Mrs. Jenkinson repeated that all would be made clear to Miss Lizzy soon enough. Thereafter, they headed to the drawing room

~~~~~~~/~~~~~~~

When it was her turn to enter the parlour where the two coffins were side by side just as Jenki had described when she had found them, Elizabeth felt a little trepidation. Not at seeing Anne and Uncle Lewis, but regarding her ability to maintain her composure. Before she entered the room she had been told there was no right or wrong way to express her grief in private, so whatever felt right to her here on her own with the remains of father and daughter, was not wrong.

She went to the side of the casket holding Uncle Lewis first. Other than his colouring not looking as it should, he just looked like he was sleeping, and as Jenki had told her, he did have a ghost of a smile on his lips.

"Look after Anne in heaven, please Uncle Lewis," Elizabeth beseeched.

Next, she walked around to the other side to stand next to the coffin containing Anne's body. She too looked like she was asleep. Just like her father, she had a slight smile on her face, and best of all, Anne looked like she was at peace.

"Annie, my dearest, best friend, I renew my vows to you. You were, and will forever be my best friend in the world and I will always miss you. May I share a secret with you?" Elizabeth waited as if expecting an answer. There was a ripple in the curtains from a movement of air which Elizabeth decided to take as a yes. "I think I like your cousin William Darcy quite a lot. You had the right of it Annie, I believe we will suit well one to the other. Once we have both completed our respective mourning periods, then I hope we will get to know one another and see if there is more than an infatuation there."

Elizabeth's face turned melancholy. "My life will not be the same without seeing you any longer. Rest well my friend and sister, and take care of your father for eternity." As a few tears rolled down her cheeks, Elizabeth reached in and took Anne's hand closest to her. It was cold like ice, but she squeezed it as a final goodbye.

~~~~~~~/~~~~~~~

Elizabeth flatly refused to return to Longbourn with her family. She was determined to remain in the house until Anne and Uncle Lewis were moved to Rosings Park for burial.

As they would all be returning in the morning for the reading of the will, her parents did not try and convince her to come home with them. The only thing they insisted upon was that Mrs. Annesley would be sent to spend the night knowing that Mrs. Jenkinson would want to keep her vigil over Anne's body.

In addition, Biggs, Johns, and the rest of the guards, not to mention the staff and servants were all present.

Hence, when the three coaches departed, it was without Elizabeth.

~~~~~~~/~~~~~~~

Mr. Horace Rumpole arrived at Oak Hollow in the morning, two days after the death of his client and Miss de Bourgh. He had arrived in the area the previous late afternoon and had taken a room in the local inn.

By the time the solicitor arrived at the estate a little before midday, all of those whom he expected to see present were awaiting him.

He first verbally verified, even though he knew them by sight, the two executors were present. There were two wills he withdrew. One was labelled "*If Anne survives me*," while the other "*If both Anne and I are no longer alive*."

"As I have death certificates attesting that both Sir Lewis de Bourgh and Miss Anne de Bourgh are not living, this document," Rumpole lifted the former, "is null and void, while this one," he lifted the latter, "Is the only *valid* last will and testament of Sir Lewis de Bourgh which will be executed. Do the executors agree?"

"Yes," Lord Matlock responded.

"I agree," Bennet added.

Rumpole began to read the will breezing past the legal parts of the will attesting to the late baronet being of sound mind, and others. He cleared his throat. "Now we reach the bequests." There were small amounts left to faithful retainers like his valet and others. Rumpole read:

*To Mrs. Jenkinson I leave the sum of £7,500 and the lifelong use of a cottage at either Rosings Park or Oak Hollow, whichever she chooses.*

*The Greens will continue to live rent free in the cottage I placed them in and until the three sons are earning at or above the wages my murdered coachman used to earn, the quarterly payment of £300 will continue.*

*Those who are named heirs of the above mentioned estates will honour these bequests.*

*I leave the estate of Oak Hollow in Bedfordshire to my friend Mr. Thomas Bennet. As it is about the same size and income (the true income) of Longbourn, if Bennet chooses to, he has my permission to have the heir presumptive of his entailed estate take Oak Hollow in return for ending the entail.*

*In that case, Bennet would offer Mrs. Jenkinson a cottage at Longbourn as a second option in case she chooses not to reside at Rosings Park.*

There were collective gasps from the Bennet sisters who had no idea of the contents of Uncle Lewis's will. As his uncle, Reggie, had prepared him for surprises, Darcy only raised his eyebrow when the disposition of Oak Hollow was mentioned.

*That leaves Rosings Park, de Bourgh House in London, the house at 12 Littlefield Street in Bath, the de Bourgh jewels, and the de Bourgh fortune. Although I can hear her protesting at this moment, which is even more reason to know she is the most deserving one to be bequeathed all of the above, all of the named properties and items of value listed in this clause are bequeathed to Miss Elizabeth Rose Bennet.*

"No!" Elizabeth interjected, "This cannot be. What have I done to deserve all of this?"

"You mean besides saving their lives and being the reason Anne lived years longer than any of us expected she would?" Lord Matlock stated.

"But you are all family by blood, it should have gone to one of you." She turned to Mr. Darcy sure she would have an ally who would agree with her.

Darcy had been impressed with her before, now after seeing her trying to refuse a fortune others would kill for, his estimation of her was to the skies and beyond. "I am afraid Miss Bennet that I, like my Fitzwilliam family, have more than enough already, and as my uncle stated, there is none more deserving than you."

Mr. Rumpole cleared his throat indicating he was not done reading yet. A shocked Elizabeth sat back down.

*I wonder if Lizzy protested as much as I believe she has.*

There was a ripple of soft laughter from some in the room.

*Yes, Lizzy, you do deserve all of this. Who should I leave it to? My wife from whose murderous scheme you saved us? I would sooner see my properties burned to the ground than her gain one penny from her plotting and manipulations.*

*Mr. Thomas Bennet and Lord Reginald Fitzwilliam will administer a trust for all of Miss Elizabeth Rose Bennet's property which she has just inherited until:*

> *a. She reaches the age of 25; or*
> *b. She marries*

*Lastly, now that the will has been read, notification of Anne's and my passing is to be sent to my widow at Rosings Park in the fashion I laid out.*

Mr. Rumpole read some final legal clauses and then he was done.

Elizabeth was in shock. How could this be? Yet it was. She was an heiress, regardless of how much she desired not to be.

"Lizzy I have your letter with me, would you like to read it?" Bennet enquired.

Elizabeth's first inclination was to refuse as she was still attempting to come to grips with the changes to her life and fortune. Then she remembered Jenki's words. She also realised this was one of the letters Uncle Lewis had wanted her to take when she had refused to do so. "Yes, Papa. I will go sit in the parlour and read it if I may," Elizabeth averred. She took the letter from her father's hand.

She made her way into the small parlour, not the one where the now sealed coffins still rested. Elizabeth recognised Jenki's hand. She broke the seal, smoothed the sheets out, and began to read.

*5 October 1810*

*Oak Hollow*

*Lizzy, my best friend and sister,*

*At least this time when I tell you how important you have been to me, how much you have given me, you are not able to argue the point with me.*

*You made the last 10 years of my life a pleasure to live. Even when I was temporarily fooled by Lady Catherine's machinations, you stood by me. When I saw the truth of the woman who bore me, you never said, or even in the smallest measure hinted at your knowing, she was beyond redemption.*

*I cannot but agree with Papa and Jenki that you gave me the will to live far beyond that which was expected of me.*

*Lizzy, I need to ask you a favour. I am fully aware Papa has made sure Jenki never has to work again if she chooses not to. Knowing her, she will not be happy without a purpose. If she decides to continue in service, please take her as your companion. Even when you marry William (as I am sure you will) as long as she has the desire, keep her with you. When she is ready to retire she will be happiest close to you given the common bond you both share.*

(Miss Lizzy, as you know I am writing for Miss Anne. If you will have me, I would love to work for you and your family. Jenki.)

*Now to explain what I meant when I said, 'You may be in danger from my mother.' You know it has always been her avaricious dream to own all of Papa's property and wealth. As you are reading this, I am sure you are fully aware all which she coveted is now yours.*

*John and Brian and their men will be with you to make sure you are safe, and I believe Papa has set in motion that which will finally have my mother pay for her transgressions.*

*Until that occurs, you must be vigilant and never go anywhere without John Biggs and Brian Johns with you. For the rest of eternity, I would never be able to forgive myself if the gift from Papa and me leads to your being harmed, even a little. I want to see you again Lizzy, but not for many decades.*

*And yes, Lizzy, you deserve everything Papa and I have bequeathed you. No one else in the family is being deprived because of everything coming to you.*

*Before he was given Cloverdell, Richard was Papa's indirect heir. As I know you are aware, Richard and Mary will have more than enough when they marry. I can hear you now; you are thinking if (when) you marry William, you too will have more than enough.*

*True but you will do something great with everything Papa has bequeathed you.*

*In closing, I would like to remind you of my request you name one of your daughters for me.*

*Remember I will always love you as my sister and best friend. Now go live your life. (yes, after the mourning period.)*

*I will always be watching over you.*

*Your best friend,*

*Anne*

# CHAPTER 32

L ady Catherine de Bourgh stared at the black edged letter written in her brother's distinctive script as she held it reverently. She hoped and prayed it was the notice she had been waiting for, but it could be one of her other traitorous family members who had died. She had been disappointed before.

She took a deep breath and began to break her brother's seal. Surely if her brother was the sender, it was the news she had waited so long to hear. With great anticipation she opened the page and began to read.

*12 October 1810*

*Netherfield Park, Hertfordshire*

*Catherine, it is with profound sadness I write to inform you your husband and daughter were both called home to God this morning. By the time you read this, we will be on our way to Kent with the earthly remains of both Anne and Lewis.*

*Elaine and I, as do the rest of those here, all condole with you...*

Lady Catherine stopped reading. She was free! Her damned husband and sickly daughter were finally dead. Ten years too late thanks to the interference of that Bennet chit, but dead nonetheless.

Now she would finally get her due! Soon enough everyone who had ever crossed her, especially the interfering Bennet girl would pay for their actions. She had waited ten long years, and now Lady Catherine was impatient to have things move in the direction she wanted. At the same time, she knew she needed to exercise a little more patience. Only a little.

Had she not been concerned for the guards seeing her, she would have danced a jig. Lady Catherine stood and walked in her normal stately way to her sitting room. As it had been since her return to Rosings Park, two of the guards—who she would soon have the pleasure of sacking—followed her and took up station in the hallway outside the room. The sooner she was rid of them and the rest of the servants, the better.

Once there, she retrieved the will she had and then dated it. She decided it would be prudent to date it two days earlier, on the tenth day of October. On presenting it, she was sure there would be questions as to how it came into her hands. She had a very plausible answer prepared; one she had made sure her man was well versed in.

She wrote a letter she would give to the solicitor to post for her. After removing the will which would give her all from its hiding place, she secreted the document and letter in her gown and returned to the drawing room where she rang for the butler.

When the butler entered, she made a show of dabbing her eyes. "The house will go into mourning. My husband and daughter have both gone to their final rewards." Lady Catherine pretended she was drying her eyes. "I need to see my solicitor, Mr. Neil Mink, whose offices are in Westerham. I must prepare for the upcoming changes."

The butler expressed his condolences and then exited the drawing room. He informed the housekeeper and sent a note to the steward. Next, he asked one of the guards to ride into Westerham to summon Mr. Mink.

~~~~~~~/~~~~~~~

By the time the solicitor arrived at Rosings Park, there was black fabric hanging from the gateposts. It was not hard to guess Lady Catherine's fondest wish had finally been realised. Mink smiled to himself when he thought of the additional fees he would earn once Lady Catherine was the owner of this and all of the other de Bourgh properties. That would be nothing when added to the amount he intended to demand for his silence about the will he had created for her. He was sure his final monetary reward would be in the many thousands of pounds.

His small carriage stopped under the extended portico. Once he had handed the butler his outerwear, the solicitor was shown into the drawing room. When he was inside, per Lady Catherine's instruction, the butler pulled the doors closed.

"Mr. Mink, here is the document. You will deliver it to me on the morrow when my family are present. You remember what I decided you will say regarding how it came to be in your hands, do you not?" Lady Catherine said quietly. The last thing she wanted was to be overheard at this juncture.

"Yes, your Ladyship, I know exactly what to say," Mink simpered.

"Additionally, I require you to send this letter by express." She handed her solicitor the missive. "You will arrive at eleven in the morning. Do not be late, you know how I demand punctuality." Mink nodded. "Now you may go." Lady Catherine waved him away dismissively.

The way she treated him only made him more determined to extract as much as possible for his silence from the pompous blowhard.

~~~~~~~/~~~~~~~

The five coaches arrived at Rosings Park in the middle of the afternoon. Mrs. Jenkinson rode in the coach which bore the two coffins back to the de Bourghs' ancestral home. She was determined to escort her Miss Anne's body until it was placed in the family crypt in the morning on the morrow.

Mr. Jamison—Hunsford's rector who had received a letter from Lord Matlock—was waiting for them in front of the doors to the mansion.

Once everyone had alighted from all of the conveyances, Lord Matlock nodded and under the command of Biggs and Johns, the guards reverently extracted the two coffins from the lead coach. Each casket was then carried on their shoulders by four men. The parson led the way to a parlour which had been prepared for the coffins to be rested until they were carried to the crypt in the cemetery in the morning.

Lady Catherine was conspicuous by her absence; no one repined not seeing her.

Fanny and Bennet joined Mrs. Jenkinson to sit with the coffins for a spell. The rest of the party made their way to the drawing room where they found Lady Catherine.

She had demanded the servants place a platform under her favourite seat so she would be higher than everyone else. They had simply ignored her. She could not wait to sack all of them.

"Catherine," Lord Matlock inclined his head. "I think the only two you have not met are the two youngest Bennets, Miss Kitty and Miss Lydia."

"What are these lowborn Bennets doing in my house?" Lady Catherine spat out as she glared at Elizabeth.

"Your house? At this moment things are as they always were, that is until we have a reading of the will after the interment on the morrow," Lord Matlock drawled.

She berated herself for allowing her anger at the Bennet chit to override her need to be patient just one more day. "You are of course correct," Lady Catherine managed through gritted teeth. "Now that *dear* Anne is gone too; we will have to see what the disposition of my husband's assets are on the morrow."

"The family solicitor is in Hunsford and will join us in the morning once the condolers depart," Lord Matlock shared.

"You will not object if I have my own man of law will you? Lady Catherine asked slyly. "Mr. Neil Mink of Westerham is here to see to my interests. I have been much ill-used with unfounded accusations and kept like a prisoner in gaol, so excuse me if I have him make sure everything is as it should be."

"Your lawyer is more than welcome," Lord Matlock agreed.

Lady Catherine fought to school her features so she would not smile. Everything was going just as she planned. Her letter would have been delivered by now, yes, all was—or very soon would be—as it should be.

~~~~~~~/~~~~~~~

That night Elizabeth joined Jenki to watch over Anne while Andrew, Richard, and Darcy sat next to Uncle Lewis.

Even had someone tried to convince her she needed her sleep—which no one had—Elizabeth would have spent the night—the final one before Anne's body would be consigned to the crypt—next to her best friend's earthly remains.

*'My best and dearest friend and sister Annie. My prayer is that you are running free in the fields of heaven now you are not bound to your body and its earthly restrictions,'* Elizabeth intoned silently, her eyes lifted to the heavens where she was sure the souls of both Anne and Uncle Lewis were. *'It seems there will be a confrontation with your mother on the morrow. I will be well. In addition to those guarding her, John, Brian, and their men are here and as you well know, they will not allow any ill to befall me or anyone else. I miss you Annie, all the time, but at least I get to speak to you when I need to. As much as not being able to see your physical form pains me, I am pleased you are no longer suffering, both you and Uncle Lewis.'*

Some tears ran down Elizabeth's cheeks unbidden. She felt Jenki take her hand closest to where she was sitting and felt the comforting, gentle squeeze as Jenki silently told her she was not alone.

~~~~~~~/~~~~~~~

Elizabeth did not miss the pinched look on Lady Catherine's face when she was not only not allowed to take the lead in greeting the condolers who sat with the ladies, but she was restricted to her chambers until the guests departed. During this time, the men were at the cemetery to see Uncle Lewis' and Anne's bodies consigned to their place of eternal slumber.

As sad and sombre as the day was, Elizabeth would not have been able to look at Lady Catherine before she returned to her chambers if she wanted to refrain from laughing at the woman. It was good the lady was where she was as any temptation for mirth had been removed.

As the other younger ladies were all fighting to maintain their equanimity, Jane and Elizabeth led them out into the gardens to watch Tommy who was being chased around by his nursemaid.

Lady Catherine watched her niece and the Bennet sisters exit the house with a gimlet eye from the window in her bedchamber. Only a few more hours and everything would be hers. She would order everyone out of her house and then put her revenge in motion. For the first time since her brother and sister-in-law had denied her the honour of being the hostess to the callers and sent her to her rooms like an errant young girl, she smiled to herself as she thought about everything which would be hers.

How much pleasure she would have dividing the estate in Bedfordshire into farms and selling them off one by one. She would finally be able to order the gardens as she wanted, and redecorate her houses to reflect her status. Everything she desired was a few hours away.

~~~~~~~/~~~~~~~

Mink's small conveyance arrived right behind Rumpole's; neither knew who the other was.

Even though Lady Catherine had objected to Mr. Bennet

being present for the reading of the *will*, he was present with her brother and three nephews.

When she was joined by her solicitor, Lady Catherine looked around the room triumphantly as if she knew something no one else did. "Shall we begin?" she suggested not able to hide the anticipation in her voice.

"Catherine, when we arrived, you intimated that the house was yours," Matlock began evenly. "As you had not heard de Bourgh's will read, how could you know that?"

"That is because Mr. Mink had sent me a note telling me he received a new will from my late husband only a day before his unfortunate death," Lady Catherine asserted. It went over her head any note sent to Rosings Park would have been checked by one of the guards.

The Earl turned towards the man standing next to Lady Catherine. "What is the date of the will you hold Mr. Mink?"

Mink made a show of opening the forged document and perusing it. "Ah, here it is. The tenth day of October of this year, my Lord."

"That is indeed dated after the one I have for my late client," Rumpole confirmed.

"Then we agree the one I hold is the most recent one," Lady Catherine crowed. "What did my late husband write, Mr. Mink?"

"Mr. Mink, before you inform us of the contents of the document you hold, are both you and Lady Catherine willing to swear it is genuine?" Rumpole questioned.

"You are not interrogating a witness at the Old Bailey now, Mr. Rumpole," Mink sneered. "However, yes I will attest to that fact."

"As will I," Lady Catherine added with a smug smile.

"How is it you came to be in possession of it? The late Sir Lewis never mentioned you to me," Lord Matlock queried.

"When he wrote and told her he wanted to revise his will, Lady Catherine requested he send the document directly to my office. It arrived with his letter of explanation only yester-afternoon." Mink held up the letter Lady Catherine had written to accompany the will. He was sweating a little now, not as sure of himself as he had been.

"What does it say?" Rumpole enquired.

"It lists all of the de Bourgh property, the houses, estates, and liquid assets, and leaves all to Lady Catherine de Bourgh née Fitzwilliam," Mink summarised the contents of the forged will.

"As such I want all of you off my property forthwith," Lady Catherine demanded.

No one moved. How was it that her orders were being refused, they were trespassing.

"We have a slight problem, well a few actually." Rumpole nodded and one of the footmen relieved Mr. Mink of the will and letter he had been holding and handed them to Rumpole who held the forged documents next to the genuine one on the signature page.

Matlock, Bennet, two Fitzwilliams, and Darcy all reviewed what Rumpole indicated. "The signatures are forgeries on both documents, they are not even close to the real one," Matlock announced.

"Of course, they are not the same," Lady Catherine barked out as she thought how to save all which was her due. "My late husband was sick, why would you expect the signatures to be exactly the same?"

Bennet turned to Matlock with an amused gleam in his eye. "What say you Matlock? Is it possible the signature is not even close to de Bourgh's due to the fact he was already in heaven on the day these works of fiction were dated? The fact the signature on the *supposed* will was not witnessed is immaterial at this point." He turned around and looked at the cringing solicitor and a shocked Lady Catherine.

"That cannot be! I dated it two days before..." Lady Catherine blurted out before she realised what she had said and closed her mouth.

"Your late husband and daughter passed away on the ninth of this month as the signed death certificates attest," Matlock boomed. "Did you think your husband was not aware of your forged will and of this scoundrel who assisted you? Why do you think my late brother planned you would be told he and Anne passed away some days after the real date? In addition, he had a genuine copy of his will filed with the courts, just in case. And Catherine, one of our men was engaged as the express rider to deliver your secret letter you had this useless man post for you." Matlock held the offending missive up. "By now your hired assassin will be in custody. Do you think he will trade his neck to tell us all about what you paid to have done ten years past?"

Mr. Mink tried to run towards the doors but he was knocked down by a footman and was soon bound and carried away.

All Lady Catherine could do was splutter. "My plan was perfect," she mumbled.

"You always had an overinflated opinion of your intelligence," Matlock nodded his head sadly. "Before you are taken away, and Catherine you will be tried for the murder of the coachman Green, you should know that Rosings Park and most everything, other than Oak Hollow, was bequeathed to Miss Elizabeth Bennet." Matlock watched as his sister's eyes grew huge and her eyebrows disappeared under her hairline.

"Yes, that is my daughter. The same one who foiled your murderous plan ten years ago," Bennet confirmed.

Lady Catherine promptly fainted as all of her dreams of wealth and revenge turned to dust.

# CHAPTER 33

"You will never allow the scandal of a trial," Lady Catherine blustered the next day before she and her lawyer were to be sent to the assizes which was meeting in Canterbury. Her brother had come to visit her in the small, windowless room she had been locked in since all her plans had come to nought. She was sure he was too afraid of the Fitzwilliam name being connected to something as plebian as a public trial.

"Catherine you always overestimate the cards you are holding," Matlock shook his head at his sister's abject stupidity. "I am honour bound to see you stand trial. I made that promise to my late brother and I intend to keep it. There is but one option you have to save yourself from trial and the hangman's noose when you are found guilty. It is the only one de Bourgh authorised me to offer you."

"I knew you would be reasonable," Lady Catherine trilled.

"You may not think so when you hear your option," Matlock stated derisively. "Firstly, if you refuse what I am about to offer you, there are no other options, to the assizes and then the Old Bailey you *will* go."

It was a look on her brother's face Lady Catherine had seen more times than she cared to remember over the years. It showed he had made an irrevocable decision. "What is my other choice?" Lady Catherine asked defeatedly.

"You will be stripped of your courtesy title and transported to Australia. All you will have is one year's allowance, which as you know will give you forty pounds. You will have to find work to provide for your needs once your money runs out. And Catherine," the horrified woman looked up at her brother, "two last things. You will not use either the de Bourgh or Fitzwilliam names and if you ever return to England, you will be tried for murder."

"B-but I am y-your sister." Lady Catherine tried to play on her brother's familial sympathies.

"The day you employed that man Younge and his witless cousin to murder your husband and daughter you ceased being my sister," Matlock barked. "No sister of mine would ever attempt something so heinous. What will it be?"

Clay Younge had turned over the letters from the very first one she had sent him. He had never followed her orders to destroy them. In doing so, he and his cousin would be spared from the gallows and were awaiting transportation to Australia with the maximum hard labour sentence possible. With all the evidence against her, Lady Catherine now knew if she stood trial, her neck would be stretched. As much as she abhorred the option of being transported, at least she would be alive.

"Transportation," was the soon-to-be former titled lady's reply.

"Very well, you will be taken to Southampton and placed on a ship for New South Wales. The captain will be given your money and he will turn it over to you before you disembark in Australia," Matlock stated dispassionately. "If you want to survive the journey, never mind once you arrive, I would not try any of your distinction of rank nonsense. Remember, you have always been a commoner, now you will not even have your courtesy title any longer."

Without looking back at her, the Earl turned on his heel and exited the room, nodding to one of the guards to lock the door again.

Within two hours Miss Catherine Smith was being transported towards Southampton in the back of a cart.

~~~~~~~/~~~~~~~

Since Penny did not accompany them into Kent, Elizabeth elected to walk in the morning even though there were a few riding horses in the stables. She made this decision starting with the day after that despicable woman had been sent to the ship which would take her far away from all of them.

The permanent removal of Catherine Smith and her complete defanging did not reduce Elizabeth's guards' vigilance. Although she enjoyed having John Biggs and Brian Johns close by, Elizabeth did not love the need for their continued presence in her life. With everything she had inherited, she was now one of the wealthiest heiresses in the country. Try as they may to keep her wealth secret, word would leak out and then she would be a target of every fortune hunter in the realm.

It was a cool autumn morning when Elizabeth made her way down to the entrance hall. Even though her dress was black, her pelisse and scarf were a royal blue, while her thick gloves were a shade of beige.

On arriving where the butler was waiting to assist the new mistress into her outerwear, Elizabeth was very pleased to find Cousin William, as she called him now, waiting for her. He was already dressed for outdoors; his heavy greatcoat with its black armband on his left sleeve. It was buttoned closed and he too wore a scarf and thick gloves. His beaver was atop his head and he smiled when he saw her.

Not that it was important to him, but Darcy was now aware of the Bennets' true position regarding dowries and wealth. After the reading of the genuine will Bennet had taken him into his confidence.

Now he stood watching this enticing beauty

approaching him. She glowed when she saw him and Darcy was well pleased he had been able to bring her out of the melancholy she often slipped into when she had time to think of her sadness at Uncle Lewis's and Anne's passing.

"Cousin Elizabeth, if I am disturbing your intention for a solitary ramble, I will not bother you, but if you do not object, I seek your permission to walk with you," Darcy gave a half bow.

"Other than John and Brian," Elizabeth saw Cousin William's brows knit in question. "You know them as Biggs and Johns, I was planning on walking alone with just my escorts." Darcy nodded his comprehension. There was no missing how his face fell at her statement. "However, your company would only enhance my enjoyment of my walk."

A wide smile of pleasure lit up Cousin William's face displaying his dimples in all of their glory.

'Five weeks of mourning to go,' Elizabeth reminded herself. Regardless of Anne's belief they would do well together, she would not explore a relationship with him until the six weeks had passed. Besides, by then his deep mourning period for an uncle and cousin would also be concluded.

Biggs and Johns were waiting for their new mistress just out of the front doors under the portico. Mr. Darcy was well known to them so they knew he was no threat to Miss Lizzy.

Elizabeth accepted the offer of his arm and rested her hand on his forearm. Even through the layers of clothing and her thick gloves she could tell the arm underneath was well defined. She shook her head as she lifted her eye to the brightening sky. 'You are not going to make this easy for me, are you Annie? How will I last not showing my feelings for five more weeks?' Elizabeth enquired silently. She swore she could hear Anne's laugh on the breeze.

Luckily, Cousin William was happy to walk in companionable silence until they reached the southern end of the groves. Many leaves were already on the ground, but the trees still held a magnificent display of brown, red, orange, and golden leaves waiting their turn to fall to the earth. Interspersed were a few pine trees proudly displaying their green needles among the sea of autumn colours.

"I understand from Andrew and Richard on previous visits you brought that speed demon of a mare of yours with you to Kent," Darcy stated as he looked down on the petite woman he was now sure he loved.

"Yes, I loved riding her through the groves. She has taken me to the glade a few times," Elizabeth responded. "We depart in but two days on Wednesday so I will see my Penny soon enough."

"Unfortunately, I will not be able to return to Hertfordshire, I must to away to supervise the preparations needed to make Pemberley ready for the winter, which as I am sure you know is far more severe in the north," Darcy related.

He so much did not want to be apart from her, but he would not eschew his duty. There was the added advantage that he would be away from her during their mourning periods and when he returned, if he saw she was at all receptive, he fully intended to declare himself for Miss Elizabeth Bennet.

While they walked along the widest path in the groves, the one if they continued northward would bring them to the Hunsford parsonage, there were little periods of inconsequential conversation, but for the most part they were both happy with a companionable silence. After about twenty minutes of walking, the path to the glade was reached. They turned onto it and made for the clearing in the middle where the pond and benches were located.

Biggs and Johns waited at a point just before the access path reached the clearing. Elizabeth and Darcy took a seat on one of the three benches their late uncle had had placed around the pond.

"Did Anne ever tell you about the time, about six months before she became ill, Richard, Anne, and I came here?" Darcy asked. Elizabeth shook her head. "Mayhap she was still embarrassed. We were playing here when she *accidently* bumped into me which sent me into the pond, much to the chagrin of the frogs and toads who were residents. I was wet head to toe!"

For the first time since Anne's passing Elizabeth laughed. She had no idea how much the man sitting next to her on the bench was thrilled at hearing the sound he loved. The image of a wet William soaked from head to toe and an impish Anne before she was taken ill was too much for her not to laugh.

"You can laugh if you want," Darcy stated with mock severity, "but to this day I am convinced Richard put her up to it. When we were younger, we loved to prank one another."

"Having witnessed Richard's humorous side, I am surprised those pranks are a thing of the past." Elizabeth cogitated for a moment. "Surely you did not let the prank go without response?"

"Most certainly not!" Darcy returned with put on arrogance. "I made sure a few of the residents of the pond in the glade found their way into Richard's bed that night. No, I did not do the same to Anne, no matter how tempted I was. Even then I was a gentleman of sorts."

"Was any punishment meted out?" Elizabeth enquired laughingly.

"Both of us boys were punished but Anne was spared." Darcy had not thought of those carefree days for many a year.

Until recently, it had been the last time he had been at Rosings Park. He did not want to spoil the mood by telling Elizabeth how the then Lady Catherine had demanded an engagement claiming somehow by three young cousins playing together he had compromised Anne. From that day on, any contact between the families had been away from Rosings Park and its single-minded mistress.

Not long after, they left the glade and walked to the end of the grove near the parsonage. From there, they cut across the park for the less than half mile walk back to the manor house.

~~~~~~~/~~~~~~~

On their return to Longbourn, Bennet made for his study to see what correspondence was awaiting him after being away for about a sennight.

There were letters from the steward at Oak Hollow. Even though he had known what de Bourgh intended to do since he had been made an executor of his will, it was still strange for Bennet to think of Oak Hollow as his own.

The letter with the most potential for amusement, he left for last. Before he broke the seal on that letter, Bennet rang for Hill and instructed him to request the mistress join him in the study.

"Thomas?" Fanny stated questioningly when she entered the study.

"My cousin has replied to my letter," Bennet related as he held up the still sealed missive.

"How do you think he reacted to your explaining now was not a good time to visit, and that in future we would extend an invitation, if and when, we desire to meet him?" Fanny asked with a smile. "I am sure he loved being told we would not accept him as a son-in-law."

"Rather than speculate, let us sit on the settee and I will open it," Bennet suggested. Fanny nodded her agreement.

As soon as they were comfortably seated next to one another, and with more than ample light entering via the windows behind them, Bennet broke the seal and opened the letter holding it so they could both read it.

*11 October 1810*

*Thornburg's Theological Seminary, Wiltshire*

*Mr. Bennet:*

"No more 'Dear Sir' I see," Fanny noted amusedly. After a little laugh they both turned their attention back to the letter.

*How dare you throw my offer to heal the breach between our families back in my face in such a manner? I can only thank the good Lord above I did not dishonour my father by bestowing my olive branch on one with whom he was correct to be at variance!*

*You refuse to extend me hospitality; to a clergyman like myself. You also spurned my request for you to prefer me to the living in your gift even though it should be mine. Further, you tell me that I will never be allowed to marry any of your daughters!*

*Given your ungenerous words, the day you pass from this world can only be into the fires of hell. Your widow and unmarried daughters will be turned out of the house. For all I care they can starve in the hedgerows. In fact, so much the better.*

*Be on notice I will check and see that every stick of furniture, every piece of silver, plate, etc, etc. is where it should be according to the inventory. If one item is missing, I will have your widow and daughters arrested for theft.*

*Just because your eldest daughter used her arts and allurements to entrap a viscount, it does not follow any of your other daughters will be disposed of in marriage. The offer I was willing to make would have been the only offer any one of the rest of them would ever receive.*

*God will be good to me and see to it that a Collins assumes his rightful place as master of Longbourn sooner rather than later.*

*I take no leave of you, Mr. Bennet. I send no compliments to your wife or daughters. You deserve no such attention. I am most seriously displeased.*

*W C Collins, Curate*

This letter decides it. I will pursue a simple recovery," Bennet stated as he shook his head at William Collins' childlike reaction to being denied what he had decided he deserved.

"You have no choice Thomas," Fanny agreed. "No matter how many estates we own, we cannot allow such a man to be master over our dependants. He is a bully and I am positive he would destroy the estate inside of a year."

"You will hear no disagreement from me, Fanny my dear. I will go see Philips in the morning on the morrow."

# CHAPTER 34

While Darcy supervised the harvests with his steward, his heart was more than a hundred miles to the south. Occasionally when he and his steward were speaking, Chalmers had to repeat something to gain his attention.

One evening he was seated in his study, a tray on his desk with a dinner plate thereon. He saw no point in using one of the dining parlours when he was alone at his estate. He looked at the calendar. It was but a few days to the one-month anniversary of Anne's and Uncle Lewis's passing.

In less than two weeks he would enter half mourning, but more importantly, Cousin Elizabeth's mourning would be complete. By this time though, he thought of her as simply *Elizabeth*.

Darcy did not want to make assumptions, but in his opinion, she was not indifferent to him. She had taken as much pleasure from their walks in Kent as he had. Even though he had given her a choice each time, she had always chosen his company over a solitary ramble on her walks.

When he made his way south in about a sennight he would know more based on the way she would react to his return to her presence.

Not wanting Cook to scold him for not eating enough, Darcy turned to the delicious smelling meal on the tray in front of him. Once he began to eat, his body reminded him how hungry he was and soon he had cleaned his plates leaving Cook no cause to repine.

~~~~~~~/~~~~~~~

At the militia encampment just outside of Oxford, the officers were supervising their soldiers who were striking the camp.

Ordering soldiers around and not having to do anything himself suited Wickham just fine. He sauntered over to where Denny was imparting some instructions to a sergeant who was listening attentively. The sergeant gave a smart salute and made for a group of men to carry out the lieutenant's orders.

"Tell me Denny, did you see pretty girls in the town where we are moving to?" Wickham enquired nonchalantly.

"Some, however we were told there is a group of sisters who are the jewels of the county, and are in mourning for someone in their family. Hence, we never met them," Denny responded.

"Any one of the locals with a dowry of interest?" Wickham questioned.

"No, the estates in the area are not large, and from what I heard tell, the largest dowries are only one, mayhap two thousand pounds," Denny related. "There is one larger and more prosperous estate in the neighbourhood, called Netherfield Park, but the owner lives at his primary estate and leases out the local one."

'Such a pity there is no one there with a decent dowry. If only my plan to acquire Georgiana Darcy's had not gone awry. However, if these jewels are pretty enough I would not mind taking a tumble with some of them,' Wickham thought.

"I will return to my men," Wickham stated as he inclined his head. Denny had no useful information to impart so he had become bored talking to him.

"Do not forget we depart at first light on the morrow," Denny reminded Wickham as the latter walked away.

Wickham nodded. He knew what time they were to

begin their move to Hertfordshire in the morning. The early mornings were one of the things he detested about the militia.

His illusion about strutting around in his uniform charming young ladies with his good looks, regardless of the angle of his nose, and doing nothing much else, had been shattered in Wickham's first days of being an officer. Much to his chagrin he was expected to perform his duties, which included—some days—rising from his warm bed at the crack of dawn and others being up all night.

The first and only time he had missed relieving another officer from his overnight duties, a bucket of cold water had been emptied on him as he lay in his bed. If that were not bad enough, the Colonel had punished him by giving him a fortnight of consecutive night duty.

Any thoughts of sleeping on duty had been erased when Wickham had been informed of the ten lashes which would be the punishment for *each* such infraction.

At least none of the shopkeepers to whom he owed money in the area had approached the Colonel regarding Wickham's debts. The fools had believed he and his men were remaining another fortnight after the rest of the regiment departed and he would have the money in but a few days.

He was sure the merchants in the town of Meryton where they would move to on the morrow were as gullible as those in Oxford.

A more difficult task was keeping the demands from his fellow officers from whom he had borrowed money, or to whom he owed debts of honour, or in some cases, both, at bay. He had played on their sympathies to borrow money from a few fellow officers.

Knowing none of them would ever meet any of the Fitzwilliams or Darcys, he told a story of how he had been cheated out of his rightful inheritance due to jealousy. Wickham claimed a solicitor was working on his behalf to recover his *stolen* money and was confident of success. He had pledged to make repayment as soon as the expected funds were received.

When the questions began, Wickham would simply tell them it was taking longer than expected.

~~~~~~~/~~~~~~~

"Good morning, Philips," Bennet welcomed his brother into his study at Longbourn. "Does your call to see me portend good news?"

"It does indeed," Philips averred. "You may recall I told you that Sir Norman Randolph was the barrister I retained to represent you in the Court of Chancery, do you not?" Bennet nodded his head. "I received a report this morning. The current heir presumptive appeared *pro se*, in other words, on his own behalf. He is far more ignorant and a worse simpleton than we had imagined. He mistook bluster for facts and the judges ordered him to hold his peace if he had no salient facts with which to rebut our case."

"Based on his letters I would assume not speaking is not something this Collins is capable of doing," Bennet observed.

"In that you would be correct. His Lordship had your cousin bound and gagged so he would not disturb the proceedings again. Without Collins's performance, the deliberation may have lasted for some days, even weeks. Fed up with the idiot's antics, an immediate judgement in your favour was entered. The entail is no more. Longbourn is your property. You are no longer a lifetime tenant."

"Under normal circumstances, I would not imbibe at this time of the day, but this is anything but a regular day!" Bennet rung for Hill and waited for his butler to enter the study. "Hill, please summon Mrs. Bennet."

The butler bowed and left to carry out his orders.

"Thomas? Good morning, Frank," Fanny greeted both gentlemen as soon as she entered the study. "By the look on

Thomas's face I assume you delivered good news Frank, did you not?"

As soon as the wonderful tidings were shared with Fanny, she joined the men in toasting the future. She had a small amount of sherry while the two men indulged with less than a finger of brandy each.

With many thanks for his assistance, Philips took his leave.

"We own three estates now," Fanny shook her head in wonder.

"It is not a problem I ever imagined would be ours," Bennet stated stoically. "Jane, Lizzy, and Mary have no need for one of the estates. Who knows whether Kitty's or Lydia's future husbands will own their own estates."

"Only time will tell," Fanny stated.

She had noted the attention Mr. Bingley had paid to Kitty before he had left to situate his youngest sister. Since his return to Netherfield Park during the final week of October, he had been in company with the Bennets once or twice. He had sought Kitty out each time, but so far, he had been restrained enough during their mourning for Anne that there had been no need to speak to him regarding Kitty and the fact she would only come out in London in May of the following year. Fanny shook her head. It was barely more than six months before Kitty's presentation. Thereafter, it would only be Lydia who would still not be out.

After kissing her husband and agreeing they would share the news with the girls together, Fanny returned to her daughters who were in the drawing room. Lizzy, Mary, and Kitty were sitting on a settee working on samplers. Mrs. Annesley and Mrs. Jenkinson were seated off to the side also working on some embroidery. From the sounds coming from the music room Lydia was with the pianoforte master.

Jane, Andrew, and Tommy had returned to Hilldale

for the harvest, and the Fitzwilliam parents had made for Snowhaven for the same reason. Richard had reluctantly departed to Cloverdell, but would return in a few days. Before the leave-taking between the engaged couple, they had selected the date of Friday, the eleventh day of January 1811, for the wedding. The day selected was beyond the three month mourning period for Anne and Sir Lewis, therefore all mourning periods would be completed for everyone in the family. It also gave Fanny two more months with her middle daughter still residing at Longbourn.

As she sat down, Fanny looked at Lizzy. It was easy to see how much she missed Anne, but she was holding to her promise of not allowing the sadness to stop her from living her life. Like the rest of the Bennets, Elizabeth was dressed in the muted colours of half mourning.

She smiled to herself as she remembered Lizzy's reaction when anyone mentioned William Darcy's impending return. Lizzy would light up with pleasure and blush deeply whenever her opinion of his coming back was canvassed.

Just then, as if she knew her mother was thinking about her, Elizabeth looked up and smiled at Fanny.

Before either could speak, Bennet entered the room and his wife joined him. Lydia was summoned from the music room and Jenki, Mrs. Annesley, and Miss Jones asked to leave them, and close the door on the way out.

Bennet and Fanny broke the news regarding Longbourn. The four sisters were happy the estate they loved would never fall into the hands of the man who had written the letter their parents had shared with them. They cared nothing for the financial implication, rather the fact the dependants on Longbourn would be well protected. Elizabeth especially did not think of the added wealth given she owned her own property in abundance.

"Thank you for warning that man off before he came to

importune us in our home," Elizabeth addressed her parents.

"There was no scenario your mother and I could imagine where we would have allowed such a man to pay his addresses to any of you, never mind sanction such a match," Bennet responded.

"What if he arrives uninvited, especially now he has lost his future inheritance?" Mary wondered.

"Sir Norman, the barrister who argued our case, has informed him verbally before witnesses as well as presented him with a letter. If Mr. Collins brings himself to Longbourn uninvited, he will be arrested for trespassing," Bennet shared.

"Papa, may I go into Meryton to see the militia arrive on the morrow?" Lydia asked.

"With the soldiers and officers joining our society, it is more important than ever to be well escorted when you go into the town," Fanny warned her daughters, looking pointedly at her youngest.

Why Lydia had decided only a man in a uniform would do for her, no one in the family knew. Fanny felt it was time to lay out the reality of what life as an officer's wife would be like for her youngest to cure her of this unreasonable infatuation. Her experience of almost being importuned by an officer many years previously precluded her remaining silent on the subject.

"No, Lydia, as you are not even out locally, you will not be in company with the militia members, even well chaperoned and guarded," Fanny stated firmly. "Why is it you are enamoured of a man in uniform?"

"In pictures of officers I have seen they look so dashing," Lydia responded dreamily. "It would be a great and fun adventure to be married to such a man. Life would be full of society and balls."

"Lydia dear, you are not even fifteen yet, why would you even be thinking of men and marriage?" Fanny pushed. "You know it is two more years before you come out locally and then another year after that before you enter London society, do you not?"

"But surely if I meet a handsome officer and we fall in love, you will allow me to marry before I come out," Lydia averred. Both her parents shook their heads emphatically. "What if I eloped?" Lydia asked petulantly.

"Then Lydia dear, I hope you are able to live on about two pounds a month," Fanny said while she maintained her equanimity. "How many ball gowns, for that matter, any gowns or dresses, do you think your husband would be able to afford to purchase for you? What of servants? On such a monthly amount you would not have any. You can forget about balls and society as you would be confined to the small, dingy room your husband would be able to barely afford. You would not have a conveyance to take you where you desired to go at any rate."

Lydia turned paler and paler as her mother spoke. "B-but I will have my fortune," she managed weakly.

"No, you will not!" Bennet responded decisively. "Did you forget the terms attached to your dowries?" Lydia nodded her head as tears began to prick her eyes. Bennet reminded his daughter of the terms to which he was referring. "Like we did with Mary, and will for Kitty, we will not approve of even a courtship until you are nineteen. And then, unless I am convinced the man is able to support himself and you in a style you are accustomed to, *without* your money, which would tell me he is not after you for your fortune, I would not approve of him."

By now Lydia was sobbing. Fanny sat next to her youngest and pulled her into a hug. "Lyddie, as much as I hate to see you upset, you needed to know the reality of what life with a poor officer would be like before this infatuation you have with men in scarlet coats causes you to do something irrevocable you know you should not."

"There is no hurry for any of the three of you who are unattached to think of a partner of your future life until you are well and truly ready for that step. You must know we would only approve of a man who will love, protect, and respect you, one who you love and respect in turn," Bennet explained.

"You may not want to hear this Lyddie, but I know from experience that not all the men who join the militia are honourable or have good intentions. One day, when you are older, I will share what occurred with an officer in Colonel Millar's regiment of the Sussex Militia who visited Meryton before I met and fell in love with your father," Fanny related as she dried her youngest's tears. "All I will tell you now is I am lucky your Uncle Edward was there to rescue me before anything untoward occurred."

Thankfully Lydia was not an unintelligent girl and was able to assimilate what her parents had told her. The prospect of living in poverty just because of the colour of a jacket made her feelings about officers dim considerably, in fact they were well on their way to being extinguished completely.

"In that case I am happy to remain home and not meet the officers," Lydia decided.

When she was ready, Lydia went to find Miss Jones to continue her lessons.

"One good thing has come out of Lydia's former obsession with men in the army," Bennet stated. "I will make sure Biggs, Johns, and their men are well aware of the militia and when any of you are out, you will have a minimum of two of the guards with you."

"Yes, Papa," the three daughters present chorused.

# CHAPTER 35

Richard was able to leave Cloverdell a few days before he had expected to. He was as happy as he had ever been to arrive in Hertfordshire. He rode directly to Netherfield Park where his valet and carriage would arrive later.

Not wanting to waste any time travelling, he had elected to ride Invictus. An added advantage was he was able to use paths his coachman would not be able to negotiate so he arrived at Bingley's leased estate without having to use the road which would have taken him through Meryton.

His friend and his aunt met Richard in the entrance hall. "Welcome back, Fitzwilliam," Bingley stated jovially. "I take it you want to wash and then make for Longbourn and your fiancée?"

"That, Charles is a silly question," Miss Bingley teased her nephew. "What man violently in love would not prefer his betrothed's company to yours and mine?"

Richard coloured slightly at Bingley's aunt's accurate assessment of the situation. Not that he objected to their company, it was simply too many days since he had last been in company with his Mary.

"Do you object if I ride with you?" Bingley enquired.

"Not at all, allow me to wash and change," Richard agreed. "And there will be no racing. Although I did not push my horse, after my ride here I will not go above a trot until he is well rested."

Bingley knew Richard was serious, he took very good

care of his horses, especially Invictus.

"So be it, a nice slow three mile ride," Bingley accepted.

~~~~~~~/~~~~~~~

Wickham had tried to garner credit from three shops plus the Red Lion Inn where he intended to drink in the tap house, but so far, regardless of how much of his vaunted charm he had employed, he had been refused. When Colonel Forster had informed his officers the local merchants did not issue credit to anyone who was not well known to them, Wickham had been confident he would be able to bypass that particular impediment. Much to his chagrin, none of the stratagems he had employed had won him an account to gain what he wanted on credit.

What was he to do, he had less than five pounds to his name so unless he convinced some of his *friends* to buy his grog for him, he would soon be without.

The same officers were getting more and more insistent Wickham pay his debts to them. He of course, had no intention of doing so. Perhaps he would have to think about leaving the militia sooner rather than later.

Leaving presented two problems. Unless his resignation was accepted, he would be counted a deserter, which in time of war meant death if one was caught. The problem was he had signed a contract to remain an officer for one year complete. The second, more pressing problem was his lack of funds, and so far, his luck had not turned with the cards so all he had gained were more debts.

Thankfully he had heard some cryptic talk around the town about one of the Bennet sisters having inherited an estate and possibly much more than that. If he could find out which one it was, and compromise her, all his financial woes would be a thing of the past.

Based on the gossip supplied by a serving wench who had allowed him to tup her, the Bennets had begun to frequent the town again as they had completed their deep mourning. The same girl had mentioned the older one was married some two years ago to some noble, and another was engaged, to whom she knew not. If the one who was betrothed was the sister who had inherited the estate, her being spoken for would not affect his plans.

He would be on the lookout for these supposedly comely Bennet sisters and he was sure it would not take him long to discover which one was the heiress. Wickham could smell wealth like a pointer could detect the prey its master was hunting. His secondary plan, which he had already begun to put into practice, was to *borrow* the purses and valuables of as many of his fellow officers as possible before he ran in case he needed to make his escape.

~~~~~~~/~~~~~~~

"Should we walk into Meryton?" Elizabeth proposed to Mary and Kitty. "It has been some time since we have visited the stores in the town."

"I have no objections," Mary agreed. "It is not too cold today and I do not expect Richard for some days yet, so there is no need for me to await his call at home."

"Could we not use one of the carriages?" Kitty, who did not like the cold, asked.

"It will be a brisk walk, as long as Papa agrees," Elizabeth responded. "However, if you are dead set against walking, we may use a conveyance."

Knowing how much Lizzy and Mary enjoyed walking, Kitty agreed to walk as well. Elizabeth made for the study to seek their father's permission for the outing.

"Even though who the heiress is has not been discovered, there are whispers in Meryton about one of you gaining an estate," Bennet responded after Elizabeth made the request for her and her sisters to hie for the market town. "We know not of the characters of the militia men, so as long as you have Mrs. Jenkinson as well as Biggs, Johns, and at least two other men escort you, you have my consent for your walk."

"Thank you, Papa," Elizabeth enthused as she kissed her father's cheek.

Soon a party of nine was making the one mile walk into Meryton. Before they entered the town, Biggs stopped them. He explained he would remain close to the three misses with Mrs. Jenki, as long as they stayed together while Johns and the other three men would appear to not be a part of their party but would be close by in case they were needed.

Thus, when they made the turn onto the main road which ran through the town, Johns was walking ahead of them on the other side of the street with one of the other guards close to him. One man walked ahead of the sisters on the same side of the street while Biggs was where one would expect an escort to be. The fifth man was a little farther back.

~~~~~~~/~~~~~~~

Just when Wickham thought the Bennet sisters were a myth, three of the most beautiful young ladies he had ever seen began walking up the other side of the street from where he was. Two were blonde, one tall and willowy, the other shorter like the dark haired one. He guessed they were the Bennets as they were dressed in the colours of one who was in half mourning. They were followed by an enormous oaf of a footman. Wickham was sure the huge dullard was mentally and physically slow.

Wickham's mouth fell open when he really looked at the one with the raven coloured curls which protruded from under her bonnet. She had bewitching emerald-green eyes and was the most gorgeous woman of any age he had ever beheld. If only that one was the heiress. What he would not give to bed one as comely as her. He decided even if she was not the one with the estate, he would have her anyway.

As they walked, none of the three Bennet sisters missed

the way one officer was leering at them. Elizabeth shifted her vision to where Johns was on the same side of the street as the drooling man. Johns gave an almost imperceptible nod telling his mistress he saw the man and was watching him carefully.

From behind the three sisters, the officer staring at them had caught Biggs's attention as well. He issued a non-verbal command to the man who was on the same side of the street as Miss Lizzy and her sisters.

His man sped up and once he was well past the leering lieutenant, crossed over and took up position a few yards behind the officer.

Not seeing the man behind him mirror his action, Wickham crossed the street. He decided he would *accidently* bump into one of the young ladies, preferably the dark haired one, which would allow him to introduce himself as he *apologised profusely*.

~~~~~~~/~~~~~~~

Bingley and Richard reached the main street of Meryton and turned their horses so they could continue on until they reached the turnoff towards Longbourn. Richard had not mentioned the possibility of arriving sooner than he had planned in his last letter to Mary. He wanted to surprise his fiancée and see the look of pleasure on her beautiful face when she saw him.

As the sun was shining in his eyes, he lifted his hand to shade them. Although they were twenty to thirty yards away, he could swear Lizzy, Mary, and Kitty were up ahead.

It was then Richard noticed an officer walking towards them. At the last instant he saw the officer change his direction and bump into one of the sisters, but which one he could not tell from there. He kicked Invictus into a canter and Bingley followed suit with his stallion.

Before Biggs or one of the other guards could reach the man, he had bumped into Miss Lizzy, however, it was not enough to cause her to fall. He and the other men were about to step in when they all saw Miss Lizzy shake her head. That stayed Mrs. Jenkinson as well who was about to come stand next to her charge.

"Please excuse me, Madam," Wickham bowed as he removed his hat with a flourish. "I was blinded by the beauty before me and did not pay attention. If I may be so bold, I am Lieutenant George Wickham at your service and would like to make amends..."

"You are perhaps the George Wickham whose father was steward of a large estate in Derbyshire?" Elizabeth asked calmly.

He was not sure how the lady would know that, but she had not mentioned the name Darcy so Wickham judged it was safe to answer her truthfully. "Why yes, my father was steward to Mr. Darcy of Pem..."

Whatever Wickham was about to say was lost in the crack of a slap to his face as his head jerked back. Instinctively he lifted his hand to respond.

In a flash, the large man he had thought slow was in front of him and planted his enormous fist in Wickham's gut, doubling him over. With all the air knocked out of him he fell to the ground. At the same time, Mrs. Jenkinson stood between Elizabeth and Kitty.

As he saw the officer go down, Richard vaulted off his horse followed closely by Bingley. "Richard," Mary fairly squealed with excitement.

Before he could react, a colonel and some of his officers arrived on the scene. It was then Richard identified the man Lizzy had slapped. "What is the meaning of this, why has one of my officers been accosted?" Colonel Forster demanded.

Wickham was getting some air back in his lungs and managed to sit up. He was about to feel better about things when he saw who was standing in front of him. None other than Richard Fitzwilliam!

"Has the militia sunk so low they take a debaucher, a defiler of young girls, and leaver of debts into their ranks," Richard drawled. "An officer no less, I thought an officer needed a gentleman's education."

"You cannot believe anything this man says, Colonel. His lies are likely the reason this young lady accosted me. You remember I told you of the family who cheated me out of my inheritance." Wickham could only hope he would be believed and then he would escape.

"Nothing Richard said caused me to slap you!" Elizabeth insisted.

"Then why did you, Miss?" The Colonel enquired.

"I am Miss Bennet, the eldest unmarried Bennet sister," Elizabeth responded. "This man is a liar and a fraudster. My reaction was because he tried to have his paramour lie to gain the position of companion to a young lady of my acquaintance in order to seduce her and lay claim to her dowry."

"Come now Colonel, surely you see this poor young lady has had her head filled with lies..." Wickham began when Richard interjected.

"I am Richard Fitzwilliam, second son of the Earl and Countess of Matlock who are guardians to the young lady alluded to," he stated. "My father holds the signed confession of Wickham's paramour wherein she admitted to the whole scheme, including how her characters were forgeries written by this excuse of a man. Also detailed in her confession, was his plan to take my father's ward to Gretna Green so he could gain her dowry. We hold debt receipts of his for well over a thousand pounds. I will wager if you send some men back to where you were previously encamped, you will soon discover he has left debts and despoiled young girls behind him. Do you think you and your men will ever be welcomed back again where you were?"

By now Wickham had begun to sweat and he had lost his look of confidence.

"What of his claim of being denied an inheritance after he completed his studies at Cambridge?" Colonel Forster enquired. Based on the looks from Wickham, he had a feeling he and his other officers had had the wool pulled over their eyes by a practiced deceiver.

"First of all, Wickie here never completed his studies, he had hardly begun them at *Eton* when my late Uncle Darcy withdrew his patronage because of the blackguard's perfidy. Yes, we have proof," Richard related.

As Fitzwilliam spoke, Wickham looked for an avenue of escape. He was about to try and run when he felt himself being held in place by rather large hands on either shoulder. He looked and he was being restrained by the big man who had hit him as well as another equally large man who had materialised out of nowhere.

Richard gave a brief rundown of the truth behind the phantom inheritance.

"We were all taken in by this dastard," the Colonel shook his head.

"He has borrowed money from many of us based on his expectation of what he is owed, and that does not count his heavy debts of honour," Denny revealed ashamedly. How had he allowed this man to work on him in that fashion.

"Colonel, if you will lock this man in the town gaol or your brig if you have one, until my father arrives, it would be appreciated," Richard requested. "He must answer for trying to defraud a peer of the realm. You might also search his belongings; chances are your men will be able to claim some of their possessions of which I am sure he has relieved them."

Wickham knew he was sunk. The defeated man was transferred to some of the officers who marched him back towards their encampment to lock him away until the Earl arrived.

The Colonel dispatched some men to Oxford to discover what debts Wickham had left in his wake. "Thank you for your bravery, Miss Bennet. Your action will lead to a snake in our midst being excised," Colonel Forster stated gratefully.

Elizabeth did not think she did so very much, however she inclined her head to the officer in appreciation for his words.

"Now that Lizzy has saved the day, how is it you are here Richard," Mary enquired.

"If you would prefer I could return to Cloverdell…" Richard teased.

"Silly man," Mary slapped her fiancé on his arm playfully.

"That is more than enough excitement for one day," Mrs. Jenkinson suggested, "should we make for Longbourn?" The three Miss Bennets nodded their agreement.

"You do not object if Bingley and I join you for the walk back, do you Lizzy?" Richard questioned.

There was no objection voiced. The expanded group began the walk to the Bennet estate with the stallions being led by two of the guards.

~~~~~~~/~~~~~~~

"Only you, Lizzy," Fanny exclaimed as she kissed her daughter's cheek. "You think he walked into you on purpose, do you not? What could he mean by it?"

"I think I can elucidate Aunt Fanny," Richard averred. "If as you say word about Lizzy's inheritance is abroad, then I am sure he wanted an introduction so he could—what he would consider such—make subtle enquiries to discover who the heiress is. The way your daughters report he was leering at them I am sure he would have wanted to have his way with each of them. As much as it pains me to say it, had he succeeded, it would not have been the first time he forced himself on an unwilling female."

"I suppose I should have allowed John to take care of him right away," Elizabeth sighed. "I knew he had caused the accident purposefully."

"No harm was done, except to him by you," Bennet assured his second daughter. "Richard informed me there is a nice print of your hand on his cheek." Bennet turned to his soon-to-be son. "Will you write to your parents and Darcy and ask they bring all proof against this wastrel with them?"

Richard nodded.

"Enough about that waste of a man," Fanny declared. "I need some time with you two so I may begin to plan your wedding."

That was Bennet's cue to stand so he could return to the study. "No speaking of lace in my presence, please Fanny dear," Bennet requested playfully.

Fanny smiled indulgently and herded Mary and Richard towards the small parlour.

# CHAPTER 36

George Wickham was stripped of his lieutenancy and reduced to the rank of private without delay. He was informed once Lord Matlock arrived, he would be cashiered out of the militia, but until then he was under their control, including the administration of a punishment of twenty lashes, he was to receive later that morning.

Wickham tried his best to talk the Colonel out of delivering the discipline, but the man could not be moved in the least. Claiming he had not known the penalty for not being truthful about himself when joining the regiment fell on deaf ears.

None of his former friends, not even Denny, were willing to speak on his behalf. Oh yes, they had spoken, but against him! For some reason, they were not appreciative of him having played them for fools and his *relieving* them of some of their belongings. Sitting in his cell in the brig, he wished he had never heard the name Bennet nor joined the army.

How was he supposed to know the regiment moved to a town where his attempt to have Karen Younge gain the position of Miss Darcy's companion was known. If that was not enough, Richard Fitzwilliam was residing in the area. He would have never told the story of his supposed ill-usage by Darcy had he known someone in the neighbourhood would be able to contradict him and offer proof as well.

Unable to consider he played a part in his downfall, Wickham chalked everything up to the bad luck which had dogged him at the tables and when he played cards with his former brother officers.

From the window in his cell, Wickham could clearly see the two posts with the metal rings on the inside edge of each. There were chains attached to each ring, each of which ended with a manacle. The two at the top were for the wrists, the lower two for the ankles. Having seen a soldier suffer in this manner while he was lashed for some infraction in Oxfordshire, Wickham was well aware of the purpose of the rings and chains. He hoped he would lose consciousness before too many strokes had been administered.

He saw the two soldiers guarding the door to his cell come to attention which told him the time to be taken to the posts was nigh. Denny and Carter stood waiting for one of the soldiers to unlock the door. Once it was open, Denny nodded to one of the men who handed his weapon to his mate and then entered.

"Off wif yer shirt," the soldier commanded roughly.

"Come now Denny and Carter, this is not the way to treat a friend is it. Let me go and I will not hold these offences against you," Wickham tried. He was desperate but he needed to exude confidence.

"You do not have friends, only those you feel you can use. I was a fool once, but never again," Denny spat out. "My missing fob watch was found secreted in your former quarters, so unless you want to feel my retribution before your lashes, remove your shirt as Johnson commanded."

Wickham looked to Carter and saw heavy disdain in his eyes. His last avenue for escape was lost.

~~~~~~~/~~~~~~~

Lord and Lady Matlock, along with their ward, arrived at Netherfield Park the Friday after Lizzy's now famous slap which had unmasked the wolf in sheep's clothing. Accompanying them was their nephew, William Darcy. He had ridden in the coach with them while their personal servants and the companion followed in the coach behind. Zeus was led by one of the six outriders.

Although he tried to hide his anticipation of seeing Miss Bennet again, especially as his full mourning and her mourning had ended the day before, he tamped down his desire knowing he and his uncle needed to deal with Wickham first.

On the journey into Hertfordshire, uncle and nephew had come to a consensus regarding the punishment which would excise the blight—Wickham—forever.

Bingley and his aunt welcomed the arriving party very warmly. Richard was also waiting to welcome his parents, although he would have preferred to be at Longbourn.

Once the travellers were washed and changed, Lord Matlock met in Bingley's study with Richard and Darcy. "Is that bounder ready to be moved?" he enquired. "It has been more than a sennight since he was whipped."

"I spoke to Mr. Jones this morning," Richard reported. "The seducer will be able to travel in two days at the most."

"It must have been a shock for him to answer for his crimes for once," Darcy opined.

"Yes, I believe it was," Richard averred. "From what I was told, he even tried to charm his way out of his lashing. He failed...miserably."

"It seems he still has a talent for making friends but not keeping them," Darcy shook his head.

"I suppose we must get this unpleasant business behind us," Lord Matlock stated as he rose from the chair where he had been seated. "Giana is with Mrs. Mayers and Elaine. Our ward wanted to make directly for Longbourn but she was reminded she needed to finish a lesson before that would occur."

Darcy smiled to himself. If he succeeded in wooing Elizabeth, he knew his sister would be well pleased. He did not want to get ahead of himself, but once he was married he wondered if his aunt and uncle would permit Giana to live with him and his lady, at least part of the year.

Richard and Darcy followed the Earl out of the study and the three men made their way to the front doors where the butler and a footman were ready with their outerwear.

~~~~~~~/~~~~~~~

Elizabeth had felt butterflies in her stomach since she woke that morning. Although the day was cold, it had not rained for the preceding three days, so she was able to ride out on Penny to expend some of her nervous energy.

The punishing ride had temporarily helped to take her mind off that which had dominated her thoughts for a few days now. As soon as she had returned home from watching the sunrise from Oakham Mount, escorted by John and Brian, she bathed and dressed. By the time she was ready to go down to join the family in breaking their fasts, the clarity she had found while riding had been banished from her mind.

She was aware of what—or more accurately who—was the cause of the disturbance to her equanimity. Cousin William was to arrive at Netherfield Park that morning. She had a few hours to wait; the residents of Netherfield Park would join them for a family dinner that evening. Elizabeth had a feeling Anne was smiling down on her. Rather than feeling melancholy thinking of Anne's passing, she was concentrating on the future.

It was not that Elizabeth did not think of Anne all through the day—she did. Each time she saw Jenki, she could not but think of Annie. Rather she was taking her promise to live for both of them very seriously.

Always having been a rational being, the feeling of instant attraction to William Darcy was still something with which she was not sure she was sanguine. Surely love at first sight was a construct of the gothic romance novels she did not read, at least not very often.

After the morning meal, Elizabeth had taken herself off to the still room where she tried to keep herself busy and quiet her mind for a while.

~~~~~~~/~~~~~~~

George Wickham had never experienced the degree of pain he had after his punishment was administered. Thankfully, he had fainted dead away by the time the third stroke of the cat had found its mark. Since that day, he had been lying on his stomach, the wounds on his back were packed with a salve to ward off infection. One of the nights since his lashing, while in a fitful sleep, he had turned onto his back. The pain had woken him almost instantly. Since that one and only time, he had not repeated that error.

Denny had come by a few days after the lashing had been administered to gloat at his pain. It was then his former friend had informed Wickham how Mr. Fitzwilliam had purchased all his non gambling related markers, including the extensive debts which had been discovered in and around Oxford.

There was talk of a trial for the few things he had *borrowed* from his—at the time—brother officers.

This was the day the Earl of Matlock, Fitzwilliam, and Darcy were to come to see him. All Wickham hoped for was his ability to trade on the former warm feelings the late Mr. Darcy had for him.

~~~~~~~/~~~~~~~

The three family members waited in the Colonel's office while Wickham was brought to them.

When the miscreant shuffled into the office he was shackled by his ankles and wrists. As the gouges on his back had not all healed, he wore no shirt. The two soldiers who had escorted the prisoner into the room stood Wickham in front of the three men and his colonel, and with a salute to the latter, withdrew pulling the door closed behind him.

"Your father would not want to see me suffer..." Wickham tried when Darcy cut him off.

"Do not mention my late father. You know as well as I do from the time his eyes were opened to the truth about you, he wanted nothing further to do with you! Had he been alive, and you had attempted your plan against my sister, you would no longer be living!" Darcy barked at the cowering man.

"Before you waste your breath, you have a choice to make," Lord Matlock stated firmly. "Do not fritter away my valuable time trying to plead your case because I have no patience for a man who would try to move against a young girl like my ward."

Wickham stood with his head down. He knew his life was in the hands of the men before him.

"One of the options is for you to be tried by a military tribunal for theft and when you are found guilty, you will be shot," Colonel Forster stated dispassionately.

"The *only* reason we are offering you an alternative is the esteem my father and I held for your late adoptive father. As disappointed as he was in the path you chose for yourself, he would not have wanted to see your life end in front of a firing squad."

For the first time in his life, Wickham knew when not to speak.

"Your one chance is transportation," Lord Matlock informed Wickham. "It is either a one-way journey to Van Diemen's Land, with fourteen years hard labour, or you may remain and face military justice. If you do and you are sentenced to gaol and not the firing squad, then the day you finish serving your prison sentence will be the day you find yourself in one of the debtor's prisons for all the vowels we hold in the amount of more than one thousand five hundred pounds. Thanks to what you borrowed from the officers and your debts from Oxfordshire, you owe a pretty penny. In other words, if you are not sentenced to die, you will spend the rest of your life in a gaol cell."

"Transportation," Wickham chose without raising his head.

"If you should ever be simple enough to return to the United Kingdom once you have served your hard labour, you will be arrested and tried as you would have if you chose to stay here" Richard added. "Do you understand Wickie?"

Wickham nodded his head, again without lifting it. The Colonel summoned the guards who escorted the defeated man back to the brig.

"I want to thank you for restoring my regiment's honour both in Oxford and here. I have been informed we will be welcome to return to Oxfordshire thanks to your family paying the merchants that bastard cheated," Forster said gratefully. "And here, thanks to Miss Bennet and Mr. Fitzwilliam, he was stopped before he could cause any harm to the local ladies, although the shop owners' policy of not allowing credit to unknowns must have put a crimp in his plans."

After shaking the Colonel's hand, the three men took their leave. The Matlock coach was waiting for them outside of the office.

"What do you think the chances of Wickham and your sister meeting in Australia are?" Richard asked once they were underway. "I am not sure who I would cheer for if those two met."

"From what I understand though, your wayward aunt will arrive in New South Wales, and Wickham is for Van Diemen's Land. Given the latter is an island and the other is somewhere in the vastness of the Australian colony, the chance of their meeting is infinitesimal," Lord Matlock opined.

"If they do, they deserve one another," Darcy added.

"On a more pleasant subject, I have never seen you so keen to travel south as you were this time," Lord Matlock ribbed his nephew. "I wonder if it was just disposing of Wickham which brought you back to Meryton."

"I know not of what you speak," Darcy responded all the while fighting to keep his face neutral.

"That is brown Mr. *'I abhor disguise'* Darcy," Richard joined his father in funning with Darcy. "Unless one is blind, and even then a blind man would notice, it is my sister Elizabeth who has Darcy entranced as a moth is to a flame."

Darcy harumphed and turned to stare pointedly out of the window.

Father and son released a round of rather loud guffaws with a snort or two interspersed. "Come now William, surely you are not put off by some light-hearted ribbing, are you?" Lord Matlock questioned.

It was not many seconds before the corners of Darcy's mouth turned upward.

# CHAPTER 37

I t was a merry party enjoying dinner at Longbourn that evening.

Darcy made sure he was in position to escort Cousin Elizabeth into the dining parlour. He pulled a chair out for her across from Bingley, who had made sure he was seated between Darcy's sister and their cousin Kitty, with Cousin Lydia next to her older sister. Next to Giana were Mary and Richard, who were as was common for them, lost in their own world.

Bennet had Elaine on one side and Miss Bingley on the other. Opposite him, his wife was in conversation with Matlock. The three companions and Miss Jones filled in the gaps along both sides of the table. Mrs. Jenkinson could not but smile thinking how happy Miss Anne would have been to see the interactions between Mr. Darcy and Miss Lizzy.

The Bennet patriarch watched Bingley's interactions with his second youngest daughter and as was his wont, Netherfield Park's tenant kept his attentions to Kitty appropriate. He spoke to Giana and Lydia, as much as he did Kitty. Bennet was pleased Bingley was not doing anything which would necessitate a conversation with the young man regarding his second youngest daughter.

Darcy leaned a little towards the bewitching lady next to him. "If there is no rain or snow on the morrow, will you and your speedy horse be in the field where we raced?" he asked quietly.

"No, I plan to walk to Oakham Mount on the morrow,

weather permitting that is," Elizabeth replied as her cheeks pinked a little. "I will be with Jenki, Biggs, and Johns, and we will leave the house a half hour before sunrise."

"Would you object if I were to meet you on the path to the hill in the morning?" he asked keenly.

"As I will have more than adequate chaperonage, I do not see why not," Elizabeth granted. Seeing the wide smile that spread across his face at her response, revealing both of his dimples, Elizabeth blushed a deep shade of red no matter how much she tried not to.

"I look forward to our exercise in the morning. Now I need to ask the Lord for no precipitation on the morrow," Darcy returned.

Even though she had been speaking with Reggie regarding the miscreant who would be permanently removed from their lives, Fanny did not miss the interactions between her second daughter and William. Lord Matlock also watched his nephew for a minute or two. "That boy has lost his heart," he opined.

"And Lizzy, who has never looked at a man romantically before seems to be just as lost as he is," Fanny posited. "She may not know it yet, but I have a feeling we are looking at the next Mrs. Darcy."

"Elaine and I have seen the mooncalf look William gets whenever he talks about Lizzy, never mind when he looks at her," Matlock mused.

"All those years ago when we first met, who would have imagined two of my girls would marry your sons, and probably another your nephew," Fanny averred wistfully. "God has been very good to all of us in so many ways, but I never expected two more daughters would join Janey in the married state so soon, one after the other."

"William has not asked her, and Lizzy has not accepted yet," Matlock pointed out.

"He will and she will, and soon," Fanny predicted. "I believe they will love and respect one another just like Jane and Andrew, and Mary and Richard. We know it is not her fortune that interests him. He has more than enough of his own and I noted his interest in Lizzy well before he was aware of our true financial state, and long before she inherited all of her property and wealth."

At his end of the table, even with the stimulating conversation with Elaine and Miss Hildebrand Bingley, Bennet had not missed the interactions between Lizzy and William. Without knowing what his wife and Matlock were discussing, he reached the same conclusions as they had.

'When he takes Lizzy away to the north, at least there is that magnificent library I have heard so much about for me to visit when we are at Pemberley,' Bennet thought as he watched his second daughter interact with Darcy. 'Not even a marquess turned her head. At least when the day comes, and he asks for Lizzy's hand, I will know it is for the right reasons. She may not know it yet, but Darcy is totally and completely in her power.'

As those still mourning were in half mourning, the Bennet sisters and Giana entertained everyone on the pianoforte and harp once the men joined the ladies. It was the first time Darcy heard Elizabeth's perfect contralto voice swell with song.

She had the voice of an angel as if her multitude of attributes were not already more than enough. He could not wait for the hours to pass until he met her the next morning.

~~~~~~~/~~~~~~~

Darcy was not alone in having to struggle to fall asleep that night. Elizabeth had the same problem for a very similar reason. While he was imagining how he intended to declare himself to Cousin Elizabeth in the morning, she was dreaming of him making a declaration. No, it was more than that, she was imagining him proposing to her.

Both were out of their beds and preparing to dress at about the same time, which was around an hour before either had intended to rise.

Once she was dressed, Elizabeth pulled a book from the small bookcase in her chamber. It was Samuel Taylor Coleridge's *Love*, the 1800 edition. She thought it was a very appropriate book to attempt to read on this of all mornings. Once she had unsuccessfully tried to read the same page five times, she gave up, closed the book, and placed it on the little table next to her bed. She had to wait some more time before Jenki would knock on her door.

Just like Elizabeth was unable to read, Darcy sat in the library at Netherfield Park looking at the page of an agricultural journal but not seeing the words thereon. He admitted defeat, and returned the journal to the shelf.

He was amused when he remembered how surprised he was Bingley's leased house had a very decent library. Now aware of the name of the landlord, and the man being a fellow bibliophile, Darcy was not at all shocked the house Richard's friend lived in had such a well-stocked library. Before the first time he met Bingley, his cousin had warned him an affinity for the written word was not something they shared.

After giving up on reading, Darcy lifted his eyes to the heavens. '*Mother and Father, you remember I had told you I thought I found my match, the other half of my heart?*' Darcy communicated silently with his parents in heaven. '*She is the one. You remember how I told you about the woman who made that inept attempt to entrap me and how I would not marry her if she were the last woman alive? It is the exact opposite with Elizabeth. She is the* only *woman I will marry. If she refuses me, and I do not think she will—at least I hope she will not—then, I simply will not marry and Pemberley will go to Giana's son.*

"*I pray that will not be my fate, but until I ask her, all I can do is hope. I love you both and I hope you are spending time with*

*Anne and Uncle Lewis in heaven.'*

At the same moment Darcy began to speak to his parents, Elizabeth was addressing her best friend. *'Annie, my dearest friend Annie. I think I have gone and fallen in love with Cousin William—William. Ours is not a long acquaintance, but I think I knew when we shared the dances at the assembly in October. Do not ask me when I fell in love with him, I was in the middle before I realised I had started. Yes, Annie, you had the right of it,'* Elizabeth smiled as she told her friend that. *'My feelings are not driven by anything other than my belief he is the only man who will ever own my heart.*

*'He is truly the best of men! You know how Mary and Richard balance one another, with her being more sombre and him being the jovial one, do you not? I believe in the opposite ways that William and I are one another's perfect foils. We are so well matched in so many other ways, our love of nature, horses, intelligence, and I can go on. It does not hurt that he is exceedingly handsome, and when he smiles, and his dimples show...oh my.'* Elizabeth blushed as she told Anne the last. If she did not know better, she would swear she could hear Anne giggling. *'I love having Jenki with me, we are able to find solace in our shared memories of you and she has told me so much about when you were a child before we met.'*

A knock on her door caused Elizabeth to look at the clock on the wall where she saw it was time. Jenki's arrival had pulled her from her reverie. Soon she would see him, and she was sincerely hoping he would speak.

~~~~~~~/~~~~~~~

"Good morning John, good morning Brian," Elizabeth trilled to the two huge men waiting for her and Jenki just outside of the kitchen door. "Mr. Darcy will be joining us along the path this morning." She could not help her colour deepening when she mentioned him.

Biggs and Johns gave knowing grins which matched the

wide smile on Mrs. Jenkinson's face.

As was to be expected in the latter half of November, the morning was cold but Elizabeth's prayers had been answered. There had been no rain overnight, and the sky, which was becoming streaked with the first fingers of the new day's light, was clear.

With the temperature and the season, there was no welcoming birdsong as there always was in spring, summer, and even early autumn. The non-evergreen trees, which were most of those at Longbourn, were stark with very few brown leaves still clinging to the branches determined not to let go until there was no choice.

Another positive was the absence of wind. There was a slight breeze, and it was cold, but nothing like a wind-driven chill. Elizabeth was wearing a heavy overcoat, thick sheep's wool lined gloves, and a heavy wool dress. Her bonnet was also lined with sheep's wool and had little flaps which covered her ears in case there was a cold wind. Between her stockings and half boots, she had worn a pair of thick wool socks, so she was fully prepared for a colder day than this one was turning out to be.

As was her wont, her first stop was at the stables. Hector was gifted an apple and a carrot. Penny received the same. Both were as happy as they always were to see her and nickered with delight as she approached them. Elizabeth rubbed both on their foreheads and made sure the blankets they wore in the winter to keep them warm overnight were secure on them.

Once she had confirmed the horses were happy, and after greeting the stable hands already at work, Elizabeth walking next to Jenki, with the guards following, made for the gate which led out of the paddock and into a field and the path to Oakham Mount.

Halfway to the gate, Elizabeth's breath caught as she saw Cousin William standing on the path on the other side of the fence. He had a great coat on over, what she had to assume, were warm clothes, the black armband was on his left arm. His gloves looked thicker than normal, and he was wearing a beaver. From what Elizabeth could see his ears were exposed so she was pleased there was no wind.

Although she wanted to run towards him, Elizabeth regulated herself and continued to walk like the lady she was supposed to be. She did not miss Jenki's smile as she fought to regulate herself. John Biggs got to the gate just ahead of his mistress and opened it for her. Once she and her companions were past it, he fell in step behind them while Brian Johns closed it again.

"Good morning, Cousin Elizabeth, Mrs. Jenkinson, Biggs, and Johns," Darcy greeted as he gave her and the companion a half bow. The guards grunted their greetings.

"It is *good* to see you, Cousin William," Elizabeth replied with a semblance of a curtsy. Mrs. Jenkinson also curtsied. "Shall we?" Elizabeth pointed towards the path and the eminence about a mile or two distant rising out of the early morning mist.

Mrs. Jenkinson fell back to walk behind her mistress and Darcy fell in step with the lady he loved and offered her his arm. She took it without hesitation, and he saw it as a very good sign that rather than simply rest her hand lightly on his forearm, she wrapped her arm around his. He knew he was grinning like a fool, but he cared not.

For the first quarter hour of the walk, there were no words spoken between them. All that was heard was the crunching of the grass which had frozen overnight as two pairs of lady's half boots and three pairs of men's boots came down with each step the walkers took.

"Exposing Wickham was very brave of you Elizabeth," Darcy noted.

"I did not do more than anyone else would have done,"

Elizabeth protested.

"Ninety-nine out of a hundred women would not have confronted him, never mind slap his face," Darcy disagreed. "I am not surprised you are downplaying your role. It makes you uncomfortable, being given credit for your bravery. I have heard tell of that ever since you rescued Anne and Uncle Lewis from certain death."

Neither of them saw Mrs. Jenkinson nodding her agreement emphatically.

"Anne told me the same on more than one occasion," Elizabeth shared wistfully.

"Well, there you have it," Darcy responded. "Anne was never wrong," he jested.

"If she was here with us, she would be the first one to disagree with you." Elizabeth looked up as they were getting closer to Oakham Mount. "Did you know Anne came up to the summit with us some years ago?" Darcy shook his head. Elizabeth related the story to him.

"You were truly Anne's best friend," he concluded. "Before you deny it, it was you who planned it all so she could join you, was it not?"

"Yes, I did," Elizabeth blushed, "but there were many who assisted and without them, it would not have been possible." She turned and looked pointedly at the three who were walking behind them.

"I am sure that is true, but it does not change the fact it was your idea," Darcy insisted. Elizabeth inclined her head not arguing the point.

They spoke of inconsequential things until they reached the base of the hill and the path that led to the summit. Johns walked up to make sure there was no one waiting for Miss Lizzy at the top. The place was deserted so Johns whistled to let those waiting at the base know it was safe to walk up.

"I will remain her with John," Mrs. Jenkinson stated.

349

"With Brian at the top, propriety will be observed."

With that decided, Elizabeth and Darcy began the walk up the path while Jenki and Biggs remained at the base where they would wait for them.

~~~~~~~/~~~~~~~

The summit was just as it had been described to Darcy by Giana and Richard. The major difference was the oak trees were all bare. By now their fallen leaves had been, for the most part, carried away by the wind.

While Johns stood—even though Miss Lizzy had in the past told the guards they may sit, both he and Biggs told her they could see more and react much faster while standing —Elizabeth led Darcy to a flat rock on the eastern side of the hill facing the horizon where the weaker November sun was threatening to show its head to them. Both were looking forward to it rising even if the sun's rays were weaker, they would still be somewhat warming.

As the sun rose, Elizabeth removed a cloth from her overcoat pocket. She opened it to reveal two muffins and two rolls. She offered one of each to William and took the others for herself. Resting the cloth in her lap, she broke both into ladylike sized bites.

At the same time, Darcy finished the still warmish roll in two bites; the muffin took three. He wanted to declare himself more than anything he had ever wanted to do, but he knew he needed to exercise a little patience as the woman who held his heart finished the pieces of her snack.

Once she had finished, Elizabeth lifted the cloth holding all four corners together so the crumbs would not escape. Then she stood and shook the cloth out over the edge of the hill.

"Cousin Elizabeth…Elizabeth, would you mind sitting again?" Darcy requested.

Elizabeth felt her heart rate increase. She hoped he had a particular reason to ask her to be seated. "I am at your disposal," she said once she had resumed her seat.

"In vain I have struggled. It will not do. My feelings will not be repressed. You must allow me to tell you how ardently I admire, respect, and love you. I am not normally impulsive about anything, but I knew almost from our first dance that you were the only woman for me. You are too generous to trifle with me. If your feelings are not in accord with mine, tell me so at once. Regardless of my affections and wishes, one word from you will silence me on this subject forever if that is what you desire," Darcy managed, it seemed almost all without taking a breath.

"Not in accord with yours? In fact, I think I would go *further.* Rather I believe my regard matches yours closely, so no William, not speaking on this subject is the very last thing in the world I desire you to do. It has come on much quicker than I thought it could, but I too love you. I love you deeply," Elizabeth declared.

"In that case, a request for a courtship would be superfluous," William stated, and Elizabeth nodded.

"Before I make my proposals, I want you to know I intend to request all of your property and wealth remain yours," Darcy insisted.

"I do not need that, but there is one thing, and that is Rosings Park. Anne asked me in jest to name a daughter after her. If you agree I would like our first daughter to be named Anne after her and your mother. Her dowry will be Rosings Park," Elizabeth stated.

"Agreed." Darcy stood and led Elizabeth to one of the benches below the trees. Once she was seated, he dropped down onto one knee and took each of her hands into each of his. He cared not for the state of his trousers kneeling on the dead grass. "Elizabeth Bennet, you complete me and there is no other I would ever want as my wife other than you; will you marry me?"

"It is good then you are the only man I would marry. Yes, William, yes to infinity and beyond, I will marry you," Elizabeth replied.

Both members of the newly engaged couple were ecstatic. There was only one impediment to their expressing their love through kisses—a rather large one in the person of Brian Johns.

As Darcy stood, they wordlessly communicated they would find a time to experience their first kisses. For now, he removed her gloves enough to bestow a lingering kiss on the pulse of each wrist. Feeling his lips on her skin warmed her body as frissons of pleasure found their way to the farthest reaches of her extremities.

"I think we need to return to Longbourn so I may speak to your father," Darcy managed. All Elizabeth could do was nod. She did not trust herself to speak yet. She had a fiancé!

As they walked down the path with Johns following, Darcy felt like he was floating on air. His eyes were lifted to the heavens sure his parents were smiling down on them at that moment.

Standing next to John Biggs, Mrs. Jenkinson did not miss the glow of pleasure emanating from both Miss Lizzy and Mr. Darcy. She suspected an engagement, so she knew Miss Anne would be very pleased.

Elizabeth's eyes were also heavenward like her fiancé's. *'Are you happy Annie? I am to marry William, just like you predicted.'*

Just then a gust of wind whipped around Elizabeth's head. She took it as Anne responding in the affirmative. It caused her smile to grow that much wider.

# CHAPTER 38

**M**ary was sitting at the pianoforte with Richard next to her turning the pages when Elizabeth seemed to float into the music room on the wings of angels.

After she stopped playing, Mary turned to Richard and they exchanged knowing looks. "Lizzy, is there something you would like to share with us?" Mary asked.

"Not yet, he has gone to Papa," Elizabeth averred dreamily.

"Did William propose to you?" Mary prodded. All Elizabeth could manage was a nod of her head.

Given how she had felt when Richard had proposed to her, Mary could well understand the state in which her normally rational older sister found herself at that moment.

"And here I was thinking my cousin was a confirmed bachelor." Richard shook his head. "I suspected he had fallen under Lizzy's spell."

"It is mutual," Elizabeth managed, "I am as much in his thrall as he is in mine."

"As it should be. I am certain you two will do very well together," Mary stated as she shook her head at her fiancé telling him it was not the time to tease Lizzy. "Richard and I give our heartfelt congratulations. We would love it if you and William would join us the day we marry, and agree to a double wedding." She looked at Richard who nodded emphatically.

"The only thing better than marrying my Mary would be doing so in a joint ceremony with you two," Richard insisted. "You know William and I have always been as close as Andrew and I are."

"Once William has Papa's permission and blessing, I will discuss it with him," Elizabeth responded. "Jane and I always imagined a double wedding, but having one with you and Richard will be perfect."

"I do not think Bennet will refuse him," Richard opined.

"It is my hope he will not," Elizabeth replied.

~~~~~~~/~~~~~~~

Darcy entered Bennet's study on hearing the invitation to do so when he knocked on the door.

Bennet was sitting at his desk reviewing some correspondence when he looked up and saw Darcy standing nervously before him. He had a feeling he was about to lose another daughter.

He returned his quill to the inkwell and removed his spectacles. Once they were off, he pinched the bridge of his nose. "I did not realise you came with Fitzwilliam this morning. Are you to join us to break our fasts as well?" Bennet asked as he tried to defer the inevitable question.

"No, I did not join Richard. In fact, I met Cousin Elizabeth on the path on the way to Oakham Mount as she had agreed to my accompanying her when I requested the pleasure yester-evening at dinner. I was well aware she would be chaperoned by Mrs. Jenkinson, Biggs, and Johns so I knew propriety would be observed," Darcy related.

By now any doubt of Darcy's purpose in seeking him out was banished from Bennet's mind. He recognised the look of a man violently in love. He had seen it when Andrew requested Jane's hand, and then again when Richard had requested Mary's. If he were honest, he knew it was the same look which had been seen on his own face before he had proposed to Fanny all those years ago.

"I assume you have something you wish to ask me,"

Bennet guessed. "If it is for Lizzy's hand, allow me to have my wife summoned first." Darcy nodded. Bennet rang for Hill and instructed him to request the mistress's presence in his study.

A few minutes passed in awkward silence before the Bennet matron entered the room. She looked at her husband questioningly. As she followed his direction of vision she noticed William standing, shifting from one foot to the other and without being told, Fanny was sure she knew what his purpose was in being in her husband's study. The fact he had summoned her as he had when Andrew and then Richard had asked for permission to marry Jane and Mary respectively, was another clue.

"Young Darcy here has something he would like to say," Bennet drawled once his wife sat down on one of the armchairs in front of his desk.

Once she was comfortable, schooling her features, Fanny looked at William expectantly. She had hoped there would be more time before Lizzy would think of leaving home. However, Fanny knew from her own experience with her beloved husband, love would not be denied.

"Cousin Elizabeth and I spoke and discovered that our feelings mirror those of the other which led us to decide a courtship is not necessary," Darcy began. "With her encouragement, I proposed to her and she accepted me."

He looked at Fanny who gave Bennet a nod. "Fanny and I have been expecting this eventuality ever since we saw the way you reacted one to the other at the assembly in October," Bennet stated. "I will not sport with your intelligence by asking you questions to which I already know the answers. All I will say is always treasure her. Welcome to the family, son, you have our hearty permission and unreserved blessing to marry Lizzy."

Bennet stood and proffered his hand, which Darcy shook with gusto all the while his face was split by a wide grin of pleasure. When his soon to be father-in-law retracted his hand, Darcy noticed Aunt Fanny had stood. She pulled him into a warm, welcoming hug.

"You will always make sure our girl is happy, will you not William?" Fanny said softly next to one of her future son-in-law's ears.

Darcy nodded knowing it was more of a statement than a question. Making sure Elizabeth was happy was not anything anyone would have to prompt him to do. He had no doubt that of the two of them he was the fortunate one. What a thing to win the heart and love of such an extraordinary woman.

As soon as he was released by Elizabeth's mother, he reiterated what he had told Elizabeth regarding her money and property, as well as her response.

"There will be time to incorporate all of that once you bring me a draft settlement," Bennet assured Darcy. "I assume you have not discussed a wedding date yet, have you?"

"No, we have not yet," Darcy confirmed. "Are there any restrictions from your side?" Darcy asked as he looked from one Bennet parent to the other.

"Even had we wanted to, we would not have been able to delay the wedding past the fifth day of March of next year when Lizzy reaches her majority." Bennet looked at his wife again who gave a wan smile and a nod. "No there will be no embargo of when you may marry our daughter. Discuss it with her, and then inform us when you two are in accord."

"I think we should send a note to Netherfield Park and invite Elaine, Reggie, and Giana to join us to break their fasts, if they have not yet done so," Fanny suggested.

Darcy looked at his fob watch. "It is about a half hour, a little more, before they will do so," he informed his soon to be in-laws.

Fanny wrote a quick note and soon a groom was galloping towards one of the Bennets' other estates with a message to be delivered to the Countess. Another was dispatched to Meryton to be delivered to the Philipses.

Elizabeth was called into the study where with great pleasure she accepted felicitations from her parents. She had never doubted they would approve of William, but the fact they had not put any restrictions in place regarding when she and her fiancé could marry, had been most pleasurable. She had agreed not to say any more to her sisters until Papa made his announcement upcoming.

"Papa, Mama, may William and I have a few moments to discuss some things?" Elizabeth requested.

"You have ten minutes and the door will not be closed all of the way, and Jenki will be in the hallway," Bennet agreed after a nod from his wife. The Bennet parents had withdrawn and the door was partially closed after them.

Elizabeth told William of Mary's and Richard's agreement to share the date of their wedding.

Darcy agreed with alacrity. The sooner they never had to part one from the other, the better. "No one can say it is a patched up affair as the date is about seven weeks hence," Darcy stated.

"I agree and I would not pay attention to such persons who had nothing better to do than create inuendo where none exists. Those who have an imperative to marry do not wait almost two months from the date of their engagement," Elizabeth agreed.

She turned scarlet when she noted how intently William was looking at her lips. Given the lack of privacy after his proposal, Elizabeth was in great anticipation of her first kiss.

Seeing the implied permission in her look, Darcy lowered his head until his lips met hers as she turned her head up to meet him. When their lips met, the feeling was so much more than when he had kissed her wrists on Oakham

Mount. It was an electric shock, as if they had both been struck by lightning emanating from their lips, which they both felt throughout their bodies.

He pulled his head back to make sure his fiancée was sanguine with what he was doing. Elizabeth's eyes were closed and her lips ready for him. He lowered his head and expressed himself in a way only a man violently in love could when his lips met those of his one and only beloved.

They broke apart on hearing Jenki clear her throat when the ten minutes were up.

~~~~~~~/~~~~~~~

Before the residents and guests made their way into the dining parlour to partake of the morning meal, they all met in the drawing room.

Bennet did not sit and called Lizzy and Darcy to stand next to him.

Giana clapped her hands together in anticipation. She knew William loved Lizzy, but she had no clue he would propose so soon after returning from the north. She would have a sister—no five of them!

"In case there is one who has not already guessed, it is my pleasure to announce that Fanny and I have granted our permission and blessings for Lizzy and William to marry," Bennet managed before the storm of well wishes began. To protect himself from the enthusiastic young ladies who wanted to wish the newly betrothed couple happy, Bennet stepped back and joined his wife who was also off to the side.

Once the storm of congratulations, hugs, kisses, and back slapping was over, Darcy cleared his throat. "Thanks to Mary and Richard inviting us to share their wedding day, Elizabeth and I have decided to do so," Darcy announced, "unless Bennet and Aunt Fanny have an objection that is."

Fanny and Bennet looked at one another, silently communicating as those married and in love for many years were wont to do. "We have no objections," Fanny stated.

After the family had their turn wishing the couple happy, the companions and Miss Jones took their turn. The last one was Mrs. Jenkinson who hugged Elizabeth. "Miss Anne is smiling down on you from heaven," she asserted. Elizabeth just nodded.

The morning meal was an extremely exuberant affair that morning at Longbourn.

As was to be expected, news of the wedding upcoming was soon known among the happy servants who all liked Miss Lizzy very well. However, unlike many houses, it was not news which would be shared outside of Longbourn without express permission from the family. Fanny told Mrs. Hill to impart to the servants the news could be freely shared from that afternoon onwards.

Elizabeth looked to her fiancé who nodded. "Richard and Mary, as William has Darcy House, I find de Bourgh House will be left vacant," Elizabeth stated. "At some point the *daughter* of ours who will be given Rosings Park and the house in London will have need of it unless her husband has his own. Until then it is yours as you are the only ones without your own house in Town. If when this theoretical daughter marries and she has no need of it, it will become your property. It will remain de Bourgh house in memory of Anne and Uncle Lewis. And no, until then, you will *not* be paying us rent." Elizabeth looked first at her father and then Uncle Reggie. "I assume as the trustees neither of you object to this?"

"I do not," Matlock smiled. "Even if we did, if you remember the terms of my late brother's will, as soon as you marry, it becomes moot."

"It is an excellent idea Lizzy," Bennet added.

"Lizzy, William, it is far too much," Mary objected.

"You would not turn down our wedding gift to you, would you?" Elizabeth responded slyly.

Mary looked at Richard and both shrugged their shoulders knowing they could not be ungracious and reject such a gift. "On behalf of Mary and myself, I thank you and William most sincerely," Richard averred gratefully.

Soon thereafter the dining parlour was vacated.

~~~~~~~/~~~~~~~

An announcement to be placed in the papers, along with a letter for the Gardiners, would be on its way to London with a Darcy courier within the hour. Elizabeth did not want her aunt and uncle, who she loved dearly, to hear about the engagement in the papers and not directly from her.

It was then decided at eleven, that Fanny, Elaine, Elizabeth, and Mary would make calls on some of the leading families among the four and twenty gently bred ones in the area.

The first family they would call on, after a stop to visit Hattie and Frank Philips, would be the Lucases. With no embargo on sharing the news, by the time they arrived at some of the others they intended to call on, the glad tidings would be known throughout the neighbourhood.

A visit to Lucas Lodge would also allow Elizabeth to enquire regarding Charlotte's experiences with increasing since her last letter had been received.

Another decision which was reached was that Fanny would accompany her two engaged daughters to London, departing on the final Monday in November. Additionally, Lady Matlock would join them. They would meet with Madeline Gardiner in London to assist with the purchasing of a trousseau for each of the brides-to-be. The companions would remain at Longbourn.

The Earl, Richard, and Darcy would be part of the party, not counting the guards and outriders, so in addition to both sisters being able to tour their future homes in London, they would be seen by those attending the little season as one family group.

The plan was to be in London for about ten days. Thanks to their presentations and then the balls at Matlock House, the Bennets were not unknown among the *Ton*. It did not hurt that it was well known that the former Jane Bennet was Lady Hilldale and daughter-in-law of the Earl and Countess of Matlock.

Their first stop in London would be Uncle Edward's warehouse, then they would visit Madame Chambourg on Bond Street to begin to order the wedding gowns and the trousseaus for Elizabeth and Mary.

~~~~~~~/~~~~~~~

After a stop to receive wishes for happiness from Aunt Hattie and Uncle Frank, the former joined the ladies who were to call on those in the neighbourhood.

The welcome at Lucas Lodge was as warm as would be expected between families who had long been connected by friendship. The congratulations were all that was sincere. The only one who was a little reserved was Johnny Lucas who, until that moment, had nursed a vain hope Eliza would see him as more than her friend's brother. His disappointment did not stop him from conveying his best wishes .

Lady Lucas informed Eliza and Mary that they should not count on Charlotte and her husband's attendance as the former was having a rather difficult time increasing. Hence her husband, who was most attentive to his wife, had decided she was not to travel until she was well or delivered the babe, whichever came first.

Elizabeth promised to write to Charlotte when she returned home in a few hours.

As had been predicted, by the time they arrived at the third call at the Longs, the news had preceded the visitors.

# CHAPTER 39

That evening after the visits around the neighbourhood and more time spent with her fiancé, his family, and her own, including the Philipses, Elizabeth finally fell onto her bed. She lifted her eyes to the heavens. She wanted to talk to Anne to share her joy with her best friend. To make sure she was not heard by someone walking past her chamber who may think she was speaking to herself, Elizabeth spoke silently.

'Annie, how I would have loved to have you witness my wedding,' Elizabeth began. 'I know, I know, you will be there with me right here.' Elizabeth laid her hand over her heart. 'But we both know it is not the same. At least Jenki will be there, and with her here with us, I have another part of you close to me. Jane will be my matron of honour, but how I wish you were still with us physically and you were able to perform the office.

'Yes, I hear you. It is not productive for me to complain about that over which neither you nor I had any control.

'Knowing that does not lessen the pangs of sadness in my heart when I miss you each day. As I have not been haunted by you, I assume you have noted I am living my life and have not allowed the melancholy to overset it. You will always occupy a corner of my heart, but now the major portion of that organ belongs to William.

'How you knew we would suit long before we ever met, I will never know, but you had the right of it, Annie. I did not fall in love with him to make you happy or prove your prediction true, but because my heart demanded that he was the only one I would ever love as a wife loves her husband. Never did I imagine I could love a man as deeply as I love William. He is my all and my everything.'

Elizabeth told Annie about her plans for the first daughter born to her and William. She was sure Annie was pleased the first Darcy daughter would be the mistress of Rosings Park one day.

*'I told him I speak to you, and he completely understood why I feel the need to communicate with you, my dearest friend. He does the same thing and talks to his parents the same way. William told me he would be speaking to them tonight. In fact, he may be doing it at the same time you and I are in conversation.*

*'Silly me! I am sure you and Uncle Lewis are with William's parents, so you knew before I told you that he talks to them, and if he is doing so now, you were aware of it already.*

*'As my life progresses, I may not speak to you as much as I do now, but you must know I will always be thinking of you, sister of my heart. I love you Annie. Kiss Uncle Lewis for me and inform your Aunt Anne and Uncle Robert that their son is the other half of my heart.'*

Soon after talking to her best friend, Elizabeth fell into a peaceful sleep.

~~~~~~~/~~~~~~~

At the same time Elizabeth was speaking to Anne, Darcy was sitting in the wingback chair in his chambers about to speak to his parents.

*'I know you both met Elizabeth when she was a young girl, so I do not need to tell you how strong, brave, and beautiful my soon-to-be wife is.*

*'Father, you told me to marry for love, but never did I expect to find a love for the ages like you and Mother have. She is everything, and so much more than I ever hoped to find in a wife even after I decided to follow the advice in father's letter. A more loyal friend one could never hope to find.*

*'I am sure there is no need to tell you to what extent she was, and still is, Anne's best friend. When one is bestowed the gift of her love, it is for all eternity. I am sure not even death could break the*

*bonds of the power of her love.*

*'Now that I have Elizabeth's love, I understand what you two have between you. Like Father would for you, Mother, I would willingly lay my life down to protect Elizabeth. The two of us together will be able to face all the vagaries and triumphs of life.*

*'She has made me want to be the best version of myself I can possibly be because my Elizabeth deserves no less than that. How I look forward to the children we will have. I know you two are watching Giana and me from heaven. If only God's plan had allowed you to meet your grandchildren here in the mortal world.*

*'As much as I miss both of you, I pray it will be many decades before I see you again. I love you both.'*

Darcy rose from his chair, removed the dressing robe, and climbed into bed. With visions of Elizabeth sharing his bed in a little more than seven weeks, he fell into a deep, restful sleep.

~~~~~~~/~~~~~~~

## 11 January 1811

It was hard for Elizabeth to believe it was the morning of Mary's and her weddings, but it was.

As much as Elizabeth wanted to don her riding habit and gallop with abandon on Penny across the fields of Longbourn, she could not. She smiled as she thought of riding.

Twice since their return from London, William had challenged her and Penny to a race. The first time, she had held her mare back and only allowed her to go to full speed with two hundred yards to go. She had won by a full length. The second time with her fiancé crowing about how he almost won the previous race, Elizabeth allowed her horse to run free from the very start.

By the end of the half mile race, she was almost ten horse lengths ahead of William and Zeus. As soon as he had seen Penny's unrestrained abilities, William had ceased asking for another race.

He had not surpassed her abilities at chess yet either, but he would soon. The last three games were played to a draw and Elizabeth was confident William would soon begin to best her every now and again. Her father was the only player who, at this point, was able to beat her at chess almost as often as she beat him.

As her mind returned to the present, there was a knock on the door and Jane entered followed by Sarah who was carrying a tray. The latter was one of the lady's maids and would be assisting Elizabeth that morning. As excited as she was to marry William, an unladylike rumble from her tummy reminded her how hungry she was so Elizabeth followed Jane to the table under the window where they both sat to share in the cups of hot chocolate, muffins, rolls, and pastries on the plate.

"Kitty is delivering a similar tray to Mary," Jane related. Kitty was Mary's maid of honour while Giana and Lydia were attendants for Elizabeth and Mary respectively so none of the sisters would be left out. Andrew was standing up with Richard and Bingley would do the honours for Darcy. May Gardiner would be the flower girl again, but now as she was past the age of six, her mother was confident she would acquit herself with aplomb and not cry off as she had at Jane's wedding.

"Lizzy, I have a secret to impart to you. Andrew is the only other person who knows," Jane confided.

"You are with child again," Elizabeth guessed.

"I am. I just missed my third set of courses. But how do you know?" Jane enquired.

"You have the same glow about you which you had when you were increasing with Tommy. I also noticed your aversion to eggs the last two days when we broke our fasts," Elizabeth revealed. "I noticed the way Mama and Aunts Elaine and Maddie all looked at you with knowing looks."

"It seems my secret is not so secret after all. I will tell Mama, Mother, and our aunts after your wedding breakfast. They will say nothing to me until I share the news with them."

Elizabeth savoured first a muffin, then a warm roll slathered with soft butter. She left the lemon pastry, her favourite, for last. Once it too was consumed, she drank the hot chocolate slowly. She used her index finger to recover the last few drops of the decadent drink. They had stubbornly refused to oblige her by not running down the side of the cup to land on her tongue.

Her wedding gown was hanging from the door of her wardrobe. She could not wait for William to see her in it. As it was winter, the fabric was satin, in off-white. The gown had sleeves which ended just below her elbows. It shimmered in the lights thanks to the silver lamé overlay Madam Chambourg had fashioned to complete the dress. The shorter train was satin, but silver lamé extended double the length of the satin to make a long flowing train. Never one who liked bonnets, she would wear a sheer gossamer veil edged with delicate Belgium lace. The jewellery—except for the ring on the fourth finger of her left hand—she was to wear was from the de Bourgh collection she had inherited.

Her fiancé had presented her with a becoming engagement ring with a gold band and a large emerald stone. When they were in London, Elizabeth had visited the bank where her jewels were stored and selected the gold pendant with a teardrop emerald and matching earrings.

"Tommy will be very excited he will be a big brother," Elizabeth noted and Jane nodded.

Once the food and drink had been consumed, Jane kissed her younger sister on her forehead and followed the maid who came to collect the tray out of Elizabeth's chamber. It was time for her sister to bathe and then make herself ready.

As Jane closed the door to the chamber, she met Kitty exiting Mary's room.

Mrs. Jenkinson slipped into Elizabeth's bedchamber just before she rose from the chair. "You will be the most beautiful of brides Miss Lizzy and I know Miss Anne is with you today," Mrs. Jenkinson told Elizabeth.

A few tears ran down Elizabeth's cheeks as she simply nodded and hugged Jenki. The latter padded out of the door while the former headed for her hot bath.

~~~~~~~/~~~~~~~

Richard and Darcy were pacing back and forth impatiently in the retiring room off the altar in Longbourn Village's church .

Their attendants knew saying anything would not help at that juncture so Andrew and Bingley sat back and left the grooms to their pacing. It was how Mr. Pierce, the rector, found the two men he was about to join with two Bennet sisters when he entered the room.

"It is time to take your positions, gentlemen," the clergyman told the two indulgently. In his many years of conducting wedding ceremonies he had seen similar behaviour from grooms who could not wait until it was time to be joined by their brides.

The act of walking to their positions helped calm the nervous, anticipatory energy the two men had coursing through their bodies. As they watched, they saw their very soon-to-be mother-in-law enter the church with Mrs. Gardiner and that lady's eldest two children. The youngest child, Peter, was in the nursery at Longbourn.

Fanny and Maddie entered the front pew and sat next to Mr. Gardiner and the Philipses leaving a seat for Bennet beside his wife, the first one on the aisle. Across the aisle in the front pew sat the Fitzwilliam parents.

When the Reverend took his place, the hum of

conversation from the assembled congregation came to an abrupt halt. All eyes were now directed to the inner vestibule doors which allowed entrance into the nave of the church.

May Gardiner proudly entered the church when one of the doors was swung open. She seemed very pleased with herself that she was able to discharge her duties of flower girl at this wedding. May carried a basket full of rose petals which had been sent from Rosings Park's conservatory. She dropped them on the carpet as she walked.

Elizabeth had been beyond pleased the rose petals from Kent were not only in May's basket but the bouquets both she and Mary were holding were made up of roses from Rosings Park. It helped the feeling that Anne and Uncle Lewis were physically present on this special day.

By the time May was half way up the aisle, Lydia followed her. She was followed by Giana, Kitty, and finally by Jane. As soon as the grooms saw Jane, their sense of anticipation returned in full force.

The inner vestibule door was closed and as soon as Jane reached her position opposite Kitty, Mr. Pierce gave the signal for the congregation to stand. Once everyone was ready, he nodded to the back of the church which signalled that both inner vestibule doors were to be opened wide.

Bennet entered the nave of the church with Mary on his left arm and Elizabeth on his right. There was an audible gasp heard from both grooms when each beheld his bride. Richard had to fight the urge to stand still in position to receive Mary while Darcy's inclination was to run down the aisle and pull his Elizabeth into his arms. Both men kept their equanimity and their positions until it was time to stand at the head of the aisle.

As she passed the second to last row of pews on the right where the companions were seated, Elizabeth looked at Jenki and gave her a wide smile which was returned in full measure.

Between the two of them, Anne was very much present on this wonderful day. She looked back towards where William stood, heading towards her felicitous future.

On arriving at the place he would hand his daughters to their grooms, Bennet turned and kissed Mary on both of her cheeks. Mary had chosen a wedding bonnet rather than a veil so there was no impediment for him to kiss her. Thereafter, he placed Mary's hand on Richard's forearm and then turned to his second daughter. He lifted Elizabeth's veil, bestowed a kiss on both cheeks, and then lowered it. He then handed her to her groom.

While the brides and grooms took their places before the parson, Bennet joined his wife in the front pew on the right. With the couples in place, the rector gave the signal for the witnesses to be seated.

As had been agreed, it was a single service, even the asking if there were any objections. As would be expected though, each couple repeated their own vows separately. All four stressed the vow to love her or his partner. When it came time for the vow to obey, Elizabeth raised an impertinent eyebrow before making her promise. Darcy was fully aware he was not marrying one who would follow blindly if she disagreed with something. It was one of the many things he loved about her.

In what seemed like the flap of a bird's wing, it was over. Mary was Mrs. Richard Fitzwilliam and Elizabeth was Mrs. Fitzwilliam Darcy. After the final benedictions, the couples and their attendants made their way to the registry where both brides signed the name Bennet for the last time. Given there were two couples, there was no delay before they exited back into the nave where their family and closest friends waited to be the first to wish them happy.

Not long before they were to exit the church, Lady Lucas and Maria both offered their best wishes to Elizabeth. Elizabeth had not missed that although he attended the wedding,

Johnny, had not remained to convey his congratulations like the rest of his family. She understood it was hard for him to see her marry another when he had always dreamed he would be her husband. Sir William, Franklin and Jennifer Lucas were busy speaking to Mary.

"Charlotte wants you to know how very sorry she is that her increasing does not allow her to travel," Lady Lucas stated after she had conveyed her good wishes to the newly married Darcys.

"She explained all in her last letter," Elizabeth assured her friend's mother. "In my reply I promised we would stop in Lincolnshire at their estate when Mr. Darcy and I return from our wedding trip, and a month or so in London for the season."

"Sir William, Maria, and I will be departing for Smythe Bluff in a few weeks. I know Charlotte will be very happy to see you again." Lady Lucas squeezed Elizabeth's hand. "We will see you at the wedding breakfast."

Even though a large room could be configured at Longbourn with the walls pushed back it was still only about half the size of the ballroom at Netherfield Park. Therefore, the celebratory meal was being held there rather than at Longbourn. Both newlywed couples would depart for their respective destinations from that estate.

~~~~~~~/~~~~~~~

Elizabeth and Darcy sat in the Darcy coach not long after it had departed the wedding breakfast. Mary's and Richard's conveyance had left a few minutes before them on its way to Sanditon in the south, on the west coast of England. Like the Darcys, the Fitzwilliams were to spend the night at their home in London and depart in the morning.

"Hang propriety," Darcy growled as he moved himself to sit on the forward facing bench next to his wife.

"Who made up these silly rules that a husband cannot sit next to his wife in a carriage?" Elizabeth wondered.

"You know, I have not a clue," Darcy averred as he kissed his wife on her cheek. "I say we start a new way, regardless of others' opinions. Just as we agreed to sleep in the same bed each night, we will sit next to one another when we are in a coach."

His eyes were locked onto his wife's lips. As soon as they cleared Meryton, he intended to capture those enticing, pouty lips of hers.

At the same time, Elizabeth closed her eyes as she felt Anne's presence. '*Annie, it was as you said it would be. I am ever so happy you had the right of it. I have a feeling William will be requiring my attention soon. Before he does, I want you know how privileged I felt to be your sister and best friend.*'

Elizabeth felt the speed increase once they were out of Meryton. Soon William was kissing her and all thoughts of being Anne de Bourgh's best friend were temporally relegated to the back of her mind.

# EPILOGUE

## March 1826, Oak Hollow

E lizabeth and Darcy were not alone on this morning's ride. It stood to reason that the children of two who loved horses as much as they did would also enjoy all things equestrian.

Although they rode Penny and Zeus occasionally, their horses had slowed a few steps. Even though the former could still run away from the latter, the two Darcy parents rarely raced the two senior horses any longer. They both rode offspring of the two—who were far more equal in speed than Penny and Zeus used to be—when not riding their older horses.

~~~~~~~/~~~~~~~

Unsurprisingly and fittingly, their first born arrived in February 1812, only a few days after her namesake's birthday. Elizabeth and Darcy had named her Anne de Bourgh Darcy. Thankfully unlike her late cousin, Anne was as healthy as any child ever. Anne looked much like her Aunt Giana and her late grandmother who had had the same name as herself. Rather than the Fitzwilliam blue eyes like her aunt and late grandmother, Anne was gifted the same emerald-green eyes as well as her mother's stature.

From her birth, Jenki had been Anne's nurse and later her, and the rest of the Darcy children's governess. She felt a special affinity to Anne and with Miss Darcy's fourteenth birthday, Jenki had become her companion.

On her birthday past, Anne had been informed Rosings Park was part of her dowry. Her sisters had forty thousand pounds each while Anne had a quarter of that, but when added to her estate, her dowry was enormous. Like her mother before her, the estate would be managed by trustees, made up of her father, grandfather, and some of her uncles, until she reached the age of five and twenty or married. Their firstborn, Anne, was recently fourteen, and thankfully as yet, had not shown any interest in the opposite sex besides as brothers, cousins, or other relatives.

Ben, named Bennet Edward, had been born in April 1814. At the age of eleven—or as he reminded one and all— almost twelve, he was already taller than his petite mother and older sister. If one looked at a portrait of his father at the same age, it would be hard to tell them apart.

Having relinquished his pony to one of the twins, Ben had just graduated to a cob. Like Anne before him, he had begun riding Hector until the pony was put out to pasture. Hector's life had ended three years previously. He had been mourned as much by Elizabeth as her children who had all ridden him. The faithful pony had been buried under a tree in one of the fields near the stables at Pemberley so he could be visited at will.

Robert and Bethany had joined the family in November 1815. Much to her father's delight, firstborn of the two, Beth as she was called, was very much like her mother in character and looks, except for one thing, she had the Darcy height and would be as tall as her Aunt Giana one day. Ben's pony had been seconded by Beth as it was larger than hers, which had waited for more Darcys to be born before being ridden regularly again.

There had been no more little Darcys for four years after the twins, but in January 1820, Jane Darcy had arrived. She had been followed by the babe of the family—so far—Franny, named Francine, in May 1822.

Jane was very much like her namesake in character, and would be tall just like Aunt Jane, but she had her mother's hair colour and father's slate blue eyes. Franny was her mother in every way except hair and eyes. She had golden blonde hair with hazel eyes.

As they had for many years now, John Biggs and Brian Johns, among others, were watching from not far off. They would go wherever the mistress went, but they had a large team of guards. Over the years, with each addition to the family, Darcy had told the two to employ more former soldiers, marines, and sailors. Thankfully to date they had never had an incident where the men had needed to employ their particular skills.

~~~~~~~/~~~~~~~

"Elizabeth, dearest, it does not feel strange for you to be at Oak Hollow when it belongs to our sister and brother, does it?" Darcy asked his wife as she sat on her mount which stood next to Zeus.

"No, it seems right that the estate should have been purchased by one of the family. My Mama and Papa had no need for three estates and as we have seen, Catherine and Charles have been excellent stewards of Anne and Sir Lewis's estate," Elizabeth replied as she looked over the field where their older children and some of their cousins were racing reminiscent of the races she and her beloved husband used to have.

"Bingley quickly became a very able and conscientious estate manager," Darcy opined.

~~~~~~~/~~~~~~~

The riding party on this day included some of the Bingley cousins. The now Catherine Bingley, then still Bennet, had asked not to be called Kitty after she came out in London.

Like her sister Mary, when Catherine came out, her parents had informed her suitor he could not declare himself until after her nineteenth birthday. Just as had been the case with her sisters before her, by the time Catherine turned nineteen she had no doubt of his constancy or of her own feelings. Bingley had proposed and been accepted at the end of May 1813. The wedding had been in August of that year.

Bingley had been looking for an estate to purchase and both he and his wife had preferred to stay in one of the counties around Hertfordshire. Fanny and Bennet had offered them Oak Hollow at a much reduced price, which the Bingleys had accepted after trying to argue, and losing said argument, they should pay the market price. With the money he saved, Bingley purchased a small to medium sized neighbouring estate which added thirty percent more land to his estate and a commensurate increase in his income.

Their first child, Charles, called Charley, had been born two years, almost to the day, after their wedding in August 1815. Being only a few months older than the Darcy twins they and he were very close.

The first Bingley daughter was born in April 1817. She was named Hildebrand, called Hildy, for Aunt Bingley who lived with the family at Oak Hollow. Hildy's sister Mariane was born in December 1818. A second son, James, joined the family in May 1821.

Until Catherine had felt the quickening which proved she was increasing again, she had thought she would not bear another. She was at the manor house heavy with child and being attended by her husband and their mother while their father relaxed in the library.

~~~~~~~/~~~~~~~

Bennet and Fanny were as happy and in love as they had been at any time in their long, loving marriage. Longbourn was more prosperous than it had ever been, thanks to a combination of the master and his extremely competent steward. Longbourn was willed to the oldest grandson who would not receive his own estate. The will requested, not demanded, that grandson add Bennet to the end of his name to carry on the Bennet name at Longbourn.

For travel purposes, their family was thankfully situated in only two general geographic areas. As travel became harder with age, it was gratifying that those distant from Hertfordshire were to be found within a few hours of one another. With three daughters and their families in close proximity to Longbourn, it was very seldom the Bennet matriarch and patriarch were not surrounded by grandchildren.

Even though he was approaching his eighth decade—he would reach it two years hence—Bennet still felt as healthy as he had for the last few years. He could not do as much as he had been able to when he was younger, but that was to be expected and the natural order of things.

Although her hair was streaked with grey, just past the middle of her sixth decade, Fanny felt well. She was as beautiful as she had ever been, a few wrinkles notwithstanding.

Over the years the Bennet parents had become much closer with Lady Elaine and Lord Reggie. In addition to sharing a good number of grandchildren, they very much enjoyed one another's company.

Lord and Lady Matlock still lived at Snowhaven, but the plan was to turn it over to Jane and Andrew in the next year, and then Tom would take possession of Hilldale as soon as he graduated from Cambridge in some few years.

Lord Reginald Fitzwilliam felt his age as everything hurt much of the time and he had slowed down in the last half year. When his time came for God to call him home, he was prepared. He had had a good and long life seeing that he was more than halfway through his eighth decade so he had nothing to repine when it was his time.

Lady Elaine was still a vital and spry lady. She was more than ten years her beloved husband's junior so she had only begun her seventh decade recently.

~~~~~~~/~~~~~~~

"Our children have all benefited from Jenki as their governess," Elizabeth noted as she smiled thinking about Anne's former companion.

"She is more like an aunt to them," Darcy pointed out. "She has no need to work. Anne is very excited she is to have Jenki as a companion like her namesake did."

"No she does not, but she loves it. I am not sure who is more excited about that, Anne or Jenki. As Anne pointed out in her final letter, Jenki would never feel easy sitting and wasting the day away with no occupation. I know Anne is pleased that the daughter we named for her has always been so close to Jenki." Elizabeth cogitated for a moment. "Jenki is younger than Mama and could you imagine her doing nothing all day?" Elizabeth responded.

Even though Elizabeth had married soon after Mrs. Jenkinson came to work for the Bennets, she was companion to Kitty while Mrs. Annesley had been with Lydia. The latter had chosen to retire after Lydia married, while, as expected, the former had come to work for the Darcys as soon as Anne had been born.

Much to her delight not only the Darcy offspring, but all of the children in the family called her Jenki. One day when she chose to retire, she had a cottage waiting for her at her pick of family estates.

~~~~~~~/~~~~~~~

"When do Mary, Richard, and their brood arrive?" Darcy enquired.

"I believe on the morrow," Elizabeth averred.

"It has been three months since we saw them; I am looking forward to hearing about the latest horses Richard has acquired for breeding stock," Darcy stated.

"You have seen how close Mary and Catherine are, have

you not?" Darcy nodded. "Growing up, Kitty, as she used to be known, was always closer to Lydia while Mary gravitated towards Jane and me. It does not hurt that Cloverdell is less than three hours by coach from here."

"For me, I would have loved Mary and Richard's estate to be that distance from Pemberley," Darcy mused. "Charles and Richard are as close as Richard and I are. I am pleased that over the years Bingley's friendship with me has deepened beyond that of just a brother-in-law."

~~~~~~~/~~~~~~~

With the proximity of Cloverdell in southeastern Northamptonshire, the Bingleys and Fitzwilliams saw one another rather often.

About seven years past, Richard had added even more land to his estate, and with it, additional stables and breeding stock. For some years now, Cloverdell had been the premier horse breeding programme in the country.

The first child Mary and Richard had been blessed with was a large, strapping babe and heir, Andrew Lewis, in December 1811, just a few weeks before their first wedding anniversary. In February 1813, Rosemary Elaine had joined the family. She was followed in September 1815, by Thomasina, called Sina.

Mary had not become with child again for a little more than two years, when she felt the quickening in October 1817. On the final day of March the following year, Philip Frank made his appearance in the world. He was followed by two more sons, Harry in June 1819, and Ian in May 1821. Mary had thought she was done bearing children when Madeline Elizabeth arrived in October 1825.

~~~~~~~/~~~~~~~

"I am sad Jane, Andrew, and some of their children will not attend the Easter gathering this year because of Andrew's broken leg," Elizabeth stated wistfully. "At least it was not like someone, whose name I shall not mention, who broke his leg to stop meeting us and attending Jane and Andrew's wedding." Elizabeth arched one of her eyebrows playfully.

"You and I met at the exact right moment," Darcy responded as he leaned across the small gap between the horses and kissed his wife on her lips.

At one and forty he had not lost a step, and his hair had only now begun to grey around the edges in the back. Elizabeth was more in love with her husband today than she was the day they had married. Darcy worshiped the ground his wife walked on.

"Besides," Darcy continued, "I was riding my horse who was frightened, while my *much* older cousin (by three years) slipped and fell down three steps on the veranda at Hilldale."

~~~~~~~/~~~~~~~

Lord and Lady Hilldale's eldest child, Tom—he had asked not to be called Tommy on turning sixteen—was in his final year at Eton and would finish at that school in May upcoming. At the age of seventeen, he would enter Cambridge in September.

In early August 1811, Jane had delivered their second son, Reginald Andrew. He was finishing his first year at Eton. In April 1814, her wish for a daughter had been granted. Elaine Frances had been born. Her facial features were very much like her mother's, but she was shorter like her Aunt Elizabeth, and had her father's sandy blond hair.

In June 1817, and then again in October 1819, Jane had delivered two more sons, Henry and Rupert, respectively. Like her parents, she and Andrew were blessed with five children, but unlike her mother, four of them were sons.

Given the relatively short distance between Hilldale and Pemberley, not to mention the less than one mile between their London homes, Jane and Elizabeth saw one another with regularity and their children were more like siblings than cousins. That did not take into account the times the family would meet at various times of the year.

~~~~~~~/~~~~~~~

"When will our youngest sisters depart Netherfield Park?" Elizabeth verified.

"Unless you know something I do not, they will be here on Friday," Darcy replied.

"Ever since they came out together, those two have been the closest of friends and sisters," Elizabeth observed.

"When our uncle and aunt allowed Giana to come live with us for a significant portion of the year, she and Lydia built their friendship which is why they chose to come out together," Darcy pointed out.

~~~~~~~/~~~~~~~

As he had planned to do after their wedding trip, Darcy had met with his aunt and uncle and presented his request that his sister come live, at least part of the year with him and Elizabeth. They had presented Darcy with a letter from his long dead father in which he had directed that when William married and Giana's guardians felt it would be beneficial for her, he gave his permission for her to live with her brother. From then on, other than for a few months in London, she had lived with William and Elizabeth.

The two girls had come out during the little season of 1813, when Giana was already eighteen and Lydia was only a month or two away from that age. Like their sisters before them, they were not allowed to accept a courtship until they had passed their nineteenth birthdays.

It was not until the season of 1815, that the two best friends had met brothers. The older one was James Carrington, Viscount Amberleigh, heir to the Earl of Holder, who at the time was nine and twenty. He and Giana became engaged in July of that year. The younger was a major in the regulars which, given her brief, but long past fascination with officers, was deemed ironic by those who knew Lydia.

His father, the Earl of Holder had gifted his younger son a healthy legacy so he was no poor officer. Major Stephen Carrington proposed to Lydia a fortnight after his brother secured Miss Darcy. The Major resigned from the army before the wedding.

The two were married at a double wedding ceremony in October 1815.

Even though Major Carrington had offered to purchase Netherfield Park from the Bennet parents at full price, they had, in the same vein as with Bingley and Oak Hollow, sold the estate to their new son at a greatly reduced price.

Much to her brother's delight, Amberleigh was in Nottinghamshire, less than four hours from Pemberley.

Giana and James Carrington had three sons so far and Giana was with child again, hoping for a daughter this time. Their first son and heir had been born in November 1818, a second son in February 1820, and a third in September 1823. They were named Paul, David, and Robert, respectively.

To date, Lydia and Stephen had two daughters and a son. Their first daughter, Annabeth, arrived in April 1817, and Sarah Catherine in January 1819. Their son, Theodore, called Theo, was born in August 1823.

~~~~~~~/~~~~~~~

There were some people about whom no one in the family thought or spoke. Miss Catherine Smith, formally Lady Catherine de Bourgh, George Wickham, Karen Younge, Caroline Bingley, and William Collins.

The first of the villains, the former Lady Catherine, had not made it all the way to her new home in Australia. She had not been able to supress her imperious nature. Hence, it took no time at all before her fellow transportees could not stomach more time in her company. One day she had been shirking her duty of swabbing the decks when she had mysteriously fallen overboard. Two women had been seen walking away from the place where Miss Smith had fallen, but no one had witnessed any foul play.

Wickham reached Van Dieman's land and suffered through his fourteen years of hard labour. Unfortunately, he did not learn anything from his punishment and within a year of his release, he had been shot dead. He was caught trying to cheat at cards.

Karen Younge ran the boarding house on Edward Street with her sister-in-law. It was rumoured she had turned it into a brothel, but no one in the family cared enough to verify or refute that.

Miss Caroline Bingley was still a resident of the asylum on the Isle of Arran. She was even more divorced from reality than she had ever been. She existed there in her own world, happy in her own way.

Collins had attempted to arrive at Longbourn some months after his legal loss. Just as he had been warned, he had been arrested, and gaoled, for trespassing. After a fortnight in the Meryton gaol, he returned to the seminary where he had been sacked for missing weeks of work with no notice. As he had very little money, he had written to his cousin, and this time rather than making demands, he had begged for assistance.

Fanny and Bennet had felt a level of sympathy for him and gifted him a thousand pounds. Collins could not find work as a clergyman in England so he took a position with the Dutch East India Trading Company to minister to its workers in the Cape of Good Hope. He remained there for the rest of his life.

~~~~~~~/~~~~~~~

It was with immense pride Elizabeth and Darcy watched their children enjoying one another's company, Not only was Anne the oldest, but she was the natural leader of the group.

Seeing her dear daughter made Elizabeth think of her best friend, the late Anne de Bourgh. Just as William still spoke to his parents from time to time, Elizabeth continued to speak to Anne, especially when they were at either Oak Hollow or Rosings Park.

'*My dear Annie, at this estate which I know you and Uncle Lewis loved so well, I can feel your presence even more than when we are at Rosings Park. I still miss you and I always will, but it has been many years since I reconciled myself to the fact you and your papa are at peace and no longer suffering,*' Elizabeth told Anne silently. '*You always told me what I did for you, but I gained as much, if not more, from the privilege of being your best friend. I trust you approve of the life I am leading by living my best life just like you charged me to do. Please know you are in my heart and always will be. I love you Annie and one day I will see you again.*'

When Elizabeth looked at William, she saw his eyes were lifted to the skies as hers had been. It often occurred that he would speak to his parents at the same time she was talking to Anne.

When he was done communicating with his parents, Darcy smiled at his beloved wife. They both urged their horses forward to join the children, nieces, and nephews who were playing under the watchful eyes of some grooms, and those of Jenki, Biggs, and Johns.

## ~~~*The End*~~~

# BOOKS BY THIS AUTHOR

Her Grace

A Change of Heart

Colonel Fitzwilliam Takes Charge – 7$^{th}$ book in the 'Take Charge' Series

The First Mrs. Darcy

A Change of Fortunes (Republished & Re-edited)

Much Pride, Prejudice, and Sensibility - Without Enough Sense

Lady Catherine's Forbidden Love & Love Unrestricted Combined Edition

A Curate's Daughter

Mary Bennet Takes Charge

Admiral Thomas Bennet

Separated at Birth

Jane Bennet Takes Charge - 6$^{th}$ book in the 'Take Charge' series

Lives Begun in Obscurity

Mrs. Caroline Darcy

Lady Beth Fitzwilliam – Omnibus Edition

Anne de Bourgh Takes Charge – 5$^{th}$ book of the Take Charge Series

Mr. Bingley Takes Charge – 4<sup>th</sup> book of the Take Charge Series

The Repercussions of Extreme Pride & Prejudice

Miss Darcy Takes Charge- 3<sup>rd</sup> book of the Take Charge Series

Banished

Lady Catherine Takes Charge – 2<sup>nd</sup> book
of the Take Charge Series

A Bennet of Royal Blood

Charlotte Lucas Takes Charge – 1<sup>st</sup> book
of the Take Charge Series

Cinder-Liza

Unknown Family Connections

*Surviving Thomas Bennet*

The Discarded Daughter - Combined Edition

The Duke's Daughter: Combined Edition

The Hypocrite

*Coming Soon*

Fanny Bennet Takes Charge – February/March 2024